PUFFIN BOOKS

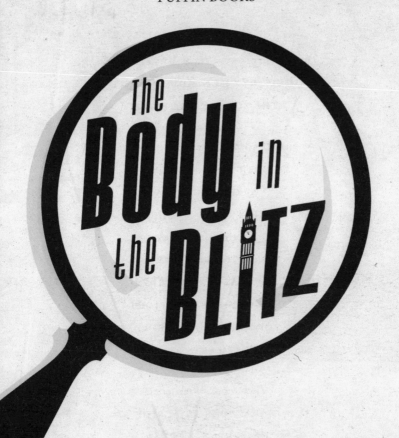

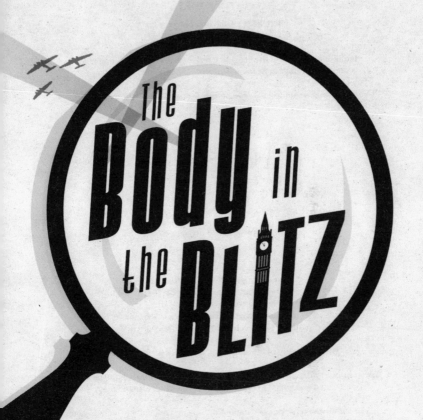

The Body in the Blitz

ROBIN STEVENS

PUFFIN

PUFFIN BOOKS

UK | USA | Canada | Ireland | Australia
India | New Zealand | South Africa

Puffin Books is part of the Penguin Random House group of companies
whose addresses can be found at global.penguinrandomhouse.com.

www.penguin.co.uk   www.puffin.co.uk   www.ladybird.co.uk

First published 2023

001

Text copyright © Robin Stevens, 2023
Illustrations by Jan Bielecki
Map illustration by Sophia Watts
Illustrations copyright © Penguin Books Ltd, 2023
Author photo copyright © Chris Close, 2018

The moral right of the author and illustrator has been asserted

Typeset in 11.38/16.84pt ITC New Baskerville Std and 10.92/16.84pt Melior LT Pro
Printed and bound in Great Britain by Clays Ltd, Elcograf S.p.A.

The authorized representative in the EEA is Penguin Random House Ireland,
Morrison Chambers, 32 Nassau Street, Dublin D02 YH68

A CIP catalogue record for this book is available from the British Library

ISBN: 978-0-241-42991-4

All correspondence to:
Puffin Books, Penguin Random House Children's
One Embassy Gardens, 8 Viaduct Gardens, London SW11 7BW

For Nat and Harriet:
Detective Society Forever

To the Shelter

To the British Museum and the Ministry

Gower Street

To Oxford Street

Store Street

Mansions 9–12

Mansions 5–8

Mansions 1–4

Hogarth Mews

2

3

4

5

6

Bedford Square

Hogarth Mews Houses

1. The Lowndes family; house bombed
2. Miss Figueroa
3. Colette, Margot, Olivier and Mrs Mortensen
4. Miriam, Samuel and Cecil Goodchild
5. Miss Charney and Miss Wimpress
6. Mr Harris

Hogarth Mews Mansions

1. George Mukherjee and Alexander Arcady (and Eric)
2. Zosia Stosic (and May and Nuala)
3. Mr Abiola

TOP SECRET

From the case files of the WOE
(Women's Operation Executive, also known
as the Ministry of Unladylike Activity)

April 1941

PART ONE

OUR ADVENTURES BEGIN AGAIN

I

This is my report on the missing spy and the murder in Hogarth Mews. It's about the time that Eric, May and I discovered a dead body, and a lot of secrets too, and almost – well, you'll see. I don't want to give it all away just yet.

I can't believe it's me writing the *official document* this time, the one that Hazel will put in the Ministry's records when it's done. This makes it really important. And secret. We can't tell anyone anything about this case, or about anything we do for the Ministry. We all signed something to say so. I asked May if she wanted to help out because she did it last time, and she said once was enough, thanks very much. Then I asked Hazel what I should write, and she said that it's always best to begin at the beginning and say what's happened since your last case. That's what she does, anyway.

Winding back to last year feels weird, but sure I will. I've been at school – *real* school – at Deepdean since January, with May. I didn't really believe her when she told me she hated it – how could anyone hate learning stuff? But it's true. She's *awful* at it. It's honestly funny. She just can't sit still or follow the rules, and most of the girls and *all* the mistresses (that's what we call teachers; there are an awful lot of ridiculous made-up words at Deepdean) don't like her.

For a while, I wondered if I should hate it too, but I just couldn't. Deepdean's fun, even if you have to do a lot of pretending to fit in there. And one *extra* thing that I have to pretend is that I'm a normal schoolgirl, and not a . . . spy.

But I really *am* a spy, and so is May! We're part of the Ministry of Unladylike Activity, and we're helping the British government win the war, even though I'm only eleven and a half and May's not even eleven yet. That sounds strange, but it's true.

Here, let me explain.

Our first mission was last November at my family's house, Elysium Hall. That was when I thought May was my enemy. It's funny to think about that. May and Eric, our other friend, turned up as new evacuees, acting so suspiciously I thought they were spies for *the other side*. But they weren't, obviously. (Actually, they weren't officially spying for *our* side, either. The Ministry had turned them down as agents for being kids, so they were working on their own to try to prove they were good enough to be hired. May doesn't like

4

remembering that part.) They found out that someone at Elysium Hall was on the Nazis' side, and they were trying to work out who it was when my uncle Sidney was murdered.

Yes, seriously, murdered. It still gives me chills to think about that. You can read about it all in the Ministry's records. Hazel, who's May's big sister, collected the diary I wrote back then, along with May's notes, and put them together. I've seen it. It looks very official in its handsome red binding.

To cut a long story short, I helped May and Eric uncover the Nazi spy, and the murderer, and even though it meant the end of Elysium Hall it was worth it. I always kind of hated that place, anyway.

Now the army's requisitioned Elysium Hall, and my family have been given a little house in the village instead. That's where I'm supposed to live during the school holidays. But I'm not there right now, because Hazel wrote to me and May at Deepdean, towards the end of the spring term.

The letter was addressed to me, which made sense because May is always losing things. She's really careless, even with stuff she loves, and she usually forgets things the moment she puts them down. But she got snakey when she saw Hazel's looping handwriting in my pigeonhole: For Fionnuala.

'Why's she writing to you?' she asked me. 'She's *my* sister.'

I turned over the letter. I'd been hoping for one from my mam, so I felt a little strange about it.

This is for May too, it said on the back.

We both laughed, the tension between us vanishing for a second, and if May had been anyone else she'd have looked embarrassed. But because she's May, she just said, 'See?'

Then I opened the letter and didn't feel like laughing any more.

Dear Nuala and May,

Something's come up. You're needed in London – family emergency. Telephone me at the number I taught you and be ready to go.

Hazel

I felt scared, but not for the obvious reason. '*Family emergency*' was just the code phrase we'd agreed on, for crucial Ministry business. This was *spy stuff*.

May gripped my arm.

'This is it!' she hissed. 'They need us! We can finally leave!'

'But there's still weeks of term left,' I said. I didn't want to leave school yet. I felt like I was getting really good at it. Some of the other girls in our dorm even liked me.

'So?' said May spikily. Like I said, she'd been spiky with me all that term. I didn't know why. 'School is a waste of time. Anyway, even if they try to stop us, I ran away before. I can do it again.'

'Sure, they're going to be looking for you this time,' I pointed out. 'You're on their list.'

I think May *is* their list.

'Nuala,' said May. 'They need us. And when the Ministry needs us—'

I looked down the corridor towards the dorm, where I knew Eloise Barnes and Mariella Semple were planning a midnight feast for that night, and back down at the letter that May and I had been waiting for. I couldn't think of what to do – and then May shouted, 'MATRON!'

Matron stuck her head out of her study. May looked at me beadily. I did my best not to sigh.

'Matron, it's my aunt,' I said, crumpling the paper in my hand so she couldn't see it, and making my face as agonized as I could. I don't have an aunt, but Matron doesn't know that. 'Something dreadful's happened. I must call her at once.'

Matron stood over me as I dialled, and May hung around, breathing anxiously down my collar. Everything she does is loud, even breathing.

'Hello?' said an English woman's voice on the other end of the line.

'Hello,' I replied in my posh Fiona voice, the one I use at school, in case someone was listening in. 'Auntie? It's me. I'm so sorry – I got your letter, and I feel terrible that I've been *swanning* around while you've been so ill.'

'Nuala, love! You got my message.'

7

Swan is my code name, you see, so the Ministry's telephonist, Miss Lessing, knew immediately who I was.

'Yes, this morning. Are you worse?' I asked, making myself sound anxious. 'Really? How dreadful.'

'I'm suffering,' said Miss Lessing. 'I need you in London, urgently. You're to pack at once – both of you.'

'Oh no, I'm so terribly sorry! *Really* urgent?'

'I think you can catch the Saturday train. I shall be wiring you some money. Tickets these days are absolute *piracy*.'

My heart skipped. *Pirate* is May's code name – and Saturday would be *the next day*. The last we'd heard from the Ministry, we thought we *might* be coming to London some time around Easter for more training. This was all entirely new, and really exciting.

'We'll be there,' I said, thrilled.

'Do stop jabbering – let me speak to her,' said Matron impatiently. She snatched the mouthpiece away from me and barked 'Hello?' into it.

May squeezed my elbow, her sharp little fingers making me wince.

'Yes?' said Matron. 'Who is— Oh. Yes. Hello. How – how terrible. Yes, I understand. And . . . really, *both* of them? Did Mr Mountfitchet say so?'

She gave me and May a very suspicious look. 'You're sure? Oh – well – *tomorrow*?'

And that was how May and I ended up in London on a Saturday afternoon in early spring. We should have been watching Deepdean beat St Chator's at hockey again, but instead we were about to be spies.

That's where this story starts, really. The rest of this account is my diary entries from that time, things I wrote before I knew what'd happened. The Nuala in these pages doesn't know what I know now. Sometimes she gets things wrong. Sometimes she doesn't behave entirely well. And sometimes—

—but I won't spoil it for you.

You'll see soon enough, anyway.

I've let Nuala do the writing in this account. Writing so much of the last one made me bored. It's just not as interesting to write about a murder as it is to solve one. It's been funny to read Nuala's diary (the bits she's shown me, at least) – sometimes she wrote down things that don't seem important but I know will be later.

I haven't always agreed with her, on this case. Sometimes she's been a beast. You'll see. Just remember that I am <u>always</u> right. She understands that now.

– May Wong, 23rd April 1941

2

From the diary of Fionnuala O'Malley

Saturday 22nd March

I'm writing this in the blue lights of the London train as it creaks along at half-speed. I haven't been in London since the end of last year, Diary, and I'm a little nervous about being back.

There was a big air raid on London while we were at the Ministry last December, before we got whisked out again to Fallingford House, the Ministry's country headquarters. That night felt like being stuck in an oven, the whole sky roaring with fire, and then the next day the air was just powdered ashes and dust. That was the first raid I'd really been in, apart from the one on Coventry in November. I've been having nightmares about them both, ever since.

Sure, I know by now that nowhere's safe, not really. We just have to pretend it is, because otherwise we'd never do anything. But it still feels scary to me, to be going into the middle of a big city today. And scary to be doing spy training too. I'm afraid of a lot of stuff right now.

The good thing, though, is that May and I get scared in different ways. I think if she met Herr Hitler she'd just . . . bite him. Nothing bothers her – nothing but enclosed spaces, anyway, but don't tell anyone I told you that. So I'm worrying about raids, and what London's going to look like, and what the Ministry will be like, and whether maybe they'll regret hiring us as spies and kick us out and I'll have to go back to the little house in the village. But when I said all that to May, she just grabbed my hand and said, 'Stop talking or I'll be sick on you.'

May gets sick on trains, even the ones that go slow because of the war.

'I don't know if I can do that,' I said to her. 'I keep thinking of stuff to tell you about.' It's still weird to be on my own with her again. We have to pretend not to be good friends while we're at Deepdean, so we don't blow our cover.

'All right, if you promise to stop saying stupid things, you can talk,' said May. 'Read me the paper, here. I stole it from that old woman on the platform.'

'MAY!' I said.

'She didn't need it,' said May through gritted teeth. 'If you disagree with me, I *will* be sick on you. Read the best bits.'

So I read to her about a body that had been found in a bombed-out church hall, and about thieves who had stolen paintings from a stately home, and about the new play at the Rue Theatre—

'The theatre's not important!' said May.

'It is to me!' I said. Diary, you know Da had a theatre company when I was a little kid. I grew up travelling all over the world with him and my mam and the rest of the Company. Then my da died, and Mam and I came to England – which is how we ended up in Elysium Hall with all my English relatives, which is how May and I met, which is why I've ended up on a stuffed-tight slow-moving train to London reading the newspaper to May while a woman's gas-mask case presses against the side of my head and some soldiers have a singalong in the corridor. But my point is, I care about plays, just the way May cares about murders.

Lookit, I guess I care about murders too. I solved one, last year, with May and Eric, so I'm a detective as well as a spy. That's a secret, Diary – so don't tell anyone.

But this time the detective part of me won't matter. We're going to London to help with spy stuff.

There won't be any murders waiting for us this time.

We were met at the station by May's big sister, Hazel.

She looks a lot like May, but calmer and more comfortable, instead of being spiky with rage – she's fat, with a round, pretty face and long dark hair up in a bun, and a really nice smile. She was arm in arm with a tall blond man who kind of reminded me of one of those bouncy blond dogs that fetch sticks. He was wearing a Navy uniform, and he had a battered detective novel sticking out of one of his pockets.

'I'm Alexander,' he said, shaking my hand enthusiastically. I flinched a little. It surprises me when someone's so friendly so quickly, when I don't know exactly how to behave around them yet. Then Alexander picked up our bags like they were nothing. 'You must be Fionnuala. Little May I know.' He had an accent that blurred in and out of American and English like a radio tuning between stations, kind of like how mine is if I don't pay attention to it. But he pronounced my name right, like *Fin-noo-la*. I was impressed.

'I'm not little!' snapped May at once. 'I'm almost eleven! Don't be an idiot, Alexander.'

He just grinned at her and started to lead the way out of the station.

'Alexander's my . . . friend. He's on leave,' Hazel told me, motioning us after him. 'He wanted to come and meet you both.'

'*Is* he going to marry you?' asked May. '*Have* you told Father you're marrying a gweilo?'

Hazel's cheeks went pink. 'May!' she said. 'Don't be rude!'

'I'm not! Rose says hello, by the way,' May carried on. 'And have you heard from Father? He hasn't sent even one letter to us, and I think it's the least he could do after he LEFT US IN ENGLAND DURING A WAR.' Her voice rose.

'May!' Hazel's kind face flickered and fell. 'You know he's busy in Hong Kong. I'm sure it's important. Anyway, he's with Teddy – don't you want him to keep Teddy safe?'

'I want him to keep *us* safe!'

And then she and May started to talk very fast in Cantonese, looking even more alike than ever. Sometimes I wish I had brothers or sisters. It must be nice to have someone who knows you so well, without any pretence. I stared around at the station. It echoed with noise and light – it was a bright afternoon, and the sun struck down through the panes of glass (and the gaps where glass used to be) in heavy stripes.

Then we stepped out of the station and we were back in *real* London.

I came to London just once before the trip last December, when I was really little, with Da and the Company, but I don't have much memory of it. Sure, everything looks bigger when you're small, and you don't know how anything fits together because you're just following adults around. But this spring London's turned into an unfinished theatre set: buildings sheared off as cleanly as cut paper, doors open like they're waiting for their cue forever, a painting hanging sideways on a wall that's cracked through and useless. There are weary, determined-looking people in uniform everywhere, and dust has got on everything, so that none of it looks quite real. But then again, life doesn't always feel real these days.

I thought we'd be staying with Hazel and Daisy in the flat they share in Bloomsbury, but we weren't.

'Why?' asked May.

'The Mountfitchets' baby,' said Hazel briefly. 'Their flat is right below ours, and she's . . . noisy.' Hazel paused, then added, 'And Daisy will be back soon. Anyway, Zosia has a spare room you can use.' We wound through the grey, cracked streets, dodging past adults in uniforms and children pushing scrap carts and ambulances on their way to their depots and newspaper sellers and women carrying shopping and a man with sergeant's stripes on his shoulder walking with crutches, one trouser leg folded up emptily.

'Where's Daisy?' I asked. It's confusing when people you know talk about lots of other people you don't. It makes me feel awkward, like I'm in the wrong room by mistake. When it happens, I have to pretend to be someone completely different – jolly English Fiona, the sort of person who fits in at Deepdean – so when I asked that question I made my voice as radio-English as I could. I know Daisy, at least. She helped me and Eric and May in our last case; she was actually the person who put together all the clues we'd found out and revealed the murderer. May's still mad about that.

I was sure I'd said it in a friendly way, but Hazel's face fell again and her fingers gripped her handbag nervously.

'She's on a business trip,' she said briefly.

I thought I understood what she meant. A *business trip* was code for mission. Daisy's a spy, see, just like Hazel.

'Where's she gone?' May blared. 'Is it important? When's she coming back? What—'

'May! *Quieter!* And you know I can't say here. *Loose lips.*'

Then Hazel rushed us all the way across a park and past tiny shops and huge white marble buildings and down busy, dirty roads, all the way to the place we were staying, and where our friend Eric was waiting for us.

3

I haven't said much about Eric in this new diary, have I? Well, that's all wrong because Eric's important. He's the third member of our Detective Society, and the nicest. That's not an exaggeration. He's a lot nicer than May, and for sure nicer than me. He just *gets* people without even trying. He always knows what someone needs to hear, and he says it. He's very sensible and clear, in a way that makes everyone – people and animals – like him.

He's round, with dark skin and short curly hair, and he's always got a pet somewhere on him. At Elysium Hall he had Emil the hedgehog, but he put Emil back in his field when we all had to leave. He can't go to Deepdean with me and May because he's a boy – which is a pity because he'd love it, and we'd love having him with us – so he goes to a school called Weston. He got a scholarship, because his family aren't rich, not like my English family are, and definitely not like May's are. May comes from the kind of family where you don't just have one house; you have lots, *and* a boat, *and* servants. She's *rich*. Her father has a boat back in Hong Kong, and when she told me so a few months ago I could tell she didn't even know how weird that is.

Eric came to London from Germany with his mama and papa and twin sister, Lottie, just like I came from America, so we've got that in common. His mama and papa were musicians, famous ones, in Germany, but his papa's in prison now, because the government here is afraid he might be a Nazi – which he's absolutely not. His sister, Lottie, goes to Deepdean, in the year above me and May, and his mama runs a nightclub in London. People are sometimes weird about that, Eric says. I don't know why; a nightclub's just like a theatre, but with music instead of a play. It makes me like Eric more, that his parents and mine are kind of the same – or, at least, they were.

So that's Eric. And, Hazel told us, he'd been brought out of school too, and he was staying in the same place we were: Hogarth Mews.

I guess I should explain what a mews is, in case you're like me and have never even heard of one before now. That's the thing about English people: when they talk it's a test, every time. If you know what they're saying, you're allowed in, and if you don't, you never will be.

When I heard Hazel talking about Hogarth Mews, I got really confused at first. Sure, I thought she must have adopted another cat called Hogarth, as well as Eric's big orange cat Pfote who lives at the Ministry.

But a *mews* has nothing to do with a cat. It's a pocket

18

side street filled with cute little houses. The houses used to be garages or stables for horses, way back when the Victorians were around and even stables were two floors tall.

Hogarth Mews is tucked into one side of a wide street near Oxford Street and the British Museum. You have to kind of dive down between two big houses that have been blackened by London smoke. The street level drops as you come out into the mews. It feels like being in a cobbled toy street: dark little doll's houses with white-painted windows and shiny black barn doors on each side.

At least, they're houses on the left-hand side. On the right, the houses have been turned into flats. They're called Hogarth Mews Mansions, but, like a lot of things in England, they're not anything like what they're named for. Each flat has two bedrooms, a tiny little kitchen and a bigger living room. May and I are sharing a room in Flat Two on the first floor, and Eric is right below us in Flat One – but I'll tell you more about that in a second.

The far end of Hogarth Mews is blocked off, so once you're in, you have to go out the same way, and the mews houses look really small because ordinary London houses shoot up behind them on both sides like cliffs. It's always a little darker in the mews than it is outside it – although I guess it's not quite as dark as it should be, because of the bombed-out house.

I said that when you come into the mews, you see two

little rows of houses stretching away from you. That's not totally true, because, actually, when you come in the first thing you see is the smashed space where the first house on the left has been hit. It looks like someone came in and cut a slice out of a loaf cake. There are still a few crumbs of wall on each side, and you can see cracks biting into the second house along. It doesn't look like anyone could live in that one any more, either.

I've learned by now that you don't ask about bombed-out houses – what happened to the people in them, I mean. You just don't want to hear the answer most of the time. But when we walked into the mews this afternoon, Alexander pointed at it and said, 'That happened last year, before George and I came here. It's all right – the family weren't in it. They were down in their house in the country. The woman who used to live in the house next door's gone away somewhere too. So you don't need to worry about it.'

'Why would I worry about it?' asked May, who was still in a bouncy mood after her argument with Hazel.

Alexander looked at me and smiled.

'Thank you,' I said to him.

Eric is staying in Alexander's room, and a friend of Alexander's called George has the other one. I asked where Alexander was staying, if Eric was taking his room. Alexander and Hazel both flushed, and Hazel said, 'Oh, Alex has Daisy's room in our flat, while she's not here.'

This was suspicious, and I could tell May had sniffed it out too. She had the little-sister glint in her eye that she gets whenever she's around Rose at school.

'Hazel—' she started, but right then we walked past the third house on the left and a dog started howling. I turned my head and saw it bouncing up and down in the front window. It was a fat black one with a curly head of hair and long, floppy ears. There was a little girl in the window too, a tiny kid maybe four years old, and she stuck her tongue out at me. An adult voice started yelling at the dog, and I saw an arm grabbing at the dog as it bounced. Then, somewhere upstairs, a baby started to sob.

'Babies!' said May, making a face. 'We can't escape them!'

'That's the Mortensen house,' said Alexander in a low voice. 'Mrs Mortensen, her daughter-in-law Colette, and *her* two kids, Margot and Olivier. Mrs M's lived here for years; Colette and the kids came over from France last summer. They're nice people, but the dog gets kind of excitable when you walk by. Next to them are the Goodchilds. They're great. Mr Goodchild works at the British Museum. Their son Cecil's a few years older than you three, and then Anna— Oh, hey!'

I looked up at him, wondering what had made him change tack. I'd already worked out that he was the kind of person who calls everyone *nice* and *great*, even when maybe they aren't.

21

He was waving across the mews at two people who'd just come out of the entrance to the flats at the end, on the other side. One of them was a tall, brown-skinned man with smooth dark hair and an eye patch. His trouser leg was folded up to his knee like the sergeant we'd seen earlier. A lot of soldiers come back like that, these days, but I'd never seen one making it look so stylish. He could have been the lead actor in any play.

He waved one of his crutches back at Alexander, a cool salute, and then nodded at me and May. I felt just a bit overwhelmed.

'Nuala, that's our friend George,' said Hazel.

'I know!' said May.

'I know *you* know! Be quiet, May!'

And next to George was Eric. He looked taller than I remembered, but still shorter than me. His round face was crinkled up into a smile, and he waved at us both.

May obviously went running forward at once and threw her arms around him. I went a bit more shyly. I always get worried that people might have forgotten me when I see them again. Usually they have. It's hard making friends, and even harder keeping them, and I guess I wasn't totally sure whether we really were friends, yet.

But then Eric's smile got wider and he held out his free arm and I found myself hugging him too.

'I missed you!' he said to me.

'Oh!' I said. 'Me too!'

'We're all back together,' said Eric happily. 'I'm so glad.'

'Ugh!' said May, even though she was still hugging Eric. 'Well, I'm going to be the best spy of all three of us – just you wait and see!'

'First of all,' said George, looming down at us, 'don't say things like that outside the Ministry. That's important. Especially here – you can't escape the neighbours. And second: May, Nuala, hurry and drop your things at Zosia's. You're needed for your briefing this afternoon.'

Zosia, whoever she was, wasn't in her flat. Hazel let us in with an extra key, and May and I put our bags on the bed in the spare room and left our ration books on the table. Food's always important in a war, and it's not polite to move in with someone without giving them your ration book to use too.

'I get the bed and you sleep on the floor,' said May to me.

'I get the bed!' I said. 'That's no fair!'

We both glared at each other.

'You can sleep one at each end,' said Hazel. 'Calm down. Now hurry up.'

Obviously we were both madder for being told to calm down, but the others were waiting for us outside. We hurried back out into the mews, me braiding my hair and May pulling up one of her socks that'd got shoved down on the walk over from the station.

When we were back outside, I realized how right George had been. The dog was still barking inside its house, the little girl pressed against the window, and in the house next door, the one closer to our flat, another window opened and a plump, friendly-looking woman with grey hair up in a loose chignon leaned out into the mews to water her window boxes, which were full of really beautiful spring flowers.

'Hello, George,' she called. 'Are these your new lodgers?'

'Yes, Mrs Goodchild,' George called back. 'Hazel's sister May and her two friends. Their schools have been bombed out, so Zosia and I are taking them in for a few weeks.'

'That's kind of you,' said Mrs Goodchild. 'Children, if you want cake, I've usually baked one. Stop by any time, if you don't mind being bored by Samuel talking about art.'

'See? I told you they were nice,' said Alexander to us, as we all walked out of the mews together. 'And great cake too. All right, Hazel, I guess this is where I leave you.'

'Will you be all right?' asked Hazel. 'Sorry to be working on a Saturday.'

'Oh, I'll be fine. Grandmother wants to meet me for tea, so you're not missing much.'

He turned left, and the rest of us turned right, towards the museum and the Ministry headquarters, and the answer to what we were doing in London.

4

Wednesday 26th March

I haven't had much time to write in you this past week,
Diary. I'm sorry. I'm going to have to do some more
explaining. I've got nothing else to do until this raid's over,
anyway. I keep hearing that we're through the worst of it,
but then the planes come back again and again. Last week,
just before we arrived in London, there was an enormous
raid that went on all night. People are still talking about
how awful it was. That scares me, because we don't ever
know what's going to happen next. So to distract myself I'll
begin with what Hazel and George explained to us on
Saturday afternoon, once we were safely inside the red
door of the Ministry.

When we started our training last year, after the end of
the Elysium Hall business, no one really thought the spy
stuff was urgent. We were still really too young (that's
what everyone said, anyway), and so we thought it'd
be years before we were needed to go on our first spy
mission.

But something's happened at the Ministry these past few months. The war has got more dangerous, and more and more agents aren't coming back from their missions. They're missing in the field. That makes me shudder, because that means they're either *captured* or they're *dead* – and *that* means the Ministry's short on agents and coders in the London office. Because of that, Mrs Mountfitchet's ordered that everyone on the books get trained up properly, in case they're needed – and that means *us*. That's why we're here.

It feels like we're back at school, except that the lessons we're learning are a lot harder than normal school lessons. I'm used to finishing all my schoolwork early, but here everyone's struggling – even Eric, who's been studying codes for years. He's way ahead of me and May, even though I've been practising this term at Deepdean. He can take down eighteen words a minute in Morse code, and he can put coded words into Morse almost as fast.

We have coding lessons with Hazel, in a little study room on the ground floor of the Ministry. I really like them, but May always gets so frustrated – her note paper gets scribbled all over and she writes in bigger and bigger letters until they explode over the side of the page and Hazel tells her to start again. Then she sits panting furiously through her nose, tongue sticking out of the side of her mouth, grumbling to herself.

'Is this NECESSARY?' she asked Hazel this morning.

'Absolutely,' Hazel said calmly. 'I've told you. We're short coders, and there's a big push coming this spring. You're essential. Go again. I know you can do it if you listen properly.'

'ARGH!' May shouted, squishing up her face. 'I can't THINK like this!'

She got up from her seat and began to stalk about like a cat, hissing.

'Sit down!' said Hazel. 'May, really, if you just focus—'

I put my pencil down and watched them. Eric was sitting quietly in the corner, working evenly through his twelfth page of decryption. 'Codes just make sense to me,' he told me yesterday. 'They're so clear. I can think in Morse code sometimes, just like I can think in English and German. I can hear the beeping. It's nice.' That sounds kind of like magic to me. But sometimes I can – oh, it's hard to explain – catch the shape of a sentence that's still half decoded, like I'm hearing someone recite a speech I know in a play.

And sometimes, even more interesting, I can see where they've gone wrong with their lines. The best thing about codes – I think so, but Eric disagrees – is that they're made up by people, so they're not perfect. I can't ever spell *chief*, so if I was encoding that word I'd write the coded letters down wrong. So when I look at a code and it isn't making sense, I imagine the person who might have written it, and I can kind of feel the mistakes that they might have made, just like when I feel my way into different roles.

Anyway, my point is that the way someone writes or cracks a code is as different as each person is. And I wondered whether May was trying to crack codes in the wrong way for her.

'Is she allowed to walk about while she works?' I asked.

'No, she has to sit *down*—' Hazel began. Then she looked at May, and at me. 'That's actually a good idea, Nuala,' she said. 'May, go for a walk and don't stop until you've worked out six words.'

'FINE!' snapped May, snatching up her pencil and paper, and she began to walk between the chairs in the room, humming to herself. 'Sunday thirtieth March,' she said, after two minutes. 'Leave package at – er – at usual drop point.'

'MAY!' cried Hazel. 'That's right! You did it!'

'Well done, May,' said Eric.

'It was easy,' said May, sounding surprised. Her cheeks had gone pink. 'Thanks, Nuala.'

I felt pleased. Sure, I've known May for almost six months now. We share a dorm at Deepdean, and when you do that, it's hard *not* to know a person. But May's *so* spiky – and sometimes I'm not sure how friendly we are right now, even outside school. It's been tough, at Deepdean. It's hard to fit in there *and* be friends with May, and I'm worried she doesn't understand that.

We decode for an hour, and then the lesson always ends with us reciting our poem code lines to Hazel. We've all had to choose and memorize a poem, or a bit of a play. This isn't just for fun or to keep us occupied. It's to use in our coding, and it's going to be crucial when we do go on a mission.

Before I became a spy – when I'd only read about them in books – I thought that codebreaking was just taking ordinary words and putting them into code. The thing is, though, spies have had to get more and more clever. Most people know simple codes now – Morse code, Pig Latin and all that – so, to keep your messages safe, real spies have to do more than just decode them. And that's where poem code keys come in.

I've chosen Caliban's speech from *The Tempest*: *Be not afeard; the isle is full of noises.* Eric chose a poem about a tiger, and May chose a horrible little poem about a man on the stairs who wasn't there.

Every time we want to send a coded message, we pick five words from our poem and use them as the key to create an entirely new code, one that can only be decoded if the person we're sending the message to already knows what our poem is (or if they can work out the poem we are using).

We're also learning languages – because, of course, fighting against the Germans means you have to be able to read German, as well as French and Polish and all the other countries they've invaded. Fully trained spies, the ones who are trusted to go into the field, have to know other languages so well that they can speak only them during their missions. When I think that might happen to me some day, my heart kind of clutches in my chest. It's so big, and so scary, but I really want to do it.

The language lessons are given by George. He's one of the most interesting people at the Ministry, I think. He's *really* good-looking, but it's not just his features that make him handsome. It's the way he moves – he's paying attention to his whole body, trying to be in control the whole time. Most actors aren't as good at that as he is. And he somehow makes his Air Force uniform look like the most incredible fashion plate.

Even though he wears the uniform, he isn't in the Air Force any more. He told us he was in the Battle of Britain. He was an ace pilot, and he shot down ten German planes, but then his plane was hit, and when it crashed his leg got caught in the – I don't know, some part of it. They cut him out before the fire really took hold, but they couldn't save the leg. He walks with crutches now, while he waits for a false leg to be made, and he's got an eyepatch over his left eye, and the Ministry recruited him at once.

He's very funny, and he's got the whole Ministry running after him adoringly, but when we were supposed to be working on our translations yesterday I saw him squeezing the pencil in his hand like it's the only thing holding him up. I think that some of his control is because he's afraid of what will happen if he stops watching himself for even a second. I can tell the leg still hurts him.

He and Eric have been arguing about Pfote. She's Eric's cat, the one he found last year and brought into the Ministry, and now whenever Eric sits down to do lessons she comes running in and curls her big fluffy orange body around him. George thinks it's distracting, but Eric shrugs and says, 'I can't tell her what to do. She does what she wants.' Eric knows German already, and French, so he's got time to argue. I'm way behind. I know a couple of sentences of Irish, and a couple of Japanese, and how to say hello and thank you and where is the theatre in ten different languages, but that's not really the kind of thing the Ministry wants.

George has started me on French and Polish. Zosia, the woman we're staying with, works at the Ministry too, and she's Polish and Serbian, so she helps me with the Polish stuff. Not that she's a huge amount of help. Zosia's one of those people who you can *feel* the temper pouring out of, even when she seems still. She's really pretty, short and curvy with amazing dark-brown hair and perfect red lipstick always, but it's a daunting kind of prettiness. May and I try to stay out of her way in the evenings, and spend as much time as we can downstairs in Eric's flat.

May's even worse than me at the language lessons – not because she's not good at languages (she's fluent in two of them already) but because she's upset that knowing Cantonese doesn't count at the Ministry.

'It *is* useful!' she said to George.

'Of course it is,' said George, 'but not *here*, May.'

'Yes, here! It's uncrackable unless the other side has someone who can read Chinese!'

'How do you know they don't?'

'They don't. I know. I'll just send a message in Chinese to Hazel! She can read it!'

'May, that is— Can you not just work on learning German?'

May, as you can tell, is just as awful at lessons at the Ministry as she was at Deepdean. The only thing she really likes is our combat training. I like it too, if I'm honest. Eric isn't sure.

We don't have combat training in the Ministry building. We go down into its basement, and then through a long tunnel that brings us out inside the British Museum. It's mostly closed now – only a few people like Mr Goodchild work there still, but they're in far-away offices and aren't allowed to know that we're using the museum. The galleries are pretty much empty, apart from the big Egyptian statues which are too heavy to move (they've got sandbags draped round them in case of bombs) – so we have huge echoing spaces to ourselves to practise. It's incredible.

A woman called Bridget teaches us. Bridget's also incredible. She's Irish, like Da, and she's fierce. She knows ju-jitsu, and she can use a knife in very alarming ways, and shoot straight. (Eric refuses to shoot anything; he says he's going to be a pacifist spy. Bridget asked what he'll do if he comes across some Germans who want to kill him, and Eric said, 'Hide. And have May with me,' which I think is a really good point.)

I'm a pretty good shot, although knives make me woozy – I can't help thinking about the knife in the moonlight, that night at Elysium Hall – but May's amazing. She usually has all that energy (she can't keep still), but when she's lining up a shot she goes totally calm and focused. She *never* misses.

Then in the afternoons we get special sabotage lessons from – I guess I'll call her the Cook. She's skinny and quiet, and she doesn't look like much, but that's the thing about people; you can't always tell what they're going to be like inside from what's outside. Anyway, she's Austrian, and she's learned a scary amount about explosives and poisons. She told us about poisons that can be put in fabrics, and in spray bottles and pencils, that can be eaten and drunk and licked and smelled. Some are so deadly that someone can just brush against it once and die. Then she showed us a chocolate bar that explodes, and a cookie that explodes (the Cook's baking is great, when it doesn't explode), and even a teddy bear that explodes.

'I don't think I want to hold that,' I said anxiously.

'Ooh, I will!' said May. 'It won't blow up unless you squeeze its foot, Nuala – haven't you been paying attention?'

I had, but I still don't like the idea.

Our first few days in London have flown by, all surface-busy, and I fall asleep so fast whenever I can (which isn't always, when there's a raid like there is now). But I've got this funny feeling. The Ministry seems so fun, and exciting, and busy, but I know that, like George squeezing his pencil tight, a lot of that's just an act. Eric and May and I are only here because agents who should be here are missing. *Daisy's* missing. Everyone's rushing around trying to teach us things, because if they slow down it might be too late.

And not just that. It feels like something's about to happen.

But I'm not sure exactly what it could be.

5

Ooh, this is a good bit! This is the bit where we find the body! – May

Thursday 27th March

I was right, Diary. Something's happened – but not at the Ministry. In Hogarth Mews. Something completely unbelievable. Except, somehow, I can believe it. I just don't *want* to.

It happened this afternoon, just after we'd been sent home from the Ministry for the day. Mrs Goodchild had invited us round for tea and cake – and you don't say no to cake in a war, not ever, especially not Mrs Goodchild's Victoria sponge.

Eric came out of his flat dressed tidily – long trousers and a nice white shirt. I'd tried to dress up too, because I wanted to impress Mrs Goodchild with pretty clothes. Not that most of my clothes are pretty; they're all the stuff from our Company wardrobe, and Mam's old clothes, and some things we got in Coventry that I've not quite grown out of yet. It's getting hard to buy new clothes these days with only coupons, and all the things that are in shops don't feel very like *me*. I was wearing a purple drapey dress and Da's old waistcoat, and I had my hair in a braid down my back. May, though, was in shorts and a pullover. She's been wearing shorts more and more often since we came to London. They're borrowed from Eric and tied up with string. It's hilarious how much they don't fit her.

'I look so unladylike!' she crowed, spinning to look at herself with delight in our bedroom mirror, and I didn't say anything, because I guess we all need a costume. It would have really annoyed me back at Elysium Hall. I would have thought she was just doing it to upset me. But now I know that's not how May works. She only bothers with things she really, really likes.

So May was in shorts, her knees all dirty, and she totally did not look like someone ready to have a nice tea. But Mrs Goodchild didn't even notice while she was serving us the most enormous slices of creamy sponge cake. Mrs Goodchild's cakes are honestly great. You wouldn't know that eggs and sugar and butter are rationed right now, while you're eating one.

We said the polite stuff that you're supposed to, about the weather and about Mr Goodchild's paintings that are hanging on all the walls, and about Mr Goodchild's work at the museum – he's really busy right now, something to do with art and the war. The Goodchilds' son Cecil came wandering in, nodded vaguely at us, picked up a slice of cake and walked back upstairs.

Cecil's maybe a few years older than me and Eric and May, one of the big boys that I'm never totally sure how to act around. It doesn't help that he's got eyebrows like wings and the kind of face that'd look amazing lit up on the stage. His clothes are always ripped and a little dusty but good, and he has a device clipped onto his right ear, a wire from it snaking away down into his big army jacket. I'm curious about that, but I don't want to ask.

And then May piped up about the bombed-out house at the end of the mews.

'When did it happen?' she asked. 'Did you see it? Was it awful? How big was the bomb? Were there incendiaries? Have you ever put out incendiaries? Isn't it true that you can just cover them with your coat?'

'It was last November,' said Mrs Goodchild, sighing. 'Thank goodness the Lowndes family weren't there when it happened. They were in their house in the country; lots of people left last year when the bombing got bad, including Mr Harris, the lawyer at Number Six, and most of the people in the flats. But Samuel and I decided to stay. We were really so lucky – we *are* so lucky. And you mustn't try to put out incendiaries, dear. They're putting explosives in them these days. You could get hurt.'

'This cake is very good,' said Eric.

'Oh, I'm glad you're here to enjoy it,' said Mrs Goodchild, giving him a little half-smile. 'Our daughter loves that cake, and it hasn't been the same since—'

At that point the dog next door started barking again.

'That dog!' said Mrs Goodchild. 'Who's out there now? Oh, it's Primrose coming back from work. That means Samuel should be home soon.'

'Poor General Charles de Gaulle!' said Eric. 'Everything upsets him!'

'What's happened to him now?' I asked, confused. General Charles de Gaulle is the leader of the Free French movement – the people who hate the Nazis, and are angry that they invaded France and took it over last summer. He's gathering his forces in Britain and Africa now, while he works out how to get France back and get rid of the horrible fake government that did a deal with the Nazis.

'Oh, not the real one. He's all right as far as I know,' said Mrs Goodchild. 'The dog's name is General Charles de Gaulle. Colette from next door supports the Free French and I think she was feeling patriotic when she named him. He gets so distressed when anyone walks by. I don't think he gets much attention at the moment, with the babies in the house.'

'He might like someone to say hello to him,' said Eric brightly. 'I thought he looked lonely yesterday.'

Mrs Goodchild laughed. 'Go on then,' she said. 'I can't

compete with a dog, can I? But take another slice of cake before you go.'

Eric jumped down from the table and May pushed back her chair with a squeal. I followed them, wrapping my bit of cake in my handkerchief.

Outside was a bright early spring day, with pale cloud floating high above our heads and the air smelling of dust and smoke but also of the flowers from the Goodchilds' window boxes. It's hard to remember the war on a day like this. It feels so normal and so hopeful. And then you see something like that bombed-out house.

Eric knocked on the Mortensens' front door, Number 3, and when it opened the dog burst out at him, licking his face. He – the General, I guess I should use his name now that I know it – is a big black poodle, and of course he loves Eric. I'm not so sure about him. He barks a lot, and when he jumps up he's almost as big as me. The little girl, Margot, came out too, holding on to the General's fur, and the mews suddenly seemed very full. 'Margot!' called Colette from somewhere inside. 'We are leaving in five minutes to get Mormor! Be ready!'

I turned to May and saw that she wasn't watching Eric and the General. She was looking over at the bombed-out house.

'What is it?' I asked.

'That house,' said May. 'It's interesting.'

'It isn't really,' I said. 'You heard Mrs Goodchild. It's been months since it was hit. It'll all have been cleared out.'

You see, civil defence people go through houses after they're bombed, to make sure there's no one left in there, dead or alive, and then people come by to pick the rubble for scrap and useful bits of furniture and so on. The people who went through this house left ropes behind, strung across it and the next house over, with KEEP OUT signs hanging from them. It was very obvious that we were supposed to leave them alone.

'Hmm,' said May. 'But imagine if you're wrong! If the family wasn't there when it was hit, they might have forgotten things. There might be treasure! They were rich, weren't they, if they've got a house in the country too? Maybe they left . . . gold.'

'The Lowndeses didn't leave *gold*,' I said. May really is ridiculous sometimes.

'How do you know? You're so boring.'

'I'm not boring!'

'You are. Well, I'm going to take a look. And when I find gold you'll be sorry you didn't believe me.'

'You are NOT going to find GOLD!'

'Don't worry,' said Eric to the General and Margot. 'They don't mean it when they argue.'

'YES, WE DO!' May and I both yelled at him.

May started to walk over to the bombed-out house. I was really riled. She never thinks through anything, May. She just does it.

'You're being silly!' I snapped, and I lunged after her and grabbed hold of her arm.

'Leave me ALONE!' yelled May, flailing. The General must have thought it was a game, because he bounced forward and began to gallop around us, yipping. Then May pulled herself out of my grip and ran towards the house, the General scampering in front of her.

He wriggled under the rope, got to the edge of the pile of rubble, and then – it's still hard to explain, even though I saw it with my own eyes – he just disappeared.

We all stood frozen with shock.

There was a yelp, from somewhere below us, and the General began to bark. Each bark echoed.

'What did you *do*!' cried Eric. 'You've hurt him!'

'He's obviously fine!' said May, but I could tell she was shaken. 'He's just . . . fallen somewhere underground.'

I saw her face go pale as she said that. I told you, May hates small, dark spaces. They make her twitchy.

'We have to get him back, quick! He might be in danger!' said Eric.

'I – I—' May stammered.

I had to do something. I took a deep breath and put ice in my spine. I wasn't Nuala, I told myself; I was the person I always am when I get scared – Gráinne the Irish pirate queen. I was fearless. I could not be bested, and I was not afraid.

'Eric, you go and find Colette,' I said. 'May, you stand guard. I'll get the General.'

Before they could tell me not to, I'd already ducked under the rope and marched over to the last spot we'd seen the General. It was only a little way up the rubble, a place where half a sofa had slid down and knocked over some rotten beams, leaving a gap in the pile of bricks. It only looked a small hole – but I reminded myself that the General was a big dog. If he could get in there, so could I.

My boots slipped and slid around. My palms were sweaty and claggy with dust, and somehow I'd got a cut on my wrist. It stung. I leaned forward into the dark gap, pulling the flashlight out of my pocket and spinning it around.

I saw the General almost at once, his big dark eyes shining up at me in the glow of the light.

'Come here to me!' I said to him, and he yipped and backed away from me.

Then I saw what he was standing on: stairs, leading down. I realized that this was the way down into the basement.

I pulled the cake out of my pocket and waved it at him. 'Come here!' I yelled. The General huffed and backed away further. I took a deep breath, leaned forward and lowered myself onto the top stair.

'What are you doing?' May called from behind me. She sounded nervous.

'Going to get him!' I puffed. 'I'll be grand.'

42

I didn't necessarily believe that, but the stairs seemed pretty solid, and all I needed to do was to grab the General's collar.

I went down one step, then two, holding the cake in front of me, and then in four steps more I was down in the basement. It was dark and earth-cold and it made me shudder.

I swung my flashlight, looking for the General, and then ... I saw something huddled in the corner of the room.

6

I had a weird moment when I saw it but I couldn't *see* it, if you know what I mean. I wondered why that pile of clothes in the corner looked kind of like a body, and then I thought, *But that IS a body!* And then I remembered that it couldn't be, because there aren't just *bodies* lying around, and *then* I thought, *But of course there are. We're at war, aren't we? Everything's real now, or nothing is. Of course I'm in the basement of a bombed-out house, staring at someone who's dead.*

All of that went through my head in the time it took me to catch my breath.

I couldn't speak. I kept sucking in air, but it didn't seem like it was filling up my lungs. My legs felt like water, and the whole basement felt like it was at sea. I remembered being in the study in Elysium Hall, and seeing the bloodstains on the carpet, and hearing Granny cry.

'What's happening?' called May from outside. 'Do you have the dog?'

'May,' I said. It came out very thin and breathy. 'There's someone down here. I think they're dead.'

'WHAT?' screamed May. I heard a rattling noise and shifting bricks, and then I saw her face upside down at the top of the stairs. 'HONESTLY?'

'Yes,' I said, because if May yelling hadn't made whoever it was move, they were definitely dead.

'ERIC! THERE IS A DEAD BODY DOWN HERE!' shrieked May.

'Don't let Eric come down!' I shouted. My voice still wasn't working properly, but I couldn't let Eric see this. *He* was the one who found the body in the study last year, after all. I know it still scares him. 'You stay up there too. Go and get help.'

I saw May wavering between her excitement at the thought of a dead body and how much she hates small spaces.

'Go look at it!' she said at last. 'Go look! You have to!'

'No! Don't be an eejit!'

'I am not! Nuala, listen. You've found a body. You have to look at it. It's *important*. Do it for me! Please! Oh, this isn't fair!'

I thought that was a bit rich. The General was still avoiding me and the cake. Instead, he was pattering around near the body, sniffing at it thoughtfully.

'You're not thinking properly!' May went on. 'When the grown-ups come, they'll send us away. We won't be able to look at the scene any more. But you've discovered a case. A real case. We have to detect it! We have to get all the clues!'

'We're spies! We're not detectives. Last year was . . . a one-off, because we had to.'

'We *are* detectives. Being a detective is a calling,' said May severely.

'Who told you that?' I asked.

'Daisy.'

'She did not!'

'All right, she didn't. I heard her say it to Hazel last year.'

'Yes, but we're not Daisy, are we? We're kids, May. We're not real detectives, not like adults are. And we're busy, so. We're in training to be *spies*. We can't also be solving a murder mystery.'

'I AM NOT LISTENING TO YOU,' said May. 'GO AND DETECT.'

I wasn't going to. I swear it. But just then the General stretched out his neck and nuzzled the body's elbow, and I had no choice but to stop him.

'General!' I shouted, leaping towards him and dropping the cake. He skittered away from me and started to lick bits of cake off the ground, and I . . . ended up facing the body.

It was leaning back against the basement wall, sort of slumped over. I didn't want to touch it – I actually don't think I could have made myself touch it – but I could definitely tell it was dead, and it had been for a long time. It had almost stopped being a body and become a skeleton. Even its smell had faded.

I knelt down in front of it and looked closer.

It had long curled hair. It was wearing slacks, an untucked shirt that must have been white once but was greyish now, and a stained brownish pullover. The laces on one of its boots were hanging untied, and that made me so sad, to see it. Maybe whoever this used to be had come down here and had been in the middle of taking off their boots when they'd – no, *she'd* – died.

I realized I was thinking of her as a person then. I crossed myself, the way Da had taught me. It felt so heavy that someone had died here.

'I'm sorry,' I said into the quiet basement.

'NUALA, HAVE YOU FOUND OUT ANYTHING IMPORTANT?' May bellowed down at me.

Oh, I was mad at her.

'LEAVE OFF!' I yelled back. I swept my flashlight around the scene, and something on the front of the body's pullover glittered – a gold necklace. I reached forward and touched it. It was a pretty little heart-shaped pendant with a red jewel at its centre. I stared down at it and wanted to cry.

'I'm sorry,' I said again. Then I turned and walked towards the stairs, and May.

'I looked,' I told her crossly. 'I can't believe you made me look! But it's nothing, May. The person – I think she's a woman – probably died in the Incident.' I haven't been in London for long, but I already know that *Incident* is what people say to avoid the word *bomb*.

'Don't be stupid,' said May. 'You know what happens after Incidents. You said it yourself. Wardens and ambulance people go through houses to look for bodies. That's their job – in case someone needs to be rescued. They wouldn't miss a perfectly obvious body in a not-very-destroyed basement of a house.'

I bit my lip. She was right.

'Maybe she came down to get out of the cold and just . . . died here, sometime *after* the Incident?' I asked.

'Maybe,' said May. 'Or maybe this is a suspicious death. Until someone tells me otherwise, I'm going to *suspect* it. And if you were committed to the Detective Society, you'd help me.'

'I *am*! What are you talking about?'

I was shocked. But then—

'You've been behaving strangely at school,' said May angrily. 'You *abandoned* me. You know it's true.'

I felt myself go red. It wasn't fair of her to bring it up, especially not here. It's just that, like I said, May hates school. And I don't. And that makes May mad at me. It's like I've betrayed her whenever I try to join in with the other girls. I don't know why.

No, that's not true. Maybe I do. It's like I said before: to fit in at Deepdean you have to act a part. You have to be the English version of yourself, watch how you speak and what you wear and how you behave. I don't mind doing it, and being Fiona all the time, even though that's hard, but

May can't. She thinks I'm being fake, and she gets so angry at me.

So I . . . Maybe I did ignore her, a little. I felt bad about it, but I just thought that I had to. I thought it was part of our Ministry cover. And even people who aren't spies pretend to be different people sometimes. I mean, Eric pretends to have the last name Jones, so English people aren't frightened of him because he's German. Only, now I think about it, May is the same wherever she goes and whoever she's with. That's possibly the problem. I was acting, and she wasn't.

'I haven't abandoned you!' I said. 'Look where I am! Who's more committed to the Detective Society now?'

This was unfair, I knew, but it shut May up for a second.

And right at that moment someone came up behind her, someone large and deep-voiced, who said, 'What's all this, then? Can't you children read?'

7

'*Curses*,' said May quietly.

'Hello!' I called up. 'I've – I've found something. I need help.'

'Right then,' said the person. 'Move aside, young lady, and let me down.'

May shuffled over, then the newcomer climbed down into the basement.

I held up my flashlight and saw a big, burly man with very dark skin. He was wearing a cheap and worn-looking blue suit of rough fabric, a tin helmet with a white W printed on the front, and an arm band with several white stripes across it. A whistle was hanging around his neck, and he was holding a flashlight in one of his hands.

'What are you doing?' he asked. 'Why did you let the General down here? Can't you see it's not safe?'

'He came down here on his own!' I said. 'I tried to stop him!'

The man frowned. 'You shouldn't have followed him. You know that?'

I nodded my head, ashamed. 'But look!' I said. 'I found it when we got down here.'

I pointed at the body. The man looked and sucked in air through his teeth.

'That's not good,' he muttered. 'That's not good at all. All right, you need to leave. You can't be here.'

'But she found it—' May began to protest from the top of the stairs.

'Absolutely not,' said the man. 'Enough. You, young lady, are going back up above. You can watch from the mews like everyone else. You're Zosia's new lodgers, aren't you?'

'We are,' I said. 'I'm Nuala, and that's May.'

'Nice to meet you, then. I'm Mr Abiola. I'm the warden around here. I live in Flat Three. I was just on my way to start my shift – so you can leave me to sort this out. It's in safe hands, I promise.'

He seemed like he knew what he was talking about. He boosted the General, and then me, up the stairs, then turned back towards the dark corner where the body was.

Once I was out in the fresh clean air, Eric rushed at me, his face crinkled up with worry.

'Nuala! You're all right!'

'Of course she's all right,' grumbled May. 'It's not as though the body down there could have hurt her. It was already dead.'

'*She* was,' I said. 'I'm glad you didn't see her, Eric.'

Eric had turned pale. 'Thank you,' he said to me quietly. 'Was she— Could you tell what had happened to her?'

I shook my head.

'We must look into it, though,' said May.

'MAY!' said Eric.

'I know,' I said to him. 'She wants to be detectives again.'

'*May. No.* This isn't anything to do with us.'

We could all hear Mr Abiola digging through the basement. Most of the mews had come out to crowd around the bombed-out house.

There was Mrs Goodchild, her hair coming out of its usual chignon, and her nice patterned dress rumpled. She looked horrified, and she was clinging to the arm of Mr Goodchild, who must have just come back from work. He was leaning on his cane, his eyeglasses glinting, and murmuring something to his wife. His voice sounded reassuring, but I could see the line of worry down his forehead.

One of the women from Number 5 was there too, Miss Wimpress – she's the one Mrs Goodchild had called Primrose. She's tall, with fluffy fair hair, and she moves like a dancer – I heard Mrs Goodchild saying that she fences. She always seems kind of distracted when we see her, which isn't often – she works at the British Museum with Mr Goodchild, and she volunteers with the ambulance service too – but today she looked as though she was watching her own home burn down. Her hands were clenched together and her cheek was twitching.

I was curious about that.

The Mortensens came through the passageway into the mews then, Margot scampering ahead. Colette had the baby in a carrier on her hip, and was pushing Mrs Mortensen in her bath chair. She stopped when she saw the commotion, and Mrs Mortensen exclaimed in surprise, her knitting rolling off her lap. And then someone else came into the mews behind them. It was Zosia. Her bright red lipstick looked more vivid than ever in the sunshine, and she was wearing her glossy brown hair in beautiful rolls. I always wish I could wear lipstick that bright, but I think it might clash with my hair. Maybe when I'm older I'll be able to do it anyway.

And seeing Zosia made me realize that this case might actually have something to do with us, after all.

Because that's the thing, isn't it? May and I have the spare room in Zosia's flat, the one that should belong to her friend. And I've found out some things about that friend. Her name's Anna Goodchild, and she's Mr and Mrs Goodchild's daughter, the one who loves Victoria sponge. And she works for the Ministry, and she's . . . missing.

8

I have to go backwards a bit here to a few days ago, Diary. I've said, haven't I, about the missing agents? Daisy was one of them, obviously. We knew she was gone, but we didn't get told where, or why. It was frustrating; the Ministry knows what we can do, but we still sometimes get treated like kids – not told things, even when it'd be useful for us to know them.

And that bothered me, Diary. I liked Daisy. I met her at Elysium Hall last year. She'd been undercover, but even then, when she was just around me, May and Eric, I could see how *weird* she was. She's got the same kind of strong personality May has, although, like I said, May can't ever hide who she is. People like May and Daisy make life feel interesting, and they make you feel like *you* might be interesting too, if only you spent your life with them.

I wanted to know what'd happened to her. And so – I admit it – I've been putting our spy training to use. I told myself it was all good practice. After our coding lesson was done a couple of days ago, I said I needed the bathroom and snuck into Hazel's study at the Ministry, feeling very Nancy Drew-ish.

Hazel's desk is comfortably tidy: books lined up across it and an organized pile of letters in her drawer (once I'd picked the lock). Most of them were from Alexander, but there was a faded old note in Morse code in a different handwriting. It read *Detective Society Forever* – I was proud that I can read Morse code so quickly these days. There were other notes in the same handwriting too: *Hazel get milk* and *Hurry up with the Waverley documents – I need them.* And then one more, marking the page in the book Hazel was reading, that said: *Au revoir, Mamzelle Watson – back soon! Don't worry.* It had been folded and refolded, the paper fuzzy under my fingers.

Then I turned it over and saw that it must have been written while pressed against newsprint, because there were ghostly letters on the back of it. And part of a date: 3 Mar—.

So, Daisy had gone somewhere, earlier this month. And the evidence of the note – *Au revoir* – told me that the place she had gone was most probably France.

But why wasn't she back yet? She'd been gone for weeks, after all, but she'd said she'd be back soon.

And then I heard George and Zosia talking, the next day. I was at the top of the Ministry stairs, on my way with a message for Miss Lessing, and they were on the ground floor, so they couldn't see me.

'Still nothing from Daisy. She's missed her latest sked too,' said George. 'I'd have thought—'

'She shouldn't have gone off looking for her,' said Zosia tightly. 'I told you, Anna'll be all right on her own. She'll come back.'

'Zosh, you can't expect Daisy not to care about another agent in the field! When Anna missed the plane home, Daisy couldn't just focus on her mission as though nothing had changed. You know Daisy – she has to find out what happened to Anna. And she will; you'll see. But I don't understand why you're not more worried about Anna. You're her flatmate, and—'

'Leave it, will you? You're right; you don't understand.'

'Fine!' said George. 'I will. But if you're ever ready to talk about Anna, and you want a charming ear to listen to you, I'm here.'

'Thanks, George, but I'm quite all right,' said Zosia sharply.

And I ran away before they could notice me.

So that's how I found out that May and I were staying in a missing woman's room. I mean, I'd worked out that Anna was *gone*, because why else would May and I be sleeping in her bed – but now I knew that she was one of the missing agents, and Daisy was in France looking for her.

I got kind of fascinated by Anna after that. Once I knew to look for her, it was as though she was everywhere. There was a scarf hanging in the Ministry's entrance hall with *AG* embroidered on it and a few dark, curling hairs still tangled into it. And the rota for feeding Pfote the cat had *Anna* written on it, and then scrubbed out. Of course, Anna's a common name, but I *knew* it was her. And then I had another revelation, an even more important one. The exercise book I'm using to take Morse code notes has a list of crossed-out names on it, and one of them is *Anna Goodchild* – small, shy script, very heavily scratched out, but there all the same. That's how I worked out that Anna wasn't just Zosia's flatmate; she was Mr and Mrs Goodchild's daughter. She was tied to Hogarth Mews twice. That felt important, somehow. It made my skin prickle.

I didn't talk to May or Eric about any of this.

So when Zosia came walking into Hogarth Mews earlier today, carrying a bag of shopping, I got a jolt of knowing, somehow, that *this* is where all my investigations have been leading.

Anna Goodchild, who's missing. Anna Goodchild, who can't be found. Anna Goodchild, who Zosia didn't want Daisy to look for.

And right then the thought jumped into my head. What if Anna wasn't missing at all? What if . . . we'd just found her?

9

When I finally told May this afternoon, she was really angry at me, of course.

'You hypocrite!' she cried. 'Going on and on about not wanting to be detectives when all along – all along you've been on a case without us! Eric, can you *believe* her?'

We were in our little bedroom – *Anna's* bedroom – sitting on the bed (at least me and Eric were, May was pacing about the floor as usual) while we waited to see what was going to happen next with the body.

'It's not very nice of you,' said Eric to me. 'I thought we were supposed to be a team?'

'I didn't want to say anything until I was sure about it all,' I said, and I knew as I said it that it was a lie. The thing is, I got so used to being on my own when I lived at Elysium Hall, before May and Eric came, that it's still hard sometimes to remember I'm part of a team now.

'We could have helped,' said Eric, staring at me. 'You know we could.'

'You're right!' I said, flustered. 'I'm sorry.'

'You are a traitor to the Detective Society,' said May.

'I've told you now, haven't I?' I asked. 'Lookit, I'm sorry. I really am. I won't do it again. But, listen, don't you see what this means? What if – what if it's *Anna* in the basement? What if Daisy's in France chasing after nothing? Isn't that important? And isn't it something that we have to look into?'

'Should we not tell the Ministry?' suggested Eric.

'Why would we tell them?' asked May incredulously. 'You think Hazel will let us detect a murder, even if it's the murder of a spy? No, we have to wait until we've worked it all out, to bring it to the Ministry.'

This was suspiciously like what she'd said during the Elysium Hall case. Eric and I glanced at each other dubiously.

But her excitement was infectious. And, besides, hadn't I found a mystery at the Ministry that they were trying to keep from us? I had to admit that May was most likely right. If we went to them now with a half-piece of maybe-information, they'd probably shut us out, and I didn't want that.

Suddenly I wanted to be like Daisy. I wanted to be weird.

'All right,' I said.

'All right?' May asked.

'All right,' I said again. 'Let's do it. Let's be detectives. And if it doesn't come off—'

'It will!' said May, beaming at me.

'I do think there's something to it,' said Eric.

'I *know* there is,' said May.

I looked at them both, and I liked them such a lot that it almost choked me. I'd missed this at school. I'd missed . . . my friends. My real friends. That's still hard to say, but it's true.

And now the Detective Society were on a new case.

PART TWO

WE UNCOVER ONE
VICTIM TOO MANY

10

Thursday 27th March, continued

May went back to being mad at me almost instantly, of course.

'I just can't believe it,' she kept hissing. 'If Anna's the dead body, then we've been sleeping in a crime scene, and you didn't tell me! We might have destroyed important clues!'

'We don't know her bedroom's a crime scene,' Eric pointed out sensibly. 'It might not be. And, anyway, we can investigate it now. There's no point in imagining what *might* have happened.'

'There's always a point!' May and I said together, and then we glared at each other.

We went digging through the room. It'd been cleaned up before we arrived, obviously, so there wasn't much, but we did find an interesting pile of romance novels at the back of a shelf with the name *Anna Goodchild* doodled on their flyleaves, a pair of boots, some blouses and a blue dress in the wardrobe, and a quick sketchy drawing of a woman reading in a chair, her head and neck tipped back so you could see the line of her jaw, and her legs dangling. She had long curly hair and bony wrists and ankles, and she was smiling a little. *My beautiful Anna, by her father*, it said in the corner of the drawing.

I was staring at it thoughtfully when Eric leaned over and pointed.

'Look!' he said. 'Her necklace!'

I'd told them about the necklace I'd found on the body, the little pendant. And there it was in the drawing, hanging from Anna's neck.

So the body had to be Anna.

I felt suddenly really sick. The woman in this drawing, who looked pretty and happy and was obviously loved very much, was *dead*.

'Oh *no*!' I said.

'Oh yes!' said May. 'Excellent work! You see, we're already getting somewhere! We've practically cracked the case.'

'Of course we haven't!' said Eric. 'You're running ahead of yourself. We need to be logical. To crack the code we need the key. We might have the victim, but we're missing most of the other important facts in the case.'

May huffed. 'Like?'

'Like *when* she went down there. Nuala, you said it looked like she'd been there for a while.'

I nodded, swallowing.

'Yes, you said her skin was sort of—' May started.

'ARRA, WILL YOU STOP?' I yelled at her. She hadn't seen what I had. She didn't understand.

'So, when was the house bombed?' wondered Eric. 'Mrs Goodchild said it was the end of November last year, when the Lowndes family weren't there, but we don't know more than that. It isn't likely that the body was already there when the bomb hit, so when *did* she go down into the basement? Or did someone else put her there? *How* did she die? Was it a murder – or something else? We can't do anything more about this case without finding those things out. We shouldn't start by assuming anything, otherwise we'll miss something.'

'So what should we do, then?' May asked sulkily.

'Go down and listen to what everyone's saying,' said Eric at once. '*Be spies.* You know what they told us at the Ministry – if you listen to a conversation for long enough, someone will say something important. Loose lips. We just need to *be* there.'

Eric was right. I knew it and, from the chuntering noises she was making, so did May. We had to pretend to be company members, just part of the crowd. We had to let our suspects reveal themselves to us.

First, though, I needed to start a fresh set of case notes.

I turned to the back of the notebook I always keep in my pocket in case an idea for a play hits me and wrote down:

THE BODY IN THE BASEMENT
Time of discovery: Approximately 4:50 p.m., 27th March 1941.
Victim: Anna Goodchild (we think, from the evidence of her gold
necklace). Body had been there for a long time. Likely after the bomb
hit (in November 1940) — but is this right?

— WHEN did she end up in the basement? Was she alive or dead?
— WHEN EXACTLY did the bomb hit the house?
— WHO else was there with her, if anyone?
— HOW did she die? Was it murder? An accident? The bomb?
— HOW are we going to work this one out?

Eric looked over my shoulder and nodded approvingly.

May grumbled and said, 'That's a lot of questions. I think we know she was murdered. It just *feels* like a murder.'

'*OK*,' I said. 'Come on, let's go.'

11

Outside, the ambulance had arrived. One of the ambulance women was picking her way across the rubble of the bombed-out house, looking cross. She was young, with bushy black hair and broad shoulders, and her face was set into a frown.

'Elfie!' she called back at her partner. 'Hurry up, can't you?'

'Will you just wait, Lavinia?' the other ambulance woman shouted up at her. She was dark-haired and quick-moving, her hairstyle so daringly short that it barely peeked out from under her helmet, and she was wearing beautifully cut slacks. I'd seen her before – her name was Miss Charney and she lived with fair-haired Miss Wimpress in Number 5, the house beyond the Goodchilds'. She was standing among the other people in the mews, and had one arm around Miss Wimpress now. She was talking gently to her, offering her a handkerchief. 'Can't you see Primrose's upset?' she said to Lavinia.

'Is Primrose *injured*?' roared the bushy-haired woman. 'No, she is not. So why are you worrying about her instead of the *dead body* we've been called to look at?'

I wanted to get closer to Miss Wimpress and Miss Charney. Both of them were civil defence volunteers, and so I wondered whether either of them had been the people who had looked through the house when it had been bombed last November. And I wondered too why Miss Wimpress was so upset. She must see bodies all the time. But she still had the stricken look on her face that I'd seen before we'd gone back into our flat.

I went sidling towards them, half turning my body away so it looked like I was talking to Eric. They were whispering really quietly, and it was hard to tune my ear in to their speech, especially as they were pausing halfway through sentences in that way that adults who know each other really well do. It's a seriously annoying habit. But I did catch a couple of sentences.

'—worried,' murmured Miss Wimpress.

'Nonsense, Prim, you mustn't be,' said Miss Charney, louder. 'Listen to me. It's nothing. I—'

Then whispering again.

'—for months!' said Miss Wimpress. 'If it's *her*—'

'WILL you be quiet, darling!' hissed Miss Charney. 'Stay here, can't you? Temple is about to scream. I must go and do my job. *Don't worry.* It will all come right, I promise.'

Miss Wimpress had said *her*. Was that the body? But if so, how did Miss Wimpress know it was a woman's? Nothing had been brought up from the basement yet.

Lavinia – Miss Temple – and Miss Charney hadn't even lowered themselves down through the hole. Maybe when Mr Abiola had reported the body, he'd said it seemed to be female, but— No, the way Miss Wimpress had said it just wasn't right.

I was highly suspicious, and when I looked at Eric, I could see he was as well.

May, meanwhile, had wriggled her way over to Mr and Mrs Goodchild. I could tell she was trying to avoid Colette and the kids. She doesn't like kids much, which is funny since she's got a little brother. She hasn't even asked to see the Mountfitchets' daughter. (I've only seen her once, if I'm honest. Most babies are dotes, but Tess is not. She looked right at me with a witchy little face and threw up all over my skirt.) So I nudged Eric and started to wander over towards the Mortensens while Miss Temple carefully moved down the stairs into the basement.

Margot was asking for a biscuit and Mrs Mortensen, who had levered herself out of her bath chair and was leaning on a walking stick, was complaining that the cobblestones were very uneven. The baby Olivier was writhing like an eel in Colette's arms, kicking his arms and pointing frantically at the ground.

'Don't drop him, Colette,' said Mrs Mortensen.

'I will try to avoid it,' said Colette tightly. Her hair was pulled back into an unhappy bun, and she had a stain running down her skirt that looked a lot like what Tess had thrown up on me. The long red birthmark on her cheek was starker than usual – or maybe it was just the pinched, worried look on her face making it seem that way. She knelt down and put one arm around the General, who licked her face. Margot tapped at her leg and whimpered.

'Tais-toi, Margot,' said Colette, more gently than I'd heard her talk before.

'These stupid cobbles!' said Mrs Mortensen, wobbling a little. She still has a bit of an accent when she talks English – I've heard her speaking Norwegian to the kids, the way Da used to speak a bit of Irish to me. 'What is happening? Can you see?'

'Just wait – they'll be coming up soon.'

At that moment, Miss Temple stuck her head up through the gap to the basement. 'NO ONE GO ANYWHERE,' she bellowed. 'WE SHALL NEED TO TALK TO YOU *ALL*.'

'Talk?' asked Colette. 'What for?'

'I expect they think there's been a murder,' said Mrs Mortensen cheerfully, and for the first time I saw her face break into a smile.

'No! But . . . they wouldn't,' said Colette. 'We don't even know— The authorities don't know anything.'

'What is there to know? There's a body,' said Mrs Mortensen.

'Was it squished by the bomb?' asked Margot.

'Oui, bien sûr,' said Colette. But I saw her face falter. She didn't believe what she was saying – adults often don't when they talk to kids, but they usually hide it better.

'Don't worry, Margot – it's nothing to do with us, I'm sure,' she added. And I could tell that Colette knew she was lying.

12

That was when the body came up on a stretcher. Mr Abiola lifted it out, with Miss Temple and Miss Charney pushing it up from the basement. It was covered in a white sheet, and everyone went quiet as it passed, apart from the kid Margot, who yelled 'SQUISHED BY THE BOMB!' again, and was shushed by Mrs Mortensen.

Then Cecil strolled out of the Goodchilds' house into the mews.

'What's all this?' he asked, yawning and looking around at the crowd and the ambulance volunteers carrying the stretcher down from the bombed-out house. 'I was napping. What did I miss?'

As the body was carried past us all, the sheet shifted to one side so the body's stained pullover was revealed, and I saw the gold necklace glinting in the sun.

Cecil saw it too, and he froze.

'That's Anna's necklace!' he shouted. 'Mum, Dad, look!'

Mr and Mrs Goodchild turned to him. 'Cecil, dear, of course it isn't—' Mrs Goodchild began, looking concerned.

'It is!' cried Cecil, looking from them to the stretcher.

'It's from her birthday, two years ago. I know it is. What's wrong with you? Don't you remember? That's *Anna's necklace*. What if – what if that's Anna?'

'Cecil, no!' said Mr Goodchild. 'I'm sure it's just – well – some poor person who lost their home.'

'Then why do they have Anna's necklace?'

'Did you say *Anna*?' asked Mr Abiola, coming up to him and putting a hand on his shoulder. 'Cecil, lad, did you say Anna?'

'What? Yes, I did!' said Cecil. 'You know she's been missing since December.'

'She's not *missing*,' murmured Mrs Goodchild to Mr Abiola. 'She has a most important job. We can't know more than that, and you didn't hear it from me.'

'Stop muttering, Mum – I can't hear you! Mr A, what if this is Anna? What'll we do?'

Cecil looked terrified, and I felt so sorry for him. I knew how he felt. I know what it's like to lose someone so close to you, someone you can't imagine ever being without.

'Don't panic yet, lad,' said Mr Abiola, turning his face down to Cecil's. 'We'll look into it. I'm sure Anna is quite all right, and this person simply bought a similar necklace.'

'But—'

Cecil's parents put their arms on his shoulders and guided him backwards as Mr Abiola turned to follow the stretcher.

I wanted to go after Mr Abiola. May was already scuttling along behind the stretcher, and Eric was loitering in the entrance to the mews. I was proud of us right then. We were working as a team again, just the way we had in Elysium Hall.

'Do go away,' said Miss Charney to May. 'This isn't nice to look at.'

'But I want to see!' cried May, unsubtle as always. 'It's interesting!'

The other woman, Miss Temple, turned and blinked down at her. 'Am I hallucinating?' she asked. 'Are you any relation to Hazel Wong?'

'NO!' cried May. 'Yes. She's my sister. It's not my fault!'

'So you are! And just as annoying as she is. D'you know she once attacked me on a hockey pitch?'

'*Hazel?*'

'It made me respect her, actually,' said Miss Temple. 'But never mind that. What are you doing here?'

'If you know Hazel, can I look at the body?'

'Absolutely not. Go away!'

They began to bicker, and I suddenly wondered whether May was being unsubtle at least slightly on purpose, dragging the spotlight onto herself so no one would notice me and Eric. I slipped backwards into the shadow of the mews entrance, playing my best Crowd Member 5. The trick of playing a crowd member is being so dull that no one in the audience can even be bothered to rest their eyes on you, and I played it for all I was worth until I'd slunk all the way out of the mews to where the ambulance was parked and hid behind its back wheel. Eric was hovering by a newspaper seller, a few feet away. He's not as good as I am at being inconspicuous, but he's obviously been practising. May, just as obviously, is still extremely bad.

I waited, breathing lightly and floating on the balls of my feet.

At last, there was the *thunk* of the ambulance doors opening and the rattle of the stretcher being pushed into it.

'Got rid of her at last,' said Miss Temple's voice. 'Can you believe it? Little fool.'

'Your school friend's sister?'

'I suppose I shouldn't be surprised. Hazel and Daisy always managed to come across the most ridiculous things. We actually had— Well, never mind that. It's all in the past now. How about this, then, Charney?'

'It's the oddest thing,' said Miss Charney. 'I attended the Incident myself. November the twenty-fourth. Swept the rubble, looked down in the basement. Our old warden Fig was there too, and she didn't miss a thing. Never did. There definitely wasn't a body there. I suppose it's a poor bombed-out civilian who got an injury, wandered in out of the cold and died somehow. Terribly sad. I'm sure the coroner will confirm it.'

'So you don't think it's this Anna person?' asked Miss Temple.

'I shouldn't think so. I've told you about her before – she's the daughter of one of the families here, the Goodchilds. No, she's quite all right. Don't worry about Anna.'

I heard new footsteps then, and a voice saying, 'Be off, lad! No more hanging around.'

'Abiola,' said Miss Charney. 'We'll take this straight to the coroner – a nice easy one.'

'I just wanted to say,' said Mr Abiola, 'it's the strangest thing, isn't it?'

'Mmm,' said Miss Temple. 'Very. Can we get on?'

'Yes, now, wait a moment. I know the Goodchild boy is very set on it being Anna. And the necklace – I can't really square that. I remember Anna wearing it. But, look, I'm wondering something. What about *Miss Fig*?'

'Fig?' said Miss Charney. 'The old warden? I was just telling Temple she was the one who cleared the mews house with me. It can't be her. She left London a couple of weeks after the Incident, remember? Cracks all up her own house, Number Two, so she went to join the Lowndes family in the country. You saw the note at Post. No, she's not our problem any more.'

'Well, yes, I did . . . but her leaving was so sudden—'

'Hardly sudden! She wouldn't shut up about it. We were hearing about her packing up for a week at least. She's gone, Abiola – and aren't you glad?'

76

'What do you mean?' asked Mr Abiola sharply.

'Well, you're the warden now, aren't you? Moving up the ranks. More responsibility and more money – and I know you need the money, don't you? I'm sure you don't want her back. So be careful what you wish for.'

'Now—'

'I'm sure we'll see you down at Post when your shift starts,' said Miss Charney. 'If you'll excuse us, we've got a dead body to take to the coroner. Add to his backlog. Come on, Temple.'

That was my cue. I retreated as fast as I could, and then turned and began to walk casually across the road, like I had somewhere to be but wasn't too urgent about it. The important thing about acting is that you have to make a story in your head, about what you're doing and why you're doing it. That time I was a girl who was going shopping for tinned tongue, which she didn't like, so she was being slow.

I was getting really into that story, so that I didn't even notice Eric rushing up to me at first, until he grabbed my arm.

'Hey! Nuala! They've gone!' he said. 'Did you hear it? I missed most of it. What did they say?'

I shook back into myself.

'They said,' I told him, becoming Nuala again, 'that there's more than one person who might be missing from Hogarth Mews. Have you heard of someone called Miss Fig?'

13

'Miss Fig?' said Zosia.

We were all sitting at the table in her little kitchen, eating an early dinner, which was spam and potatoes and not very nice. Zosia had an apron over her silky blouse, and she looked as annoyed as she always does at having to cook for us.

'It's a name we heard,' I said carefully.

'What do you want to know about her?' asked Zosia. 'She's gone.'

We all flinched. The body had to be Anna's, surely – but now we'd found out that another person in Hogarth Mews had left after the bomb. It felt strange.

'She lived in Number Two,' said Zosia. 'She moved out last year, in December, I think. When the Lowndes family at Number One were bombed, her house was damaged too, so she left. Not a particular loss. She was the warden, and she thought that meant she was allowed to be rude to the whole mews. She was always banging on our door telling us that light was showing in the windows, and then coming in and snooping around. Anna was nicer to her than I ever was.'

'People keep talking about Anna,' said Eric. 'If she was Mr and Mrs Goodchild's daughter, why did she live here with you?'

'And where is she?' I added. 'It's not true, what Cecil said, is it?'

Zosia scowled.

'Of course it isn't true!' she said. 'She's perfectly fine. *She's away on business. Ministry* business. That's all I should have to say to you, and I hope you'll understand me. And she *lives* with me because she's a grown adult, and when you're an adult you want your own space.'

Then she glared round at the three of us meaningfully. 'Don't you want to go and play? I have to get on with the washing-up.'

'We're not *six*,' said May scornfully.

'Fine, then go and work on your translations,' said Zosia. 'I don't care. I've a programme on the wireless I want to hear later.'

'She's mean,' May whispered as we crept out of the kitchen.

'I CAN HEAR YOU,' called Zosia. 'Don't be rude!'

We all crowded into mine and May's bedroom – the one that used to be Anna's. It creeped me out now, to be in it.

'What if we climbed out of the window?' asked May. 'Oh, we need to go investigate the scene again! Nuala, I don't think you looked at it properly!'

'We don't!' I said.

'We really don't,' agreed Eric. 'We do have more to consider, though. Are we sure about that necklace? Because I think we've got *two* possible . . . is the word "suspects"?'

'No, I think it's "victims",' I said. 'And yes, I'm sure. I know what I saw – it's the necklace from the drawing of Anna. And Cecil confirmed it!'

'It does seem as though the body is Anna's. But we can't be certain yet, can we? Not until it's identified by the coroner – and that might be a while. Miss Charney said there was a backlog.'

'Of course we can be sure,' said May. 'It's Anna, we agreed. We just need to work out how she died, and when, and why.'

'We do know more about that! We know she died *after* the Incident,' I said. 'There was no one in the house when the civil defence crew looked through it after the bomb in November – Miss Charney said so. So Anna was put there – or went there herself – after that.'

'All right then. How and why?' asked Eric.

May didn't reply, and I turned to see her standing by the window, craning upwards with her mouth open.

'What are you doing?' I asked, annoyed.

'I'm watching Cecil Goodchild climb down the wall to us,' said May.

'WHAT?' I said.

'Oh, shh, come and look!' said May.

Eric and I rushed over to her and peered upwards – and, sure enough, there was a pair of feet wriggling down towards us, weirdly huge and the body behind them foreshortened. The end of a rope tapped against the top window pane.

'I'm going to open the window,' said May.

'No—' Eric began, but she was already turning the catch and pushing the glass open.

'Hello!' she called up to Cecil. 'What are you doing?'

The rope swung backwards, the feet kicked and then, with a thump, Cecil dropped onto our window ledge.

'Hello,' he said, crouching down to look at us all. 'I need to talk to you. Are you brave enough to come up on the roof?'

'No thank you,' said Eric.

'Isn't that dangerous?' I asked. From up close, Cecil smelled like rust. I could see the dirt under his nails and the unusual device in his ear.

'Oh, *absolutely*,' breathed May. 'Eric, I'll lift you up.'

'You can't do that!' Eric and I both said together. We remembered what had happened at Elysium Hall last year.

'*I'll* lift you up,' said Cecil. 'I need to talk to you. You – you're Nuala, right? You saw the body.'

I nodded, starstruck.

'I have to know what it looked like. I need to know – I need to know if it was Anna.'

14

The top of Hogarth Mews Mansions was flat, with a funny little roof garden that had some scrubby sooty trees in pots and a couple of sad little clumps of grass. It was like being in a secret bird's nest, looking down on the mews itself, and it hadn't been that hard to climb up, once we tried. Eric had squeaked a bit, but it wasn't worse than climbing a tree. We all just held on to the rope and the drainpipe, and tried to go as quietly as we could.

'So, what do you want from us?' asked May, sticking out her chin and glaring at Cecil once we were all up safely. I knew she was just acting, and I could also see that it didn't really impress him.

He gave her a funny little sideways grin and said, 'Tough kid, are you? Don't worry. Here, have this cake. I brought it for you. All I want is to talk about Anna.'

I noticed something, watching him talk to May. He twisted his head a little, to the side with the device on his ear, when she spoke. It made him look a little bored, like he was half watching something else, but I didn't think that could be it. The thing in his ear was helping him listen to her – and, as

I realized that, I remembered the way his parents and Mr Abiola had turned towards him as they spoke to him.

'She's eight years older than me,' Cecil went on. 'And she's – I mean, she's the best person I know. That's sappy, and you'd better not tell anyone I said that when we get down from here, but it's true. She's so brave, and she's clever and funny, and she always manages to get out of tight spots. I'm still waiting to join up, but when the war started she went and got some job. She said it was a typing pool, but *I* think that it's something important and hush-hush. Anyway, she did that until last summer, and then she started being sent away. Just for a weekend at first, and then longer. And then, in December, my parents told me she'd gone away again – but that time she never came back.

'My parents aren't worried, but I am. I made her promise me that she'd write to me if she went away, but she hasn't. I haven't heard from her since then, and it's been months. And now this body's been found – I need to know if it's her. Did it look like her?'

'You haven't actually told us what she looked like,' said May, taking a piece of cake – even though, of course, we knew from the drawing. She was testing him. 'And what's that in your ear?'

'What's it to you?' asked Cecil. 'None of your business, is it? Anna looked like me, but a girl. Dark curly hair, skinny, big feet, five feet nine inches tall, twenty-four years old. So? Was it her?'

'The body . . . it'd been there for a while,' I said cautiously, biting into the cake myself. It was sweet and nutty, with little bursts of raisins in it. I don't get where Mrs Goodchild finds all these ingredients. 'I don't know. It could have been. She had on that necklace, the one you saw – so if that's Anna's . . .'

I didn't want to finish the sentence. I felt, then, that we all knew. The body had to be Anna's, didn't it?

'Who's Miss Fig?' asked May.

Cecil started. 'What?' he asked. 'Did you say *Miss Fig*?'

'Yes. Mr Abiola was talking to the ambulance drivers about someone called Miss Fig,' Eric explained. 'He said that she's missing too.'

'She's not *missing*!' said Cecil. He looked really surprised. His eyebrows went up in winged points. 'She was our warden – you know, she made sure we all went to the shelter during air raids, and checked the blackout, and helped at Incidents. But she left after the Lowndes' house was hit. Went to the country. Look, no one misses her. She was a real busybody, always upset at everything. She watched out of her window, all the time, and spied on us. I think she worked out— Well, never mind that.'

'But if she left,' said Eric, 'how do you know she's *not* missing? Have you heard from her?'

'Ugh! No! Catch me writing to *her*! She was always telling Mum and Dad off for letting me run around on my own. Like they could stop me! But I went into her house last

84

December, and she'd moved out. I was looking for scrap – I collect it from bomb sites and other places, see. Scrap collecting's good money, and it's fun. You can't imagine the stuff you find, and then the council pays you back for it. So I know Miss Fig's gone, *not* missing. All her stuff's gone too. Can't we get back to Anna? How can you not know whether it was her?'

'Because—' May started, but I cut her off.

'Hey, that's not the right question to ask,' I said to Cecil firmly. 'We've told you we're not sure, because we're not yet. But we're going to find out – if you just give us a chance.'

'What, you? You're kids!'

'We're not kids; we're dete—' started May.

I slapped a hand across her mouth. Obviously, she bit me. I guess that was my fault, but I didn't want her to keep being so loose-lipped. Cecil seemed like he really was looking for his sister, but I'd suddenly had a moment of worry. What if *he* was responsible for the body in the basement? Sure, wouldn't someone guilty do this very thing – try to find out how much we knew? Could we really trust *anyone* on a street where a dead body had been found?

'When did you last see Anna?' I asked, as May sputtered and hissed like a kettle on the stove.

'*And* Miss Fig,' Eric put in. He was making his most turtley face of concentration, so I knew he was putting something together in his head. I couldn't understand it.

No matter what I was saying to Cecil, I thought we *did* know that the body was Anna. I just didn't want to upset him before the coroner identified her.

'Anna – the morning of the sixth of December,' said Cecil at once. 'I was going to school just after eight and I waved at her; she was looking out of the window of her flat.'

That was really precise, and that surprised me. It's hard to remember back even a month ago, and if I didn't have this diary I'd get so confused. Your brain sometimes sticks different days together, especially when you're doing the same kind of thing over and over again, like going to school. Some stuff you just know, like fish on Fridays and Games on Tuesday afternoons, but then it's hard to remember *which* Friday Mariella Semple threw her hake on the floor and told Matron she was a vegetarian.

'How do you know?' I asked.

'Because that day was a Friday, and she wasn't there when I got back from school to get her for Friday night dinner,' said Cecil. 'We're Jewish, and so that meal's important. It's—'

'We know about that,' said Eric, and he was right. We knew from our Elysium Hall case. Friday evenings are a special time for Jewish people, like Sunday is for Christians.

'It's *important*,' said Cecil. 'She'd never missed making Shabbos before, even when she was travelling for work. And, anyway, I remember the sixth, because it was a Fog.'

He said that as though fog was an important person, *Fog*, which was weird. May looked confused too, but Eric was nodding.

'You two aren't Londoners, are you?' asked Cecil. 'Hah! If you stay here until the autumn, you'd better be careful. You can't see *anything* in a pea-souper. It's worse than the blackout. Imagine a sheet over your face, and it's woolly and yellowish and it *smells*. People end up walking right out into the river, or out in front of a car. Last autumn was so clear, though – good for the Germans, bad for us – which is why I remember the Fog on the sixth. It started to come in after lunchtime, I think. And that's the thing – because there was a Fog, I knew Anna couldn't have gone anywhere that afternoon. So where was she? Where *is* she? Something's happened to her, I know it.'

His fists were clenched.

'And what about Miss Fig?' asked Eric.

'Will you stop asking about Miss Fig? I don't know!' Cecil grumbled. 'It must have been around the same time – the Incident happened at the end of November, and Miss Fig kept on complaining that her wall had cracked and it was dangerous. She said that she was going to go to the council for compensation, but that mustn't have worked out, because then I heard she went to stay with the Lowndes family. I don't know why they'd invite her; they didn't like her either, but she would go on and on until she got what she wanted usually. And she left a note. Mr Abiola told us about it, and that's why I went looking around her house. Here, you three are no help at all. If I find out that you've been holding out on me—'

'We're not!' I protested.

'How do we know *you* aren't?' asked May. That was kind of interesting – that she was thinking along the same lines as me.

'Oh, I give up!' snapped Cecil. He looked really mad. 'All right. The three of you can get back down on your own. Go on, down the rope again.'

'Where are you going?' asked May. 'Why can't we come? Is it secret?'

'Again, it's none of your business. You're as nosy as Miss Fig!'

'Why's she called Miss Fig?' I asked, as Cecil practically shoved us towards the rope again. I couldn't work out why she'd been named after a fruit.

'Short for Figueroa,' said Cecil. 'I think her father was Spanish. But I don't care. All right. Stay here, if you like. I'm leaving.'

15

'Useless!' fumed May when he'd gone. 'How dare he! I hate him!'

'I think he's worried about his sister,' I said. 'Probably, anyway. And he brought us cake.'

'Oh, he's worried about his sister, is he? I don't see why he should be – he's such a – a—'

'Because she's probably dead,' said Eric quietly, taking another piece of the cake. Cecil'd left it behind. Fruit cake isn't my favourite, but, like I said, you never say no to cake in a war.

'It has to be Anna, doesn't it?' I asked him sadly. I was trying to think back to the body. It'd only been a few hours and I was already getting mixed up. I'd just seen a hunched-up shape, a pair of slacks, some curls and that necklace. I felt kind of hopeless. How could we prove anything? On our last case, it'd been . . . not easy, and not fun; it'd been awful actually – but *contained*. We'd known it was a murder. We'd known when the murder had happened. And we'd known all the people it could have been. This time we didn't know anything.

'I think we know a lot of things,' said Eric.

He said it so firmly that I looked up at him in surprise. I'd been feeling pretty low, but he was sitting with his arms folded and his head up, his eyes gleaming.

'First of all, we have a timeline. The Incident, the bomb, happened on the twenty-fourth of November. Miss Charney said so, and I remember because that's my birthday. There wasn't a body in the basement then. The last time Cecil saw Anna was –' Eric quickly counted on his fingers – 'just under two weeks later, on the morning of the sixth of December. The fog happened that afternoon, and Cecil said Anna wasn't there that evening to make Shabbos, or any time after that. Everyone else seems sure that Anna's lost in the field, on a mission somewhere – everyone including the Ministry – but if that's not true, and the body *is* Anna, then she was probably put there some time on the sixth. And Miss Fig went away at about the same time, because she left a note that Mr Abiola saw, and then Cecil went looking around her house and saw she was gone.'

'Don't we *know* the body is Anna by now?' I asked. I didn't get why he kept coming back to Miss Fig.

'Maybe,' said Eric. 'But it's a logical fallacy to assume that only Anna matters.'

'Ooh, big words!' said May, making a face.

'Hazel told us about that yesterday,' said Eric. 'You just weren't listening. It means assuming something and making a mistake because of that. We have *one* body, and so you think we need only *one* missing person. But that's not what we have. There are two people in Hogarth Mews Mansions who no one's seen since the end of last year – actually, there are more than two. Anna, Miss Fig and the Lowndes family.'

'The Lowndes family went to their house in the country, and so did Miss Fig!' protested May.

'But how do we *know*?' asked Eric, maddeningly calm. 'We don't. So we have to find out. I think you're right, and the Lowndes family are safe. But we need to make sure, because Miss Fig is supposed to have gone to stay with them. If she did, she's safe too, and then we *do* know that the body is Anna. But if she didn't, then we don't have just one problem to solve and one person to find. We have two.'

'Well, we've found one of them,' said May. 'That's obvious. Oh, come on, Eric – this is all too complicated. We've got a body and it's obviously Anna's.'

'It *isn't* obvious!' said Eric, sounding almost annoyed – which means a lot, coming from him. 'And we still ought to find them both. Otherwise who's looking for them? Imagine being lost, in a war, with no one realizing you're gone. This is *important*.'

THE BODY IN THE BASEMENT

Time of discovery: Approximately 4:50 p.m., 27th March 1941.

Victim: Anna Goodchild (we think, from the evidence of her gold necklace). Body had been there for a long time. ~~Likely after the bomb~~

hit (in November 1940) — but is this right? NB: Miss Figueroa is also missing. Is this important?

- WHEN did she end up in the basement? Was she alive or dead? Anna was last seen by Cecil Goodchild on Friday 6th December 1940. Miss Fig left a note saying she went to the country with the Lowndes family in early December.
- WHEN EXACTLY did the bomb hit the house? 24th November 1940.
- WHO else was there with her, if anyone?
- HOW did she die? Was it murder? An accident? The bomb?
- HOW are we going to work this one out?

16

Today we were at the Ministry, Diary, but we couldn't just focus on learning. We had a theory – that Anna wasn't on a mission for the Ministry at all but lying on a coroner's slab somewhere – and we needed to prove it. We had to get a look at the Ministry records for December somehow.

This morning was languages and codes again. We're doing a lot of decoding, because that's what the Ministry needs. There are endless messages coming in right now. I was chipping away at a message in French that I thought was probably about information on a boat, or an agent arriving on a boat – unless it wasn't *boat* at all but misspelled *hat*, and then everything made a lot less sense. Eric had just decoded his third message (remember, he knows German as well as English, so he's way ahead) and May was wrestling with a very short code in Polish that she'd turned into a graveyard of angry black scribbles.

'We do need to know what that says, May,' said George,

peering down at her from where he was sitting at the front of the room, his amputated leg propped up on the teacher's desk in front of him, eating an apple. He did it like there was a spotlight on him, even though there was no one else in the room apart from the three of us and Hazel.

'You don't care!' said May. 'It's all just games, not real.'

'May, I've told you, we're overstretched,' said Hazel. She was sitting next to George, working away at a code of her own, poking and prodding and sighing at it. I don't know Hazel well, but I can tell that she's a leader, the kind of person who acts warm and easy to keep everyone else calm, and hides how she's actually feeling. So the fact that I could see worry lines on her forehead was concerning. 'We've got too many agents in the field, so we need everyone here to be working. That message *is* real, and you're ruining it. Focus, can't you?'

'If I do, will you tell us where Daisy is?' asked May.

'MAY,' said Hazel and George together. I saw George put out his hand to cover Hazel's, and I saw her shoulder lean against his arm for a moment. So it wasn't just Hazel who was worried about Daisy.

'She's always been all right before,' said George to Hazel, and then the telephone rang, the one that communicates between different rooms in the Ministry. He picked it up.

'Ralph!' he said warmly. 'Hello.'

'George!' murmured Hazel. 'I told you to stop calling each other unless you need to.'

'It's about work, Hazel, shh— Ralph, did you say that there's a code you need help with? I'll be over in just one second—'

As George got up and went out of the room on his crutches, Hazel put her pencil down on the table quite hard and said, 'MAY! Look, you've ruined it – you'll have to start again!'

'I have not!' bawled May. 'I've almost got it, I swear!'

And right then she kicked me, hard, in the ankle.

May has a really strong kick, like a baby horse, but this time I got what she meant, and got that she didn't (probably) want to hurt me at all. She was telling me to go, now, while George and Hazel were both distracted.

I leaned over and poked Eric in the stomach, and then I said, 'Eric, did you forget to feed Pfote?'

Eric would never forget to feed Pfote. Neither would the rest of the Ministry, so Pfote is very generously sized these days. But Eric nodded and said, 'Oh! I did, yes!'

He's really bad at acting, Diary, but Hazel didn't notice. She just waved her hand at us while she leaned crossly over May, and we scuttled out of the room together.

'Quick!' I said once we were outside. 'The records office!'

I'd wanted to get there to look for Anna. I'd been hoping to do that, even before I found the body. But it's tough getting there on your own. There are always people watching it, and I never got close. But now that I wasn't alone, I thought I had a chance.

'Follow my lead,' I whispered to Eric, as we went rushing through the dark wood corridors of 13 Great Russell Street. 'When I've distracted them, go and look at December 1940, all right? We need to know if Anna really did have a mission around the sixth.'

When we opened the door, red-haired Miss Lessing was there, taking notes on a sheet of paper. Zosia was sitting next to her, a headset around her neck, frowning unhappily at a piece of foolscap paper.

'Miss Stosic, help them,' Miss Lessing said. 'I need to run this over to Mrs M. I'll be back in ten minutes.'

'Yes, Miss Lessing,' said Zosia. 'What do you need, Nuala?'

'Hazel's asked for records from May 1940,' I said, doing my best uninterested act.

'Which country?' asked Zosia. I pretended not to remember if it was Poland or Czechoslovakia, and as I dithered I saw Eric out of the corner of my eye, sidling towards December 1940.

I finally pretended to remember that it was Norway, after all, and we went together to the logbook in the next room. You see, you can't just take records away – that's another problem. You have to sign them out, so there's no way that I could ever just walk out with the records I wanted, or even look at them without a note made of it. Without help, that is.

I tried to take as long writing out the request as possible, and I knew I was doing a good job because Zosia looked

96

crossly at her watch. At last I couldn't dawdle any longer, and we came back into the main room – just in time to see Eric smiling and holding out a piece of paper.

'This fell off your desk,' he said.

'Thank you, Eric,' said Zosia. 'Is that everything, Nuala?'

'Yes, thank you,' I said. 'Come on, Eric.'

I felt kind of bad about lying to Zosia, even though she has been pretty mean to us. But we had to.

'Did you get it?' I hissed to Eric.

'Under my pullover,' he said, patting his stomach, which rustled.

Together we ran to the bathroom on the first floor. Eric locked the door, while I ran the cold tap as hard as I could, and then Eric pulled a thin file from under his jumper.

It said TOP SECRET on it in red ink.

'We're going to really be in trouble,' said Eric to me. 'You know that, don't you?'

'I know!' I said. 'But we have to! We have to find out what's happened to Anna!'

Eric nodded and flipped it open.

17

ASSIGNMENT LIST, it said at the top of the paper. NOVEMBER/
DECEMBER 1940.

I scanned down it like I was reading a script, picking out
names I knew.

AGENT SHERLOCK (Daisy Wells) – Cairo, Egypt,
16th November (Operation Iskander) RETURNED

AGENT SIDHE (Bridget O'Connell) – Galway, Ireland,
25th November (Operation Merryweather) RETURNED

AGENT TROY (Helen Mountfitchet) – Southampton, England,
29th November (Operation Basking Shark) RETURNED

AGENT SHERLOCK (Daisy Wells) – Uppsala, Sweden,
4th December (Operation Christina) RETURNED

AGENT GENTILESCHI (Anna Goodchild) – Paris, France,
6th 7th December (Operation Modigliani)

My heart dropped. I can't explain it any other way. This
didn't make sense. It read as though Anna *had* left.

'But—' I said. 'There must be a mistake. The sixth must have been called off because of the fog, so they rescheduled it for the seventh. But – but she can't have *left*.'

'Of course she left,' said Eric, who's always really logical. 'They'd have made a note about it if she hadn't. Zosia keeps careful records. She's good with details. You know that. And look, they've put "Returned" on everyone else, but not Anna's.'

'Yes, so—'

'So Anna *did* leave, but she hasn't come back,' said Eric. 'Otherwise Zosia would have marked it down the way she has with the others. So the Ministry story is true. Anna *is* missing, but she's missing in the field. She's not the person you found down in the basement.'

'But I don't understand it!' I said. 'The necklace! It was Anna's – you saw the picture!'

'I don't know,' said Eric, shrugging. 'I can't explain it. But these records can't be wrong.'

I was still struggling – it just didn't make sense – when someone kicked at the bathroom door from the outside.

'HEY!' said May in her blaring whisper. 'I NEED A WEE.'

'Shh, May! You'll give us away!' Eric hissed back.

'Oh good, it is you,' said May cheerfully. 'Let me in, I want to see what you found! And also I do need a wee, actually.'

Our lesson this afternoon was with red-haired Miss Lessing. She works on the telephones, and she's also the person in charge of preparing agents for missions and sending them out into the field when they're ready (oh, I really want to be ready soon), and tracking them until they come back again. Zosia helps her, and she's the one who marks down the notes on each agent.

As Miss Lessing was talking to us, with Eric listening intently and May nibbling at a bit of her nail and fidgeting her foot, I realized that this was absolutely the perfect opportunity to find out more about what could have happened on the night that Anna had apparently left. Was there any way the Ministry might have got confused? How could Anna be in France but her necklace be on a dead body in a basement in London?

'Now, there are three things you should NEVER bring with you on a mission,' said Miss Lessing. 'What are they, Nuala?'

'Your real identity papers,' I said, thinking. 'Any personal objects. And—'

'Ooh, ooh, I know!' said May, coming out of her trance. 'YOUR REAL UNDERWEAR.'

'Thank you, May,' said Miss Lessing. 'Helpful as always. You're quite right, you mustn't wear anything from your real life. Anything could have a laundry stamp on it, of course, and things like handkerchiefs might have your real initials. And yes, Nuala, you're right too. You must collect a new wardrobe from the costume department and leave every important personal item behind. That means no keepsakes, no charms or messages from loved ones – agents have been caught because they've forgotten or refused to leave a necklace or watch that can be traced back to their real identity.'

Eric coughed and shuffled, and I knew he was thinking of his father's watch, which had nearly ruined things for us at Elysium Hall. I'd had a thought too. Of course – if Anna had gone on the mission, she'd have had to leave her necklace behind. Did that mean someone else had found it? Someone had stolen it?

'You will then meet your contact at the pre-arranged place. Eric, how will you identify yourself?'

'With a code phrase,' said Eric promptly.

'Excellent. Remember you are testing them too – you need to make sure they are who they say they are before you agree to go with them. You will then be taken to the airfield in an unmarked car, and from there onto the plane that will fly you to your destination. What will you do when you get to the airfield?'

'Get on the plane?' asked May.

'*Use your second code phrase to make sure that you are still in the right place*, May. You will be given your kit, including your radio and new identity papers; you will get into the plane and you will sit quietly and not distract the pilot, who is going to a lot of trouble to get you to your destination. May, are you listening?'

'D'you know, I thought that the Ministry would be better

than school,' said May, scowling. 'But you all believe what Hazel told you about me. I'm not *six* any more.'

'Then maybe you shouldn't have worked so hard to join the particular agency that your sister helps to run, May. And I'd say that wasn't fair or true, either. It isn't about who you were before you joined. It's about who you are now. Aren't we training you up? Would we do that if we thought you were still a baby?'

'HUMPH,' said May.

'What would you do if the agent – I mean, if we didn't arrive where we were supposed to?' I asked. My heart was thumping. 'Would you make a note of it, or—'

'Of course we would, Nuala. We keep careful records, you know that.'

'And what if – what if we were *caught*?'

'We'd know that too. We're watching, I promise. Listen to me. Sometimes things go wrong. I won't lie to you about that. This is a dangerous business, and when you become an agent you have to know that – that we can't guarantee you'll see the end of this war. But we do everything we can to keep you safe. We don't just let agents go out without keeping a watch on them. Like I said, we have careful records. It all goes into our notes.'

'Then what about Anna Goodchild?'

I really thought I'd been the one to ask that. But Miss Lessing was staring, open-mouthed, at Eric.

'Where is she?' he asked. This was unlike him. It should

have been me or May blurting that out. I glanced at her and saw that she was just as shocked as I was. 'We talked to her brother. He's worried about her.'

Miss Lessing blushed. She's even more of a redhead than I am, so her blush turned her whole face pink. She suddenly looked kind of young and not like a teacher at all.

'You mustn't tell anyone this, not even her brother – Official Secrets Act, you know. But Anna is missing in the field, in France,' she said. 'That's— You must have heard that's where Daisy is. She's looking for Anna, and she will find her, if she can be found. *We don't leave agents behind.*'

And I really thought she was telling the truth.

So Anna *had* got on the plane and gone to France on the seventh of December. That meant that, despite everything, she wasn't the person I'd found in the basement. She *was* missing, but she wasn't our victim.

And if she wasn't the victim, then . . . Well, there was another person we knew was missing from Hogarth Mews, who had vanished at about the same time. Someone who *could* have found Anna's necklace – or stolen it.

Miss Fig.

18

Friday 28th March (well, early hours of Saturday 29th March)

The air-raid siren went off right on cue this evening.

At Deepdean your life is arranged around bells. There's a bell for each meal, and one for each lesson, like we're all being called on and off stage. But in London our lives are split up by air-raid sirens. Just the way your stomach starts to growl because you know that the lunch bell is going to go in ten minutes, the longer you spend in London, the more your body just knows that it's almost time for the siren to sound.

Everyone goes straight for the shelters when they hear the siren – which is funny, because the public shelters are nothing to write home about. They're dingy and smelly and chilly and damp, even though the spring is warming up now.

There's a shelter space at the Ministry, below the basement, in the tunnel that leads to the museum. It's way better than the public shelters, and so we've been using it while we've been in London. But tonight May turned to Hazel and said, 'Can we go to the Mews shelter?'

I knew what May was doing when she asked Hazel that. She wanted to go and find out more about Miss Fig from the person we'd first heard mention her name: Mr Abiola.

Hazel looked at her sharply. 'You hate public shelters, May,' she said.

'I'm trying not to,' said May, which was obviously nonsense because when has May ever tried to do anything she didn't like? 'It's closer to the flat, anyway, so we can get more sleep afterwards.'

'All right then, go on,' said Hazel. 'But behave yourselves! And take your pillows; you don't want to have to borrow them. Do you want some cake?'

That's the great thing about Hazel. She thinks about stuff like pillows and cake, even when she's distracted. She's very sensible and she knows what really matters.

So off we went to the shelter.

The one most people in Hogarth Mews use is kind of close to the big University College building that looks a little like a temple but isn't. It's down below the ground – which I like, even though May obviously wishes it was a surface one. But I've heard stories about the walls of surface shelters getting caught in a blast and being swept away, so the roof pancakes down on top of all the people sheltering there. I really don't want to go in a surface shelter after those stories.

Mr Abiola's job, as the warden in charge of the shelter, is to go around all the streets in the area when the siren sounds to check that everyone's safe and out of their houses, and then to come down to the shelter after us. So we knew he'd definitely be there. What we didn't know is that he'd turn out to be a great shelter warden, as well as maybe a suspect. He lets people play the wireless and sing and play tiddlywinks, and it almost made me forget the noises going on overhead.

The bunks were all full, but May and Eric and I found a space on the floor where we could pile up our pillows and eat the cake Hazel had given us (not great; I could taste the powdered egg in it, but I didn't mind). The Hogarth Mews people were all in a group together, sitting in a half-circle of chairs the way girls from the same dorm all sit together in the common room at school. I could see Colette Mortensen and the two little kids, Olivier asleep in his carrier and Margot smashing a wooden train into Colette's chair; Miss Charney slicing and eating an apple; and the Goodchilds.

Mrs Goodchild was sewing something – the button of a shirt, I think – her head bent close to the lamp propped on the bunk next to her, and Mr Goodchild was sketching in a little notebook. Their elbows rested against each other, so they kind of looked like two parts of a single figure, one of those strings of dolls you can cut out with folded paper. When I was a kid, I used to cut them out and draw different costumes on them and imagine they were part of my own theatrical company.

Cecil was next to them, fidgeting at a bit of wood with his pocket knife. Miss Wimpress was missing – she must be on shift – and so was Mrs Mortensen. Miss Charney said something to Mrs Goodchild, and she nodded and then looked up from her sewing. She caught sight of us and smiled.

I hadn't been sure how to approach them – it really felt a lot like watching a dorm of friends, and you don't just go up to friends and begin talking; it's awfully rude – but this solved the problem.

'Come over here, you three,' Mrs Goodchild said. 'Not with Mr Mukherjee and Miss Stosic tonight, then?'

'We decided to come here,' I said, grabbing May's hand and pulling her forward. She had the glazed expression she always does in a shelter, like she's trying so hard not to scream that she turns off.

I felt Cecil staring at me, and I knew he was still mad about our talk yesterday. I tried not to look at him, and felt myself blushing.

'Is Mrs Mortensen all right?' asked Eric. 'She isn't here.'

'She doesn't come down to the shelter,' said Colette, shrugging. 'It isn't easy for her because of her chair, so she prefers to stay in the house, with the General. She refuses to be carried, and no wonder – she wants the dignity of being able to come down herself, but people don't think of it that way. Mr Abiola's not happy about it, but she doesn't care.'

I thought about this. It made sense to me, but it seemed very sad. 'Why *did* you name the dog General Charles de Gaulle?' I asked, trying to change the subject.

'We had to come over to England last year, after France fell to the Nazis,' said Colette. 'I wanted to remember what had happened, and remind myself that one day we'll be able to go home again.'

It makes me so upset, what's happened to France. I told you about it before, Diary. The Nazis rolled into Paris last summer and took over half the country. There's a Nazi government there now, just like there is in most countries in Europe. Lots of French people are even helping the Nazis, which shocked me when I first heard about it. After what happened at Elysium Hall last year, though, I've realized that there are people in every country who're willing to work with the Nazis, either because they believe in the horrible things the Nazis think, or because they're too afraid to do anything else. It's pretty weak of them, and I'm glad that some other people aren't like that, and are doing everything they can to resist. The Ministry's helping with the resistance too.

'I remember the boat,' said Margot, running her train over my foot, which hurt. 'It smelled bad. There was a boy who came for tea. The General almost jumped overboard.'

'Margot! Attention!' said Colette, pulling her away. 'Play quietly!'

'Apple, anyone?' asked Miss Charney, holding out slices to us on her penknife. I took one. It was a little soft but still sweet. That's the thing about Hogarth Mews – everyone really is kind to each other. They give each other things, like apples and cake. Maybe they're always watching each other, like George said, but that's because they care about each other.

'And would you three like cocoa?' asked Mrs Goodchild, putting down her sewing and reaching into her bag. 'Cocoa's a tradition in the mews. I began it last year. I'd start with Mr Harris at Number Six, then go all the way down to each house till I got to the Lowndeses. We've fallen off a little this spring, but I still usually bring it to the shelter when there's a raid. I'm afraid I don't have enough mugs, but you three can share.'

She poured it out of a flask into a tin mug, and we drank it: Eric first, then me, then May (I had to shove it into her hand, and of course she drank up the whole rest of the cup). It was delicious, warm and sweet, although it was made with water.

After a while I realized Mr Goodchild was sketching us. He kept looking up at me, May and Eric, little bright glances, the rims of his glasses flashing and his mouth frowning a little with concentration. That was weird, because I'd been making notes about him in this diary. It feels strange, being watched when you're trying to be the one watching.

'What are you drawing?' asked May, licking her lips and sticking out her slightly messy chin. The cocoa had shaken her out of her state enough to notice things again.

'The three of you children,' said Mr Goodchild. His voice was soft and precise, just like the way he'd looked at us. 'You make a charming group.'

'I'm not charming!' protested May. 'Can I look?'

'Be my guest,' said Mr Goodchild.

'Oh,' said May, squinting down at his paper. 'It does actually look like us. You've made me look *nice*!'

'Don't be so affronted,' said Mr Goodchild, chuckling. 'Everyone has something nice about them, I've found. I used to draw my children all the time, but these days—'

He paused there. I saw Cecil flinch angrily, and remembered: *My beautiful Anna, by her father.*

Eric and I were obviously curious by this time, so we went round to look too. And we *did* look nice. Mr Goodchild had caught May's fierce face, and Eric's curious stare, and me – it was a shock to see my face from the outside, the way I must look when I'm imagining something super hard and not remembering to pay attention to the real world.

'Not bad, Sam,' said Miss Charney, peering down at the page and then grinning up at him. Mr Goodchild pursed his lips thoughtfully and said, 'Thank you, Elfie.'

'Hah, Nuala, he's got your mouth right,' said May. 'It goes all gormless like that when you're thinking.'

'How did you do that so quickly?' asked Eric. 'We weren't even sitting still!'

'Oh, it's a skill. It can be taught, though. It's all about the lines. Are you interested in drawing?'

'A bit,' said Eric. I was surprised. I mean, I guess I know that Eric did the sketches of the crime scenes in our first case, but he's never talked about liking drawing otherwise.

'Well, I'm delighted to hear that,' said Mr Goodchild. 'An appreciation for art is important. It's one of the things that really makes us human, our ability to— But there, Miriam's telling me off for talking too much.'

Mrs Goodchild had jabbed him gently with her elbow.

'Samuel, you're boring the children,' she said.

'I'm not, am I? At least, not young Mr Jones. Now, sir, if you'd ever like a lesson or two, you're more than welcome to come to our house.'

'Thank you, Mr Goodchild,' said Eric, looking pleased.

May was wiggling in annoyance, though, and I knew it was because she thought we were wasting time. The Goodchilds weren't who we were here to talk to; we needed to interview Mr Abiola. He was the one who Cecil had said had seen the note from Miss Fig. He'd worked with her too, and he'd been the first person to mention her name yesterday. He was our best lead.

'Excuse me,' I said. 'I— The cocoa, it's made me need—'

This was really embarrassing, because Cecil was staring at me with one of his eyebrows raised, but I had to do it.

'Over there,' said Colette, waving her hand. 'By Monsieur Abiola.'

Which, obviously, I knew.

We wriggled our way across the singing, talking, sleeping, crying shelter until we got to Mr Abiola.

He was sitting on a rickety little chair that looked tiny beneath his big legs and wide coat. His tin hat with its white W was on his head, and his regulation whistle was hanging round his neck.

May went marching up to him, all her nerves turned into energy, and just as someone on the other side of the shelter started up a new singalong she came to a stop in front of him, folded her arms and said, 'Hello. Where's Miss Fig?'

19

Mr Abiola had been slouched, but as May spoke he sat up with a shock. The lines of him went sharp up and down and anxious, and I could feel him staring at us.

'What do you mean?' he asked. 'Where did you hear that name?'

'*You* said it,' May told him. She's never subtle, and I really wish she was sometimes. We're being trained to be sneaky, after all. But I guess May wasn't paying attention during those lessons. 'Yesterday. With the *body*. We heard you talking about her. So where is she?'

Mr Abiola looked around him as though he was hunting for the exit. 'That isn't any of your business,' he said. 'What you overheard—'

'I overheard you saying that you thought the body was Miss Fig's,' said May. 'I know what I heard and I know what you said, so you can give over pretending you didn't. All we want to know is if that's true, and, if not, where she is now.'

Her voice was rising over the chatter of the shelter, and heads were turning towards us. This was all going pretty wrong. I can read people, better than May, and I could tell that Mr Abiola was hardening. He wasn't the kind of person who can be yelled into doing something. He needed to be prompted with a reason *why* he should.

'May,' I said.

'DON'T—' May began furiously. Then Eric reached out and wrapped his arm around her shoulders, making the kind of gentle sound he does when he's trying to calm down an angry cat. May huffed out a surprised breath and, while she was wriggling and distracted, I said, 'I'm sorry, Mr Abiola. We're just worried, you see.'

'There isn't any need to worry. You must have misunderstood what you heard yesterday,' Mr Abiola said, clearing his throat and pressing his hands together. 'Miss Fig lived in Number Two, next to the Lowndes family. Her house was damaged in the Incident in November last year, so she had to move out in early December. I gather she went to live with the Lowndes family in Buckinghamshire. She left a note for me at Post, explaining. The damage at her house was too bad, and she didn't want to wait for her compensation from the authorities.'

'What *is* Post?' I said. People kept talking about it, and I wasn't sure what it was.

'That's what we wardens call our headquarters. Miss Fig was a warden – and, in fact, this was her assigned shelter, but, as you can see, it was passed on to me when she left.

She suggested it, in her note. So, you understand, there's nothing to worry about.'

May opened her mouth indignantly, but Eric pulled her from one side and I shoved at her from the other and together we got her away from Mr Abiola, who sank back into his chair with relief.

There was a *thump* and then some screams from far away. The ground rolled a little, and then went still again. It's weird how little we all notice bombs these days unless they're close by. They're kind of like background travelling noise, the same as the underground trains and the buses going by.

'Eric, stop treating me like one of your pets!' hissed May, shaking herself free from his grasp at last. 'I'm not an animal! It's rude!'

'He had to shut you up, though,' I said. 'You were upsetting Mr Abiola.'

'But you saw him, you both saw him – he was clearly lying. He *does* think the body is Miss Fig – maybe he *knows* it is, because he killed her! He took her job, didn't he? This shelter used to be hers and now it's his! What if he did it because he needed the money and he's terrified that we're about to find it out and—'

'Calm down, May,' said Eric. 'Talk quietly, otherwise everyone else will hear.'

'I *am* talking quietly!'

'You aren't,' I told her. 'But I think you're right. It's really suspicious, isn't it?'

'It is,' said Eric, nodding. 'But the adults all keep hiding behind one thing, don't they?'

'The Lowndes family!' I said, understanding. 'Sure, everyone keeps talking *about* them, and saying that Miss Fig went to live with them, but we don't have any way to find out if it's true.'

'Of course we do, though,' said Eric. 'We can telephone them. We know their name, and Mr Abiola told us where they live. We can ask the exchange to connect us.'

'*Can* we?' I asked.

'Oh, we *can*!' cried May. 'Eric, well done!'

The all-clear went then, a shrill noise that cut through all the singing and laughing and arguing in the shelter.

'We can do it now!' said May.

I wasn't so sure about that – it was past eleven, past our bedtime, although bedtimes don't really mean anything, not here in London when we're all half nocturnal. Sometimes this past week I've slept at my desk at the Ministry. Once I fell asleep in the bath, which is usually dangerous to do, but in the war it doesn't matter. We're only ever allowed to use a couple of inches of water.

'Oh, of course we can,' she went on. 'Quick, there's a telephone at the end of the street.'

It was true, there was, and I couldn't think of a reason why not – so suddenly we were out in the fresh air, the buds in the trees rustling above us as we ran down the street, flickering our blue-tissue-paper-covered flashlights low down in front of us so as not to fall over a kerb or someone's foot. We linked arms so we wouldn't lose each other in the dark, and as we ran I looked up at the halo of bright orange in the sky away to the left, incendiaries burning in some other building, far away. You feel really small in the dark after a raid, like a hidden little animal who got lucky this time.

We all three squeezed ourselves into the booth, which was a tight fit with our pillows and blankets. I could smell that May hadn't washed that morning. Eric dropped in some pennies (Eric's always got money – he's the responsible one) and dialled the exchange.

'*You* speak! Do a voice!' said May, shoving the receiver at me just as there was a hollow clicking noise on the other end of the line, and a woman said, 'Who do you need?'

'Lowndes residence, Buckinghamshire, if you please,' I said, trying to sound like a posh, polite adult English lady.

'Is that Lowndes, Bletchley, Buckinghamshire?' asked the woman after a pause. 'Or there's a Lowes in High Wycombe.'

'Lowndes in Bletchley, please,' I said. 'Do connect me. Thank you.'

'You're ringing awfully late, aren't you? Hope they're happy to hear from you. Connecting you now.'

There was a pause and a thudding noise, followed by someone on the wrong line saying, 'Really, Gloria darling, it's been such a shock—' then five rings and the operator's voice saying, 'Call from Bloomsbury, Mr Lowndes,' and, at last, another voice, an angrier one, saying, 'For heaven's sake, you're calling late. Can't you keep to a normal time? You've woken Miranda.'

'Mr Lowndes?' I asked.

'Anyway, you're awfully early. We weren't expecting another delivery until April— Wait, who's speaking?'

'Many apologies, Mr Lowndes, I think there's been some mistake,' I said, trying to make myself sound as much like the woman from the exchange as I could this time. 'I'm calling from the telephone exchange. I'm testing the connection – the lines went down earlier today and I need to make sure it's working again.'

'Bloody telephones! I don't know why we even have a line some days. Look, you've disturbed us thoroughly.'

'Mr Lowndes!' I said. I knew I had to talk fast. He was about to put the phone down. 'Goodness, I thought I recognized the name. You aren't Miss Figueroa's neighbour, are you?'

'What? Who *is* this? If this is some prank—'

'Oh, no, Mr Lowndes – I'm Amelia, Miss Fig's friend. She's staying with you, isn't she? Can you give her a message?'

'Now, really, I know this is a prank. Miss Figueroa was our neighbour in London, but we haven't seen her since we came down in early November. She certainly doesn't live with us. I'm ringing off now, and I will certainly be contacting your supervisor tomorrow to report you for disturbing us. Good EVENING to you!'

With that, he hung up.

I put the telephone receiver down and turned with a squeeze to May and Eric.

'What did he say?' cried May. 'Does he know Miss Fig?'

'He did,' I said. 'He thought I was someone else at first. It got confusing. But he hasn't seen Miss Fig since *early November*. She never went to live with them. She *is* missing. I think . . . I actually think we're right. I bet she never left Hogarth Mews at all. She's the body in the basement.'

We'd found our victim; I was totally sure of it now. Even Eric agreed as we made our way back to the mews. And did we have a suspect in Mr Abiola? He'd been talking about a note from Miss Fig saying she was going to the Lowndes family's house – but if she was the body in the basement, could that be true?

'But what do we do now?' asked May, when we were back outside our flats.

'Keep talking to people,' replied Eric. 'We're already finding out a lot. Look at what we've managed so far!'

'I guess you're right!' I said, a little surprised.

'Well, we're getting good at spy stuff,' said Eric, smiling at me. 'Haven't they said so at the Ministry?'

Somehow, when he said that, I thought about our Ministry training and something occurred to me.

'Here! I know what we have to do!' I said. 'Tomorrow night, when the siren goes, we need to go to Miss Fig's house and look around.'

And oh, I felt so good as I said it, Diary. I felt like a real spy at last.

PART THREE

WE PIT OUR WITS
AGAINST A POLICEMAN

20

From the diary of Fionnuala O'Malley

Saturday 29th March

So we waited until the air-raid sirens went off this evening, just before nine. It was only a little bit scary, running *away* from the shelter while we could all hear the electric hum in the air from the planes on their way. Actually, it was very scary. May wouldn't have admitted that, but I'm not May.

We had a mission.

We told Zosia and George that we were going to the Ministry shelter with Hazel, and told Hazel that we were going to the Mews shelter with the other two. Then we hid next to some railings down the street until we heard the heavy tread of Mr Abiola going by, after he'd been round to check all the houses were clear.

It felt so wicked but also at the same time really natural. We've been trained for this, after all. We did a whole lesson on it last week: how to escape detection when you're surrounded by enemies in a hostile environment.

I still can't really believe I'm the kind of person who knows how to evade enemies, when I won't even be twelve until September.

Anyway, the only thing we had to worry about was that General Charles de Gaulle might bark if he heard us. Like we heard Colette say last night, he can't go in the public shelter. So we went really quietly – or at least we tried to, until May dropped her flashlight on the cobblestones.

'MAY!' I hissed at her, as the General started shrieking with excitement. We all froze, feeling like the worst spies in the world. But I guess Mrs Mortensen must have thought the General was barking at the German planes, because she yelled at him once and then everything went quiet again.

Eric pushed the door of Number 2 and it clicked open, just like that. It wasn't locked – the door didn't even really fit into its frame. I'd heard of that happening to houses when bombs have landed close by and made the walls shift. So anyone could have got inside this house after the Incident. The door doesn't lock, and doesn't even close properly. It must have been easy for the murderer to get in.

We slipped under the rope and crept inside.

It's always kind of startling, going into one of the mews houses, because they don't have hallways or anything. The door opens straight into the living room, so if you're not careful you'll walk right into a chair or a lamp or an occasional table.

We all switched on our flashlights, still covered with blue tissue paper to make them dimmer, and shone them very carefully across the floor.

The carpet was stained and musty, and the legs of the small table looked kind of warped. I could see big cracks across the wall that the bomb had made, and pale sections of wallpaper where prints had fallen down. It was spooky and kind of sad. It didn't feel like a house that had been lived in for a long time.

All the same, it was tidy. You could tell that someone very neat and organized had lived here. The books (some in Spanish, some in English) were arranged by the authors' last names, the magazines were piled up in a perfect tower, and the furniture was straight against the patterned rug.

We walked gingerly through the house to the kitchen at the back, the cold striking up at us through the tiles.

I went looking around the room. One of the cupboards was hanging loose. The crockery had been tidied away into the cupboard that was still upright, and cutlery was in neat rows in a drawer. There was no food anywhere – it was all empty, cleared out. That fitted with Miss Fig having really left. But then—

'Look!' said Eric, gesturing at the closed kitchen door. There was a paper calendar hanging up with a pretty woman on it. 'Look at the dates!'

I looked. It was a calendar from 1940. Each day had been carefully filled in with appointments and notes, and then crossed off in blue ink – until December. The first six days were crossed off, and then the crossing-out stopped. There was a note on the seventh of December: *Council – appointment 9:30 a.m.* It was circled in red, but there was no blue line across it.

'Oh!' I said. 'That has to be a clue, doesn't it?'

Eric nodded. 'If she had an appointment with the council the next day, why didn't she go? Why would she go to the country? It doesn't fit.'

'May!' I called. She'd wandered off somewhere. 'Come and look at what we found!'

I heard creaking upstairs, and then:

'Don't want to!' May yelled back. 'I've found some things here!'

We crept back through the house and into the living room, where May was dangling over the side of the rickety stairs, one foot and an arm out into the air. It made me feel sick.

'*May*,' said Eric reproachfully.

'It's not that far to fall,' said May. 'Anyway, come and see what I found in the bathroom!'

21

May grabbed Eric by the hand and towed him upstairs. I ran after them – that made me nervous, because the stairs creaked and little pieces of plaster were falling like flecks of soot. I could smell the dead-skin rot of a house that hasn't been lived in for months. My flashlight flickered over the steps and the wainscoting, and I saw layers of spiderwebs and something scuttling behind them, either rats or really, really big spiders. There was nowhere I wanted to be less than upstairs, but May was already on the way, and since she'd captured Eric I figured I needed to go with them to show solidarity.

'I don't think this is safe,' said Eric quietly. 'I think it's fairly possible we might all die if we step in the wrong place.'

'Weak!' hissed May as a bomb whistled down and hit somewhere close by. The house shook and groaned. How much more would it take to knock it down totally? May didn't seem worried at all, but I was. 'You can't think about that! I've got something to *show* you – I *said* so!'

'Yes, but I don't want to fall through the floor, May,' said Eric.

'You won't! You won't! Oh, come on, look!'

She pulled us into the little bathroom and pointed. I couldn't see anything – and then I had it. In the shadow under the loo, there were two scraps of paper with a few letters on them.

I leaned down and picked them up.

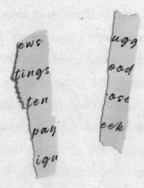

May wrinkled up her nose, and next to her Eric made an almost identical expression. It was funny seeing Eric take on her mannerisms like that. It reminded me that we do know each other pretty well by now, actually.

'I think someone tried to flush a message away, and dropped these bits,' said May.

'What does it say?' I asked Eric. I knew it was a stupid question, but Eric's so good with codes, Diary. If anyone could get it, he could.

'I don't know,' said Eric after a careful moment. 'I need to study it. *Ten* and *pay* – that could be about money? And *ews* – that could be *Mews*, couldn't it? But I don't know the rest yet.'

He put out his hand and took the pieces from May, sliding them very carefully into the sketchbook he always carries, and slid it back into his pocket. I like how gentle he always is. He treats everything so nicely.

This was a great clue. I was excited.

We crept out of the bathroom and across the hall into Miss Fig's bedroom, where I had a surprise.

The rest of Miss Fig's house was so muted: dull patterned wallpaper, boring faded prints of parts of London, even the lampshades were a pale nothing pink. But on her bedroom wall was a big bright painting of a sunny afternoon. The colours glowed, even in the darkness, and when I turned my flashlight on them they were dazzling. They were bright and fresh, the brushstrokes sharp, the hill in the picture shining, studded with flowers, greens and yellows and purples and blues.

For a minute I got lost in its brightness. I was feeling a little weird. The room suddenly felt really small, with its door shut and the lights off. My flashlight beam seemed like the only bright place in the world, the only real thing, and when it moved across the hill in the picture I started to imagine that I wasn't in London at all, but there, among the flowers, in the summer afternoon sun. It was nice. It made me forget that I was in a crumbling house, in the middle of a London air raid, trying to solve a months-old murder.

'Her bed's made,' said Eric, behind me. 'And all the clothes have been taken out of her wardrobe. It's all so tidy. It's almost as though she did go away— Oh!'

I turned round to see that he'd pulled back the covers. And on the sheets . . . was a big rusty stain. *Blood*.

'It *is* blood, isn't it?' I whispered, and Eric looked at me with his most serious expression, and said, 'Yes. Nuala – I think we just found the crime scene. She was killed *here* somehow, in her room, not down in the basement.'

'Hey!' cried May from the doorway.

I yelped.

'What?' said May. 'Oooh. Is that blood? Do we have another clue? Excellent. And I've got something else to show you. I got bored again and I went into the back room and I *found* something.'

22

She dragged us through the house again. These houses are two storeys: the kitchen and living room on the ground floor, then two bedrooms up the stairs at the front and at the back a bathroom and a tiny box room. Miss Fig had her room at the top of the stairs, and the other rooms were mostly empty. I could see a few bits of luggage and a chair in the box room, but not much else.

'SO,' said May, bouncing on her toes and pointing into the box room. 'THREE things. First of all, look at that.'

Eric and I looked.

'So?' I asked.

'Oh!' said Eric. 'Well done!'

I couldn't see it, which was really annoying, because May was looking very smug – and then I did.

'*Luggage!*' I said. 'The story everyone believes is that she went to visit the Lowndes family. But if she really had gone somewhere she'd have taken her luggage, and she didn't.'

'Exactly,' said May. 'We know that was a lie, but we've just *proved* it. And, well, that's the second thing. Go and look in the luggage.'

I padded over to it (carefully, because back here you could see the cracks in the walls again – big dark fingers reaching down like they wanted to grab us) and pushed the biggest case open.

'OH!' I said.

It was full. Dresses, slacks and blouses, blue warden uniforms, a silver whistle, a silver brush set, a set of identity papers for Paula Figueroa – Miss Fig's whole life was piled into it. It was all thrown together like whoever'd put it in hadn't cared how it landed or whether any of it had been damaged. I could see an old romance novel in the pile, its pages curled up and stained. It still had a bookmark tucked into it. So Miss Fig wasn't the kind of person who bent the spines of books or folded over pages. I'm not either – I won't ever damage books I'm reading. It feels like I'm hurting them.

'SEE?' said May. 'From the other rooms, it looks like she's left. Anyone just glancing in would have thought she'd really gone. But the *second* you come back here and see those suitcases, you ought to know that she hasn't gone anywhere. She can't have done. If anyone with sense had looked properly, they'd have realized she had to be dead, not in Buckinghamshire.'

'Well, we know someone did come in,' said Eric thoughtfully. He can sometimes pick up on stuff that May hasn't exactly said, quicker than I can. They only knew each other for a few days before the three of us met, and a couple of weeks before we met properly as detectives on the same case, but I still feel like they've got a head start on me and I'm always catching up.

'Cecil,' said May, nodding. 'He said he came to the house looking for scrap. So why didn't he spot this? That's suspicious. When I ran away from Deepdean, Rose told me she went to my dorm and went digging in my tuck box that evening to see if she could find any clues. And she wasn't even the first person to do it. That annoying Mariella Semple had already looked. And isn't a street a sort of larger dorm?'

It was exactly what I'd thought before, in the air-raid shelter.

'You're right,' said Eric, nodding. 'At least, this street is. It's like George said, someone's always watching. So she should have been reported missing months ago, but she wasn't.'

'Maybe Cecil didn't come back this far,' I said. 'Or didn't think properly about it. Maybe he got distracted.'

'*Maybe*,' said May. 'But, come to think of it, why's this stuff still here at all? Why leave it where someone might notice it?'

We all heard the whistling noise from outside then, and we half crouched, waiting for the hit. I thought it sounded close, but the explosion was streets away. The house shook, the ack-ack guns rattled and screamed, and then there was another hit, even further away.

'I know!' said Eric. 'Because of *that*. This house should have come down a long time ago. It should have fallen onto the rubble of Number One and buried Miss Fig. If another bomb had hit nearby, this would be the perfect crime.'

My heart jumped with excitement, or maybe with nerves. Someone'd got away with murder for months. Someone *here*. Finding the luggage proved it. Maybe we weren't in the middle of the country, stuck in a house with a murderer, but now that there's a war London's almost like each little street and building is its own isolated place, everyone jammed together unable to get out.

And now Miss Fig's body had been found, instead of buried. What did that mean for her murderer? What would they do now?

I remembered something else.

'What was the third thing you wanted to show us?' I asked.

'Oh, that,' said May, her face brightening with excitement. 'Well. Look up there.'

Our eyes followed where she was pointing – at a darker black square in the darkness of the ceiling. A chair had been dragged under it.

'It's an attic,' said May. 'And I went up into it.'

'I'm beginning to think you *want* to die,' said Eric.

'WE ARE IN A WAR,' blared May. 'Danger is all around! We might as well live a little. Anyway, *I went up into the attic* and here's the thing: it doesn't end.'

That sounded kind of like a nightmare to me. I blinked at her, and so did Eric.

'No, listen, you're not listening to me – I mean that the attic space doesn't end. It looks like it does. There's a wall at the end of it, but there's this kind of little gap at the side that you can wiggle through if you're small. And, well, the thing is that if you get in you can *just keep going*. I went on for ages and I couldn't really work out where I was, but I definitely wasn't in this house any more.'

'You were only gone for a few minutes,' Eric pointed out.

'It was hard to tell – I said so,' May replied crossly. 'Listen, what's important is that if you start here, you can get anywhere. I bet you'll be able to get into all the rest of the houses on this side of the mews. Don't you see? We can spy on *everyone*. This case is going to be *easy*!'

23

I had to admit that this was pretty big.

'How did you deal with the small space?' I asked. I was impressed that May was coping so well. One thing I have worked out about May is that she's all front. She acts big and fierce (OK, maybe not *big*– she's too tiny for that), but inside she's a scared little kid.

'Ugh, don't ask that! It was perfectly fine,' said May, which told me that it wasn't. So I was even more impressed. 'Come up and see – come on!'

Eric and I glanced at each other, and I could tell what he was thinking – that it sounded like the kind of thing *May* would think was brilliant, something tough and scary and probably covered with spiders.

'Sure,' he said.

'All right!' said May. 'Now, look. You just need to climb up like this, balance on one foot and then *hop*—'

The chair bounced alarmingly and scooted to one side a few inches. May made a huffing noise as she gripped with her fingers and dragged herself upwards into the blank black space.

'I definitely can't do that,' said Eric. 'How did you do that?'

'I've been practising,' said May, her voice echoing down to us. 'Nuala knows. Fifty push-ups, every day.'

'She does them in our dorm,' I agreed. 'The other girls think she's weird.'

'*Nuala* thinks I'm weird,' said May. 'She doesn't stick up for me.'

I felt my face go red. It was true. But the thing is, it's hard to be brave enough to stand out at Deepdean. You have to really have something burning in you, the way May does, and not want to hide it. You really have to not care what people think, and that feels hard to do.

'I said I was sorry, didn't I?' I called up to her.

'Yes, well, prove it next term. Anyway, look – it was useful, wasn't it? I'm up in the attic and you're not because you have no upper body strength.'

'I do!' I said angrily. We were arguing with each other again. I clambered up onto the chair – it wobbled beneath me – and I reached up to the side of the attic hatch. I'm way taller than May, so I guess I had an advantage, but still my arms burned and I had a panicky moment before May grabbed my collar and hauled me up over the edge.

I gasped and rolled over, then pulled my flashlight out of my pocket to wave it around the attic.

Just like I'd suspected, there were spiders everywhere, swags of web with horrible black dots at their centres. The attic was tall and pointed, and at the top of it one part had been blasted open by the Incident. I could see the strange London night sky through it – no stars, just a flat orange glow from a fire somewhere nearby.

I stared up at it, until May said, 'Help me with Eric, will you, if you're not too tired?'

So she was still mad at me.

I turned onto my stomach and shuffled round, and we both dangled our hands down to grab Eric. We lifted him up next to us, and he made an unhappy huffing sound, which really reminded me of the time May had almost tipped him down the well at Elysium Hall.

Once he was up, we began to look around the attic space. It seemed ordinary – four sloping dingy walls, but there was a little dark opening at the back that I thought was a cupboard at first, until Eric shone his flashlight down low into it.

'Oh!' he said. 'I see what you mean, May! This crawl space – it must go right through the line of buildings.'

'Exactly,' said May. 'Go on – go and look. I think I'll stay here.'

Eric went first, and I wriggled after him. It was a very small space, only a foot or two wide – it would be a tight squeeze for adults, but for kids it was pretty easy. It was a little gap in the eaves, a fluke of the way the roof had been built that made a wooden tunnel you could crawl through on elbows and knees. It went along the far side of the attic, with little gaps to look out of every ten feet or so. I was mostly staring at Eric's shorts and his pink socks in the flickers from my flashlight, but every time the wall to my right ended I looked out into a different space. We'd gone in at the last gap in Miss Fig's empty attic, and so I knew the next house over was the Mortensens'.

It was pretty empty, but there were still some broken bits of furniture – an old bath chair, some walking sticks, a table and chairs – and boxes of what looked like clothes, knitted woollens in lots of different sizes and colours. I remembered Granny and the way she knits and knits for the troops, and I realized Mrs Mortensen must be the same.

We moved on again. Then Eric suddenly stopped, and I almost bumped into his behind.

'Hey!' I said.

'Sorry,' said Eric. 'The Goodchilds'. You'll see!'

And I did. When I got to it, the gap showed me an attic space that was full of *stuff*. Packing crates, some closed and some open with their sawdust leaking out. Paintings, all piled against the walls. An easel with a half-finished brightly coloured painting, and art materials scattered around. This must be where Mr Goodchild made his art – and, as I thought that, I realized why the painting in Miss Fig's house had looked so different to her other things. It was by Mr Goodchild.

Eric was already wriggling forward again, and I followed him. Two more gaps filled with the Goodchilds' things, and then we were in another attic. I was shining my flashlight out at piles of books and what looked like some parts of a car, when without warning a light clicked on in the room below.

24

It shone up through the attic entrance. Just like Miss Fig's attic, this one opened directly into the box room below, and that was where the light had turned on.

Eric kicked me, and I dropped my flashlight. It bounced out of my hand and rolled across the attic floor, and I scrabbled after it. I managed to catch it and click it off – and then I had a horrible frozen moment when I was sure I'd been heard by whoever'd turned on that light.

I listened, and I knew the person below me was listening back. You know the way a silence can be full of attention, Diary? It was like that. Then—

'I thought I heard a person up there! But it can't be, can it?'

'Rats, darling, that's all. At least they're having a good night,' said a woman's voice – Miss Charney. 'I'll put down poison for them tomorrow. D'you have your respirator?'

'Of course I do! Don't fuss so.'

'Well, you did forget it until just now. You'd forget your head if it wasn't screwed on!'

'I know,' said the other voice – Miss Wimpress. 'I just— There was an Incident over on Torrington Place. Two families. We had to hurry. And, you know, *Paula*. My head hasn't been right since they found her.'

'*Paula is Miss Fig*,' whispered Eric in my ear. Sure, I almost died right there, Diary. I'd forgotten he was there – or, if I'd remembered, I'd guessed he'd still be in the crawl space. But he'd come over to where I was, close enough to touch my hand.

I grabbed Eric's fingers and squeezed, just to make sure he was real, and also to show him how mad I was at him.

'Why have they come home?' I whispered.

'The all-clear went five minutes ago. Didn't you hear it?'

I hadn't. But, of course, Eric would have noticed.

The voices below were still talking. 'Don't think about her! Just don't, Prim. It'll only upset you, and she did enough of that while she was alive. Now, I'm on late shift tonight, so I shan't be home until morning. Will you be all right?'

There was a sniff, and Miss Wimpress said, 'Yes, Elfie. Don't worry. I'm only being silly. It's just – I really thought it was all over. I thought . . . you know . . .'

'I know, darling,' said Miss Charney heavily. 'Stupid woman. She won't leave us alone, will she?'

'I keep thinking, now she's been found – what if it all comes out? I mean, about *us*. They'll be looking at everyone. You know that, don't you?'

'Nonsense. We are quite safe – as safe as anyone could be during this war – and you mustn't worry so much. Chin up and hold your nerve, eh? It's important.'

'Chin up,' murmured Miss Wimpress. She still sounded anxious to me. 'I know. All right.'

'Good girl.'

There was the sound of a kiss, and Miss Charney said, 'Good luck. Tonight's a big one.' Then she went hammering down the stairs.

I made to move, but Eric squeezed my hand tighter and whispered, 'Wait.'

As usual, he was right.

Miss Wimpress sighed. Then—

'There *isn't* anyone up there, is there?' she asked. 'I was sure it was too early, but – hello?'

My heart was beating so hard I thought it would fall right out of my chest. I couldn't breathe, because I knew that if I did I'd gasp like a racehorse. Miss Wimpress was talking to us – or, no – talking to someone else who she *thought* was us. Someone in the attic.

'Ah well,' said Miss Wimpress after a long pause. 'It must only be the rats, then.'

And I heard her sigh again and walk away downstairs after Miss Charney.

We had to get out of that attic *now*.

'Quick!' I hissed at Eric. 'Go!'

We wriggled as fast as we could back into the crawl space,

moving by touch since we couldn't switch on our flashlights. I could feel Eric shaking, or maybe that was just me. It was probably both of us.

As we went, though, I kept thinking about the other stuff we'd heard, the stuff that Miss Wimpress and Miss Charney had said to each other.

I really thought it was all over.

She won't leave us alone.

What if it all comes out?

And: *I was sure it was too early.*

Someone else had said something about it being too early, hadn't they? I couldn't quite remember, but it felt important.

And what did the other stuff mean? I knew it might have a totally innocent explanation. That's something they're teaching us at the Ministry – to always look for the innocent explanation, to make sure we don't jump to stupid conclusions. There were people like Miss Charney and Miss Wimpress in the Company, and they hated the police looking at them too. I knew that. But what if the explanation wasn't innocent at all? What if Miss Charney and Miss Wimpress knew something about what had happened to Miss Fig?

What if we'd overheard something really important?

25

Diary, I was not prepared for what was about to happen today. Because today a *policeman* arrived in Hogarth Mews.

The first May and I knew about it was when someone hammered on the front door of the flat this morning. Zosia yelled for us to open it, and May went to the door, still pulling on her jumper. I was trying to finish braiding my hair.

'Oh!' I heard her say. 'Eric!'

I rushed to the door.

Eric was standing there, pink in the face with excitement, his collar sticking up. 'Come outside!' he said. 'Something's happened.'

'Who is it?' called Zosia. 'Come and get your breakfast, the two of you – I'm not making it for you! It's jam *or* butter, remember!'

'Come outside,' Eric hissed to us. 'No time for breakfast. Hurry!'

We dashed down the stairs of the apartment building and out into the mews, May's shoelaces clattering against the stairs and my hair streaming behind me out of its braid. I caught air into my lungs and felt so sharp and awake. I didn't get much sleep last night – it was another heavy raid after we got out of Miss Fig's house, going on for hours – but somehow it's always amazing, just being alive the morning after a raid. Sometimes I look at the tips of my fingers and think, *I could die any time.* The next moment, the very next second after I've written this sentence, a plane could come along and drop the bomb that has my name on it. It makes my heart jolt with amazement.

'What's happened?' I gasped as I ran.

'I looked out of the window and— Oh, come on!' Eric puffed back.

'You're very annoying, Eric!' May yelled at him. 'It had better be good!'

And it was. I could tell that May was a little upset about that, because she loves to be right, but also excited, because – oh, it was *really* good.

A policeman was in the mews. Actually, three police officers were, but I could tell from the way that two of them were standing, kind of hunched and sideways-facing, like they were waiting to be told they could speak, that only one of them was in charge.

That one was a tall man with dark hair, a long nose and a greatcoat that swept behind him. I was impressed by that. I could tell that he knew how to move in it, to make everyone look at him. He was staring around at the mews, his forehead wrinkling up like he was really thinking.

This man wasn't like PC Cuffe, I could tell. This one was serious.

May bounced on her toes with excitement, and that made the policeman turn and stare at us. He frowned, and then I saw him gaze directly at May. His eyes widened, and he took a step forward.

'Miss Wong?' he said. 'But . . . you've got *smaller*.'

'I'm NOT HAZEL!' snapped May. 'Why does everyone – why does everyone keep thinking I'm her?! She's my sister, and I'm better than her and anyway it's good to be small; you can get anywhere.'

The policeman blinked, then shook his head, and his forehead became even more wrinkled. 'My apologies,' he said. 'I'm getting old. I should have known you weren't *my* Miss Wong at once. You do look quite different, now I look properly. I first met her when she was much younger, you see, and I forgot that she's quite a grown-up now. It's – well, I won't say nice to meet you, because I suspect that there's a reason you've just appeared at my crime scene with two very smart-looking friends. It runs in the family, does it?'

I wasn't sure whether he was teasing or not. Eric and I didn't look very smart right then. My clothes weren't tucked in properly, and my hair was down around my shoulders. Eric rubbed one shoe against his sock to try to pull it up, and then he reached out gently and began to braid my hair.

'I'm Chief Inspector Priestley,' said the policeman, which I guess made him more important than just a policeman. I wondered what on earth someone with such a long title was doing at a regular crime scene.

'I'm May,' said May. 'And this is Eric, and Nuala. We're staying here. So, you see, we have every right to be here. You can't send us away.'

'I suppose you're the children who found the body?' asked Chief Inspector Priestley. 'I should have known.'

'It wasn't our *fault*!' said May. 'I mean, it was. But not on purpose!'

'Be that as it may. I'll need to speak to you, but after that – you really can't be here. Don't you have school? Miss Wong, shouldn't you be at Deepdean?'

'We have school in London at the moment,' said May. '*None of your business*. So, who's the body?'

'Now, please understand that I am only telling you this because I assume you will hear about it in an hour or so anyway,' said the Chief Inspector. 'I am not allowing you to have anything to do with this investigation – which, even as I'm saying it, sounds ridiculous; you all look about twelve – but, then again, I've met your sister too many times, May Wong, and if you're anything like her and Miss Wells, you're going to be trouble. The body was discovered on

148

Thursday last week and appears to have died in suspicious circumstances. It has since been identified by dental records as Miss Paula Figueroa, a local warden. The authorities don't like that much, so I am here.'

'Ooh!' said May. 'I knew it! She was murdered!'

'Stabbed, unfortunately.'

I gasped. So the police knew too.

The Chief Inspector went on. 'All I ask of you is that you stay well out of it while I conduct my other interviews. Can you do that?'

'NO,' said May. 'We're not talking to you. You can't interview us. So there. And we won't stay out of anything.'

'Yes, we *will*, May,' I said, swallowing and crossing my fingers behind my back. Eric must have seen me, because he let out a little chuckle that he tried to turn into a cough. I thought I saw the Chief Inspector smile.

I've seriously got to teach them how to act better than this, the next time we have a case.

Unless we don't have another case. After all, maybe there's a limit to how many exciting things can happen in a person's life. I think I've already had most of my lot.

But we couldn't stay out of *this* case – no way. Because we'd been right. There had been a murder – and Miss Fig was the victim. She'd been dead, stuck in a basement, since December. We knew *how*. I wanted to know *who* – and *why*.

THE BODY IN THE BASEMENT

Time of discovery: Approximately 4:50 p.m., 27th March 1941.

Victim: ~~Anna Goodchild (we think, from the evidence of her gold~~
~~necklace). Body had been there for a long time. Likely after the bomb~~
~~hit (in November 1940) – but is this right? NB: Miss Figueroa is also~~
~~missing. Is this important?~~ Miss Fig!!

- WHEN did she end up in the basement? Was she alive or dead?
  ~~Anna was last seen by Cecil Goodchild on Friday 6th December~~
  ~~1940. Miss Fig left a note saying she went to the country with the~~
  ~~Lowndes family in early December.~~ Anna went to France on 7th
  December. She's not the victim. Miss Fig was last seen in early
  December – she did not go down to the Lowndes family's house in
  Buckinghamshire. She was murdered, we think on 6th December.
- WHEN EXACTLY did the bomb hit the house? 24th November
  1940. Miss Fig was put in the basement afterwards.
- WHO else was there with her, if anyone? The murderer, obviously.
- HOW did she die? Was it murder? ~~An accident? The bomb?~~
  MURDER! Miss Fig was stabbed in her bed!
- HOW are we going to work this one out?

26

'Did you hear him?' May asked. We'd gone out onto the main street, cars shooting past us, on our way to the Ministry. 'He thought we were twelve! That's not bad, is it? I'm not even eleven yet.'

'May!' said Eric.

'I know, I know, the murder,' said May. 'Ooh, it's a real murder! Someone *stabbed* her.'

'I can't believe it,' I said. 'It seems so ridiculous. We found a *murder* in someone's basement.'

'Yes, and now what are we going to do?' asked Eric. 'If there's a chief inspector here, we can't do anything else. He won't let us. You heard him.'

'I don't know,' I said. 'Sure, he's heard of Hazel. Maybe he was mixed up in all the stuff she and Daisy used to do. Maybe he's used to kids solving cases.'

'But that's worse,' Eric pointed out. 'If he's used to it, then he can stop us.'

'If he's used to it, we just need to be *very* sneaky,' said May. 'Hazel's mentioned him before. He's quite clever for a grown-up, apparently. But we're cleverer. We solved a murder case on our own, didn't we?'

Had we? I know May's proud of us, but Daisy did help us out at the end. We were most of the way there, but we'd never have solved it in time without her. So . . . how good were we, really? Could we go up against a real chief inspector? *Should* we, even?

'You're wobbling,' said May to me. 'I can tell. *Don't* wobble.'

'Don't yell at me! What do we do, though?'

'We solve the case, obviously. We know almost everything we need to. We know the victim's name, and how she died, and when. We just need to know who killed her.'

'Almost anyone here could be a suspect,' I said. 'No one sounds as though they liked her very much. Maybe she wasn't the kind of person who had friends.'

I realized I kind of felt sorry for Miss Fig.

And I *really* wanted to find out who'd murdered her.

We ran all the way back to Hogarth Mews as soon as we were let out of the Ministry at lunchtime. This morning we had a dead-letter drop lesson with Hazel, as well as our coding practice. The Ministry seemed even more anxious and busy than usual – though maybe that was just us.

We've been doing a whole lot of running today, and my legs are feeling pretty wobbly. I know what Miss Lessing would say, that spies need to stay fit. I need to work harder.

Anyway, the mews was quiet when we got there, apart from General Charles de Gaulle barking away in the living room of Number 3, his breath steaming up the window and his fluffy black topknot bouncing. We thought we'd missed the action.

But then we went to our flat and found the Chief Inspector standing outside it, in the main hallway, writing something in his notebook. He looked up when we came up the stairs, frowning in annoyance.

'What are you three doing here?' he asked.

'What do you mean?' cried May. 'What are *you* doing here? You can't just break into people's flats!'

'I haven't broken in anywhere,' the Chief Inspector pointed out. 'I was given a key. I'm merely mapping out the area as part of the investigation. I like to be thorough. So you live here?'

'We're in this flat with Zosia, and Eric's downstairs in that one with George,' I said. I got two kicks on my shins, from both May and Eric. May I expected, but Eric was a surprise. I looked over at him and saw his face closed and mulish.

'Don't *say* anything to him!' May said loudly. 'We don't have anything to say to him now that he's not letting us be part of the investigation. We're just here to get our lunch.'

'Well then, I shan't stop you,' said the Chief Inspector. 'We're all busy people.'

He waved his hand, and I saw something in it, poking out from under the notebook. It was a photograph. My heart caught.

'Is that . . . her?' I asked.

'Oh, yes. That's her,' said the Chief Inspector, pointing. 'Miss Figueroa.'

May snatched it, and I leaned forward to see. The picture was of two women. The one the Chief Inspector had pointed at was older than my mam but younger than Mrs Goodchild. She had long wavy hair under a peaked cap with a W on it, and she was wearing some kind of strict dark uniform, her gas mask on her shoulder. She was eyeing up the camera suspiciously, one hand raised to shade her eyes from the sun and her other around the waist of a thin, pale woman with fluffy hair.

I recognized her, the woman in the uniform.

We came to London at the start of December last year, after what happened at Elysium Hall. You remember that, Diary. We were only here a couple of days before we set off for Fallingford, but during one of them Hazel needed me to fetch something for her. I was hurrying along a street close to the British Museum, thinking about ten things that weren't where I was going, and I ran straight into someone. She started yelling at me and telling me off, and I couldn't stop her even though I said sorry at least five times. I was so embarrassed I just ran away, and I didn't tell anyone about it.

But it was *her* – this woman. Miss Fig.

I must have gasped.

'What?' asked May at once.

'It's just – it's just I wasn't expecting to see her,' I lied, as hard as I could. 'It's upsetting. She's dead.'

The Chief Inspector was looking at me curiously, and I felt all over again how different he was to PC Cuffe.

'We're going to get lunch,' said May firmly. 'Come on, Eric, Nuala. We don't have anything more to say.'

She dragged us both through the door into Zosia's kitchen and slammed it behind her, putting her finger to her lips. Then she managed to sign out ROOF NOW in surprisingly respectable semaphore code. Bridget's been teaching us.

I nodded and looked at Eric, who still had his mulish face on. I thought he looked pale too. We put together sandwiches – not very well; the tomatoes were squishy and the bread quite old – and as fast as we could climbed out onto the roof, using the rope Cecil had left the other day.

27

'What's wrong?' I asked Eric, as soon as we were up on the roof of Hogarth Mews Mansions.

'You *know* what's wrong!' yelped May. 'That policeman's going to ruin our investigation!'

'Arra, will you be quiet! I was asking Eric.'

Eric swallowed. He still looked pale.

'It's just . . . when we saw him outside the flat,' he said. 'That's what it was like, when they took Papa away. British police, outside our door. And in Germany that's how they'd— I thought they might say I'd done something, that's all.'

'Oh, Eric!' cried May, and she threw herself at him.

Eric buried his head against her shoulder, and said, 'PC Cuffe was silly, but Chief Inspector Priestley frightens me.'

'I think he's all right,' I said, but Eric said, 'No,' very firmly. I could tell how upset he was.

'Well, we don't like him,' said May, giving Eric one last squeeze. 'That's settled. Nuala, what did you see?'

'I – I've met her!' I said in a gasp, and I explained what had happened. It didn't matter to our investigation – except it made her real, to me. Not nice, but real.

'And we know the other woman with her too – that was Miss Wimpress,' said Eric.

'Oh!' I said. I should have recognized her, but all I could think about was Miss Fig. 'You're right! Well, if they were neighbours, I guess that makes sense.'

We all sat thinking and eating our lunch, sticking our heads over the side of the roof to look down at the mews. It felt like being up in the flies gazing down at a theatre set, being able to see not just the front that the audience would look at but also the side of it, the secret part that only the actors get to see.

'Pass that spam sandwich over if you aren't going to eat it,' said May. 'It's yum.'

I shook my head and handed it over. Spam sandwiches taste like the time after the money runs out during a tour. I picked up her tomato sandwich instead. May hates tomatoes.

'You are disgusting,' said May. 'Eating that!'

'Sure, you're disgusting eating that!' I said. We glared at each other.

'Look!' said Eric, waving a scone. 'The Chief Inspector!'

May and I leaned forward. The Chief Inspector was coming out of the flats below us and pacing across the mews. I thought he was going to the rubble of Number 1, but instead he stopped in front of Number 2, the house that Miss Fig had lived in, ducked under the KEEP OUT sign and pushed open its unlocked front door.

We waited, and a moment later a lamp turned on in the window. The Chief Inspector looked out, and then twitched the curtains closed.

'What's he doing?' May asked. 'Spying round her house?'

'Must be,' said Eric – but half an hour passed, and he didn't come out again. The two minor police officers went in after him, one carrying a box of papers and the other carrying a typewriter and some sandwiches in wax paper.

'He's setting up a station!' gasped May. 'He doesn't care the house might fall down – he's staying *there*!'

'Of course he is,' said Eric, looking anxious all over again.

'Don't worry, Eric – he won't get anywhere near you,' said May, sticking out her chin. 'And we'll outwit him, you'll see. We just have to keep detecting. We'll get to the bottom of this soon!'

Eric and I looked at each other – and I wasn't sure we totally agreed with her. But sometimes you just have to pretend, Diary.

28

Tuesday 1st April

This morning, when we turned the corner that brought us to the Ministry's red front door, we found that the raid last night had left a crater in the road, knocking the railings of the British Museum sideways. Two kids were trying to pull out the remaining bits of the railings for scrap, and waiting beside them with a scrap cart was Cecil from Hogarth Mews.

He looked like he hadn't slept, like all of us right now, but in a nice way. He was wearing his big army jacket again. I could see the wiring of his device disappearing into it. He had a bag on his shoulder.

'You're staring at him,' muttered May to me. 'Stop it.'

'I'm not!' I said, feeling my face flush. We turned away – and almost bumped straight into Miss Charney. It felt like the residents of Hogarth Mews were all following us this morning.

Miss Charney looked surprised. 'What are you doing here, children?' she asked.

'What are *you* doing here?' May asked, sticking out her chin.

'Primrose forgot her lunch,' said Miss Charney. 'I'm taking it to her. That woman – she needs taking care of sometimes! And then I have to drop something off at Post for Mr Abiola.'

Of course, we had to make sure she didn't work out we were going towards the Ministry. And we all knew what to do if someone questioned us. We had to pretend to be on a normal boring errand too.

I pulled out the crumpled list I always keep in my pocket as an alibi, and showed it to Miss Charney.

'Powdered eggs, tinned peas, fruit,' I said. 'We're just going to the shops for Zosia.'

'Why not the shop on Gower Street?' asked Miss Charney.

'This one's got pineapple chunks,' I said. I saw Cecil watching us, hugging his bag to him. What was he doing?

'Well, go on then,' said Miss Charney. 'And be careful. You don't want to turn up any more dead bodies!'

Which I think was a joke, but a weird one.

So we crossed the road and went into the shop. It's always best to do the thing you're pretending to, when you're under cover. You're already lying, and you don't want to add extra lies to that. It's exactly like acting – you want to use what's real as much as you can. It makes your performance more authentic.

Once we were inside, we went to the very back of the shop, where the shopkeeper couldn't see us. Eric sat down on a pile of tins and started to pet the store's skinny black cat.

'Pfote'll be jealous,' said May.

'She knows she's my favourite,' said Eric, catching the cat behind the ear, so it wriggled happily and shoved its nose against his fingers. 'Cecil was watching us, you know.'

'He wasn't!' I said, even though I knew Eric was right.

'Of course he was. And he's hiding something too. Whatever's in that bag isn't just more scrap. Oh, pretend to be shopping in case someone comes in.'

I picked up a tin of fruit and a tin of spam, for May. 'We might as well have a meeting, then,' I said. 'While we're waiting for him and Miss Charney to go away. What do you think is in the bag? And why's he watching us?'

'Something delicate, from the way he was holding it,' said Eric. 'And he still wants to work out what happened to Anna. He thinks we know something.'

'Well, we don't!' said May. 'But – but I've realized something. If he really thought Miss Fig's body might have been Anna, then he can't have killed Miss Fig, can he? That's one person to strike off the list. Oh, Nuala, we need to make a list.'

'Not necessarily,' said Eric. 'He might be trying to throw us off the scent about killing Miss Fig.'

'But he was so upset about Anna!' I protested.

'I've seen you act,' said Eric, folding his arms. 'You could pretend to be just as upset, and I'd believe you if I didn't know you.'

That felt both rude and a compliment.

'So, you still think Cecil's a suspect?' I asked him.

'Well, we can't rule him out yet.'

'Miss Wimpress and Miss Charney are suspects too,' I said. 'What Eric and I heard them say – sure, they sounded *really* suspicious.'

'And Mr Abiola,' said Eric. 'He's taken Miss Fig's job. That's four suspects, then, definitely.'

I started a new page of notes and wrote it down.

'But it's more than that,' said May. 'Colette didn't like Miss Fig, and neither did Mrs Mortensen – we heard them say it. And you have to add Mr and Mrs Goodchild too, and Zosia, and George and Alexander. Oh, and the lawyer who lives at Number Six and his housekeeper – she still comes to clean his house even though he's not there; I saw her.'

But Eric was shaking his head. 'The calendar in Miss Fig's kitchen, the one that Nuala and I saw, had all the dates crossed out until the seventh of December last year. That means we know when she died: it was the sixth of December, late enough that she'd already marked off the calendar and gone to bed. George and Alexander are ruled out, because George told us they only took the flat in January this year, and so are the Lowndes family and the lawyer, and most of the people in the flats – they all went away in October and November because of the Blitz. The Chief Inspector said she was stabbed, and the bloodstains on her sheets prove she was in bed when she died. That makes it seem like the person who did it knew her routine, and knew what time she'd be in bed. I think we should be looking at people who were in the mews on the night of the sixth of December – and remember what Cecil told us? That was the night of the fog. That makes it even more likely that it was someone who lives here in the mews!'

'Oh, nicely done!' said May, loudly enough that the shopkeeper cleared her throat and called down the aisle to us.

'Quiet or you're out,' she said. 'I've got a shop to run. Are you buying anything?'

'Yes, just a minute,' I said to her in my best English voice, then I whispered, '*Quick! What do we do now?*'

'Easy!' said May. 'We have the date and close enough to the time of the murder, and the murder method too. All we have to do is find out what our suspects remember! I vote one of us follows the Chief Inspector, and the others spread out and talk to the suspects.'

She pulled out a grubby tuppence from her shorts pocket and said, 'Heads I win, tails you lose.'

'Hey, that's not—' I began, but it was already spinning in the air and clattering down on the linoleum. Tails.

'You lose!' crowed May. 'That means I get to pick what job I want, and I bagsy the Chief Inspector.'

'That's it, OUT!' yelled the shopkeeper. 'Hurry up! Dirty little urchins, I know you're trying to steal things.'

'Sure, how are we going to get away from the Ministry, though?' I asked, as we filed out of the shop, Eric giving the cat one last pat. 'They've got us working all day.'

'We can pretend to be ill,' said May, shrugging like it was obvious.

'No, we can't!' I protested. 'They're all spies, May; they're going to realize we're faking it.'

'We'll just have to be good at faking it!' said May.

'I'm not good at faking it,' said Eric. 'And I don't think we can do that. They need us right now, especially me – I'm good at decoding.'

May made a face at him. 'All right, boastful,' she said.

'I'm not being boastful,' said Eric seriously. 'I am good.'

'Oh, we'll work something out,' said May, bouncing from foot to foot and sticking out her tongue back at the shopkeeper.

Eric and I looked at each other.

'It'll be all right,' he said.

Cecil and his friends and Miss Charney were gone, so we did one more careful circle and came back to the Ministry by its boring back door. You can't be too careful.

But we were late, obviously. And when we got in, Hazel was waiting for us in the downstairs hallway. I was scared she'd worked out what we'd been doing, but it was obvious she hadn't. She looked way too tired and worried.

'There you are!' she said. 'Something's happened. A message's just come through. We think – we think Daisy's made contact with us, from France.'

29

'Are you going to go get her, then?' asked May.

Hazel made a face. She was biting her lip, worry radiating off her.

'We're still deciding,' she said. 'We need to make sure nothing's wrong.'

'What might be wrong?' asked May sharply.

Hazel rubbed her hand across her face, the way she's been doing more and more since we arrived.

'We think – we don't know – we got the message last night. It's asking for extraction, and using Daisy's poem code, the one from "Goblin Market", but there are . . . mistakes. She's missed out the extra code we agreed on.'

I suddenly got a sinking feeling. I knew what the problem was before Hazel even said it. See, poem codes aren't really so secure. They have to be pretty famous poems, otherwise we wouldn't remember them, and that means other people might be able to work out which poem we're using and crack the key. That's why sometimes agents agree extra codes, like writing S three times at the beginning of a message, or always ending with the word *turnip*.

Daisy had skipped her extra code. Which meant Hazel thought that it might not be Daisy at all. She thought Daisy might have been caught.

'No!' said May. 'No! Daisy'd never let that happen.'

'I just don't know, Mei,' said Hazel. 'I can't tell. That message – it's not enough to go on. She's always so sloppy with coding, and if she's in a hurry she might have forgotten. But she's asking to be brought home, in three days' time. So we're scrambling to see if it's a valid request before we send an agent into the field.'

'Who's the agent who might go into the field?' I asked.

'Me,' said Hazel shortly. 'George did ask to go, but he – he's retired from active duty. He knows that.'

'I *don't* know, Hazel!' George yelled suddenly from a nearby study. 'I don't agree! You know I could go. It's *Daisy*.'

'Be quiet, George,' said Hazel, grinning and looking as though she wanted to cry at once. 'I have to focus on this, today and the rest of the week. That means your training will have to pause. You'll all be in the message pool instead – yes, even you, May. We need everyone right now. So, will the three of you be good?'

I looked at May and Eric. Oh, I felt so bad, Diary! But this was it. Our perfect opportunity.

'We'll be *so* good,' said May fervently. 'The best.'

'You can trust us,' I said.

And I knew I was lying.

*

I remember how tough it was to be a normal kid and also a detective, back at Elysium Hall. It's funny how different but the same it is in London. We're not having to pretend to be normal kids now – but we're still kids, and that means that adults still sometimes look right through us, as though we don't matter.

I was all ready to keep a low profile, and actually use it – be Crowd Member Number 5 again – but that isn't May's style. We stayed at the Ministry to help with the messages. But then, after lunch, when we were sitting down decoding while Hazel and George were in the next room having a meeting, May nudged Eric and me.

'Look at this!' she whispered, and she pulled something out of her bag. It was one of the Cook's exploding chocolate bars.

'May!' I yelped. 'You eejit! You'll blow us all up!'

'I will not!' said May. 'I'm just going to blow up the supply cupboard a little bit. Make them think it's an accident. They'll be too worried to notice where we are after that. All right. I'll see you two whenever you can get away.'

She grinned at us, slipped out of her seat and pattered away down the hallway. Thirty seconds later there was a dull explosion.

Everyone exclaimed, jumped out of their seats and ran to find the door of the supply cupboard splintered and hanging open, the pots of pens and compasses and clothes and shoes and gas masks inside all dusty and marked. This was a pretty bad idea, I thought, even for May.

Except . . . Hazel and Zosia and George and Miss Lessing were so busy trying to work out where May was and how she'd set the charge in the supply cupboard (Hazel worked out it was May at once) that they didn't pay much attention to me and Eric.

I felt kind of annoyed about that, even though I should have been pleased. I sat back down in my seat and fidgeted and couldn't focus on the message I was supposed to be decoding. I tried to remind myself that this was real, that there was someone out there, somewhere in Europe, who needed me to turn this string of letters into their words. They were speaking to me, and all I had to do was tune my ear in to hear them.

I picked away and picked away and then I blinked and *saw* it. CALLING HOME STATION, I read. SUPPLIES NEEDED ADVISE DROP POINT.

I yelped, and George, who'd come back into our room, looked up and said, 'Got it?'

'I *got* it!' I said, and I couldn't stop myself beaming.

'That took you a while,' said George. 'Look, you can go if you like. It's chaos here, and you're not focused. You'd usually crack that in half the time. Eric, you can leave too.'

I was kind of embarrassed that he'd noticed I wasn't focused, but I wasn't going to say no. We slipped out of the

Ministry door and began to run towards Hogarth Mews. Pfote had followed Eric out of the door, the way she does sometimes, and she was trotting along beside us, her long orange tail fluting like a fan in the breeze. My gas-mask case bumped against my back and the barrage balloon a few streets over shone above us, twisting from side to side slightly. The air smelled of spring and burning. I wanted to skip, suddenly. I was having fun.

And I don't know why that should be, since Daisy was in danger and we were on a terrifying secret detective mission – except maybe it wasn't so terrifying. It wasn't worse than the war, I guess. That's the thing about this war: all the time, you're trying *not* to think about dying. You're trying not to burst out screaming at the thought that *the* bomb might be getting loaded onto a plane at that very moment. You never hear the one that gets you, apparently. How scary is that?

So having the chance to think about something else, something as human-sized as a murder, was kind of amazing. We could solve a murder, couldn't we? Easy.

THE BODY IN THE BASEMENT

The facts in the case: victim is Miss Paula Figueroa. She was murdered (stabbed) in her bed in her house, Number 2 Hogarth Mews, on the evening of Friday 6th December 1940, during a heavy fog. She was then moved down to the basement of Number 1 at some point after her death.

SUSPECT LIST

- **Mr Abiola.** Has taken Miss Fig's position as shelter warden after her death. Does not seem to have liked her. Needed money?

- **Miss Charney.** Does not seem to have liked Miss Fig. Overheard talking suspiciously to Miss Wimpress by Nuala and Eric in the attic after Miss Fig's body was found.

- **Miss Wimpress.** Seems very upset by Miss Fig's death. Is this a ruse? Overheard talking suspiciously to Miss Charney by Nuala and Eric in the attic after Miss Fig's body was found.

- **Colette Mortensen.** Does not seem to have liked Miss Fig.

- **Mrs Mortensen.** Does not seem to have liked Miss Fig.

- **Cecil Goodchild.** Behaving suspiciously. Is he looking for Anna to throw off the scent about Miss Fig? What was in the bag? Why was he watching us?

- **Zosia Stosic.** Does not seem to have liked Miss Fig.

- **Mrs Goodchild.** Motive unclear.

- **Mr Goodchild.** Motive unclear.

- **Anna Goodchild.** Motive unclear, especially as Zosia told us that Anna was nice to Miss Fig. Miss Fig's body had Anna's necklace on it – why? We know that Anna went on her Ministry mission the next day, Saturday 7th December, and missed making Shabbos with her family on the evening of the 6th. Where was she that evening? Is she a suspect or not?

PART FOUR

WE HAVE SOME CLOSE CALLS

30

From the diary of Fionnuala O'Malley

Tuesday 1st April, continued

When we got back to the mews at about half past five, I saw shadows moving in Number 2 and heard voices, and I knew the Chief Inspector and his officers were inside. They'd pushed aside the string and moved the KEEP OUT sign so it dangled sadly on the ground.

I linked arms with Eric and walked slowly by, being someone in the back of a scene sauntering along a street, a bit part not worth caring about. Eric looked at me anxiously, but I squeezed his hand and whispered, '*Shh*,' and then we were past the window.

Of course, then General Charles de Gaulle heard us coming and started to bark frantically in the window of Number 3. I sighed. Pfote's tail puffed out and she scampered away crossly.

'Pfote!' cried Eric.

Margot stuck her head out of the front door. The paint on it was scratched, and I noticed that most of the flowers in the Mortensens' window boxes were dead.

'Salut!' she squeaked. 'Come in for tea!'

'Margot!' called Colette behind her. 'Stop inviting the police in! Oh, it's you.'

She'd seen me and Eric. She didn't look a lot happier that we weren't police, to be honest, but this was exactly the opening we'd been looking for.

The General shoved Colette aside and leaped on Eric, and after that there was pretty much nothing else for Colette to do but invite us in.

The house was laid out just like Miss Fig's and the Goodchilds', but it was a mess. There's no other way to describe it. There were pawprints on the chintz sofa, pencil lines on the floral wallpaper, scratches on the mahogany table and big stains all across the tufted rugs. Some of Mr Goodchild's paintings were hanging on the walls. Toys were cluttered across the floor, most with their heads pulled off or their stomachs ripped out, and I could smell something burning in the kitchen.

I sniffed, and Colette saw me and said, 'Nom de nom! The biscuits!' and fled.

Eric and I were left standing in the middle of the dirty rug, the General bouncing around us happily. Olivier was in a little pen at the side of the room, sucking on a wooden pig and saying, 'BababaBABABA,' and Margot had gone back to working on some sort of colouring on the floor. Red marks were going all over the floorboards.

Mrs Mortensen was sitting in a big chair at the table, sorting through a huge pile of woollens. 'Colette,' she was saying. 'This afternoon's Woollies for Families of Soldiers committee meeting was very productive. We really are getting somewhere with it!'

So I was right, I thought. She must be one of the people who organizes everyone's knitting and sends it off to be used by people fighting the war in different countries.

'I'm glad, Mormor,' said Colette, rushing back into the living room with a plate of biscuits and sandwiches.

The biscuits smelled burnt, but I still took one politely when she shoved them at us. I took a sandwich too.

'What are *they* doing here?' asked Mrs Mortensen, glaring at us. 'What are you two doing here?'

'We're—' I said, and paused, biting into the biscuit. Underneath the char, it was surprisingly good – light and sugary, with a strange tang that I couldn't place. 'We're—'

'We're hiding from the police,' said Eric suddenly. 'The Chief Inspector keeps trying to interview us, even though we don't know anything.'

I looked at him, and he stared straight back at me meaningfully.

'Hah!' said Mrs Mortensen, pleased. 'Good for you! He's already come by twice, but I fended him off. He's not going to find out much, I can tell you that.'

'But – but they're trying to get justice for – for the body!' I said. I'd realized what Eric was doing, and I'd seen enough plays about the police to know that, if there are two of you, you want to have one person buttering up the suspect, and the other arguing with them. If Eric was taking Mrs Mortensen's side, then I needed to take the other point of view.

'So?' asked Mrs Mortensen. 'I don't trust the police. Now we're at war, they have become unpleasant about my name, even though I have been English for thirty years at least, and so is my son. Quisling has much to answer for! And if it is Miss Fig, as they say, then she was the most insufferable woman. Just because she was our warden, she thought she was God or something. And the way she loved rules. Coming into our houses three times a night to check the blackout! Telling me I should go down to the shelter, when I could never manage the steps! Going through our ration books! We had to—' She paused, and her eyes flicked to Colette, and then to the plate of biscuits. 'Never mind that.'

I knew that was important. That's the interrogation technique that Hazel's told us about: if you're trying to get someone to tell you something, just let them talk. People think that the more they say, the more they'll be able to fool you, when really the more they say, the more they'll tell you without meaning to. So I pretended I hadn't noticed anything, and took another bite of my biscuit. It really did taste good. It had to be almost Colette's whole sugar ration.

'And she kept trying to get us to get rid of the General!' Mrs Mortensen went on. 'Said it was irresponsible to have a pet when there are food shortages.'

Eric gasped, and squeezed General Charles de Gaulle so hard that he yelped. 'No!' he said.

'And, I mean, the General's a dreadful dog. He pees on the furniture – and the barking! But still, you don't say that kind of thing, do you?'

I looked over at Colette. She was stepping into the pen to pick up Olivier, who'd fallen over on top of some blocks and was whimpering. She looked furious. 'Trying to get me to get rid of him! Because there's *a war on*! As though I don't know that already!'

'It's all right, Maman,' said Margot, looking up from her colouring. 'Papa's going to kill all the Germans and end the war.'

Next to me, I felt Eric flinch.

'That's quite right, Margot,' said Mrs Mortensen, then she turned to us. 'My son enlisted in the English army last year, after he and Colette and the children came over from Normandy. He'll be back soon.' She looked proud as she said it, but I caught the flash of fear in Colette's face.

'I wish you wouldn't say that to her,' she said to Mrs Mortensen. 'You know it might not – it might not be true.'

'*Pfft*, Colette,' said Mrs Mortensen. 'He'll be back. We have good luck, this family. *You're* here, aren't you? You got out!'

'We got a boat,' said Margot, colouring away. 'Maman had to hold the General because he wanted to jump overboard. There was a boy.'

'Margot!' said Colette.

'I heard the Chief Inspector talking about a fog,' said Eric, changing the subject as he reached for another biscuit. 'What do you think that means?'

31

I saw Colette shiver as Eric mentioned *fog*.

'Ridiculous man,' Mrs Mortensen muttered, glancing at her daughter-in-law. 'Why should he care about the fog? And which fog, anyway?'

'There was one at the beginning of December,' said Colette slowly. 'I think, anyway. With a baby, days blur together. Olivier wasn't sleeping. But wasn't it then?'

'Well, I'm not asking that man. I'm not helping the investigation. Did he say why he wanted to know?' Mrs Mortensen was staring at Eric sharply.

'He told us Miss Figueroa hadn't been seen after that,' said Eric, blinking up at her. He was doing a good job of keeping his face looking casual. I was proud of him.

'Well – no,' said Mrs Mortensen, 'but we all thought she'd gone to stay with the Lowndes family. That's what we heard.'

'Who told you?' I asked.

'There was a letter, I think – Mr Abiola saw it,' said Mrs Mortensen. 'But on this street it's hard to know where anything comes from. It's all third-hand gossip, very confusing.'

'I *did* see Miss Fig the evening of the fog,' said Colette suddenly. She was narrowing her eyes thoughtfully, gazing off into the distance. 'I remember. We came home early, didn't we? Your committee meeting at four was cancelled.'

'I suppose so,' said Mrs Mortensen grudgingly. 'But it's impossible to remember the rest of that day.'

'No, wait. I remember Mrs Goodchild coming round with cocoa at eight, the way she always does, and seeing her torch flash in the fog before she rang the doorbell. Like a lighthouse, you know? And Miss Fig must have seen it too, and known the cocoa was on its way, because she came out of her house to wait – Mrs Goodchild always started at the other end of the mews and went to her last. She said something rude about the General barking. I was angry at her. And she said, "Well, I'm sick as a dog, not that you care." But she had been complaining of feeling sick quite a lot that week, so I ignored her.

'Then I went up to bed, but the General barked and woke Olivier just before midnight – he sleeps in with me, and Margot has the little box room at the back of the house. I checked the clock when I got up to feed him. Then I went to the window to look out at the fog, to try to see what had bothered the General; it was like cardboard had been nailed across the pane, it was so thick. And I heard – I heard someone talking.

'It was a man, I think, although the fog confused everything. It must have been someone who'd taken a wrong turning in the fog and ended up in the mews. But . . . the thing about it was that somehow the words he was saying sounded . . . *backwards*.'

'*Backwards?*' squeaked Eric.

My skin was crawling. I wasn't expecting a ghost story.

'It sounded so wrong – I was afraid. So I shut the curtains and fed Olivier and then went back to bed.'

Mrs Mortensen was frowning. 'Nonsense. You must have imagined it, Colette. And what are you doing telling the children? You two, forget this immediately.'

'Yes, Mrs Mortensen,' Eric said, lying.

'Good. And don't tell that Chief Inspector any of it, either.'

'We absolutely won't,' I said, not lying at all.

'I didn't imagine it, though,' said Colette, rubbing the birthmark on her cheek thoughtfully. 'The General had been quiet that whole evening, until then. Funny how it all comes back!'

'Maman, look, I drew Miss Fig dead in the basement,' said Margot, and Colette exclaimed and said, 'Margot, no! What on earth?'

'You were talking about her!' protested Margot.

'I think that's enough talking for everyone,' said Mrs Mortensen firmly, and the conversation was obviously over. Eric and I finished our biscuits. Eric gave the General one last loving pat, and then out we went into the mews again.

The Goodchilds' house was empty and dark, and we were both hovering outside it, wondering where to go next, when the door to Number 2 opened and Mr Abiola came out.

We both saw him relax, as though he'd been holding something in. His chin dropped and his fists clenched and he breathed *out* in a rush.

'Hello, Mr Abiola,' said Eric, and Mr Abiola jumped.

'Hello, children,' he said, pulling himself back together so quickly I almost thought I'd imagined it. But of course I hadn't. 'What are you doing here?'

'We've just had tea with the Mortensens,' I said.

'Are you all right?' asked Eric.

'Quite all right,' said Mr Abiola gruffly. 'But it's never nice to be doubted. I've just been in to see the police.'

'They don't think you had something to do with it?' I cried. I was worried I was coming on a little strong, sounding like a character in a play, but I guess Mr Abiola was already feeling so unnerved that he didn't notice.

'They don't need to say anything,' he said. 'I know. It's always the way. *You* understand, lad. I walk into a room and there's already a mark against me.'

He nodded at Eric, who stuck his hands in his pockets and shifted his shoulders unhappily.

'I told him!' he went on. 'There was a note, at Post, saying she was going to stay with the Lowndes family. It was strange, I'll admit it – she had a claim open with the council for damage to her house, but she never followed it up, which wasn't like her. But I believed it, until this week.'

I thought that wasn't quite right. He'd had doubts before that, as soon as I'd found the body. I remembered him talking to Miss Charney and Miss Temple after they'd put the stretcher in the ambulance. *Look, I'm wondering something. What about Miss Fig?*

'After all, why should she stay?' Mr Abiola peered up at Number 2. 'Look at this house. It's uninhabitable. There's a hole in the roof and a crack down the side – the front door doesn't even latch properly. Anyway, just you be careful around the police. You don't need to get yourselves mixed up in this, do you hear me?'

'Yes, Mr Abiola,' Eric said.

'Good,' said Mr Abiola. Then he went striding away across the mews to his flat. He's tall, and big, but right then he looked pretty small.

'I think we need to find May,' I said. Eric nodded.

'She might have heard that interview,' he said. 'He's a good suspect, isn't he?'

It was my turn to nod.

'I wish he wasn't,' said Eric in a rush. 'I mean, I know he seems suspicious. But what if he's just scared of the police? If Mama was here, she'd be acting the same way, even if she had nothing to do with it. I know it.'

'But we don't have an alibi for him yet,' I pointed out. 'We can't rule him out until we get one.'

'I know,' said Eric with a sigh. 'Come on.'

*

To get to where May was in the attics, we had to be sneaky. We walked along the left-hand side of the mews until we got to the door of Number 6. It belonged to Mr Harris, the lawyer who'd been away last December. He was still away, but I noticed that his housekeeper was here for the afternoon, cleaning the house the way she did every week, and that was who we were aiming for.

I took off my cardigan, dangled it from my hand and knocked on the door.

'Hello!' I said when the housekeeper answered. 'I'm Nuala, and this is Eric. We're staying in the flats. Can I borrow some sugar?' I wasn't trying to sound polite or English, and I knew that it'd annoy her.

The housekeeper scowled, exactly the way I hoped she would. 'Of course you can't,' she said. 'Taking our sugar ration? The cheek! Go on, get, you little urchins!'

'Oh, I am sorry!' I said rudely, and then just as she was closing the door in my face I flicked my dangling cardigan, catching it in the doorframe.

The door didn't close, of course, but bounced a little on its hinges. I waited until the housekeeper had stomped off again into the kitchen at the back of the house, before I knelt down, pushed the door open and crept inside. Eric followed me.

We were moving as quietly as we could, softer than mice, shoes off, mine bundled up with my cardigan. I pretended I was a ghost, floating my feet above the ground, and I ghosted forward across the living room in my socks, up the stairs that were mirrors of the ones in Miss Fig's. I saw more of Mr Goodchild's paintings as I went.

The box room in this house was almost empty, and the hatch to the attic was closed. I stood on tiptoes on the unmade bed to push it open, and I was so scared that we wouldn't be able for getting up. But I managed it in a rush, hauling myself into a dark space full of crates and pulling Eric up behind me. I guessed that Mr Harris must be storing all his stuff up there.

I went wriggling forward, flashlight between my teeth, and got into the crawl space. I inched my way along, counting gaps and trying not to make noise. I remembered what Eric and I had overheard Miss Wimpress saying, and got suddenly scared that whoever she was expecting might be up here with us.

Then I saw a bright gap in front of me and to my left. May's flashlight.

'Shhh!' she said really loudly.

'Shh yourself, you pup,' I said.

'You're so rude!'

'And you're so loud! They'll hear you downstairs.'

'No, they won't,' said May, as we wiggled out of the crawl space and came to sit down beside her. She'd set up a sort of desk out of a cardboard box, and she was kneeling up against it, scribbling in a notebook. 'They're busy.'

'Are they really?' I asked.

'Yes. I've been halfway down the stairs listening to them talking and no one noticed me. They just interviewed Mr Abiola.'

She flicked through her notebook, and then she got to the bit she wanted and stabbed at it with her finger.

'Here, all right, *listen*.'

May, Eric and I bent our heads together, so close that May's fringe tickled my nose, and she read out what she'd written.

32

'So, they said some boring nothing-chat first,' May told us. 'Mr Abiola wasn't happy to be there; the Chief Inspector was polite to him, but it didn't mean anything. Then Mr Abiola said, *But you suspect me,* and the Chief Inspector said, *Truly, I don't. In fact, I don't know that I suspect anyone yet. I don't know enough about what happened on the night in question.* He definitely thinks Miss Fig died on the sixth, just like we do.

'Then Mr Abiola said, *Miss Figueroa missed her shift on the night of the sixth of December, due to the fog, and after that I never saw her again. But there was a note the next day – I saw it – at Post, about going to stay with the Lowndes family.*'

'He's still the only person who says he actually saw that note!' said Eric. 'Oh. That's suspicious.'

May nodded. 'So the Chief Inspector said, *When I made a search of this house yesterday, I discovered a trunk filled with clothes and personal items in the box room upstairs.* And then Mr Abiola sputtered and said, *What? What do you mean? That can't be right.*

'Anyway, the Chief Inspector asked about the night of

the sixth, and Mr Abiola said, *We were all sent home from Post around four o'clock due to the fog – Jerry wasn't going to attack on a night like that. I stumbled back, half as quick as usual, got into my flat and went to bed.*

'Then the Chief Inspector asked, *And no one stopped by your door? Mrs Goodchild likes to offer cocoa to residents, I've heard.*

'And Mr Abiola said, *That's very much a tradition for the other side of the street. The flats and the houses are separate worlds, Chief Inspector. I do my job. I work hard – I'm hoping to bring my family to England after the war. Why would I want to put all that in danger just because of someone like Miss Fig?*

'And then the Chief Inspector said, *Well, you do Miss Figueroa's job now, don't you?* Which made me know that he suspects Mr Abiola, for sure!' added May. 'And I think he's a good suspect – really one of our best!'

I saw Eric shift uncomfortably.

'Other people could have done it too!' I objected. 'We can't narrow it down yet.'

May deflated with a sigh.

'I know,' she said. 'The thing is that Miss Fig sounded just *so* awful. Everyone wanted to kill her!'

'No one's been kind about her,' I agreed. 'I think that's sad. I know she wasn't very nice, but . . . she's still dead.'

'But imagine having to live next to her! You know I've had to have Rowena Knightley in the next bed all term and she's always going on at me about not tidying up. It makes me want to *punch* her. She's such a do-gooder. And she always finishes her prep on time and tells me about it. If Miss Fig was like that, I'm not surprised someone offed her.'

This was typically awful from May, Diary, although privately I agreed with her about Rowena Knightley. She ratted on me for wearing a contraband tie pin once, something I'd saved from Da's things, and it went into Davy Jones until I went to Miss Barnard and begged for it back.

'Huh,' I said, so I didn't have to admit any of that. 'It's annoying that it happened on the same night as the fog. If it was really that foggy, then the murderer might have been creeping past five feet away, and no one would know!'

There was a mew, and Pfote's puffball face poked out of the crawl space.

'Pfote!' cried Eric. 'What are you doing here? I thought you'd gone back to the Ministry!'

I seriously don't know how Eric does it. Cats will never do a thing I want them to, but Pfote had somehow followed Eric all the way up into an *attic*, without even complaining.

'But you're wrong about the fog,' said Eric, picking up Pfote and cuddling her. 'It's not annoying. It's the opposite. Didn't you listen to Cecil?'

'I did!' I protested.

'You didn't. When it's really foggy, you can't move around at all.'

'Yes, but—'

'No. Nothing.' Eric shook his head. 'It's like being under a blanket in the dark. If you hold your hand out in front of your face, you can't see it. You can't see the road if you try to go outside. Even when you stay inside, it starts snaking in through the windows. And when you breathe, it feels like there's something alive in your mouth, trying to wriggle down your throat. When it's daytime, the whole world's yellow. When it's night, everything's black. You can see when the person across the street's turned on their lights, but it's like you're seeing it from the other side of the world. You can't go more than the length of a street without getting so winded you have to stop, and it's almost impossible to know where you are. If it was foggy like that, on the night of the murder, then it would have been too difficult for anyone from the outside to come into the mews. And that's why no one was seen moving Miss Fig's body either. Miss Fig *has* to have been murdered by someone here.'

33

'All right, what did you find out from the Mortensens?' asked May.

Eric and I told her about what Mrs Mortensen and Colette had said about Miss Fig, and Colette's memories of the night of the sixth.

'It was so creepy!' I said. 'That whole story about the man speaking backwards. What do you think it means?'

'It's a clue,' said May decisively. 'Eric's just explained that the fog rules out anyone from outside the mews coming in that night. So the voice has got to have been one of our suspects. Cecil and Mr Goodchild are men, and Zosia and Miss Charney have quite low voices, so Colette might have thought one of them was a man.' She frowned. 'The other part of her story's interesting too. She said that Miss Fig was already feeling ill at eight that night, when Mrs Goodchild went round with cocoa, and had been for a little while. Isn't that strange!'

It was. I'd been thinking about it ever since Colette had said it. We knew Miss Fig had been stabbed – so why had she been feeling sick that night too? Was this important?

I remembered Colette talking, and that made me remember the sharp, tangy taste of the biscuits. 'What was in those biscuits?' I asked Eric.

'Oh, lemon!' said Eric, beaming. 'I haven't had lemons for months. Wasn't it nice?'

'WHAT?' said May. 'Lemons? How did she get those?'

'Oh!' I gasped, and then covered my mouth. 'Sorry! I've just worked something out! Sure, lookit, the food here's all wrong. Mrs Goodchild's cakes have real egg in them. Colette's biscuits have sugar and lemons. The General's fat, like he's being fed properly. Where's it all coming from?'

'You don't think!' gasped May. '*Black-market food!*'

Black market is any food that people sneak in, outside what they can get with their ration books. There's a trade in it, obviously, which no one ever talks about, because it's illegal, and unpatriotic. We're supposed to be living on the ration while the Nazis try to stop food getting into the country, but it's really hard. And I should have seen it at once, because eating in Hogarth Mews hasn't been feeling hard at all.

'It makes sense!' I said. 'And – and I think I know who's bringing it in. Cecil!' I remembered the bag he'd been carrying and his suspicious expression.

'Oooh!' said May. 'That would make more sense of why he was in Miss Fig's house, and why he didn't see her luggage. He wasn't looking for scrap at all; he was looking for food from the kitchen. And what if that gives him a motive for the crime too? What if Miss Fig found out and was going to tell, so he killed her? Ooh, is that what the note is about, the one we found ripped up in her house? Eric, does that fit?'

Eric flicked through his notebook until he found the bits of paper from Miss Fig's bathroom. He stared at them thoughtfully.

'*Ugg* could be smuggling,' he said. 'And *ood* could be food? But the rest – I'm still not sure.'

'Brilliant!' said May, undaunted. 'Well, it's possible. That's good enough for now. And if Miss Fig knew about it and was writing notes, then it's a good motive, isn't it? For lots of people! Oh, we're really getting somewhere. This is excellent! We just have to keep listening in and conducting interviews!'

She's always so positive when we get on a case, Diary. She just *believes* that we can do it, no matter how huge and hopeless it might seem.

'Well, we're not going to be able to interview Anna,' said Eric. Pfote mewed to herself as though she was backing him up.

'Oh, you're too *logical*!' snapped May. 'Buck up! It'll work out; I know it will.'

'Yes, but how will it?' he asked.

'It just will. Now, come on, we're wasting time sitting about in the attic. Let's go downstairs and listen in again.'

'But shouldn't we wait?' I objected. 'Until they leave? We might be caught!'

'Yes, but waiting's boring. I'm bored. Don't you want to have some *fun*?'

'Do we have a choice?' asked Eric, grinning at her.

'Absolutely not,' said May. 'Come *on*!'

SUSPECT LIST

– Mr Abiola. Has taken Miss Fig's position as shelter warden after her death. Does not seem to have liked her. Needed money? Is the only person who has seen the note Miss Fig apparently left at Post – is it even real? On the night of the 6th he has no alibi – he says he came home and went to bed. Investigate!

– Miss Charney. Does not seem to have liked Miss Fig. Overheard talking suspiciously to Miss Wimpress by Nuala and Eric in the attic after Miss Fig's body was found.

– Miss Wimpress. Seems very upset by Miss Fig's death. Is this a ruse? Overheard talking suspiciously to Miss Charney by Nuala and Eric in the attic after Miss Fig's body was found. Who did she think was in the attic, when she heard Eric and Nuala?

– Colette Mortensen. Does not seem to have liked Miss Fig. Miss Fig hated the General, and tried to tell Colette to have him put down. And we think that Colette may be buying black-market dog food for him – what if Miss Fig found out about it? She also uses real sugar and lemons in her baking – from Cecil? Movements on the evening of Friday 6th December: brought Mrs Mortensen back from her cancelled committee meeting at 4 p.m. Spent evening at home with her (alibi).

Mrs Goodchild brought cocoa round at 8 p.m. Heard Miss Fig saying she was ill at same time. Went to bed early but woke just before midnight because the General barked and heard someone, possibly a man, talking 'backwards'. What was this?

- Mrs Mortensen. Does not seem to have liked Miss Fig. We think she may have been buying food on the black market — what if Miss Fig discovered that? Investigate. Movements on the evening of Friday 6th December: came back from her cancelled committee meeting at 4 p.m. Spent evening at home with Colette and the children (alibi). Mrs Goodchild brought cocoa round at about 8 p.m.

- Cecil Goodchild. Behaving suspiciously. Is he looking for Anna to throw off the scent about Miss Fig? ~~What was in the bag? Why was he watching us?~~ We suspect he has been smuggling black-market food into the mews! Is this enough motive for murder?

- Zosia Stosic. Does not seem to have liked Miss Fig.

- Mrs Goodchild. Motive unclear. She uses real eggs in her baking — from Cecil?

- Mr Goodchild. Motive unclear.

- Anna Goodchild. Motive unclear, especially as Zosia told us that Anna was nice to Miss Fig. Miss Fig's body had Anna's necklace on it — why? We know that Anna went on her Ministry mission the next day, Saturday 7th December, and missed making Shabbos with her family on the evening of the 6th. Where was she that evening? Is she a suspect or not?

34

May scampered over to the opening down into the rest of the house and hoisted herself through it with a grunt.

'Whisht! You'll have them all running to you!' I hissed at her.

May made a face at me and dropped out of sight.

I lowered Eric down by his elbows, Pfote hopping past me onto his head and from there onto the floor, and then I wriggled after him.

I could hear low voices in the rooms below, adults talking offstage.

May was already halfway down the stairs, obviously. She just doesn't have any fear. She's either the worst spy in the world or the best. Eric and I tiptoed after her, Pfote moving like a ghost in front of us.

We all stopped at the entrance to Miss Fig's room, where we could duck into hiding at any sign we were about to be disturbed, but could still hear what was going on in the living room beneath us. In the daylight, I saw that it must have been a nice room once – sprigged wallpaper, a wooden bedframe with a matching dresser, china ornaments on the shelves.

But even in the soft afternoon light echoing through the windows the house looked rotten now. I don't mean just awful, the way people in England use the word; I mean really rotting. The huge crack wriggled and split down one side of it, shattering some of the ornaments and ripping the wallpaper and making Mr Goodchild's painting tilt to one side. Little bugs and *creatures* (Eric would know which ones) had burrowed further into it, leaving plaster dust and droppings across everything.

Plus – and I noticed this now, while we were really trying to be silent – the house trembled. All houses creak and sigh sometimes as people move around them, but this one shook. Every little move we made spiderwebbed out from our bodies horrifyingly. I was sure the Chief Inspector would hear us at once.

'This house is falling down around our ears,' I heard him say, downstairs. He's got a soft voice, the Chief Inspector, but it somehow draws your ear in. He's the kind of person who can always make himself heard. 'Did this just come in?'

'Yes, sir,' said a woman's voice – one of the other officers. 'Sent straight from the coroner's office. Rush job, as you asked. And the Commissioner says, er, *Hurry up with this one, Priestley, and would you perhaps consider moving operations out of that condemned house before it flattens you and I lose another good man?'*

'Excellent translation, Fodor.'

'It was worded somewhat differently in the original, sir.'

'Unfortunately for the Commissioner, I need to be on the spot. There's something about this case – although perhaps it's just the appearance of those children. The little one's older sister – it's hard to explain, but she and her friend always had a knack of appearing where they were needed. Adults ignored them at their peril. Now, what about this report? Let me look at it.'

May was pummelling me, hissing, '*Big sister Hazel!*'

'Shush!' I said to her. 'Listen!'

There was a pause downstairs, and I was sure that we'd been heard.

'Really, this house sounds as though it's about to collapse. Now is this correct?' asked the Chief Inspector quietly. 'Am I reading it right?'

'Yes, sir. I know, sir,' said the woman, Fodor.

'It seems like something from a book. I've not stumbled into a murder mystery, have I?'

'Not that I know of, sir.'

'Well!' said the Chief Inspector. 'In my day, victims were only killed once. But I suppose the war has changed everything. Why shouldn't it change murder too?'

35

Eric gripped Pfote in his lap, so hard that she squeaked and shoved out of his grasp. May's eyes were like lamps in her face.

What was in the report?

'I mean – *listen* to this,' continued the Chief Inspector. 'She was stabbed, we knew that, but – arsenic in her system too, and then a heavy enough dose of chloral to kill her. Was the woman Rasputin?'

Arsenic and chloral! Arsenic I knew was a poison, Diary. I mean, it's obvious. They're always using it in plays and books, and it's in lots of household things, rat poison and weed killer and flypaper and so on. But chloral? I'd always thought it was just a sort of drug to help you go to sleep. You can buy it at the chemist's, and lots of people use it. I didn't know it could *kill* you.

'Well. We'll need poison books from all the chemists in the area. Send someone out on that, will you? But who on earth would stab someone they'd already poisoned, twice?'

'I'm not sure, sir, I—'

There was a pause, and then the sound of a sneeze.

'Is there a cat in here, Fodor?' asked the Chief Inspector.

I looked around wildly. Pfote had gone from beside Eric. I peeked down the stairs and saw her perched on the fifth step up, licking her white back paw.

'Eric!' whispered May. 'Quick!'

For a second I thought she was going to dive after her, which would have been very May and very stupid. But Eric and I both grabbed her sleeves and dragged her backwards as quietly as we could into Miss Fig's bedroom.

'There, look!' said Fodor, sneezing again. 'I'm sorry, sir – I never saw it before. *Ah!*'

'Now, how did you get in?' asked the Chief Inspector. 'I'm sure you weren't in here before. You look very well cared for too. Do you belong to someone in the mews? It must have been you upstairs, then. I thought I kept hearing noises.'

Pfote made a rumbly purring noise.

'Now, cat, no closer, please. This isn't the place for you. Fodor, please put it outside, will you?'

But Pfote apparently had no intention of going out the front door. There was a thump, and then the sound of hurrying footsteps coming up the stairs towards us.

'It won't – I've almost got it – come *here*—' Fodor panted, sniffing.

Right then I knew – I just knew – that we were about to be found out. It was about to happen. We'd be caught, and we'd never solve the case. Just when it was really getting interesting too! I was so mad at Eric for bringing Pfote.

But then Pfote hissed and let out a yowl, and Fodor yelled, 'GOT it, sir!'

And the footsteps bounced away down the stairs again. The front door opened and shut, and we were safe.

Eric, of course, was looking pale with distress. 'Do you think she hurt her?' he whispered. 'Is she all right?'

'Of course she's all right!' May sighed. 'She'll go back to the Ministry and we'll see her tomorrow. Eric, you fool, why did you bring her?'

'I didn't bring her! She wanted to come,' said Eric, folding his arms. 'You can't *make* anyone do anything.'

'Oh? Well, I can make you *sorry*!'

'Stop it!' I said. For once I was the one calming things down. 'Listen! Something's happening downstairs, something else.'

Maybe it was useful that the house was so wobbly. I'd heard not one but two people come back through the front door when Pfote had been put outside – the police officer Fodor and someone else.

'Sir! She was just crossing the mews when I came out. You said you wanted to speak to her.'

'Very good, Fodor, thank you. Miss Stosic, good evening.'

'Good evening,' said Zosia. I knew her voice, obviously; we all did. We stared at each other in shock. I checked my watch – it was almost eight. So Zosia must have just come from the Ministry. 'I'm on my way home from work.'

'And where do you work?'

'The telephone pool,' said Zosia.

'Hard hours,' said the Chief Inspector sympathetically. 'This won't take long, I promise. I'm asking everyone in the mews the same questions. Where you were on the sixth of December, for one, and what you thought of Miss Figueroa.'

'Oh yes? Well, I do remember what I was doing on the sixth, as it happens – I was taking a day off, helping my flatmate Anna. She was due to travel that day, but of course the fog put paid to that. I saw her off the next day instead, and then I came down with a fever – I caught glandular fever that week, quite badly.'

'I'm sorry!' said the Chief Inspector. 'It must have made for a memorable few days, though, I suppose. And Anna wasn't affected?'

'No, she wasn't. And yes, the fever was hard to forget. I was laid up for months.'

I could hear that Zosia was holding something back. It could just have been that she was pretending to be a typist, not a spy, but . . . I was sure that wasn't it. She'd seemed to tell the Chief Inspector where she was on the sixth, but she'd really just steered the conversation away to the seventh. Had he noticed that? I surely had.

'Where *is* Anna, by the way?' asked the Chief Inspector, and I wondered again.

'I'm not sure, Chief Inspector,' replied Zosia. 'Her trip was extended, and then extended again. I had a few letters from her, but months ago. In a war – you understand, I'm sure.'

'Does she work at the telephone pool too?'

'Oh, no – some sort of secretarial thing, I think. I never really asked. We didn't have that kind of friendship. Work stayed at work.'

That was definitely a lie, I could hear it in her voice. Her breath was caught up high in her throat. I thought to myself that the Ministry definitely should be training spies better than this.

'Hm. It must be hard to get work, at the moment, with a name like Stosic? It's – what – Slavic?'

'Serbian. My father. My mother was Polish. Listen, if you want to know about my loyalty – I want Hitler to go to hell, just like everyone else. Don't you forget it.'

'My apologies, Miss Stosic – I didn't intend to cause offence. I do always mean what I say, only people sometimes don't believe me. I was simply trying to make conversation. So you don't remember anything from that day?'

So he *had* noticed.

'I already told you! I was helping Anna, packing and so on. Then the fog closed in and we couldn't go anywhere. I do remember one thing. Usually there's a raid, or that dog starts howling, but it was too foggy for the planes – and I suppose the fog knocked out the General too. He was quiet almost all night. I think he only barked once. I slept unusually well.'

'Perhaps you were already coming down with your illness,' said the Chief Inspector. 'And what did you think of Miss Figueroa?'

'I didn't think anything of her. She was a bothersome woman. She was always coming into the flat, poking and prying about with her warden's badge and telling me and Anna some new rule we had to follow. I'm sure she made most of them up. She always thought we were up to no good.'

'And were you?'

'Chief Inspector, I work twelve-hour days. I come home and fall into bed. The most I *get up to* is eating a tin of soup without heating it first. But nosy people like Miss Fig never can believe that. In their heads, everyone is sinning all the time.'

'In my experience, most people are,' said the Chief Inspector thoughtfully. 'But I admit that my sample population is biased. So you didn't think anything of her, apart from not liking her very much?'

'I never said that! See here, I didn't care about her one way or another. But Anna was quite fond of her. She always said hello to her when they saw each other in the mews, and she lent her books – they had the same taste in fiction.'

'Which was?'

'Funny, as far as I was concerned. Extremely schlocky romantic books. Heaving bosoms and so on. It did make me laugh, someone like Miss Fig reading that! I think that's

206

why Anna felt such a soft spot for her. I can't stand the stuff. Give me adventure novels, any day! John Buchan, Graham Greene, Francis Beeding—'

'Have you read his new one?' asked the Chief Inspector. 'Good stuff, isn't it?'

'Oh, yes – I mean, Chief Inspector Priestley, that isn't relevant. I know what you're trying to do, and it won't work on me. Look, I've answered your questions. May I go home now?'

'You may. My apologies for catching you when you're tired.'

'You're not sorry at all,' said Zosia. 'Good try, though. Quite believable.'

The door slammed, and then bounced back.

'Spiky,' said the Chief Inspector to himself. 'An interesting girl. Fodor, where *is* this Anna? She's the Goodchilds' daughter, isn't she?'

'I looked into it for you yesterday, sir. On the surface, nothing doing. But I pushed hard enough to end up with a very thin file with a piece of paper in it telling me not to look further. If you know what I mean.'

'Interesting,' said the Chief Inspector. 'So she's intelligence, then, is she?'

'Something along those lines, I believe.'

'In which case – well, I shall have to make a call. That's all our interviews, isn't it?'

'I believe so, sir.'

'And we have the report too. I think it might be time to call it a day. Now—'

But at that moment a frantic baying rose up outside. It gave me an electric shock of fright. There's always just a second with a loud noise when you're sure it's the siren, or worse. And then, obviously, I realized it was only General Charles de Gaulle.

'Has he got Pfote?' gasped Eric.

'Well, if he has, you can't do anything about it without ruining our hiding place,' May told him severely. She was panting, though, and I could tell she'd been scared too.

Colette Mortensen's voice lifted above the howling, telling the General to be *QUIET, QUIET, be QUIET*.

'Someone startled him,' said Eric, relaxing. 'He's still locked in.'

'One thing we do know, Fodor, is that, whatever happened, it happened without much disturbing that dog,' said the Chief Inspector. 'Otherwise the whole street would have been roused.'

36

'He's got a point, so,' I said when the door had banged again behind the Chief Inspector and Fodor, and we'd waited five more careful minutes by Eric's watch just to be sure that no one else was there. 'How did the murderer not bother General Charles de Gaulle more? Zosia said that he only barked once that night – and that's what Colette said too.'

'Ooh, does that mean it was one of the Mortensens?' asked May.

'No, they can't keep him quiet, either,' said Eric, shaking his head.

'So it's a good question. *Why* didn't he bark more that night? The murderer would have had to go past the Mortensens' house, Number Three, to get to Number Two to murder Miss Fig. Go in, come out, put the body into the basement of Number One, and then go home again. That's three times at least. Write it down, Nuala.'

I wrote: *What about the dog??? Why didn't he bark more?*

'And what about Zosia?' I said. 'If she really was coming down with glandular fever, then she couldn't have killed Miss Fig that night.'

'Of course she could,' said May. 'She said she saw Anna off the next day, so if she was well enough to do that, then she would have been well enough to do a murder the night before. And you heard how she didn't really tell the Chief Inspector where she was on the sixth? She doesn't have an alibi at all, at least as far as she's willing to admit.'

So she'd noticed it too.

'Listen,' she went on. 'The Chief Inspector's gone. Let's go downstairs. He might have left papers behind.'

'Why would he have left anything?' I asked. 'That's official evidence! He's not that bad at being a policeman!'

'He might have! We have to go check!'

'Can't you stop arguing?' asked Eric. 'Let's go and look before you start getting upset about it.'

As usual, he had a point. So we left Miss Fig's room and crept down the creaky staircase. I took a deep breath as I did – the room had been so close that it'd given me a funny little headache, which I only noticed as we went downstairs.

The Chief Inspector had left the living room tidy. I could see that the chairs had been moved around, and someone had brought the small side table into the middle of the room to be used as a desk, but apart from that there was nothing but a police officer's bootprint just by the front door. It smelled a little, though: the mixed-up smells of a whole lot of different adults.

There were no papers, which kind of felt obvious. I

mean, what kind of policeman would leave evidence like that around? Certainly not the Chief Inspector.

'Blast!' said May to herself crossly, folding her arms.

'Um,' said Eric. 'Look at this.'

He'd sat down on one of the chairs, a sort of padded one, and then got up again fast. He had something in his hand, a pad of paper with pages all ripped out of it. But they hadn't been ripped very carefully, and part of one had been left behind. So maybe the Chief Inspector was careful, but his police officers weren't.

'It's from one of the interviews, I think,' he said.

May squeaked, and we both crowded round Eric to look.

'Oh!' she said after a moment. 'But it's in code!'

I grinned, because for once I knew something the other two didn't. 'Sure, it's just shorthand!' I said. 'It's not really code at all. I can read it!' My da had taught me to, years ago.

I cleared my throat and began.

'*Junior curator at British Museum. Volunteer with ambulance service. Lives at Number Five with E. Charney. Prior to that lived at Number Two with P. Figueroa. Bad falling-out between them?*

'*Question: what did you think of Figueroa?*

'*Answer: At first I think I liked her. She was very sure of herself, and I am usually not, you know. I like that in a person. But after a while she got too sure, and it stopped me being sure of much at all. That's why we quarrelled, you know. I felt overwhelmed by her.*

And the war brought out a side of her I didn't much like. She became very strict and quite obsessed with following the rules. I think they made her feel certain. Not understanding frightened her and upset her. She had to know what was going on with everyone around her. She was really an ideal warden. Anyway, in the summer last year I moved out of this house, and in with Elfie. But when I say we quarrelled, Paula and I – it wasn't really so bad. I was still happy to see her every day. When she had her car accident in October, I brought her food while she was laid up. We began to talk again. I never could understand why she left without contacting me. She never told me where she was going.

'*Question: where were you on the night of the sixth?*

'*Answer: That was the night of the fog, wasn't it? I remember they sent us home from work at the museum early. It was already getting quite close. I was due to go on shift at the ambulance station, but of course it was impossible to go out. You can't drive in a fog. That evening was unremarkable. It was so quiet. That dog didn't even bark. Miriam – Mrs Goodchild – brought round cocoa at her usual time – I mean, I think she did, I can't exactly remember that, but she must have done. I do remember how tired I was – it must have been the relief of knowing there couldn't be a raid. I kept falling asleep over my book. We both did – half dozing off, and then waking again to laugh at each other. We went to bed early. And that's all.*'

'According to her, the General didn't bark at all!' said May. 'Isn't that interesting. And they used to live together,

212

but then Miss Wimpress left Miss Fig. Is that a motive? She says they were beginning to talk again, but I don't know if that's very likely. People who used to be friends but aren't any more are always so cross at each other.'

And that was when the siren sounded.

37

We'd all lost track of time – it was after nine already. I yelped, Eric gasped and May bit into the pencil she was holding so hard it splintered.

'HEY!' I said. 'I need that!'

'Well, I hated how it looked,' said May, sticking her chin out. 'It's better now.'

'It's *ruined* now!'

'We should go,' said Eric. 'We don't need to spend another raid out of the shelter. Come on.'

We pushed open Miss Fig's front door and stepped out into the mews. I tried to shut the door, so that the Chief Inspector wouldn't notice anything different about it, but it was sort of pointless. It didn't even close properly; the whole door was kind of skewed sideways and wobbly.

The siren was wailing, up and down, screaming straight into my head. Way above us and far away, I could hear the buzz of planes coming up the Estuary. They sound kind of like mosquitos at first, then they turn into purring cats, and then you can hear the chugging noises as their engines turn over, the hitch in the hum that means they're close now, they're following you, they're almost here.

These ones were still mosquitos, so we were OK for now.

The mews was quiet, the sky still dark blue instead of black, all the shadows long and deep. Then, as we started walking towards the main road and the shelter, General Charles de Gaulle began to bellow behind us.

I thought we'd scared him at first somehow, even though we hadn't walked by his house, but then May said, 'Golly! It's Cecil!'

And I turned round to see she was *right*. Cecil was walking past the Mortensens' house, hands in his jacket pockets and the bag hanging off his shoulder, yawning and looking completely cool and casual.

Except I knew he was acting.

I can't really say *how* I knew; it takes a lot longer to explain than it did to have the feeling.

First of all, who'd be yawning in the middle of an air-raid siren? Even someone who'd been in London all last autumn and hasn't died yet. And second – there's a way you hold your body when you're trying to act calm but you really aren't underneath. Your shoulders are too far back, your face is too flat, and you have to hide your hands. And that's what Cecil was doing.

Actually, now I write it down, I guess it was the hands that gave him away. I could see the outline of them in his jacket pockets, and they were clenched into fists.

So he was acting. And he wasn't as good at it as I am.

'What have you been doing?' I asked him, glaring as hard as I could.

'Doing homework in my room,' said Cecil, raising an eyebrow. 'What's it to you? I'm still not talking to you, by the way. You said you'd help look for Anna, and you've spent the last few days doing nothing of the sort.'

'We never said that!' I protested.

'Nuala, you liar,' said Cecil. And look, I blush easily. It's not my fault. My da was the same. I could feel myself blushing, and I knew it wasn't dark enough to hide it.

'I'm no liar! Stop being bold. We didn't agree anything. And you're lying too. What have you been doing?'

'None of your business,' said Cecil.

'You've been smuggling food,' said May sharply.

Cecil froze.

'What did you say?' he asked. 'What's it to you?'

'It's nothing to us,' I said. 'We don't care. We just want to know the truth.'

Cecil's whole body had gone tense. He hugged the bag to his chest, and I could see that it was empty.

'You're smart for a kid,' he said at last. 'Look. You might – *might*, I say! – have hit on it. But if you say anything, I shall kill you. That's not a joke!'

'Oh!' cried May again. 'It's you! You're the murderer! You killed Miss Fig! Eric! Nuala! Get him!'

Cecil burst out laughing. 'Whatever's the matter with

you?' he asked. 'Of course I didn't murder Miss Fig. I'm not— When you say *I shall kill you* it's just an expression, not the *truth*. Don't you know that? And – look – it wasn't even my idea, at first. Colette asked me if I could get her extra meat for the dog, and then Mrs M asked for sugar, and it all went from there. I know some people, from selling scrap. Sometimes we go into bombed-out houses and pinch stuff, and sometimes we do . . . other things. It's easy. I get a cut of the profit, and everyone's happy. But please, listen to me – please don't tell Mum and Dad. Mum thinks my friend keeps chickens and that's why I'm bringing her eggs every week. And Dad doesn't notice anything that isn't Renaissance sketches unless I put it right in front of his face.'

'Maybe we *will* tell them!' said May, narrowing her eyes. 'Maybe we will, unless you prove to us that you didn't kill Miss Fig and you're not just lying about it.'

'Of course I'm not lying about it! Why would I have come to you thinking the body was Anna's if I knew it was Miss Fig's?'

It was exactly what I'd thought myself.

'Misdirection!' said May promptly.

The first bombs dropped, and we all jumped. We began to move properly then, rushing across the cobbles of the mews, the siren wailing all around us. Flares were falling now, like dropped candles across the sky. Every time I see them I'm stunned by how beautiful the world can be, even when it's trying to kill you.

'You're nuts! Look, I told you. The sixth was a Friday. When I went to get Anna for Friday-night dinner – I stopped by after I came home from school, because she'd always come home early on Fridays – she wasn't there. I asked Mum and Dad if they'd seen her and they said she'd gone on one of her business trips that day. Without telling me! We ended up yelling at each other, and I – well, I turned off my hearing aid so I couldn't hear what they were saying, and walked out of the front door.'

'In the fog?' I asked sceptically.

Cecil shrugged. 'It was still coming on. It wasn't as bad as it got later. And most people panic because the fog dulls their hearing, but it doesn't bother me so much. I did get lost three times just trying to get to my mate's house, though, and he only lives on the other side of Bedford Square. I was stuck there all evening – I didn't get back until the next afternoon. We went collecting scrap once the fog lifted the next day. I missed going to shul – I mean synagogue – and Mum was mad at me. That good enough for you?'

'We don't have your friend's story yet,' said Eric. 'So you might be lying. And you might have come back and killed Miss Fig.'

'Apart from the fact that I didn't. I did go and pinch tins from her kitchen, once Mr A told us that she'd left, but that's all. Ben's down in the shelter, you can ask him yourselves. You're silly kids. Why are you doing this, anyway? Why do you care?'

'Because someone has to!' I said, blushing again, but this time with annoyance.

Mr Abiola went rushing by us then. He snapped, 'Get down to the shelter!' and went running on towards the mews. I knew he was on his way to check the houses. We nodded at him and stopped talking until he'd gone.

'And maybe we like being silly kids,' May grumbled. We were at the entrance to the shelter now. It was time to go in. I put my hand on her arm and felt the muscles bunched. I knew she was scared of the shelter. She always is. So I slipped my arm through hers and squeezed as tight as I could. May squeezed back, and Eric came round the side of me to put his hand on her other elbow.

That was nice, that moment. We felt like a real team. We really were being the Detective Society.

PART FIVE

WE FIND OURSELVES IN AN EXPLOSIVE SITUATION

38

From the diary of Fionnuala O'Malley

Tuesday 1st April, continued

Down the stairs we went, all bunched together, with Cecil crowding behind us complaining that we were moving too slowly. I still felt that anxiety I'd spotted before coming off his body in hot, angry waves. Was he worried because we'd rumbled him as a smuggler? Or was he trying to lie about Miss Fig? I wasn't sure yet. I wanted to talk to Ben.

The shelter was mostly full already, and the warmth and smell of it pressed against me like a hand over my face when we ducked through the low doorway. I always want to put my palms over my ears when I get into shelters – there's just so much coming at you at once. But, in a way, a shelter's the perfect place to hide too, because everyone there's so focused on themselves and their friends. You still have to be careful what you say, but usually people don't notice you.

Cecil's group of friends were sitting heckling each other at the other end of the shelter. May kicked Cecil's boot with her little shoe.

'Take us to Ben!' she said. I could see she was pink-faced with anxiety, but as usual when May's worried, she gets punchy.

'I'm taking you to Ben – stop bothering me. But be normal, can't you? Don't start yelling at him or accusing him of being a murderer. Can you do that?'

'Maybe,' said May sulkily. 'Yes. Fine.'

Ben was spotty, with a big angular face and a bad haircut.

'Babysitting, are you?' he asked Cecil, nodding at us.

'Shut up, you,' said Cecil, cuffing at him. I do think boys are so weird together. I hope Eric never gets like that. Or maybe he does, when he's at school, and we're not there. Maybe school Eric's a totally different person. But I don't really think so. He's too much like May: the same wherever he is.

'Cecil's been lying to us,' said May. 'He told us he walked through that fog in December to see you. But that's stupid; he couldn't have done.'

'Course he did!' said Ben at once. 'He's always doing things like that. He's loopy. Anyway, he got to me before things got really bad, and then he was stuck.'

'See?' said Cecil to us. I'd been watching his face while Ben spoke. He hadn't given Ben any silent signals. So what Ben was saying, it must be the truth. We could rule him out. 'Now, go away, you three kids. The grown-ups want to talk.'

'Rude!' cried May. 'Fine! We don't want to be around you anyway!'

She stomped off, and Eric and I followed – straight into another group of our suspects.

May nearly ruined it, of course. She gasped and pointed, and Eric and I had to grab her and drag her behind one of the bunks. There in the corner of the shelter, in a space lit by one kerosene lamp, guttering low, sat Mr and Mrs Goodchild, Miss Wimpress and Miss Charney, and Colette. They were talking, and Miss Wimpress was handing Mr Goodchild a book.

'We have to listen in!' I whispered. 'Come on!'

We dodged from one bunk to the next, using all our Ministry training. We pretended to be chatting, to be looking for something we'd lost on the ground, to be part of the game of tiddlywinks that was going on next to us – and then we were close enough to listen in.

We were sitting down, faces turned away, watching the tiddlywinks game, half hidden by the big folding chair that someone had brought into the shelter. My whole attention was focused behind us, though. And this is what we heard.

39

'—upset,' Miss Wimpress was saying.

'Don't be ridiculous, Prim,' said Miss Charney. 'There's nothing to be upset about.'

'But she's dead,' said Miss Wimpress. 'She's dead. I can't get the idea out of my head, you know, of her lying there all alone for so many months.'

'Oh, come now. Aren't you glad to be shot of her? You weren't happy in that house at all.'

'You don't know that! You weren't there!'

'I was three doors away. I heard enough—' Miss Charney began hotly.

'Elfie, come now – there's no use arguing about it,' said Mrs Goodchild. 'It's all over.'

Miss Wimpress blew her nose with a trumpeting sound and sighed.

'And it isn't to do with any of us,' Miss Charney went on firmly. 'We've all told the truth to the Chief Inspector, about the night of the sixth. My shift was cancelled, so Prim and I had dinner together and then we went to bed early.' I glanced at her out of the corner of my eye. She had a book about fixing cars on her lap, and she thumped it for emphasis. 'Isn't that right, Mrs Goodchild?'

Mrs Goodchild exclaimed gently – she was sewing something again, and her needle had slipped into the pad of her thumb. 'Of course, Miss Charney,' she said, bobbing her head up again. 'Friday night dinner, and then cocoa, and then bed. A very ordinary night. That's what I told him.'

Mr Goodchild nodded and *hmm*ed, flicking through the pages of the book he'd been handed.

A bomb suddenly hit, very close by. None of us had heard it falling, so everyone jumped and cried out. Then we all went still, waiting for the next explosion. They fall in a straight line, you see – so you've got to wait until you know what direction the plane's going in, whether it's coming closer or whether it's already passed on further.

Almost immediately after there was another smash, further away, and then another. We all relaxed.

'CLOSE CALL!' yelled Mr Abiola from the front of the shelter, and he blew his whistle triumphantly. He'd come back by then. 'BUT THEY COULDN'T FIND US!'

Quite a few people cheered, including Zosia, who I saw had come down the stairs after him. She was leaning against one of the shelter walls, watching a game of chess. As usual, she looked very pretty, and very annoyed.

When I tuned back into the conversation between the Hogarth Mews group, they were somehow talking about art. I couldn't work out how they'd gone from murder to paintings while everyone was thinking about maybe being crushed by a bomb, but adults do that sometimes – skip between topics so fast I can't see the connection.

'—won't affect the special project, will it?' Colette was asking.

'Not at all,' said Mr Goodchild. 'Miss Wimpress and I are hard at work on it. The next stage is scheduled for later this week – all the details are ready. Mr Levy, this time – I was delighted to get him. Remember, Miriam, we worked together in '33? Some wonderful pieces of art. The Lowndes family are helping again, among others.'

'The supervision of it all is quite a job,' said Mrs Goodchild, stitching away. 'But Samuel is equal to it – and Primrose too, of course.'

'Well, yes, of course—'

'The project does need constant monitoring,' said Mr Goodchild. 'And it's always an anxious moment, waiting to see if the objects have been damaged.'

'I think you focus on art too much,' said Miss Charney. 'Aren't people more important?'

'Of course people are important. But what is there to live for if we don't have art? Why bother surviving if there's no beauty in the world?' Mr Goodchild had drawn himself up, and he looked really noble in the lamplight. 'Philistines like Miss Fig didn't understand this, but it's crucial. We're saving meaning, history, the images that tell us who we are and who we could be. We're giving a gift to the people who will see them in one hundred years, and we are telling all the people alive now that there *will* still be people in one hundred years, people who will need beauty and joy as much as we do.'

I really loved that. It's true, Diary – the war makes everything good feel so small. You can try and try to do your best, and to believe in stories about bravery and kindness, but then every night you watch as more and more of the world gets smashed to a pulp. Sometimes it's hard to get up the next day and keep going. I'd heard Mr Goodchild talk about this before – people who work at galleries and museums, like him and Miss Wimpress, are moving pieces of art into the countryside, where they'll be safer. It's helpful to know that there are people trying to save beautiful things, caring about *happiness* like that.

'Could you not arrange to have the Chief Inspector moved out of London?' asked Colette with a laugh. 'I'm sure it'd be better for him. He looks so tired. Can't someone persuade him to just . . . let it drop? If he decides she died in an accident—'

'She clearly did not die in an accident!' said Miss Charney, more angry this time. 'Otherwise he wouldn't be here. Really, Colette, you're being quite ridiculous – that policeman's going to stick around until he's found out what happened. That is, unless something happens—'

I turned my head to look at them. Miss Wimpress was looking wobbly again, Colette looked desperate and anxious, Mr Goodchild seemed as though he was upset that no one was paying attention to him any more, and Mrs Goodchild had her head bent over her sewing. Then the all-clear sounded. The baby Olivier, who'd somehow slept through everything, suddenly woke and began to howl, and the conversation was over.

40

It's weird how you don't feel like sleeping right after a raid, even though during it you might have thought you could drop through the floor with tiredness if only the bombs would stop.

It was just before eleven, and May, Eric and I sat around our kitchen table, drinking cocoa. Zosia came in and poured herself a mug. She looked tired and worn – she was rubbing at her eyes, and she had dust across her skirt. Her fingers were still covered in pencil marks from the day's coding. She had a smudge of it on her cheek, and I wanted to brush it off, but didn't. Zosia isn't the kind of person you touch.

'Are you staying out of that policeman's way?' she asked us. 'He's bad news. We don't need him knowing about the Ministry, so remember: *loose lips.*'

'He was asking about Anna,' said May, who can never leave anything alone. I kind of admire that about her.

'I know,' said Zosia. 'He's pulled her file. At least he won't find out anything from that. You didn't say anything, did you? You'd better not have.'

'We didn't!' said Eric.

'Hmm,' said Zosia. 'Good.' She rubbed her hand over her face again and sighed.

'Anna did leave on the seventh, didn't she?' I asked. 'We said that to the Chief Inspector.'

That was a lie – we hadn't. We'd just heard Zosia say it to him. But I wanted to poke at her a little. Maybe it was mean, but detecting can't always be nice, otherwise you wouldn't get anywhere. And there was something she'd said just now – something that was bothering me.

'Why can't you just— Ugh! Yes, she did. And then I got glandular fever. That's what happened.'

'Then why didn't Anna go to dinner on the sixth?' asked Eric. 'She didn't answer when Cecil knocked to get her, and then Mr and Mrs Goodchild told him she'd already left that morning. Why, if she was still here?' He said it in a very Eric-ish way – polite and curious, like he really couldn't work it out.

'She was tired,' snapped Zosia. 'She wasn't feeling well.'

'But that was you,' I said. 'Wasn't it?'

I shouldn't have said it, Diary. I guess I was just surprised. I'd thought Ministry spies would be better at lying than that. And I *knew* she was lying, again. I saw her shoulders hunch, and her lips quirk. But instead of telling me I was wrong—

'I'm going to bed,' said Zosia, and she turned and stomped away into her room. As she did so, I saw her take a piece of paper out of her pocket and smooth it between her fingers. Her face looking down at it was sharp with anxiety, and she rubbed at her forehead.

We all sat frozen until we heard her bedroom door close.

Eric leaned forward and tapped something out on the table in Morse code. May's brow wrinkled, but I got it.

COME DOWN TO MY FLAT.

I nodded. 'I'm hungry,' I said calmly, while I made furious faces at May. 'You've got some tiffin in your flat, haven't you, Eric?'

'Good idea,' said Eric, pinching May. She finally got it.

'GREAT IDEA!' she said. 'TIFFIN! LET'S GO!'

Seriously, May needs to learn to be more subtle.

'Grand, so,' I said, breathing out once we were all safely downstairs in Eric's kitchen and eating the tiffin (which was real, luckily, and brought in from the Ministry). There was a note from George on the table that read:

Gone to Ralph's tonight – work. Don't wait up – G

'Wasn't that odd?' asked Eric. 'Zosia got mixed up about her story. Do you think it wasn't true?'

I nodded. 'Definitely,' I said. 'But we don't know why. It might be a Ministry thing – something they don't want to tell us.'

'They don't want to tell us anything!' grumbled May.

'Why don't we have a meeting about what we've discovered?' I asked. 'We haven't talked about Cecil, or what we heard in the shelter.'

May perked up right away.

'Ooh! We ruled someone out!' she said. 'Cecil has an alibi! Which is good because Nuala—'

'Hey!' I said, blushing. 'We've ruled him out; that's good enough. Mrs Goodchild backed up what we've heard from other people: that she brought cocoa around at eight.'

'It's strange that Anna pretended not to be there for the meal,' said Eric with a frown. 'If she hadn't left yet. But she can't have left until the seventh, unless the Ministry files are wrong.'

'Zosia's lying about something,' I said. 'I don't know what, but she is. Something she said earlier – it wasn't right. I think she's really suspicious.'

'Ooh, and we're living with her!' said May happily. 'What if it's her? What if we've been living with a—'

'Stop it, May,' said Eric, just as May said, 'Well, it's not the first time. I did tell you both that I helped solve *three* murder mysteries before I even met you?'

She had, lots of times.

'I still don't think we've got motives for Mr and Mrs Goodchild, if they don't know what Cecil's been doing,' said Eric, ignoring her. 'But we definitely do for Colette and Mrs Mortensen, if they were buying black-market food from Cecil. We know that Miss Fig really cared about

234

rules – if she found out about the smuggling, she'd report it. Maybe one of them killed her to stop her?'

'And what about Colette?' I said. 'She really loves the General, and Miss Fig wanted her to get rid of him.'

'That's definitely enough motive for murder,' said Eric seriously. 'I'm not sure smuggling food is.'

'Of course it is!' said May, taking another bite out of her tiffin. 'It's a war. Food's the *most* important thing. The General's just a dog.'

'Dogs are people!' said Eric, turning pink with annoyance.

'And then there's Miss Charney,' I went on quickly. 'She really hated Miss Fig. She thought she treated Miss Wimpress badly when they lived together.'

'Yes, but *no one* liked Miss Fig,' said Eric. 'Apart from Miss Wimpress.'

'And *she* might be lying!' said May.

'I don't think she is, so,' I said, shaking my head. 'She really seems sad about her.'

'Hah! Don't get taken in!' cried May. 'Anyway, people sometimes murder people they like, and then feel sad about it afterwards. You know, everyone hates the Chief Inspector too. Ooh, do you think someone's going to kill him next?'

'No one's going to kill him!' I said. 'Don't be an eejit. People don't kill policemen.'

'I don't see why not. Policemen can be murderers, so can't they be murder victims as well?' Then May gave a dramatic sigh, and flopped forward onto the table. 'I'm tired,' she said. 'Can't we sleep?'

But when we finally went to bed I lay there for ages, writing all this up with my flashlight balanced on my shoulder. Now I'm trying to stop thinking and fall asleep, while May kicks my face with her sharp little toes and mutters and growls in her sleep. But I can't. Something's bothering me. This case feels all wrong, somehow. We're missing big bits of it. We just don't have all the information yet, and that scares me. How can we help going wrong?

Wednesday 2nd April

We've just woken up. And I think someone's tried to murder the Chief Inspector.

Isn't this exciting?! – May

41

Wednesday 2nd April, continued

So I woke up to May saying, 'Hey! Did you hear that?'

'Hear what?' I asked, sitting up.

That's something we've been taught about being a spy, Diary – when you wake up, you have to start noticing things at once. You can't yawn and get up slowly. Every second you take means you might miss something crucial.

So we've been practising bouncing out of bed in the mornings. May's best at it, obviously, and Eric's worst. I'm in the middle, but I get better when I imagine someone coming at me with an ice bucket full of water. It's easy after that. I guess spying is a lot like acting in that way – you just have to believe in what you're doing, and you can do it.

Anyway, I sat up as fast as I could and looked around. There wasn't any noise I could hear particularly, apart from May.

'What's wrong?' I asked.

'Something's HAPPENED!' bellowed May. 'Quick, come and look outside!'

I really wanted to believe she was making it all up, except that by now I'd heard what she must have – voices, outside, urgent and low, and the General barking, then something falling in heavy patters. I went back into the dream I'd been having when May woke me up and I felt like there was something – something loud—

'A bomb went off in the mews!' said May. 'I heard the Chief Inspector arriving, so I stuck my head out to look at him and a BOMB went off when he opened the door of Number Two!'

'You liar!' I gasped. 'You're making it up!'

'I am not! I saw it! A small one! Oh, come and look!'

I'd scrambled to the window by then, and stared down at the mews.

There was a hole where Miss Fig's door had used to be.

'I told you!' cried May.

'Someone's actually killed the Chief Inspector,' I breathed. It was horrible. Daisy and Hazel *knew* him. We should have done something, I thought, we should have tried harder, we should have realized—

'He's not dead,' said May scornfully. 'He's down there. Look.'

I looked – and it was true.

There was the Chief Inspector, standing to one side of the street with his big coat hanging off him in strips. I thought he was wearing a red shirt, at first, and then I blinked and realized it wasn't red at all but bloody. Miss

Wimpress had come running out of her house in a floral nightie and dressing gown, and was wrapping a bandage over and over and over his hand.

The Chief Inspector had his teeth gritted, and scratches across his face, but otherwise he looked all right.

'He's not dead!' I cried. 'He's fine!'

'I mean, it'd have been more interesting if he was dead,' said May. 'Then we could avenge him.'

I yelled, 'MAY!' and she said, 'What? It's true, though!'

'Come on, we have to go downstairs!' I cried.

We both dragged pullovers over our pyjamas and grabbed our gas-mask cases, and then we were rushing for the door of the flat. Eric met us there, his hair fluffy and sheet marks still on his left cheek, and we ran out into the mews.

It was a soft morning, cloudy and cool, and I shivered a little. But I had my notebook and pencil. I tried to hold myself like Nancy Drew, to pretend I was carrying off my outfit, that I'd just got out of my roadster, instead of out of bed. General Charles de Gaulle was howling as Colette poked her head out of her front door, and I could see Mrs Goodchild looking out of her upstairs window. Behind us, Zosia stuck her head out of our flat's window, her hair done up in twists of fabric and her lips pale without her usual lipstick. She looked horrified.

'Come back up here!' she yelled at us, but we ignored her.

'Not you three again,' said the Chief Inspector with a groan, when he saw us.

He was grinning, but the grin was kind of a grimace too. I could see sweat on his forehead, and he was shaking, the way people shake when they've had a shock. His shirt was turning redder and redder, and so was the bandage that Miss Wimpress was wrapping around his arm.

'What happened?' piped May. 'Is it serious? Are you going to die? Did someone try to kill you?'

'I'm not going anywhere, unfortunately,' said the Chief Inspector, wincing as Miss Wimpress pinned the bandage in place.

'You'll be quite all right,' said Miss Wimpress, who for once wasn't fluttering or pausing when she spoke. She sounded crisp and sure. 'But you'll need to get it looked at properly as soon as possible. I've done what I can, but some of those lacerations are quite deep. What happened?'

'I came in early to get some work done,' said the Chief Inspector, wiping his brow with his free hand. 'Which, apparently, was a foolish idea. Someone'd put an explosive of some kind in the doorway – I triggered it as I stepped inside. If I hadn't paused when I heard something fall – I'm naturally suspicious, after eighteen years of this job – I'd be worse off than this.'

May was nudging me and Eric furiously. I felt kind of sick. It had *happened*. Someone really had tried to kill the Chief Inspector, just as we'd thought they might. But at the same time I hadn't *really* thought it. It had been just a silly fantasy – after all, the Chief Inspector's a policeman, and how desperate do you have to be to actually decide to kill a *policeman*?

'May I use your telephone?' the Chief Inspector asked Miss Wimpress. 'I need to contact my sergeant, and perhaps you'd be kind enough to arrange an ambulance. You three – don't go near that house. It's not safe. Do you hear me?'

'We *hear* you,' said May cheerfully.

'He's obviously not feeling well,' she said to the two of us, once Miss Wimpress had led him away.

Miss Charney was standing waiting for them at their door holding more bandages, her face cool and calm. I guess she's good at not getting upset in a crisis, just like Miss Wimpress. Or was she trying to hide how she was feeling?

'Otherwise,' continued May, 'he'd never have asked anything as vague as that. He's usually much more precise. Going *in* it isn't the same as going *near* it, is it? And we didn't promise anything; we just said we heard him. Come on, let's go and look at the crime scene before someone who hasn't just been half blown up thinks to stop us.'

'I really don't think we should go in there,' said Eric, staring dubiously at the crumbling gap where the door into Miss Fig's house used to be. The room behind it was blackened and smeared with smoke, and things were still falling gently. I thought the crack in the wall looked like it'd got bigger.

'Fine, then you keep watch,' said May. 'Nuala's not scared.'

'Keep watch on what? And yes, she is. She's sensible, not like you.' This, from Eric, was about as close as he got to being mean. I was impressed, Diary.

'I am a little scared,' I admitted. 'But only because I don't want to be squished if the house falls down! It's not bad to be careful, May.'

'Oh, come on! It won't fall, I promise!'

I took a deep breath. Nancy Drew wasn't going to cut it right now. I had to be Gráinne Ní Mháille going into battle. Gráinne would keep going, even if she was maybe about to die. You don't get to be a pirate queen by worrying about stuff like that.

I squared my shoulders and put steel in my spine, and then I very carefully stepped through the door after May.

42

I knew right then that this was a bad idea, Diary, and I shouldn't have done it. But sometimes it's hard to take something back once you've started doing it, even though nothing in your brain wants you to keep going. I don't know how that happens. I felt my hands clenching into fists. The house was *shifting*, like teeth grinding together.

May, obviously, didn't notice. She went scampering through the rubble like Pfote trotting down the stairs, making interested noises to herself.

'Oh! Look! Nuala! He said that it was an explosive, didn't he? Here's a bit of the casing, I think. It's all twisted up. Hold it for me.'

She shoved it into my hand, and I blinked at it. It was still warm, and I held it gingerly. It just looked like shredded metal to me, a piece of an incendiary maybe. It's true that the Nazis have started making them with explosives inside. They used to just burn, really bright and hot, and you could throw sand or your coat over them and put them out. But then the Nazis worked out that people were doing that, and it was becoming a game for kids, to put out as many incendiaries as they could and keep the metal for scrap, so they added explosives. If you see an incendiary now, you need to run in the opposite direction – so if this had once been a German incendiary, then someone seriously brave must have put it out so that they could reuse the exploding part as a bomb.

Anyway, I wrapped the metal piece in my handkerchief, and shoved it in my pocket. There was something else in the rubble: a tiny scrap of white-and-blue paper. I bent down and picked it up, because anything can be a clue, can't it? And I didn't remember seeing anything quite that colour in the house the day before.

'Maybe we should go now,' I said, which wasn't very Gráinne of me.

'Of course we can't go!' said May. 'We're just getting to the interesting stuff! Ooh, a footprint!'

'The whole street was in here yesterday,' I pointed out. 'And the only footprints after the explosion are going to be the Chief Inspector's and ours, May.'

'Blast, you're right. Huh. Oh, look at this! Nuala, look at *this*!'

May's voice was wobbling with excitement, and she was pretty much dancing. She grabbed my hand and dragged me forward, pointing down onto the smeary black floor of the living room. I pulled my flashlight out of my gas-mask case and switched it on, and something glittered up at us:

a silver whistle. It used to be shiny, I could tell, but it had been dented and smudged in the explosion, and the cord it was on had snapped.

I scooped it up, and May and I looked at each other. And yes, maybe we aren't always doing the best job of communicating on this case, but right then we didn't need to say anything.

Usually it's May who does the ridiculous, terrifying things. But I was still thinking a little like Gráinne, and, as I've said, you don't get to be a pirate queen unless you take some risks.

I was moving before I even really knew where I was going. Up the wobbly stairs, with May yelling 'Where are you GOING?' at me, onto the landing and then up again, all the way to the tiny box room where Miss Fig's luggage was stored. I felt the house shifting again, felt as though I was on a ship, swallowed down my terror and pulled open the lid of the trunk.

And there was the whistle we'd seen before – Miss Fig's whistle – exactly where we'd seen it last. So the whistle we'd found downstairs couldn't be hers.

I scooped Miss Fig's whistle up with one of her handkerchiefs and shoved it in my other pocket. Then I paused, about to close the lid again. Something had caught my eye: the romance novel that Miss Fig had been reading. This is a secret, Diary, but I'd already read all the ones

Anna had left in her room. I tucked it under my arm, slammed the trunk closed and went hurrying back downstairs.

The weight of the whistle in one pocket, and the metal in the other, made the case we were building suddenly very real. We'd only really been working with words before this, and words can mean anything. One line can be said in a hundred different ways, and each way has a different meaning. But *things* can't be twisted up in the same way.

There was only one other person – one *living* person – who had a whistle like that in the mews.

Mr Abiola.

Mr Abiola had taken over Miss Fig's warden's job when she'd disappeared. Mr Abiola was around incendiaries and explosives all the time. He'd been holding something back during the interview yesterday. And, although we'd seen him at the shelter last night, we didn't know what'd happened after the all-clear sounded and we'd gone back to the flat. He might have had time to set up the trap for the Chief Inspector.

If it was Mr Abiola, then . . . then we'd solved the case, right?

'Look at this!' I said triumphantly when I got back downstairs. 'The other whistle was still in Miss Fig's case! So it's not hers – that one *has* to be Mr Abiola's!'

May was staring at me with her mouth open. 'Fionnuala,' she said. 'This is the most I've ever liked you in my life.'

I blushed. But I did feel pretty impressive right then.

'May,' said Eric suddenly, outside. 'Nuala! May!'

'What's he fussing over?' grumbled May. 'We've still got to look—'

Something shifted above us. I don't think I heard it exactly. I just *felt* it. I grabbed May's hand in my free one and I dragged her forward.

We travelled a lot when I was a kid, me and Mam and Da and the Company. We went all over Europe, and all over America, and when we were in California I learned about earthquakes. If there's an earthquake, you don't ever stay in the middle of the room. You *run*, fast as you can, for the nearest doorway – not necessarily to get out, but because a doorway's the safest place in any house. The frame's strong, and it'll stay up to protect you, even if everything's falling down around you. And that's also true in the Blitz.

I leaped for the doorway, May yelling at me – she's so stubborn, Diary, she never knows when someone's trying to help her – and at the same time someone ran towards us, scooping us up and barrelling back out into the mews with us, as a big section of living-room ceiling collapsed behind us. I had a brief moment of wondering whether my running up and down the stairs had done that.

The person who'd saved us had a heavy scratchy coat on. They smelled of cologne, and their arms were very strong. They dropped us on the cobbles of the mews, and I looked up to see . . . Mr Abiola, wearing his tin hat with the white W on it and a heavy greatcoat over stripy pyjamas.

'You two girls are making my job harder than it needs to be,' he said in his deep voice. 'What were you *doing*?'

I gaped at him. May was making a thin wailing noise. All I could think was, *We were just rescued by a murderer.*

43

Zosia was very angry at us. I think she was really mostly angry that she had to do something about us, instead of ignoring us as usual, but May and I had both almost died, and that kind of thing makes adults get serious. She made us all walk with her to the Ministry. I glanced at her as we marched along through the grey morning London streets – I didn't have to look up much; she's not a lot taller than me – and I saw that her make-up wasn't quite as perfect as usual, her hairstyle hurried, her knuckles white and shaking on her handbag strap. She really was upset about us. That made me feel kind of guilty.

'You really don't need to worry about us,' said May hopefully.

'I think I do,' said Zosia.

She led us right up to the red front door of the Ministry and ushered us in. It felt like being pushed onstage.

Hazel was in the hallway again, putting out more food for Pfote. I heard May groaning behind me. Hazel was just about the worst person we could have seen right then.

'Oh no,' said Hazel, looking at Zosia, and down at May, and then at me and Eric and our sheepish, awkward expressions. 'What did they do now?'

'They tried to get themselves killed!' said Zosia. 'They went running into a condemned house and the ceiling almost fell on them. I'm sorry I wasn't watching them.'

'Oh, don't apologize,' said Hazel, glaring at the three of us. 'May's already in trouble after what she did yesterday. She's a bad influence.'

'I am *not*!' hissed May, who absolutely is. 'Yesterday had nothing to do with me! And today – Nuala did most of it!'

I'd been feeling kind of fond towards May, but that made me annoyed at her all over again.

Hazel turned on us. We all flinched a little. Eric bent down and picked up Pfote as a kind of shield.

'What are you up to?' asked Hazel. 'There's something going on, May, I know it!'

'You don't know anything!' said May, sticking out her chin. 'And you didn't even ask us why we were in the house. You're being a grown-up about it! We had to go in, because someone hurt the Chief Inspector. They tried to kill him, and we found—'

'What do you mean, someone hurt the Chief Inspector? Chief Inspector *Priestley*?'

'Yes! Someone tried to kill him, I just said, but he's all

right, I think. He's probably in the hospital by now. His arm was hurt, and his stomach, but he's alive, which is good.'

'GEORGE!' called Hazel. 'GEORGE! Quick!'

'What's up?' asked George, coming out of one of the ground-floor rooms with a swinging hop.

'It's the Inspector – I mean, Chief Inspector Priestley. Something's happened. I have to go to the hospital— Oh, why can't things stop happening to people?'

'At least telephone first to see how he is,' said George. 'Beans'll be on shift, won't she?'

'Oh – yes – but—'

'Hazel,' said George. 'Give me your hand for a moment. What would Daisy say, if she was here?'

'Not to worry so much,' said Hazel tearily, squeezing his hand.

'Exactly. And since Daisy's not here, I have to speak for her, don't I? Sit down. Telephone. Things have a habit of working out. I'll watch this lot for you while you go see the Inspector.'

'I told you, he's fine!' said May crossly. 'You're getting silly, Big Sister. He's a grown-up. He can look after himself.'

'Yes, May, but he's one of *my* grown-ups,' said Hazel. 'Now, you stay with George, and don't be an annoyance! I'll be back as soon as I can. George, those new messages that came in last night—'

'Don't worry, Ralph and I are on them,' said George soothingly. 'We came in early. Go.'

As we went back into the room with him, I heard Hazel saying, 'Operator? Rebecca Martineau at St John's Hospital, please—'

44

We couldn't get away to talk about *detective stuff* all that morning. We were decoding messages again, or trying to – the message I had just wasn't coming unstuck. I shoved and shoved at it, until Eric leaned over and said, 'Have you tried it in French?'

Then, very annoyingly, it clicked, and I could take my decoded message over to George.

He was sitting at the front of the room, picking away at a message of his own, next to Ralph, the person he'd telephoned before. Ralph was freckly, with a lot of soft brown hair and a beautiful spotted necktie that I was a little jealous of.

He and George spent a lot of time whispering to each other and not decoding anything, as far as I could see. May rolled her eyes at them and hissed '*Grown-ups!*' at me.

'I heard that, May,' said George. 'Keep working. Remember, these messages are *real*.'

Zosia knocked on the door just before twelve. 'New message just came through,' she said. She was looking tired, creases under her eyes – though I guess we all were. 'It's the one you've been waiting for.'

George levered himself half up from his desk and practically snatched it out of her hand.

'Same transmission signature?' he asked.

Zosia nodded. 'I *know* it's her. The same person, I mean. It just came in. The extra code's missing again. But I'm sure it's encoded with *her* poem code – Daisy's.'

She, George and Ralph all bent over it.

'Eric, May, Nuala, take your lunch upstairs,' said George, without looking at us. 'Be back in this room in half an hour, all right?'

It seemed just too perfect. No one was paying attention to us – and when we went out into the hall, Hazel's coat was still missing from its usual peg. Only Pfote was there, sitting hopefully beside her empty food bowl and grooming her long lovely fur.

'Come on!' hissed May. 'We have to have a meeting!'

She led us up to the bathroom again. Eric leaned against the sink, Pfote around his shoulders like a scarf, and May perched on the closed lid of the toilet.

'So,' said May. 'There's been a second murder.'

'No one died!' said Eric.

'*Details*,' said May. 'Someone tried to kill the Chief Inspector.'

'Seriously, why would anyone try to kill a policeman?' I asked. 'It's so stupid!'

'But it's all a little stupid, isn't it?' said Eric thoughtfully. 'Listen – I've been thinking about it, and so much of it doesn't make sense. The murderer hid Miss Fig's body in the rubble, like she died in the Incident – but why? Everyone knows she was still alive for weeks after the bomb hit. She was poisoned, which might have made it look like an accident – but then she was *stabbed*, so almost as soon as someone found her, they'd realize she'd been murdered. And there was a letter left at Post, apparently from her, but her luggage was left up in her house where anyone could find it. It's a really stupid crime.'

'Except that no one found her for months! And they wouldn't have, if we hadn't gone down to the basement. And remember what we said before, about the house? If there'd been another Incident nearby, then Miss Fig's house would have fallen down and nothing would ever have been found.'

'True!' said May. 'So, is the murderer stupid or clever?'

'Stupid,' said Eric.

'Clever,' I said. 'No, listen, we know they're careful, at least. Didn't the Chief Inspector say that Miss Fig had arsenic and chloral in her body? Poisoners are careful, aren't they? It takes planning. You have to be smart to get someone to take poison.'

'But isn't that stupid?' asked Eric. 'Why give her chloral as well as arsenic? And *then* stab her on top of that? Why would anyone do that?'

My mind was all mixed up. I felt like Eric and I were *both* right. It was really strange. This case was all the wrong shape, and not just because it was so long since the murder had happened, and we hadn't been on the spot to gather up the evidence like we had at Elysium Hall. All the bits didn't fit together – the three different murder methods, what we knew had happened afterwards, and now the explosion that had hurt the Chief Inspector. It was a weird, mixed-up series of crimes and that bothered me, Diary.

'Can't we talk about the good part?' asked May. 'There's been another attempted murder! Isn't it exciting!'

I thought about Hazel, still in the hospital. At least someone cared about the Chief Inspector. We still hadn't really met anyone who'd have wanted to go sit with Miss Fig – except, perhaps, Miss Wimpress. And Anna, wherever she was.

'It's stupid again,' said Eric. 'It can't be disguised as an accident, because everyone knows that there wasn't an explosive in the house the day before.'

'Eric, we need to tell you something. We think we know who— Well, look what May found,' I said, unwrapping my handkerchief carefully. The whistle glinted up at us next to that twisted piece of metal and the bit of paper.

'That's a warden's whistle!' said Eric.

'*Obviously* it is,' said May. 'And it isn't Miss Fig's, because Nuala went to look. That's why the house almost fell down on us. It's *Mr Abiola's.*'

I patted my other pocket, where Miss Fig's whistle still was. It was bulging – I'd had to stuff the book I'd taken from Miss Fig's luggage in there as well. I'd kind of forgotten it in all the chaos this morning.

'So, that means Mr Abiola has to have been into the house, after we left last night,' I said. 'And after the raid was over, because I remember he had the whistle when we were all down in the shelter. Which I guess makes him the person who planted the explosive. Maybe he found an unexploded incendiary when he was on a job and kept it to use on the Chief Inspector. I think this is the answer. He had motive; he's the perfect person to cover up Miss Fig's disappearance – we keep hearing about that note at Post, but if the murderer was Mr Abiola, he might have just *told* everyone there was a letter – and he's strong enough to have stabbed her and then carried her body down to the basement.'

'Yes!' May said excitedly. 'We've solved it!'

Except ... 'We haven't solved anything,' said Eric, shaking his head. 'Look.' He leaned over, Pfote mewing at him, and pointed at Mr Abiola's whistle.

'Yes, it's a whistle,' said May. 'So?'

'You're not looking properly!' said Eric. '*Look!*'

'Oh!' I said, because for once I'd got it before May had. I felt really pleased with myself – and with Eric. 'The cord's been cut!'

Eric nodded. 'It's not frayed. It's been cut cleanly, with a knife. That means that it didn't fall off his neck while he was setting the trap. Someone cut it off him and dropped it there, so that when the police saw it they'd think it was him.'

'But – but – no!' wailed May. 'He's such a good suspect! Could it have been a double bluff? What if he's trying to make himself seem too obvious?'

'He'd never do that,' said Eric firmly. 'Not ever. He doesn't trust the police at all. He's scared of them. I know. So if his whistle was there, that means someone else put it there.'

'So you think . . . someone framed him!' yelped May.

45

'Right,' said Eric, nodding. 'I do. And that means we need to rule him out.'

Somehow we'd just crossed out another suspect. I felt so confused. Who'd done it, if it wasn't Mr Abiola?

'We just need to work out who was around Mr Abiola last night, to take his whistle – and who might have been able to find the explosive that they used in the trap,' said May.

'It has to have happened after the all-clear,' said Eric.

I nodded. 'And the trap has to have been set after the all-clear too, once everyone was back in their houses.'

'But the General didn't bark after the end of the raid!' said May. 'He didn't, did he? I didn't hear it, and I always wake up when he barks. We keep coming up against that—OH!'

Her eyes had gone perfectly round, and so had her mouth. May was practically vibrating with excitement, but for once she wasn't talking.

'What?' I asked at last.

'The ATTICS,' boomed May.

'SHH!' Eric and I both said at once.

'The attics! Don't you see! That's how – that's how *everything* works. Last night – and the sixth, when Miss Fig died. The General barks when someone walks in front of his door. So to get past him without setting him off, you have to move down the street another way. *You have to go up into the attics.* So you see, the trap last night had to have been set by someone who went up into an attic and then down into Miss Fig's house, after the all-clear.'

'Oh!' I said. I was so excited. I saw it, just like she was saying. 'So the fact that Miss Fig's front door doesn't close properly is a red herring! That means it can't have been Mrs Mortensen. She doesn't always need to use her bath chair – we've seen that – but she's not able for climbing all the way up into an attic and then back down again. And she's too wide to fit into that tiny crawl space.'

'It might be Colette, though,' said May.

'No, it can't be,' said Eric. 'Not if the murderer had to come through the attics. Remember what Colette said, that Olivier sleeps with her, and Margot is in the box room? That's the way up into the attics! Colette couldn't climb up and back again without Margot waking up – and not just that, if Olivier woke while she was gone, he'd cry and give her away. We have to rule her out too.'

'Miss Wimpress and Miss Charney could both have done it,' said May, narrowing her eyes. 'And the Goodchilds – yes to him, he's quite skinny, but she's fatter. I don't know if she could.'

'What about Zosia?' asked Eric suddenly.

'But she's on the wrong side of the mews!' I said.

'Yes, but she could have got up into the attics by sneaking into Number Six, while Mr Harris was away, like we did,' Eric pointed out. Pfote mewed, and he said, 'You too, Pfote.'

Sometimes I really wonder whether Eric can talk to animals. I mean, I know that's not real. But I *wonder*.

'But she's quite curvy,' said May.

'She is, but she's little,' I said. 'So she still might be able to fit, just about. At least Anna couldn't have done this one, since she's still on her mission. So – lookit, we only have four suspects left. We're really getting somewhere!'

'But are we sure that the second crime was done by the same person who did the first?' asked Eric. 'It's hard to set up explosives properly. We know after our lessons. It's not something just anyone can do.'

'Well, they must have done it, because it happened,' said May. 'I don't see the problem. We solve the second crime and we'll solve the first.'

Eric frowned, but I was excited. It felt like we were really getting somewhere. I thought May was probably right – we just had to work out who'd done the second crime, and we'd be able to get to who'd killed Miss Fig.

SUSPECT LIST
- Mr Abiola. ~~Has taken Miss Fig's position as shelter warden after her death. Does not seem to have liked her. Needed money? Is the only~~

261

person who has seen the note Miss Fig apparently left at Post — is it even real? On the night of the 6th he has no alibi — he says he came home and went to bed. Investigate! RULED OUT. Finding his whistle with the string deliberately cut proves to us that he's being framed by someone else!

- Miss Charney. Does not seem to have liked Miss Fig. Overheard talking suspiciously to Miss Wimpress by Nuala and Eric in the attic after Miss Fig's body was found. Motive: she seems to be jealous of Miss Fig, who used to live with Miss Wimpress. Alibi: she was apparently with Miss Wimpress that night — they went to bed early. Is this a lie or not? Opportunity for second crime: she was at the shelter just before the trap was set. She is small enough to get through the attic crawl space.

- Miss Wimpress. Seems very upset by Miss Fig's death. Is this a ruse? Overheard talking suspiciously to Miss Charney by Nuala and Eric in the attic after Miss Fig's body was found. Who did she think was in the attic, when she heard Eric and Nuala? Miss Wimpress used to live with Miss Fig. She says they argued, and she left her house for Miss Charney's in summer 1940. What if her motive is revenge and she's only pretending to be sad? Alibi: she says she was with Miss Charney that night — she was very tired, and they both went to bed early. Is this a lie or not? Opportunity for second crime: she was at the shelter just before the trap was set. She is small enough to get through the attic crawl space.

- Colette Mortensen. Does not seem to have liked Miss Fig. Miss Fig hated the General, and tried to tell Colette to have him put down. And we think that Colette may be buying black-market dog food for him — what if Miss Fig found out about it? She also uses real sugar and lemons in her baking — from Cecil? Movements on the evening of Friday 6th December: brought Mrs Mortensen back from her cancelled committee meeting at 4 p.m. Spent evening at home with her (alibi). Mrs Goodchild brought cocoa round at 8 p.m. Heard Miss Fig saying she was ill at same time. Went to bed early but woke just before midnight because the General barked and heard someone, possibly a man, talking 'backwards'. What was this? RULED OUT! Margot's bedroom is the way into the attic of the Mortensens' house — Colette could not have gone up and come back again without waking her. She has to be ruled out.

— Mrs Mortensen. Does not seem to have liked Miss Fig. We think she may have been buying food on the black market — what if Miss Fig discovered that? Investigate. Movements on the evening of Friday 6th December: came back from her cancelled committee meeting at 4 p.m. Spent evening at home with Colette and the children (alibi). Mrs Goodchild brought cocoa round at about 8 p.m. RULED OUT. She could not have got all the way up into the attic and down again to plant the explosive, especially not without waking Margot, and she couldn't have gone out of her front door without the General barking.

— Cecil Goodchild. Behaving suspiciously. Is he looking for Anna to throw off the scent about Miss Fig? What was in the bag? Why was he watching us? We suspect he has been smuggling black-market food into the mews! Is this enough motive for murder? RULED OUT! He is smuggling black-market food into the mews, but he did not kill Miss Fig — he left the mews just after 4 p.m. to go to his friend's house in

Bedford Square, and then he was stuck there all night. He mentioned again that Anna was already gone that afternoon — this seems strange! Investigate.

- Zosia Stosic. Does not seem to have liked Miss Fig. She is behaving quite suspiciously. She said that Miss Fig was nosy, and always prying into their flat. Could Miss Fig have found out something about the Ministry? Zosia told the Chief Inspector that she was sick with glandular fever that week — if so, could she have committed the murder? Opportunity for second crime: she was at the shelter just before the trap was set. She is probably small enough to get through the attic crawl space.

- Mrs Goodchild. ~~Motive unclear. She uses real eggs in her baking — from Cecil? Seems not to have liked Miss Fig much, but is this enough? Alibi: stayed at home with her husband on the evening of the 6th. Friday night dinner, cocoa and bed!~~ RULED OUT! She could not fit into the crawl space in the attic, so could not have committed the first crime or the second.

- Mr Goodchild. Motive unclear. Seems not to have liked Miss Fig much — called her a 'philistine' — but is this enough? Alibi: stayed at home with his wife on the evening of the 6th. Friday night dinner, cocoa and bed! Opportunity for second crime: he was at the shelter the night before the trap was set. He might have taken Mr Abiola's whistle then. He is also small enough to fit through the attic crawl space.

- Anna Goodchild. Motive unclear, especially as Zosia told us that Anna was nice to Miss Fig. Miss Fig's body had Anna's necklace on it — why? We know that Anna went on her Ministry mission the next day, Saturday 7th December, and missed making Shabbos with her family on the evening of the 6th. Where was she that evening? Is she a suspect or not? Opportunity for second crime: she is not here, so she could not have committed it — which also seems to probably rule her out from the first crime!

PART SIX

OUR SUSPICIONS HIT
CLOSE TO HOME

46

From the diary of Fionnuala O'Malley

Wednesday 2nd April, continued

The front door of the Ministry opened downstairs, then closed again, and we heard Hazel's voice calling, 'George?'

I pushed open the bathroom door so that we could listen.

'How is he?' asked George.

'He'll be all right,' said Hazel, and we all three heard her sniff and gulp, and George say, 'But he's going to be all right, you silly idiot!'

'Doesn't it feel too much, though? It's all too much, especially now Alex's leave is over and he's gone back to his ship. With Daisy gone—'

'We'll get her back. You know Daisy. Heroines never die.'

'But does the world know that she's the heroine?'

'If it doesn't, it hasn't been listening to Daisy,' said George.

'Where are the littles?' asked Hazel, and I heard May hiss next to me.

'On their lunch upstairs. You know, I think they're up to something?'

'They are, aren't they? The business at the mews. May was the one who told me about the Inspector. I don't have *time* to worry about them too! What if they'd been hurt?'

'I shouldn't think about it. Give them space. Wouldn't we all have liked that, when we were their age?'

'I know. But – May – it's awfully hard, when it's my sister. She's not even eleven. She's a *baby*.' May huffed, and I nudged her to be quiet.

'And you're nineteen,' said George, 'and you're helping run a spy organization. And I'm twenty, and I'm down to one working leg. War makes everyone ancient.'

Hazel sighed. 'Any news?'

'New message in – Ralph cracked it using Daisy's poem code key. It's the same as the last. Request for extraction, with a location and a time and date. But here's the thing – it's missing her safety phrase. And it doesn't *feel* like her, if you know what I mean.'

'I know,' said Hazel unhappily. 'It isn't *Daisy*, is it? So what do we do? What does it mean?'

'Well, it's one of three things. Either she's been captured, and she's told her captor her code—'

'—which she wouldn't do. She couldn't! She'd rather—'

'—die. I know. I've thought of that. But we can't rule it out, that someone from the other side might have got that code. *Or . . .* Daisy might have forgotten her own safety phrase and changed the way she sends messages. More likely, but still not very.'

'She might forget the poem code, but she wouldn't stop sounding like herself.'

'Indeed. Or, the third possibility. Someone else is using Daisy's code to get our attention. And that's interesting, isn't it? As Daisy would say.' Beside me, Eric made a thoughtful muttering noise.

'You think?' asked Hazel.

'It could be.'

'But *why*?'

'That I don't know yet. Are you ready to go?'

'I can be, if we decide it's real. *If.*'

'I wish I could go,' said George angrily.

There was a pause, and then someone passed the bathroom.

'New message through,' said Zosia's voice, halfway down the stairs. 'I think it's an important one. Do you need me on decoding?'

'Thanks, Zosh,' said George. 'If you wouldn't mind? The kids can go on transcription. We've got Ralph here too – I seconded him from his department now that we might be losing Hazel.'

'Of course,' said Zosia. 'I'll bring the decryption when it's ready.'

She sounded perfectly cheerful, on the surface. But there'd been a flicker of something in her voice that caught me. She wasn't cheerful at all. She was desperate with nerves, and only just holding it in. She was acting, and not acting well enough to fool me. George and Hazel were distracted, and they hadn't noticed. But I had, and I wanted to know *why*.

'Will you cover for me?' I whispered to Eric and May. 'I want to talk to Zosia.'

'No fear!' said May at once. 'Are you trying to detect without us? We all go.'

'Yes, but—' I stopped. I'd thought that I was being helpful, and sneaky. But actually May was right. I *was* trying to detect without them. It still comes easiest to me, to work on my own. I get scared, relying on other people, because what if they're not always there? What if I get used to them, and then they go away? I used to try to make friends with kids I met in different tour spots, until I realized there was no point, because I wouldn't be around long enough to matter. And I knew that whatever happened, the Company and Da would always be there – until Da died, and Mam took me away from the Company forever. I haven't heard anything from the Company people since then. I guess they just thought of me as someone else who wasn't around long enough to matter.

Anyway, sometimes it's hard for me to believe that May, Eric and I are a team. It's easier to just be Nuala, alone. But—

'You aren't going anywhere without us,' said May. 'What if you find something important and we're not there? Or something dangerous? I'm not letting you take all the glory.'

'Grand, so – well, it's up to you to work out how we all get past Hazel,' I said, trying not to sound too pleased.

'Easy,' said Eric. 'You heard George – they need us on transcription. Let's eat our lunch, and then afterwards we've got the perfect excuse to work next to Zosia. Miss Lessing's helping Hazel prepare for the mission, if they decide to send her, so she won't be there. Zosia's on her own. Why do you want to see her?'

I realized I hadn't explained to them.

'Obviously, because she's a suspect!' said May.

'Yes,' I agreed. 'But also because she was acting weird, just now. I heard it. She's *really* worried about something.'

'Her friend's missing,' said May, and I felt her shrug.

'Oh no,' I said. 'She's not worried about that. This is new.'

And then I realized I'd said something true, Diary.

See – Anna and Zosia were best friends, just like Hazel and Daisy. So why wasn't Zosia missing Anna, like Hazel was missing Daisy? I know that everyone shows the same feelings differently. It's not possible to suspect someone just because they're not doing the right thing – they're not crying, I mean, or they're crying too much, or they're laughing when everyone else is looking sad.

But . . . Hazel moves like she's pushing something heavy but trying to pretend she isn't. She moves like I saw George move once, when he forgot he doesn't have two feet for just a second. Zosia doesn't. She hasn't been carrying that weight about Anna. Why?

We have to go and talk to Zosia. I need to find out more.

47

When we knocked and went into the room, Miss Lessing's chair was empty, and Zosia had her headset on, working on a message with a scowl on her face. Zosia looked up and must have caught me staring at her, because she scowled harder. I jumped, and I could feel myself blush. I wish I didn't blush so easily.

'There you are,' said Zosia. 'Come on in, then.'

'We've been sent to help you,' said May, bouncing up and down on her toes.

'We'll file those papers, if you need us to. We'll do whatever you want,' said Eric soothingly.

'We really can help,' I added.

Eric nudged me, and I shut up. I knew I was coming on too strong, but I was just so wrapped up in wondering what was wrong with Zosia.

'All right,' said Zosia. 'May, Nuala. Those papers, there, from March, put them in those boxes. Divide them up by agent, the way the other sets have been. Eric, you're on transcription. Another message is coming in.'

Eric nodded and put the big headset over his curls, and

May and I got to work. May hummed a little in the back of her throat, and I could hear the dots and dashes drifting over the airwaves, but otherwise the room was silent.

'Done,' said Eric calmly. He really is reassuring; he's naturally got that air about him that May will never have, and that I have to act. 'Here.'

'Good work,' said Zosia, a little reluctantly. 'May, run it down to Hazel, please.'

'Absolutely!' chirped May, and scampered away as fast as she could, hair flying, her shoes hammering down the stairs.

Zosia puffed out a breath and leaned backwards in her chair. 'Ah!' she said. 'It never stops.'

'Are you all right?' asked Eric – which would have sounded so phoney if May had said it, and would have *been* phoney if I'd said it. But with Eric it was real.

'Not in the slightest,' said Zosia. 'But what can I do? We're always short-staffed here – and when we do get new agents, they're *you three*. And what can we do with three children?'

I was glad that May couldn't hear that. It made me prickle, Diary. Sure, what's wrong with being children? We can do plenty; I know it from Elysium Hall.

'We're good agents!' I said.

'You're eleven,' said Zosia. I felt myself blushing again. There's no need to rub it in. 'Obviously you're clever. But we need help. *Real* help. Oh, it's all – it's all a mess!'

276

She threw her pencil down on the desk. 'It's all a mess,' she repeated. 'And everything I do just makes it worse.'

Eric and I looked at each other. I wasn't sure she was talking about us any more.

'I'm sure it'll be all right,' said Eric gently. 'Why don't you have some chocolate?' He gestured at the bar of blue-and-white ration chocolate on the desk next to Zosia.

'Yes, that's what you think when you're a child,' said Zosia, pushing the chocolate away. The fact is that ration chocolate's not nice at all, Diary, and no one really wants to eat it. Zosia sighed and went on. 'Then you grow up and realize that it won't be all right at all. And you three, you might think if you all stick together you can get through anything. But having friends – that just makes things go more wrong, because when someone hurts one of you, it feels as though they've hurt all of you.'

'You're friends with Anna,' said Eric. It wasn't a question.

'Of course I am,' said Zosia, smiling. 'Best friends. We went through the Ministry training together, and when we moved in together we'd test each other on our languages and skills and so on every evening. Sometimes we did each other's assignments, and no one noticed. I know her like I know myself. We always had each other to rely on – until we didn't. And isn't that the problem? Now she's gone, and – and I don't know what to do. I keep thinking I'm helping, but I make things *worse*.'

'That's always what happens to me,' said May. She'd come back from downstairs and was standing in the doorway, scratching her left leg with her right shoe. 'I try to help and then everything explodes. But isn't Anna coming home soon?'

Zosia flinched, and her lips squeezed together. I saw her fingers clutch her pencil, so it made a track across the paper pad on her desk. 'We're talking too much,' she said. 'There's another message coming in. Eric, back to your station. May and Nuala, keep filing, and stay quiet.'

And I thought then, Diary, that I might have been right, what I'd thought before. Zosia had been able to speak about Anna at first. She'd smiled, thinking about her – Anna wasn't a memory that hurt to poke at. She'd only flinched and pulled away when May asked if Anna was coming home. What if Zosia wasn't worried about where Anna was – what if she was just worried at the thought of her *coming home*?

But if that was true – then that meant Zosia *knew* where Anna was now. To her, Anna wasn't missing. Could that be right? And what did it mean? It felt huge.

'I'm going to the loo,' said Zosia. 'Nuala, there's another message coming in. Take it down.'

I pushed the headset over my ears – it's heavy enough to make my head ache – and Zosia got up and walked out of the room. She pulled the door shut behind her so hard that it bounced back a little on its hinges.

'Quick!' gasped May when she was gone. 'Tell me what happened!'

'I think Zosia's lying,' said Eric, pulling one of his headset's ear pieces away from his curls.

48

'I think she is too,' I said. 'She knows where Anna is.'

'Yes!' said Eric. 'I agree! But why do *you* think so?'

'I can't explain. But I think ... the way she's been reacting. She's not worried about the right things.'

'How do you two know so much?' yelled May. 'This isn't fair! Tell me!'

'We *are* telling you!' I said. 'Shh!'

'She's upset, the way my sister Lottie is when she's done something bad,' said Eric. 'She always gets really angry, to hide how afraid she is. And I think I might know what it is. I *think* that Anna and Zosia switched places.'

'What?' said May and I at once.

'Didn't you hear her?' asked Eric, like it was obvious. 'They used to do each other's assignments. They studied together. Zosia said she knew Anna like she knew herself.'

'Yes, but that doesn't mean she swapped places with her!' I said.

'Not to you,' said Eric. 'But you're not a twin. I am. It's what me and Lottie used to do all the time – she'd do my homework, and I'd do hers in turn. And sometimes I'd be her, if there was a test she didn't want to take, or she'd be me, if I had to run a race and I didn't want to. We don't even look that similar, but people see what they want to see.'

'So . . . what?' I said. 'You think – what?'

'I think Zosia wasn't ill with glandular fever at all,' said Eric calmly. 'I think she went to France on the seventh of December instead of Anna. And now she's terrified that she's going to be found out.'

'That doesn't even make sense!' said May. 'How did she get back from France? Where's Anna? Where *was* Anna, on the sixth?'

'Obviously Anna went somewhere else, somewhere secret, that only she and Zosia knew about,' said Eric, shrugging. 'And I don't know how Zosia got back. We have to work that out. But I do know that they switched places. It makes sense. Zosia went on the mission in December, not Anna, and pretended to have glandular fever so that no one from the Ministry would wonder why she wasn't showing up for work. Miss Lessing told us that no one on the mission will know who the spy is – everyone has to identify themselves with code words. If Zosia turned up wearing the right kind of clothes, with gear from the supply cupboard, and with Anna's code words, the people meeting her wouldn't know that she was the wrong spy.'

'It doesn't make any sense!' said May. 'It's stupid! You must have got something mixed up. I don't believe it.'

It *was* stupid. My brain kind of caught that word, *stupid*, and tossed it around the way it does sometimes. Something else had been *stupid* today. What was it? Then I remembered – the murder.

And *that* bounced around in my head, and then my eye fell on the bar of chocolate that Zosia hadn't wanted to eat, its blue-and-white wrapper in a pool of light from a lamp—

Then I got it. I just *had* it.

I stuck my hand in my pocket and pulled out the bit of metal May'd found in Miss Fig's living room, before the roof caved in on us. The metal – and the little bit of blue-and-white paper.

'Eric! May!' I gasped. 'Look!'

'Yes, I found that,' agreed May. 'So?'

'So! Sure, it's *part of a chocolate wrapper*! It's one of the Cook's explosive chocolate bars! It's from the Ministry! Just like the one you took, May, to blow up the downstairs cupboard. The explosive wasn't an incendiary. It came from *here*!'

'No, it didn't!' squawked May.

'But it did!' said Eric. 'I really think you're right, Nuala!'

I knew I was. And because I was – there were just two other people who lived in Hogarth Mews *and* worked at the Ministry, and only one of them who had been there during and after the air raid last night. The same person who we thought had been lying to the Ministry for months.

The same person who had been afraid that the Chief Inspector might discover too much about her and Anna. I remembered something that Zosia had said yesterday – that the Chief Inspector had pulled Anna's file. We'd known that was true, but Zosia shouldn't have done. The Chief Inspector and Fodor had only talked about that after she'd left. That meant she must have been listening in outside the house's front door – and that meant that she definitely had something to hide. It all started to fit together in my head.

'It was Zosia!' I whispered. 'She planted the explosive. We're right about everything. It was *her*. And she *does* know where Anna is.'

And the door squeaked a little on its hinges.

49

I hoped I'd imagined that, Diary. I hoped it was just the building settling. But I definitely heard that squeak. I turned to the door, and I saw a shadow passing at the corner of it, someone moving in front of the light in the hall outside.

My heart jumped in my chest. I put a finger up to my lips and waved frantically at May and Eric.

'Oh, *what*?' said May crossly. 'You're always so dramatic. No one's—'

Eric reached out and clapped a hand across her mouth. I saw May's eyes bulge – it was pretty surprising, from Eric – but I guess she decided that if Eric thought it was important, then she should listen to him.

It's so annoying that she won't just listen to me like that.

I opened my notebook to a new page and wrote: SOMEONE OUTSIDE. QUIET.

'There's a new message coming in,' said Eric loudly. 'Nuala, can you help?'

I was feeling really wobbly with panic. Who was outside? It wasn't hard to guess that. Ralph, George, Miss Lessing and Hazel were downstairs, and we hadn't heard anyone come up. The stairs at the Ministry creak horribly. So it must have been Zosia. What had she heard? Had I been whispering quietly enough when I'd said that last thing?

But Eric was right – we had to pretend to be normal. Zosia couldn't know that we knew she'd been listening. So I pulled on my headset again and tuned in my ears to the rush of static and the clicks and beeps floating through it. Dot dash dash, dot dot dot, dot dot dash dot –

Zosia opened the door and came back into the room. She was smoothing down her blouse and patting her hair, exactly like she'd just left the bathroom, but I was suspicious. She was playing it just a tiny bit too strong – dabbing at her lipstick, even though I could tell she hadn't reapplied it – and she wasn't looking any of us right in the eyes.

'How have you three been getting on?' she asked.

May made a grunting noise and scrabbled through her pile of papers. She's really no good with this kind of stuff, May.

'New message coming through,' I said, making myself look up at her and smile carelessly. 'Hold on.'

I kept on calmly writing – T, S, V, M, I, K – until the transmission was done, and then I got up, tore off the paper and handed it to Zosia. 'I'll take it downstairs, if you like,' I said, keeping my hands relaxed and my shoulders low.

'Thank you, Nuala,' said Zosia, matching my smile. 'Very helpful. Go on.'

I knew she was acting by then. And I had a really bad feeling that she knew I was too.

The rest of this afternoon has been scary, Diary, I can't lie. Everything was so normal – we were really careful to keep it normal – but inside I was practically screaming. Zosia had tried to blow up the Chief Inspector! And if the person who'd set the explosive had been the same person who'd killed Miss Fig, then we had a murderer in the Ministry too!

But why had she done it? It all must have something to do with Anna. If Zosia and Anna had switched places in December, then maybe Zosia'd killed Miss Fig, and tried to kill the Chief Inspector, to stop them working out where Anna had gone. But where *had* she gone? Where was she now? What could be so bad that Zosia was willing to kill more than one person to try to hide it?

My thoughts were going wild, and I couldn't even talk to Eric or May to calm myself down. Now that Zosia was back in the room, I could feel her watching everything we did.

The clock crawled forward, and we filed and took down messages and were helpful, and it was about the worst afternoon of my life. At one point I sat down to sift through a box of papers that May was making a hames of, and caught her eye as I did it. I was expecting her to make a mean face at me, but instead she leaned forward and bumped her shoulder against mine. It could have just been one of May's clumsy moments, but a second later we reached out for the same piece of paper, and she pinched the web between my finger and thumb. I was weirdly comforted. I suddenly knew that May and Eric were both feeling as scared as I was, and that meant that we *were* together, even though we couldn't talk.

Finally the time ticked forward to 5:30 p.m., the end of the day, and Hazel called up the stairs, 'May, Eric, Nuala, finish what you're doing! Time to go.'

We all three leaped up, and Zosia looked at us and said, 'You're in a hurry.'

'We're just very hungry,' said Eric.

'We want our tea,' agreed May. 'Mrs Goodchild said we could go round to theirs for some cake.'

This was a lie, and I was pretty sure Zosia knew that. But she just smiled and shrugged.

Why wasn't she doing anything to stop us, I wondered? Why was she just letting us leave? Or . . . was she waiting until we were out of the Ministry, and away from Hazel and George's protection, before she shut us up for good?

That was terrifying.

'Go on, then,' said Zosia. 'I'll see you back at the mews.'

The last thing I saw as we left the room was her smiling at us. Her lipstick looked so bright, and I couldn't believe I'd ever thought it was pretty.

'Goodbye, Big Sister,' called May, as we came down the stairs.

'All right, May,' said Hazel, popping her head out of an office door. 'Be *good*, will you? Whatever you're doing, do it quietly.'

'We're not DOING ANYTHING!' shouted May, as we all grabbed hold of each other anxiously and looked upwards. 'We're NORMAL.'

'That's the biggest lie you've ever told me,' said Hazel. 'You've never been normal in your life. Eric, Nuala, don't listen to her if she tells you to do something stupid, all right? And enjoy your tea.'

I grabbed May's hand, Eric picked up Pfote, and we practically ran out of the Ministry door into the brisk London afternoon.

50

'Yes, but what are we going to *do*?' asked Eric.

We'd gone to Mrs Goodchild's – we stuck to our lie – and she'd given us a plate of buns to eat. Now that we knew Cecil was giving her extra eggs and butter and things, I couldn't think how I'd ever thought that her baking could possibly be made with rations. The buns were sweet and rich, the icing crunchy against my teeth. I did wonder, though – how could she not know what Cecil was doing? She could read people; she'd given the buns to Eric, because she'd worked out that May wouldn't remember to share. And when Mr Goodchild had wandered in, she'd said something about Michelangelo that had made him laugh. So she was lots of different kinds of clever, and I was sure she'd be able to tell what Cecil was up to. Maybe it was one of those family things – you know, where everyone knows something, but everyone pretends they don't by just not talking about it. My family used to be a lot like that.

Pfote, coiled around Eric's shoulders, mewed, and he fed her a piece of bun.

We'd climbed up onto the roof of the flats with the last of the buns, and we were staring down at the mews below us while we ate. The air was cool and only a little dusty, the sun going down.

'We have to get Zosia to confess, obviously,' said May. 'We confront her with our evidence and make her tell us what she did.'

'That's a terrible idea,' I said. 'She might hurt us! She's a spy – she's been trained to fight!'

'Well, you come up with a better one!'

'We have to get proof,' I said. 'I know that much.'

'We *have* proof! We've got the metal and paper, and the two whistles, and – and – we know what she did!'

'It's all good evidence, but we're missing half the case. We don't know *why* Zosia did it. And we don't know for sure whether she killed Miss Fig too.'

'Yes, we do!' cried May. 'If she planted the bomb to try to kill the Chief Inspector, then she must have killed Miss Fig. She wanted to stop the Chief Inspector from investigating. Why else would she do it? It's all easy.'

'Probably,' said Eric. 'But we don't know for *sure*. We still don't have a motive for her to kill Miss Fig.'

'But if she swapped with Anna, and Miss Fig found out, that's good motive! It does all make sense! It does!' May was sticking out her jaw crossly.

'We need proof,' said Eric. 'And we don't have it.'

'ARGH!' said May, and she threw herself down against the ledge and crossed her arms.

I folded my arms against my stomach anxiously – I didn't know what to do – and I felt a heavy lump in one of my pockets. Miss Fig's romance novel. I pulled it out and stared at it.

'What's that?' asked Eric curiously.

'It was in Miss Fig's luggage,' I said, blushing. 'I took it this morning – I don't know why.'

May giggled. 'Funny,' she said. 'Let me look.'

She grabbed it off me and started flicking through it. Then she stopped.

'What?' I asked. 'You know you shouldn't be looking at that; you're not even eleven.'

'Don't tell me how old I am! I already know! And you're being stupid – look, LOOK!'

She brandished the book at me and Eric. It was open somewhere in the middle of a chapter, full of close-printed text.

'*LOOK!*' bellowed May, pointing.

I gasped. Someone had taken a pen and underlined words and letters. I saw BO AT and TWELFTH and OC T O P US and K LEE. I flicked through more pages, and saw more and more underlined letters.

'It's a CODE!' yelped May. 'And look who the book belongs to! Look!'

She flicked back to the flyleaf and showed us the name written there. *Anna Goodchild.*

We all stared at each other. What did it mean? Anna was exchanging coded messages that looked a lot like the messages we'd been decoding at the Ministry. *Boat* and *twelfth* made sense – but *octopus*? And what was *k lee*? A person? A thing?

'I know someone called Lee,' said May. 'But that's not important. What's important is that these messages were for – or from – Anna. And Miss Fig found them. Isn't this motive? Don't we have it at last? Miss Fig knew about . . . whatever this secret is. Maybe she tried to blackmail them, so Zosia – ooh, or Zosia *and Anna* killed her. And now Zosia's trying to get rid of the Chief Inspector so it doesn't all come out!'

Pfote mewed supportively.

I thought May might be right. We'd been wondering why Miss Fig's body was wearing Anna's necklace, hadn't we? What if this explained it? Anna had given it to her to try to pay her off. But maybe it hadn't worked. Miss Fig still had the book in her house. Maybe she'd still been threatening Anna. And maybe that was why . . . why Miss Fig had died.

'I think we should just tell everyone what we know,' said May. 'We've got enough here!'

'I still think we need to prove it,' said Eric. 'We need to be able to show exactly what happened.'

I nodded. I thought May was probably right, but I knew Eric was speaking the truth. We had to have everything at our fingertips, otherwise our case would fall apart when we tried to talk to the adults about it. Plus, hadn't we learned at Elysium Hall that, until we had all the facts, something could surprise us? We'd got confused about who'd done that crime, and we couldn't afford to get it wrong again. We had to prove that we were better at detecting than we'd been last year.

'I think we should do a re-enactment,' I said. 'To work out how everything happened.'

It was Eric's turn to nod. 'Yes,' he said. 'But first we need to write down what we think, so we know what we're proving. There are so many facts that it's getting confusing.'

'I'm not confused!' grumbled May. But then she sighed and said, 'All right. Go on, Nuala.'

I turned to a fresh page of my notebook.

The attempted murder. 2nd April 1941

Intended victim: Chief Inspector Priestley

Weapon: Explosive chocolate bar from the Cook, planted in Miss Fig's doorway.

Facts: Trap must have been set after the all-clear at 10:30 p.m. last night, after everyone came back to the mews (Mr Abiola had his whistle during the raid), and before the Chief Inspector came to work this morning at

7 a.m. The person who set the trap must have gone through the attic space and down through Miss Fig's house because the General did not bark.

The murder, 6th December 1940

Victim: Paula Figueroa

Facts: Poisoned with arsenic and chloral, and then stabbed in her bed before being carried to the basement after her death.

She was last seen at around 8 p.m. by Colette Mortensen and Mrs Goodchild, when Mrs Goodchild brought her cocoa and she drank it. Colette says Miss Fig complained of not feeling well at the time — she must have already been poisoned. But how?

The person who stabbed her must have come into her house through the attics, since the General only barked once, just before midnight, when Colette heard someone speaking outside in the mews.

'It all makes sense. Zosia went up through the attic both times,' said May at once. 'Obviously. And she dragged Miss Fig out into the basement when she was done.'

'But then who was the man Colette heard in the mews?' asked Eric. 'Could it actually have been Zosia, and Colette just got it wrong? Zosia does have quite a low voice.'

'I don't think it's important,' said May crossly.

'I think it's *very* important,' said Eric, folding his arms. I was impressed. Eric's not usually this firm. He really must think he had a point.

'I think we need to do the re-enactment,' I said again, to calm them down. (Then I thought, *It's me calming them down again!* And that felt good.)

'Fine,' said May.

'All right,' said Eric.

'Grand,' I said. 'Now we just need to think of a cover story.'

51

But, actually, we didn't need to think up a cover story at all. The sun had gone down, and right then the siren began to howl. Down below us the commotion began, people grabbing pillows and blankets and bags and rushing out of their houses.

Eric went to climb down, but May said, 'Wait! This is the perfect opportunity. Mr Abiola will think we're at the Ministry's shelter again. We can watch people, and then we can do Nuala's stupid re-enactment thing.'

Eric nudged her, and she blinked, sighed and said, 'Not stupid. Sorry, Nuala. It's a good idea.'

'Thanks,' I said tightly. The siren was rocketing through my brain. Up here it felt louder somehow, without buildings to absorb it.

I squeezed my hands over my ears so I could focus on seeing, and stared down at the mews. Again, it was like being up in the flies and looking down at the play below, everyone so tiny.

There was Colette, Margot and Olivier, coming out of the Mortensens' house as the General barked inside, while Mrs

Mortensen yelled at him to be quiet. Margot was clutching a potted plant and shouting, 'Maman! Maman! Please!'

'Put it down, Margot – the Nazis can't hurt a plant!'

'But, Maman! I *need* it!'

Colette grabbed her by her free hand and towed her forward as Olivier whimpered in his carrier. Then they almost bumped into Mr Goodchild. Both Mr Goodchild and Colette recoiled.

'Careful!' said Mr Goodchild gently. 'Here, you dropped this.'

He held out a small book to her, and she let go of Margot's hand to take it and tuck it into Olivier's carrier.

I blinked. I hadn't seen her drop anything.

Cecil was just behind his father and mother. He stooped down, as though he was about to tie his shoelaces, but instead he waited until his parents were far enough ahead of him and then he turned round and ducked back into his house.

Miss Wimpress came out of her house, hurrying, the whole shape of her body anxious. I guessed that Miss Charney must be on a shift. She rushed to catch up with the Goodchilds, and Mrs Goodchild put a hand on her shoulder as they left the mews together.

The siren noise faded to tense silence. The planes were almost here. The mews was empty for a moment, and then Mr Abiola came out of the entrance to the flats below us. His tin helmet was on his head, but (I squinted) there was no whistle around his neck. May was jostling me and Eric, so I could tell that she'd noticed it as well.

He went down to the far end of the mews, the opposite end to the bombed-out Lowndes house, and knocked on the door of the first house before stepping inside. He moved down the houses, knocking on each door, looking inside, calling out and then stepping back outside.

He reached the Goodchilds' house, and knocked on it.

His knock wasn't answered, and he pushed the door open. There was a pause, and then he walked inside. A minute later, he came out, leading Cecil by the arm.

'You interferer!' Cecil was saying, red-faced.

'I knew you were there,' said Mr Abiola. 'Your jacket's on the peg. Come on, lad. Hurry up. You can't fool a warden.'

I watched Cecil walk across the cobbles of the mews, slouching in his jacket, while Mr Abiola stopped to knock on the Mortensens' door. The General went wild, and Mrs Mortensen called out, 'Come in!'

I heard the rumble of Mr Abiola's voice, and Mrs Mortensen's flat loud one talking back. 'I'm all right here,' she said. 'I have the dog to look after. Do go away – I'm getting tired of telling you every time there's a raid! You wardens are all the same, poking around and bothering people!'

But I was still thinking about what Mr Abiola had said: *You can't fool a warden.* A warden's job is to notice things. Wardens have to spot light at the edge of windows, and people trying to avoid going into shelters. They have to pay attention, just like a detective. Were we right, that Miss Fig had worked out whatever Anna and Zosia were doing, and been murdered for it? Was that the final secret of Hogarth Mews?

We were about to find out.

52

Ack-ack guns rattled in the distance as we stood at the entrance to the flats, ready to begin our re-enactment.

'What exactly are we doing?' asked Eric, rubbing his arms with his hands and shivering. I knew he wasn't just cold. It's so noisy during a raid. All the bangs and crashes catch your heartbeat and speed it up, and make you want to *run, run, run*. It's hard not to. Everyone gets twitchy, until they're almost as bad as May is normally.

Pfote curled around Eric's legs and meeped hopefully. I guess it's a good sign when she's not scared.

The General was roaring from inside Number 3, and we had to pause while Mrs Mortensen yelled at him and flapped the blackout curtain.

'She won't come out,' May said after a little while. 'We're safe from everything except bombs. So, what are we doing, Nuala? You're the director, aren't you?'

'Oh!' I said. 'Right. We're re-enacting the first crime. So we have to go into Miss Fig's house.' If I was honest, I was kind of worried about using Miss Fig's house for the re-enactment. It made sense to, but it was so wobbly now, with pieces missing from it.

'Right,' echoed May. 'Easy. Zosia crossed the mews, got into Mr Harris's house by picking the lock, climbed up through the attics and down into Miss Fig's house, killed her, hid her clothes and things in her luggage, dragged her down into the basement next door, and then took the message to Post the next day so Mr Abiola could see it.'

'You've missed the poisoning,' said Eric sensibly. 'She also had to poison Miss Fig before eight p.m., because Colette and Mrs Goodchild saw her then, when Mrs Goodchild was taking round cocoa, and she told Colette she was already feeling sick. Zosia probably put it in something in her kitchen in the early afternoon, before Miss Fig came back from Post – Mr Abiola said that everyone was sent home at about four – and then came back later to kill her. Colette heard the person in the mews just before twelve, remember. It's very complicated.'

May shrugged. 'But it happened! So one of us needs to be Miss Fig, wandering around her house, and someone else can be Zosia.'

'What about Anna?' asked Eric. 'It doesn't seem likely that she was still in the mews that evening, because Cecil couldn't find her for dinner – but what if she was? What if she helped Zosia, and that was who Zosia was talking to?'

'Oh,' I said. 'Well – well, maybe.' I still felt weird, thinking about Anna as a possible murderer.

'We ought to test it,' said May stubbornly.

'All right! You be Zosia, I'll be Anna, and Eric can be Miss Fig,' I said. 'Though I really don't think Anna was in the mews. She'd gone somewhere else by then. So I'll be the director too – I want to see what Eric does as Miss Fig.'

'I think you're wrong about Anna,' said May. 'But we'll see. Do I stay up in the attics after I've done the poisoning?'

'Whatever you want,' I said. 'Whatever you think works best.'

'What if Mrs Goodchild's cocoa—' May started. 'No, sorry. I know. Miss Fig was already sick at eight. And, anyway, Mrs Goodchild has the cocoa in a flask and pours it into people's mugs. I've seen her do it. So that's not how she was poisoned.'

I nodded.

'I'm going in to poison and drug Miss Fig, but I don't know what I'm poisoning or how,' said May. 'All right!'

Only May could sound cheerful about that.

'If we say every hour in the re-enactment is five minutes of real time, that should work,' I said. 'Eric, you've got your watch, and May, you can use mine.'

'I can count,' said May.

'No, you can't!' I said. I've seen May's attempts at solving maths problems at Deepdean.

'I can! You don't know me!'

302

'Grand, so,' I said, giving up on arguing. 'You can count. We'll go through Mr Harris's empty house into the attics and then crawl through to get to our starting position above Miss Fig's, so we don't bother the General – and remember, it was empty that day too, so it'd have been easy for Zosia to go that way. Let's begin the re-enactment at two p.m. on the day of the murder – the fog was already starting then. Are you ready?'

'I'm ready,' said Eric, nodding.

'Ready!' piped May.

'Great,' I said, feeling seriously uncertain about this whole thing. 'Let's go.'

53

Eric, May and I all huddled in the attic space above Miss Fig's house as the raid went on around us. Pfote had refused to come with us. She was sitting out in the mews, fluffy tail curled round herself, making me feel even more nervous. We'd been lucky before, but being lucky once is no guarantee that you will be again.

'All right,' I said. 'Let's start. It's two p.m. on the sixth of December. May, remember: every five minutes is an hour. Keep count. And *go*.'

'*Obviously*,' said May cheerfully. 'All right! I'm off!' She lowered herself through the little attic opening with a bounce and went scampering away into the house. I heard it grumble and creak as she went, each of her steps making the whole place tremble.

'I don't think this is a very good idea,' said Eric.

'I know,' I said unhappily. 'But I think we have to do it.'

The planes above buzzed and the ack-ack guns rumbled and the bombs struck around us like trains passing in the Underground. They felt nearer tonight. We waited.

'Done!' said May cheerfully, popping back up. Her face was pink and excited. 'You'll have to work out what I've poisoned.'

My watch said it'd been seven minutes, which was either great timekeeping from May, or just her working to her own schedule as usual.

'Eric,' I said. 'Miss Fig came back at four p.m., so it's almost time for you to go downstairs. Are you ready?'

Eric nodded. 'I think you should come with me,' he said.

I knew this was Eric's way of asking for help, because he was scared of being in Miss Fig's house alone. I nodded back, and we climbed cautiously down. Something clicked, down below us, and I could smell burning.

'All right,' I said, trying to stay calm, once we'd picked our careful way through the house to the living room. We had to move gingerly past the wreckage from this morning's blast. Chunks of ceiling lay scattered across the floor, and a whole chest of drawers was smashed on the living-room carpet. The dust caught at my throat, and I coughed. 'It's just after four p.m. in the re-enactment. You're Miss Fig. You've been sent home from Post because of the fog. What do you do?'

'The blackout,' said Eric at once, going gingerly to the front window. 'It's early for it, but in the fog it makes sense. I'd go all round the house closing it up. And not just the blackout: all the windows and doors. You don't want anything open in a fog. Then . . . would I make a cup of tea?'

'An English person might,' I said. 'Miss Fig was from Spain.'

'All right, coffee, then,' said Eric. We walked slowly through the house to the kitchen at the back. Even more of the shelving had fallen in the explosion, and every step we took crushed bits of crockery into the floor.

'Milk could be poisoned,' said Eric, going to the pantry. 'Or coffee grounds. So it could be that. And if she had something to eat, they could poison a tin of meat, or some bread. It's possible.'

'And then they could come back later and take away the thing they'd poisoned,' I said, nodding. 'Ooh, if the arsenic was in her coffee, then it might have been poisoning her for days, a little each time she drank a cup.'

I was pretty horrified at that, and Eric made a face. 'Oh no!' he said. 'I don't like that.'

'Me neither,' I said. 'Sorry.'

Then I had a thought. I'd been sure we'd cracked the arsenic already – there would have been plenty of poisonable things in the kitchen. But she'd had chloral in her body too, and wasn't chloral a bit special? It didn't just kill you if you took too much; it made you really sleepy. If Miss Fig had gone to get something to eat or drink and been poisoned at four, or even five or six or seven, how could she still have been awake at eight?

I said so to Eric.

'Oh!' he said thoughtfully. 'You're right. What if the

chloral was in something else? Something she took while she was getting ready for bed later? Arsenic takes hours to work, so that would make sense.'

I looked at my watch. It was almost eight in the re-enactment. 'All right,' I said. 'It's time for your cocoa. Go to the door, and pretend to take it from Mrs Goodchild.'

Eric went obediently towards the space where the door used to be, mimed leaning forward and saying a few words, and then pretended to drink from a cup before trotting off to the kitchen to wash it up.

'Good,' I said when he came back. 'That's the last anyone saw her. She wasn't feeling well, but we think that was the arsenic, not the chloral yet. Now let's go upstairs, and you pretend to get ready for bed.'

We crept up the stairs, clinging to the rail, the house echoing with our quiet footsteps. We came to the little bathroom, and Miss Fig's bedroom. Eric went into the bathroom, but I got caught by that big, bright painting on Miss Fig's wall again. I skirted around the messy gap where the floor used to be, to stare at it.

It glowed in the beam of my flashlight, its summertime colours fierce and lovely. I started to imagine that I wasn't in London at all, but there, among the flowers, in the summer afternoon sun. It was nice. It made me forget that I was in a crumbling house in the middle of a London air raid, trying to solve a months-old murder.

'Hello,' said Eric, making me jump. 'Sorry! I didn't mean

to startle you. I could see the stuff that May'd been at, but I don't think cold cream or toothpaste could be how Miss Fig took the chloral. You'd have to take an awful lot of it for anything to happen, much more than normal. There was a glass, though, for water – maybe that was poisoned?'

I nodded. It was hard to think, for some reason.

'That painting smells odd,' said Eric, pointing at it.

'What?' I asked. 'No, it doesn't.'

'Really?' said Eric. 'But can't you smell it? It's strong.'

I sniffed, and then sniffed again. My head ached, and I suddenly realized that I'd been feeling weird for a couple of minutes, just the way I had last time I'd been in her room.

'It *is* the painting!' I said. I was surprised. 'Maybe it's just new, so it still smells.'

'It's at least four months old,' Eric pointed out.

Right then I realized that we were behind on the re-enactment.

'Eric!' I said. 'I think she must be going to sleep by now, if she's taken the chloral.'

'Oh, yes!' said Eric. 'So I get into bed, and read – and then—'

We both stared at each other.

'Then I guess she falls asleep, and Zosia – or Zosia and Anna – comes in and kills her,' I said, feeling sick. 'Ugh!'

'And we know she was in bed when she was killed,' said Eric. 'Because of the bloodstains on the sheets. Oh!'

'What?' I asked.

'You saw the body. She wasn't wearing pyjamas, was she?'

'No,' I said, shaking my head. 'She was in slacks and a sweater. Oh! You think – the murderer changed her clothes.'

That was a really horrible thought, but it made sense, and I could see it making sense to Eric. He made a face, and said, 'I do. To try to hide the fact that she was in bed when she was killed. It's another thing that's clever. But then the whole murder is so stupid. It doesn't all fit together.'

I didn't want to see his point, but I did. We'd solved the case, we must have done, but it was still just so strange.

'All right,' said Eric, looking sad. 'I'm asleep now. The chloral's knocked me out. I'll lie down on the bed.'

He sat and then lowered himself down onto the coverlet. He closed his eyes and put his hands at his sides. He really was getting into it, and I was impressed. And a bit upset, if I'm honest. It was eerie, seeing him like that. I don't really – I don't really like seeing people pretend to be dead any more, even in plays. It used to be fun, to play dead, but now it makes me sick. It feels wrong.

'Hey!' said May from the doorway.

I gasped.

'Hello,' said Eric without opening his eyes.

'I came back through the attics again,' said May, bouncing from foot to foot. 'It was easy. It's all been doable so far.

I think we're proving it was Zosia! I don't even think she'd need Anna.'

My heart skipped. Was she right?

'All right,' said Eric. 'So, kill me. And then dress me, and move me.'

'What?' said May.

'Kill me,' said Eric calmly. 'Then when I'm dead, take off my pyjamas and put on outdoor clothes. Then get me down the stairs and out of the house, and into the basement. Go on. Do it. On your own.'

And right then, Diary, I saw what he meant.

54

Five minutes later it was midnight in the re-enactment and May hadn't even got down the stairs.

Eric was refusing to get up and help – 'Why should I?' he asked. 'I'm a corpse!' – and May was puffing and panting and trying to drag him by one foot.

'It's not fair!' she cried. 'I'm small!'

'*I'm* small,' said Eric, not moving. 'So it doesn't matter that you're small too. Keep going.'

His head bumped off the next step down, and I said, 'OK. Stop.'

'But I've almost got it!' said May.

'You haven't,' said Eric.

'*Stop!*' I said as fiercely as I could. 'I'm the director and I say stop. May, it isn't working without me.'

'It could work!'

'It isn't working! Here, I'll help.' I had a really sick feeling in my stomach. May couldn't move Eric on her own. And if I had to help – that meant Zosia had to have help, for the real murder. And that meant . . . Anna.

I bent down and tried to grab hold of Eric. He was totally floppy, and somehow he seemed ten times heavier than he usually is. I realized right then why people say *dead weight* – carrying a moving, helpful person isn't anything like trying to lift someone who's not responding. I'm the tallest of the three of us, and I'm pretty strong I think, and there was no way I could do it on my own.

'Let's go,' I said to May. 'Come on.'

'He's so heavy,' grumbled May, grabbing Eric by the armpits and lifting with me.

Eric finally rose up from the stairs, dangling between us. Between me and May, we could carry him. We got down into the living room, stumbling over the fresh rubble and getting dust all over ourselves. Then out through the space where the door used to be, turning right so we didn't go past the General's door.

'Right,' I whispered. 'Forward. Left a bit. Lift your feet up, you're about to step on a brick. All right, up again.'

'May, can you hurry up? My arms hurt, and I can see the planes,' said Eric, staring up at the spotlit sky.

'This is hard! I'm going backwards! I can't see!'

'So *listen* to me!'

We were talking too loud. I was anxious. And then I realized – this must be what Colette had heard. *People* talking, just before midnight, in the mews. More proof that this couldn't have been a murder committed by just one person. Anna had to be involved.

'Why should I? I don't trust you! You're a snake when we're at Deepdean!' May said.

I gasped. 'I am not a snake! I'm – just because I have other friends as well as you at school! I can't just spend time with you, May!'

Suddenly this had stopped being about the murder at all. We were poking at things I didn't want to think about.

'You *can*! I thought you were going to be my best friend! I thought you were going to be different from all the other boring girls in the dorm, and hate school as much as I do. But then you didn't. I can't trust you at all.'

In the light from the fire somewhere away behind us I could see tears in May's eyes. We were balanced up on top of the rubble of Number 1, wobbling a little, the bricks and dirt under us shifting gently and the KEEP OUT sign on its string fluttering in the breeze.

'But I don't hate school!' I said. 'You can't ask me to choose! I like you and I like Deepdean, and why shouldn't I do both?'

'Because you *have* chosen. When we're at Deepdean, you aren't *you*, and you aren't my friend, and that makes you a traitor! Anyway, you always take the other girls' side.'

'Only because you're so unreasonable! And it's all part of my cover! I don't mean it!'

'That's rubbish. And you should! I always mean it! Always! So how can I trust you if I don't know when *you* mean it?'

I didn't know how to answer that. I act so much that sometimes it's hard to know which version of me is the real Nuala.

Except.

'I think I mean it when I'm around the two of you,' I said slowly. 'But it's easier not to all the time, at school. I think that cover thing's just an excuse.'

'Obviously,' said May. 'And you can't choose like that. You have to be my friend all the time, otherwise you're never my friend at all.'

'What *happened* at school?' asked Eric. 'Put me down, can't you?'

'Nothing,' we both said together, lowering him.

'I'm sorry, May,' I said. 'Seriously, I am. I was wrong. I won't do it again. I'll be this Nuala, properly, next term.'

'You'd better!' said May. 'This Nuala's nice.'

I grinned, and then Eric got up and wrapped his arms around my shoulders and squeezed, and May grabbed me from the other side and squeezed even harder.

There was a scream and a smash, as a bomb fell a few streets away. We could feel the ground shudder and roll, all the bricks under us trembling and clicking together, and Miss Fig's house creaked ominously.

Eric let go of me, but May clung on.

'Friends?' she said.

'Friends,' I said. 'For real.'

'I'll hold you to that,' said May. 'Do we have to put Eric in the basement?'

'Absolutely not,' I said. I didn't want any of us to go anywhere near that basement right now, not with the earth shaking from all those hits. 'Haven't we proved the point already? One murderer couldn't have committed the crime, no matter how big they were. Miss Fig was pretty small, but we've shown that any size body's too hard for one person to move – or at least, it would be for our suspects. None of them are particularly big and strong. There had to have been *two* people, at least, to carry her body. Zosia – and Anna.'

I felt really sick. I remembered that drawing of Anna by Mr Goodchild that we'd found. She'd looked so *nice*. I kept feeling as though I'd like her if I met her. And now I was realizing that she'd helped kill Miss Fig and get rid of her body. Miss Fig, who'd been mean to me, but who'd been *alive* until the sixth of December last year.

May nodded. 'I think you're right!' she said. 'Anna and Zosia were best friends; they were doing something underhand, and Miss Fig found out about it. She blackmailed them and they decided to kill her to cover it up. And then Zosia decided to kill the Chief Inspector when he came sniffing around. It all fits!'

'Except that the police won't stop investigating even though he's hurt,' said Eric with a shrug. 'So it wasn't a very good idea. That's it again – half of this case is very clever, and the other half is very stupid.'

'I want to know where Anna is now,' I said. '*And* how Zosia came back to England without the Ministry noticing, if she was the one who left for France on the seventh of December, not Anna. Why didn't Anna go on the Ministry mission, and Zosia on the other one?'

'That's a problem,' agreed Eric. 'It's strange! It's all too complicated.'

'*Life* is very complicated,' said May, and she said it so dramatically that Eric and I both burst out laughing.

'Did you like it?' May asked, grinning. 'I was being you, Nuala.' And, oh, I should have been mad, Diary, but I only laughed harder, until tears came out of my eyes. Suddenly the world was so funny and brilliant, the three of us standing on the rubble of a house, in the moonlight, while bombs fell all around us. Suddenly everything was great.

PART SEVEN

WE RACE AGAINST TIME

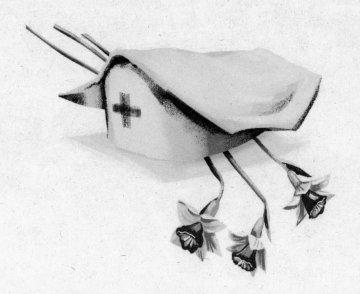

55

From the diary of Fionnuala O'Malley

Thursday 3rd April

I wrote all that up late last night, Diary, after we'd crept back to Eric's flat. I don't know why we crept – the bombs were still falling, shaking the city – but we did. We couldn't go back up to our flat, not knowing what we knew about Zosia. I didn't want to see her.

May lay down in the bed and fell asleep with her pillow over her head. Eric curled up with Pfote on the floor and snored gently, but I sat up and wrote. We'd solved the case. Surely we had. Except . . . there was still stuff missing. I knew it.

And I remembered what had happened last time – when we'd been so sure, and it had all been wrong. This felt – OK, this felt a lot like that. It felt like we'd grasped at half the case, but not the whole shape of it. We had to get more. We needed Zosia's confession. We needed Anna. It felt to me like Anna was the piece right in the middle of the puzzle. If we found her, everything would fit.

So I fell asleep still worrying about it, and dreamed that I was acting in a play, but the audience wouldn't stop stamping on the floor of the theatre, so hard that the proscenium arch trembled. I forgot my lines, and everything that came out of my mouth was wrong, because I'd mixed up the roles. My da was in the prompt box, and I needed him to tell me what to say, but he wouldn't.

I woke up crying, and saw May already awake, sitting up at her end of the bed with her arms around her knees. She looked at me thoughtfully and passed me her handkerchief. (It was dirty, obviously, but I took it anyway. I knew she was trying to be nice.)

'Wake up, Eric!' she said, and Eric woke with a snort, dislodging Pfote from his chest.

'What's wrong?' he asked.

'Nothing,' said May. 'I've been thinking about the case. You keep going on about more evidence, so today we're going to get it. Mr Goodchild invited you to his house to practise your sketching, didn't he? So we're going to go. And we're going to find out everything we can about Anna while we're at it. All right?'

As usual with May, what she was saying sounded faintly like a threat. But, as usual with May, what she was saying was a mixed-up kind of right.

'He'll be at work this morning,' said Eric. 'But we could go this afternoon.'

Which was lucky, because this morning turned out to be really busy.

George was sitting at the table, drinking tea, when we went into the kitchen. He looked drawn and a little pale; his usually smoothed-down hair was messed up and his shirt was the same one he'd been wearing the day before. That shocked me, because George is always so careful with how he dresses. He looked like he hadn't slept.

'Good morning,' he said. 'Zosia said you were here. I've got a task for you. I need you to take some messages. It's all hands at the Ministry. Here – these three, to these addresses, and then this letter for Inspector Priestley at the hospital. Pretend you're selling raffle tickets to win a cake for the first three – here, use this roll.'

'The Chief Inspector?' asked May at once, chin up, as I took the tickets. 'That one had better be important.'

'Crucially so,' said George with a grin. 'From Hazel Wong herself. And once you've been everywhere, come back to the Ministry, all right? She wants to see you.'

I felt nervous about that. The Ministry meant Zosia, and we knew she was guilty.

But I tried to forget that. We had messages to carry. It was kind of like being part of Sherlock Holmes's Baker Street Irregulars, wasn't it? It felt important.

Obviously, May had to ruin it. George had barely left for the Ministry before she was leaning over the kettle on the hob, holding the sealed letter for the Chief Inspector over its spout, trying to steam it open.

'Here, leave it!' I said.

'No fear!' said May. 'We need to know what it says!'

'No, we don't,' said Eric.

'I'm being careful!' said May. 'I just want to read it. Oh, blast, this is going wrong. It's very hot on my hands!'

'May, be careful!' said Eric.

'Got it!' said May, ripping. 'Oh.'

She held out the letter to the Chief Inspector. It said, in Hazel's writing:

May, you're a little monster. You shouldn't have opened this! But now you have. Can you please take some flowers to Inspector Priestley and see how he's getting on? Here's ten shillings. Get nice ones.

And go by the ambulance station on Oxford Street first. Miss Temple's got something that I want to give to him – collect it from her, will you, and pass it on? Thank you.

Hazel

'See?' said May. 'I told you I needed to open it!'

We got dressed (May still wearing the same shorts – it's been days, and she just won't change out of them) and went running outside, on our errands.

56

The letters really did seem to be important. The first one was for the Free French movement's headquarters – you know, the real General Charles de Gaulle (not the dog) and his helpers. That made me think about the mews again. It was really almost like the whole war in miniature – so many people, from different countries, all jammed together and arguing or making alliances.

Then there was one for a house that seemed like a nothing, just part of a long row of white London houses, but the woman who came to the door wasn't a nothing at all. She felt very important indeed, though I can't exactly say why. Then we were back on Oxford Street, handing our last message in at a shop that apparently sold umbrellas but looked as though no one apart from us had been in it in weeks.

We remembered about Hazel's message then, and bought some faded daffodils from a flower seller just outside the store. I put them to my nose and sniffed, trying to imagine the countryside they'd come from.

'You'll wear them out!' said May, snatching them from me.

Then we went to find Miss Temple.

The ambulance station was just off Oxford Street, in a yard beneath a big building. It was right behind the main Post station for wardens – the place where Miss Fig would have gone for her shift every day. All the ambulances were parked up next to each other, too close, because there really wasn't enough space for them all. Some of them weren't really ambulances, either, but milk carts and grocer's vans and people's cars that had been called into use. They all had AMBULANCE painted on them in white paint, though.

Even though it was the morning, and not during a raid, the little yard was crammed full of women in uniform, striding about and drinking tea and leaning against the ambulances and talking. I stared and stared at them, and then got worried that I was maybe staring too much. They all had their hair up in beautiful dos, or cut really short, even shorter than May's hair, and they all looked like they knew exactly what they were doing.

May, obviously, wasn't daunted. She just waved her arms and went galloping into the chaos, yelling, 'Lavinia! Hey! Lavinia!'

The woman we'd seen before, when Miss Fig's body was being carried away, the one with the bushy, dark hair and the muscular shoulders, turned and glared in confusion. Then she caught sight of May and her face became a mix of annoyance and amusement. It's a face that a lot of people get when they see it's May.

'Little Wong!' she said. 'What are you doing here?'

'Hazel sent us,' said May importantly. 'She said you've got something for her.'

'So I do,' said Miss Temple. 'Come into the break room to get it with me.'

We followed her into a little dark lean-to shelter, one of those temporary ones that are everywhere now because no one has the time to build anything that'll last – and, anyway, would you believe that anything'll last right now?

'Want something to drink?' asked Miss Temple. 'Food? Help yourselves, if so.'

She waved her hand at the biscuit tin, and we all lunged at it, because they had really good stuff in there.

'Here's Hazel's book,' she said, pulling something out of her locker.

'It's for the Chief Inspector,' said May, munching her biscuit. 'Someone tried to kill him, and now he's in the hospital.'

'Yes, I heard!' said Miss Temple, her dark eyebrows drawing together. 'What happened?'

'Zo— Uh, someone put explosives in Miss Fig's house, and he was hurt by it,' I said. 'You knew Miss Fig, didn't you?'

'As little as I could help,' said Miss Temple with a shrug. 'I didn't have any time for her. She used to come around here sometimes, though, more's the pity. We're next to Post, of course, so it made sense when she and Prim were . . . friends. But then they broke it off, and Prim moved in with

Elfie, but Miss Fig kept on appearing. We'd try to lie and tell her that Prim wasn't there, but she'd get very upset and insist on seeing her. It made Elfie furious. I don't know how they all stood living on the same street as each other.'

'Oh,' I said.

'See here,' said Miss Temple. 'There's something I've been meaning to tell the Inspector. It may be nothing, but Hazel and Daisy have taught me that if you think it is something, it usually is. If you're going to see him – could you take a message?'

'Of course!' said May. 'We do know who killed her, though, so we probably know what you're going to say.'

'May!' said Eric. 'Careful!'

'Do you really?' asked Miss Temple, leaning towards us and grinning. 'Know who did it, I mean?'

'We do,' said May. 'It was—'

'Morning, Lavinia,' said Miss Charney from the doorway. 'Just checking the rota. What are you three doing here?' She sounded suddenly sharp, like a teacher telling us off.

'They're collecting a book from me,' said Lavinia, opening it up and (I gasped) writing a message on its title page in bold dark print. 'Something for a friend.'

'Well, then, hurry it up,' said Miss Charney. 'They shouldn't be here – this isn't a place for kids.'

'Kids can be anywhere!' said May crossly, as Lavinia handed the book to Eric.

'You're already everywhere,' said Miss Charney, eyeing her. 'You're in the mews, you're hanging about on the streets, you're in the shelter.'

'The Wong family does that,' said Lavinia. 'Prim in?'

'At the museum. She's on the late shift today,' said Miss Charney. 'It's all on the rota.'

'Go on,' said Lavinia to us. 'Get! Give George and Hazel my love when you see them. And give the Inspector that book. I never much liked him, but we've been through enough together, I suppose. Make *sure* he gets it.'

57

'That was odd!' I said, once we were back out on Oxford Street, buses swooshing by us, someone sweeping up glass from the front of a shop. My skin felt prickly – what had Lavinia wanted to tell us? 'What did she write?'

'She did say it was for the Chief Inspector,' protested Eric, holding the book to his chest.

'Don't be silly. She was going to tell us. Anyway, she wrote it right in front of us, so she mustn't mind us knowing about it. Go on, show us!' said May.

We crowded to the side of the street, and Eric opened up the book. It was an old hardback detective novel, *The Man in the Queue*, and on the flyleaf it said PROPERTY OF THE WELLS AND WONG DETECTIVE SOCIETY, 1934. Lavinia's note was on the third page, and it said:

Get well soon, Inspector.
By the way, my ambulance got a ding on October the tenth last year.
I came back from my day off and found it that way. And that was the
week Miss Fig complained that she'd been hit by a car during the
blackout. Might be nothing? Thought you should know. Lavinia Temple

We all three gaped at each other. I remembered hearing about the accident Miss Fig had been in, but I never thought it had meant anything before this, Diary. Accidents do happen in the blackout all the time, I know they do. And it was months before the murder, and we knew Miss Fig hadn't been killed by a car. It didn't feel relevant.

But now . . . this.

'Wait,' said May. 'Is Lavinia saying that *one of the other drivers* hit Miss Fig – not with a car but with an ambulance? Which means – she thinks it was Miss Wimpress or Miss Charney?'

'I think so!' said Eric.

'But we know they didn't do the murder!' I said. 'Right? I mean, we know it was Zosia and Anna.'

'Well, they do have a motive,' said Eric. 'Lavinia told us. They were all fighting.'

I shook my head. I didn't understand it. It had to just be another red herring. It didn't make sense.

But I heard the Chief Inspector's voice in my head, saying, *Was the woman Rasputin?*

It was a joke, but I understood what it meant. Rasputin worked for the Russian royal family, years ago, and he was so close to the queen that a lot of the other courtiers got nervous about it. So they decided to kill him. Only everything they did (lots of horrible things – you definitely don't want to hear about them) just didn't work, so they had to keep trying other stuff. Da told me, and said that it was because he knew magic and couldn't be killed, and then Mam said, well, why did he die in the end? He wasn't magic, because magic doesn't exist. He was just different, and they didn't like that.

I remembered what Colette had said, about how Miss Fig complained of being sick a lot the week before she died. I thought about the accident Miss Fig had been in. I thought about the fact that there had been *two* different poisons in her body, and how strange that was, since she'd been stabbed as well. I thought about Eric saying that the murder felt stupid and clever at the same time.

I wasn't sure what I was thinking yet – which happens sometimes, Diary; you have to let the ideas swirl around in your head before they become a real shape. But twice on the way to the hospital I almost tripped over a loose bit of pavement, and Eric just ended up threading his arm through mine and kind of guiding me.

'Are you all right?' he asked quietly.

'Yes!' I said. 'I'm trying to think.'

'Me too!' said Eric. 'I think the ambulance clue is really important. Hey, May, careful with those flowers!'

The daffodils were looking pretty crushed by now, their stems bent and their yellow lantern heads sagging.

'We can get something else for him,' said May. 'Biscuits or something. I've still got five shillings. I'm busy *thinking*.'

'Oh, us too!' I said.

'Bet you're not thinking what I'm thinking,' said May.

'Bet we are!' I said.

'Go on, say it on the count of three,' said May, as we turned onto the street where the hospital was, red brick and finicky, already smelling of carbolic soap and sickness. 'One, two, three—'

'*Different people* have been trying to murder Miss Fig for months!' we all said together.

58

Here, the long and the short of it is that we didn't exactly say it together, because people don't all speak together like they already know their lines in a play, but the three of us pretty much said the same thing, and I knew from the looks on May and Eric's faces that they'd been thinking the same as me.

It made me really happy to know that we could be thinking *together* like that, in our three separate brains.

'So we think that Miss Charney or Miss Wimpress hit Miss Fig with the ambulance in October, but then Zosia and Anna actually committed the murder in December?' I asked. 'Unless – unless the accident was Zosia or Anna pretending to be Miss Charney or Miss Wimpress. Maybe they borrowed one of their uniforms? But—'

'Why would they do that?' asked Eric. 'It's very complicated, and it'd be hard to do. You heard Miss Charney and Miss Temple talking about the rota – everyone must check it, so it'd be difficult for someone else to just turn up and take an ambulance. Why wouldn't they choose another way of trying to kill Miss Fig that was less risky?

They already lived on the same street. But if it was different people, it makes more sense!'

We stepped through the main doors of the hospital then, and we had to be quiet.

A nurse came trotting up to us, her cap starched into perfect peaks. 'Who are you looking for?' she asked.

'Chief Inspector Priestley,' said May. 'We brought him flowers and – oh, we forgot the biscuits. But flowers!'

She brandished them at the nurse, who looked faintly disgusted. The flowers were very much the worse for wear by now.

'The Chief Inspector is on the third-floor ward,' she said. 'Up those stairs. And you have ten minutes! Visiting hours end at twelve.'

The Chief Inspector was sitting up in his thin ward bed, one arm strapped to his chest. He looked pale, and his forehead was even more crinkly than I remembered.

'Ah!' he said. 'The new Detective Society: May Wong and her friends.'

'We have names too,' said Eric crossly, at once. 'I'm Eric, and that's Fionnuala.'

'I do know that,' said the Chief Inspector. 'My idea of a joke, I'm sorry. It wasn't very funny. I— The arm makes it difficult to think properly.'

'We forgive you,' said May – which wasn't particularly fair, since she was the one who'd had her name said right in the first place. 'Look, we brought you flowers. Hazel told us to.'

'So you did,' said the Chief Inspector. 'They were certainly flowers at some point in their lives.'

I giggled. May grinned.

'We did ruin them a little,' she said. 'We had to come halfway across London, though! And we went to see Lavinia. She sent you a present too. Here. There's a note on the flyleaf for you.'

The Chief Inspector took it awkwardly with his right hand, and flicked it open. He read it, and then looked up at us.

'I assume you've seen this,' he said.

'Of course we have,' said May. 'Isn't it interesting?'

'But it doesn't make sense!' I cried. 'Why was someone trying to kill Miss Fig, months before she died? I don't understand it.'

'May I remind you that you agreed not to get involved in this?' said the Chief Inspector sharply, and then he flinched and lay back against the pillows of his bed. 'It sounds very much as though you've been investigating.'

'We haven't!' said Eric. 'Promise!'

'But Eric, we—' May started. I saw Eric pinch her arm, and she flinched in surprise. I knew what he meant – that he didn't want us to trust the Chief Inspector. It seemed so silly, because Hazel did, but . . . Eric was a Detective Society member. We had to listen to him. I caught May's eye, and she scowled but stayed silent. She'd had the same thought.

'Now, you three, visiting hours are over,' said the nurse, walking over to us and clapping her hands. She was very tall and willowy, with big eyes in a shy, pretty face.

'A few more minutes, Rebecca, surely,' said the Chief Inspector.

'Not with your arm,' said the nurse Rebecca, frowning at him. 'You know you're more hurt than you let on. Now go on, you three! You can come back later.'

'You'd better go,' said the Chief Inspector. 'Give Hazel my best.'

'And mine too,' said Rebecca, smiling. The smile made her face bunch up into a huge chipmunk grin – for a second, I'd have thought she wasn't much older than we were. 'Now go on!'

So we ran.

59

'It's all getting very confusing,' said May, as we walked back home.

It was a warm spring day, the sun making me squint when I looked up at the sky. It's weird to walk through London these days – every time you do, it's like you're seeing it for the first time, because new things have happened to the skyline. One of the shops on Oxford Street had been blasted away overnight, and I suddenly noticed a run of coloured bricks on the house behind it, a perfect little turret sticking up into the air.

'I thought we'd funnelled it all down, but now it's expanding again!' exclaimed May.

'What if we never solve it?' I asked. 'What if it keeps on being all wrong?'

'We'll solve it,' said Eric solidly. 'I know we will.'

'You're being Dramatic Nuala again,' said May. 'Of course we'll solve it. Eric's right. We're clever!'

She grinned up at me, putting her arm around my waist and squeezing, and right then maybe I did believe them both. It's good to have other people there, to make your fears squash down to normal size when they start to get out of control.

Pfote came running out to meet us as we arrived at the Ministry. She jumped up into Eric's arms, and he petted her little lion head.

'How do you make her do that?' I asked.

'I don't *make* her do anything,' said Eric with a shrug. 'She just likes it.'

'Did you see the Inspector?' called Hazel, as we stepped into the front hall. 'How is he?'

'He's still alive,' said May. 'How is he supposed to be? He loved the flowers, by the way.'

'May!' said Hazel.

'He's better,' said Eric. 'Your friend Rebecca's watching him. They both send their love, and Lavinia sends her love to you and George.'

'See? May? This is all I wanted. Now—'

Zosia came down the stairs then. Eric, May and I all moved closer together. It was scary, seeing her right *there* like that. She was still free. She might do anything.

'Hazel,' said Zosia. 'Can I have a word?'

'Of course. You three, can you go and find George? He's got something for you.'

'Oh, we'll wait,' I said. 'There's something else the Chief Inspector said he needed to tell you.'

The lie came out of my mouth so fast I was surprised at it. It didn't even feel like acting. I stepped away from

May and Eric, in case their nervousness made me look nervous.

'All right,' said Hazel. 'Zosia, what is it?'

'It's private,' said Zosia. 'There's something I need to tell you. It's about those messages that have been coming in. The ones with Daisy's code.'

'What about them?' asked Hazel.

'I really do need to talk to you in private,' said Zosia. 'It's important.'

'Why?' asked Hazel. She was frowning, tucking her hair behind one ear the way she does when she's confused.

'I— You'll understand when I tell you. Please.' She gestured towards one of the closed office doors.

The three of us stared at each other, panicked. What was about to happen? Then—

'Don't LISTEN to her!' shrilled May. 'Big Sister, no!'

Zosia turned on her furiously, and May, of course, took that as a provocation.

'May!' I gasped, just as May hit Zosia with a *thump*. They sprawled backwards on the threadbare red carpet of the hallway, Zosia holding up her hands while May pummelled her with her little fists. I was yelling, Hazel was bawling, 'GET OFF HER, MAY! WHAT ARE YOU DOING?' and Eric squeezed Pfote in horror.

George cried, 'What's going on out there?' and then Ralph came sprinting out of one of the rooms, saying, 'What's up, chaps? Hey, Miss Wong, get off her!'

'MAY! Really! What are you doing?' cried Hazel.

'I'm SUBDUING THE ENEMY!' screamed May, still hitting. 'She's an ENEMY! She tried to kill the CHIEF INSPECTOR! You can't TRUST HER!'

'That isn't true!' snapped Zosia. 'Ralph, *help* me.'

Ralph dragged May off her, and May tried to turn on him, but he held her out in front of him so all she could do was wriggle like a bug and hiss furiously.

'What do you think you're doing?' he asked.

'Why is everyone asking *me* what I'm doing and not *her*?' yelled May, pointing at Zosia. 'She's a TRAITOR! I told you!'

'I am not!' said Zosia, scrambling to her feet. 'They've got confused. This is nonsense. Hazel, if I could just speak to you—'

'We aren't confused!' I said. I tried to sound as serious as possible, Nancy Drew catching the criminal at the end of the book. 'May's right! The explosive that hurt the Chief Inspector – it's one of the Cook's special explosives. It came from the Ministry! It has to have been Zosia who set the trap, and that means she was the person who killed Miss Fig too. We think she and Anna were working on a secret project together, something they couldn't tell the Ministry about, and Miss Fig found out and tried to blackmail them, so they killed her. So it might be something for the *other side*! What if they've been working against the Ministry? You see, Zosia's dangerous – you can't trust her!'

'What do you mean, the explosive came from the Ministry?' asked Hazel.

I dug my hands in my pocket and held out the twisted-up piece of metal and the scrap of blue-and-white paper.

'It's true!' said Eric. 'Look at it!'

And here's the thing, Diary. Hazel's an adult, and sometimes she doesn't listen. But sometimes she does. This time she did. She reached out and took the two bits from me, turning them in her hands.

'Where did you get this?' she asked carefully.

'In the mews!' I explained. 'Miss Fig's house. Where the Chief Inspector got hurt. We found it afterwards, before the ceiling fell in. It has to have been taken from here. And George wasn't in the mews that night!'

'That's true enough,' said George, bending his head forward to look. 'I was at Ralph's that night, working on some code. I left you the note, didn't I? No opportunity to set the trap.'

'So you see, you *can't* trust her!' said May. 'Not even a little bit.'

'That's not true!' said Zosia. 'You can! This is important. I just need to talk to Hazel. No one else.'

'Zosia,' said George. 'You're not making sense, and I hate when things don't make sense. I know you think you have a reason to only want to talk to Hazel, but can't you just be clear with us all? Come on.'

Zosia sighed. Her hairstyle had been messed up by May, and her lipstick looked like she'd been worrying at it.

'I know who's sending the messages,' she said. 'I've known all along.'

'It's not Daisy,' said Hazel. She didn't make it sound like a question.

'It's not,' said Zosia. 'It's Anna. But I think Daisy's with her.'

60

'Do we believe her?' Hazel asked George, five minutes later.

Zosia's been locked in the basement – she didn't fight much, which I could tell May wasn't impressed by. We're lingering just inside the downstairs office, listening in, and I'm writing all this up. It's amazing how much adults will forget that you're around if they can't exactly see you.

'That it's Anna?' George replied. 'I do.'

'Yes, but what does that mean?' said Hazel. 'If Zosia did set the explosive for Inspector Priestley, and murder Miss Fig – the children could be right. She and Anna might be working for the other side. What have they been up to? Is this why Anna's been missing? If we go to the location in the message and proceed with extraction, we might be walking into a trap. Daisy might not be there at all.'

'Well, we've known for a while that the person sending the messages isn't Daisy.'

'I've known all along,' said Hazel unhappily. 'I kept hoping that she'd just forgotten her extra code, but . . . the messages never sounded like her. *You* know. There's still a chance that Anna is above board, and she really has found Daisy like Zosia says, though.'

'So interrogate Zosia! If you're not happy, you don't have to leave on the mission this evening.'

'But what if I stay here tonight, and then Daisy . . . Daisy doesn't come home? I keep thinking about what Daisy would do, and I know she wouldn't give up on me. Not ever. Are we giving up on her if I decide not to go? We're running out of time, George.'

'Hardly! We just need to get all the information first. There's still time. Go and talk to her. I'll stay up here and supervise Ralph.'

I knew he meant that he didn't want to have to go down into the basement on his crutches, and I knew Hazel understood it too. She said, 'Very well. May! Nuala! Eric! Come down with me.'

So we haven't actually been forgotten, after all.

Zosia had been handcuffed to a chair at the back of the basement, the part where we usually pretend to get interrogated. And now it was happening for real. I got one of those weird slip-sliding feelings I have sometimes when we're doing Ministry stuff, where I can't remember what's real and what's made up, and the two things seem to mix together until I can't see the difference.

Hazel flicked on the Anglepoise lamp that we use to dazzle people's eyes and turned it on Zosia.

'Keep behind me,' she said to me, Eric and May. 'Imagine this is another training exercise.'

But we all three knew it wasn't.

'I could get out of these handcuffs if I wanted, you know,' said Zosia. 'I've got my hairpins.'

'*Ralph!*' said Hazel crossly. 'I've told him—'

'Never mind that. I'm still here, see? I'm not going anywhere. I'm honest.'

'Did you set the trap for the Chief Inspector?'

There was a pause. 'I had reason to,' said Zosia. 'I *had* to.'

'You *had* to? You could have killed him!' Hazel doesn't get angry often, but I could feel it rolling off her in waves. Her shoulders were set and her hands were clenched. 'Daisy and I – we've known him since we were little. He's family. He's always been good to us, even when he didn't need to be, and you almost *killed* him!' She was shaking with fury.

'I didn't mean to hurt him! I just set the charge to try to make the house fall down. I wanted to bury the whole place – as a warning to stop the investigation, nothing else. I didn't mean for him to be caught in it.'

'Well, that was stupid of you,' said Hazel, hands on her hips. 'Didn't the Cook teach you anything?'

'I was rushing,' said Zosia.

'You *did* mean to hurt someone!' said Eric, popping out from behind Hazel, his fists clenched. 'You stole Mr Abiola's whistle and put it in the living room, so he'd be

344

framed if anyone found it. He could have been arrested, and he didn't do it!'

Zosia looked embarrassed. 'That was a bad idea on my part,' she said. 'I was rushing, like I said. I was panicking. I saw him wearing it during the raid that night and cut it off his neck. I didn't think.'

'Yes, but *why*?' asked Hazel. 'Why did you set the trap? Why did you and Anna kill Miss Figueroa? Zosia, I thought we were part of a team. Why would you do it?'

'Anna and I didn't *kill Miss Fig*! What are you *talking* about?'

The hairs on my arms felt prickly. Either Zosia was suddenly really, really good at acting, or she was telling the truth. I heard how her voice had snapped with passion. But if that was true, then why had she set the trap?

'For goodness' sake, stop being so cryptic! What's going on?'

Zosia took a deep breath, and the hairs on my arms prickled again, because she was *crying*. Tears stood at the edges of her eyes.

'If I tell you,' she said, 'you'll kick me out of the Ministry. You'll kick us both out, me and Anna. But – if I don't – Anna's in trouble. I think it's serious.'

'How do you know?' asked Hazel.

'Do you have the decoded version of the latest message?' asked Zosia. 'I only took it down; I didn't decode it. Let me see it.'

'No!' said Hazel.

'All right,' said Zosia. 'Does it have the word *art* in it? You can just look; I know you have it.'

'I— Fine,' said Hazel. She shook out her shoulders, tipped her neck to the side, breathed in again. She put her hand in her pocket and pulled out the decoded message – just a flimsy piece of paper from a code pad, a little bit yellow, one side torn off. Light dazzled through it, and Hazel bent her head to read it. I saw her give a start.

'What does it mean?' she asked.

'So it is there!'

'Yes,' said Hazel. Her voice was suddenly wobbly.

'It's our code – mine and Anna's. We agreed that if either of us were ever in danger, we'd send a message with "*art*" in it. It means just one thing: *save me*.'

61

'Yes, but what does Anna need to be saved from? What have you been doing? Zosh, please!'

'Listen to me,' said Zosia. 'I'll explain as much as I can. You have to believe me on the rest. Can you do that?'

'I don't know,' said Hazel slowly. 'Try.'

'Anna and I – we've been on a mission of our own,' explained Zosia. 'It's not legal but it's – it's right. It's good. That's all I can say. We've been doing it since last summer, and for a while it was all going well. But in November something went wrong. Our contact across the Channel stopped responding to messages. We didn't know what was going on – so someone needed to go to France to find out what had happened. Anna was the right person to do it because of her— Oh, never mind that. She was going to tell the Ministry that she had glandular fever while she was away, so you wouldn't suspect anything. But then, at the end of November, she got a field mission from Miss Lessing. It was to leave on the sixth of December, and she had to be embedded in Paris for two months – absolutely the wrong part of France for what we needed. We thought it was all over.'

'And then we realized there *was* a way to make sure that Anna went on her mission for the Ministry in Paris, and *also* went to do what we needed her to in Calais. We just needed to split her in two. If I pretended to be Anna and went on the Ministry mission in her place, she'd be free to go to Calais to find out what had gone wrong. Like I said, it wasn't something I could do. But I knew I could pretend to be Anna, for the Ministry. I know her poem code, and how to speak French, after all – I've done all the training she has. We could use the same fever excuse and pretend I was convalescing for two months, so that the Ministry wouldn't think it was strange that I didn't show up for work.

'We didn't think – we didn't really think about how we'd sort it all out again. We thought that Anna and I could swap back, and no one would notice. But it didn't work out that way. When I was due to be extracted, I sent Anna a message. I waited for her at the airfield that night – but she didn't show up. I couldn't get on the plane – I realized Daisy was being dropped by the same plane that was supposed to pick Anna up, and she would have spotted me at once and rumbled the whole plan, so I had to run away. I ended up having to get back to London another way, through our contacts – they told me that Anna had left to look for someone, I can't say who, and she hadn't come back. And that's the last I heard of her until those messages began coming through in Daisy's poem code, but with that extra word that Anna and I had talked about before we left.

'I heard you thinking about calling off the mission because it's not Daisy, but I *know* it's Anna. She's found Daisy, somehow, and she's trying to get them both out. Please, you have to listen. She's lied to you, but she's still a Ministry agent.'

Hazel huffed and folded her arms. For a moment she looked a lot like May.

'Yes, but what about Miss Fig?' I asked. 'You two killed her! You had to have done!'

'I told you, I didn't!' said Zosia. 'We didn't. But Miss Fig did find out what we were doing. She was such a busybody! We realized because . . . well, in mid November, Miss Fig began to act differently. It frightened us both. She'd come to our flat door and just . . . smile at us. And then she spoke to Anna one afternoon, and told Anna she'd found out what was going on.'

'She'd found the codes in a book Anna had lent her,' I said.

Zosia stared at me. 'Not quite. Yes, it was one of the books we were using, but Anna didn't lend it to her on purpose. Miss Fig would come into our flat to borrow books sometimes, and one day she picked it up from the kitchen table. I didn't notice until she came by to tell us what she'd discovered. She asked for – for money, to keep it secret; otherwise she'd go to the authorities. She kept sending us threatening letters. We gave her money, and then everything valuable we had, which wasn't much; Anna even gave Miss Fig her favourite gold necklace, but it wasn't enough. Miss Fig always asked for more. We hoped that if Anna went away she'd stop – we couldn't think of anything else to do.

'I took Anna to the train station on the morning of the sixth, and then I went home to get ready to leave myself. When the fog came in, I was terrified – I thought I'd never get away. But of course the mission was rescheduled for the next night, and everything went off without a hitch. And that's the last I heard about any of it, until Miss Fig's body was found last week.'

'Anna left on the sixth?' I said. 'But – the fog—'

'She left London in the morning,' said Zosia. 'The nine thirty-three to Folkestone. She wanted to miss Cecil, so he wouldn't get upset saying goodbye. She gave me the other half of her ticket – it's in my purse. Go and look, if you like.'

I gaped at her. But if Anna hadn't been in the mews on the night of the sixth, then she couldn't have helped with the murder. It made sense of why she hadn't been at dinner that night, but it ruled out one of our killers. And if Anna wasn't there – then Zosia *couldn't* have done it all on her own. We'd proved that there needed to be at least two people involved.

'We're not working against the Ministry!' said Zosia. 'You have to trust me! Please!'

'It's not as simple as trusting you,' said Hazel. 'You know that. We'll have to discuss it upstairs.'

After that, things at the Ministry got even more panicky.

Zosia was left down in the basement, while everyone else talked in one of the offices. No one could agree whether Zosia was telling the truth, and what it meant, and whether the mission should still go ahead.

'Can we at least look in her purse?' said May. 'I bet she's lying about that!'

So I ran to get Zosia's handbag, abandoned beside her station, and when I opened up her crocodile-skin purse I saw half a ticket, worn and yellowed with handling.

'It's true!' I said, showing it to May and Eric. I couldn't understand it – none of us could. We'd gone wrong again.

'Go back to the mews for a while,' said George, coming out of his office. 'We'll come and get you if we need you. Try not to get into trouble.'

Which was a pretty ridiculous thing to say. I knew he was distracted. George is usually a lot better than that.

But, actually, this was useful for us. I looked at May and Eric, and knew we were all thinking the same thing. We were all desperate to have a meeting, to discuss what we'd found out, and we knew that Zosia's flat would be empty.

Pfote tried to come along with us out of the front door, but Eric crouched down on the pavement in front of her and said very seriously, 'I think it's best you don't come with us, Pfote. I think they need you here.'

Pfote mewed and padded back inside.

'I really think he can talk to animals,' whispered May to me.

'Everyone can talk to cats,' said Eric, shrugging. 'It's just that most people don't say anything they want to hear.'

62

We rushed back to the mews as fast as we could. May kept trying to start the meeting in the middle of the street, until Eric or I hissed at her. We didn't know who might be listening.

The door of the Mortensens' house was open, and the General was dozing in the spring sunshine. He opened one eye when we came clattering over the cobbles, barked and fell back asleep. Mrs Goodchild was out on her front step, spraying her plants. She waved at us and smiled.

'Good afternoon!' she said. 'Are you three hungry? I just baked a new cake!'

'No!' cried May, shaking her head. Mrs Goodchild looked confused.

'May!' I hissed. '*Don't!* This is a good opportunity! We can have the meeting afterwards. *Come on!*'

'I'm sorry, Mrs Goodchild,' said Eric. 'We'd love to, thank you.'

'Wonderful!' said Mrs Goodchild. 'Let me just wash my hands. I've made a carrot cake. I'm not sure about it – it's quite carroty – but it'll have to do, and then there's some potatoes and a bit of bread, and Cecil got some eggs in yesterday. Samuel, look who's here! It's the children – didn't you want to talk to Eric about drawing?'

Mr Goodchild stood up from his chair. He was wearing a beautiful three-piece suit, his little gold glasses perched on his nose.

'Ah! Eric!' he cried. 'You remembered!'

I felt pretty bad at that, and I could tell Eric did too. He swallowed and nodded.

'Now, lad, show me your drawings,' said Mr Goodchild.

Eric pulled a little notebook out of his pocket and handed it over. I was surprised – I hadn't realized he'd have anything with him – and I was even more surprised when Mr Goodchild opened it and began to flick through it. There were pages of drawings – buildings, mostly, in Eric's careful, logical lines, everything beautifully detailed, even down to the cracks in the brickwork, the way a bomb had sheered away half a wall. But there were figures too. Whole pages of Pfote, sitting up with her tail around her paws or curled on her back. The General, mouth open barking. And me and May – May hunched up with her gas mask dangling from her shoulder, me bending down to peer at something, my glasses slipping down my nose. Eric hadn't got May's mouth quite right, and my hair looked kind of weird, but it was definitely us.

'These are good, Eric!' said Mr Goodchild, and I nodded.

'They're all right,' said May with a sniff. 'You've done the hands wrong.'

'Hands are difficult!' said Mr Goodchild. 'Here, let me show you something. You need to look at the *structure* of the hands – don't see them as separate parts. Fetch me that book over there. I want you to see how the masters manage.'

He and Eric bent over the sketchbook, and May and I were left alone to look around the room. I could hear Mrs Goodchild in the kitchen, singing as she worked.

I went up to the mantelpiece and stared at the family pictures. There was Mr and Mrs Goodchild on their wedding day, standing under an arch and shining with happiness, then photos of two different wrinkly little babies in white, then a family portrait – Mr and Mrs Goodchild and two little boys in trousers. Cecil, about six, staring angrily away to one side, and another child, about our age, looking directly into the camera. This child had dark, curly hair, cut short, a hungry face and a fierce expression, and I could see Mr Goodchild's hand, holding them in place. The inscription underneath the picture read: *Samuel, Miriam,* ▆▆▆ *and Cecil Goodchild, 1931*. The third name had been blacked out heavily and the name *Anna* written above it in the same looping, careful script that I'd seen in the picture in her room.

This is who it's all about, I thought. Anna. This whole mystery – it's because of *her*. She wasn't the victim, or the murderer – I knew that now. I thought I understood who she was at last. But where did she fit in? I still wasn't sure.

'Nuala,' said May suddenly in my ear. I jumped. I usually hear May coming, but I'd been so focused on the photos that I hadn't noticed her. She was standing right next to me, brows lowered and mouth in a frown. 'Nuala, *listen*.'

63

I wasn't sure what she meant. There wasn't anything weird going on, as far as I'd heard. Just Mr Goodchild and Eric talking, the swish of pencils on paper and the purr of pages being turned over, and, behind that, Mrs Goodchild singing in the kitchen along with the click and tap of things being put onto plates.

'—and of course, once you've learned all this, you'll be able to move on to your own style,' said Mr Goodchild to Eric. 'More recently, painters have been doing very interesting things with form. Kandinsky, of course, and Klee, and Matisse— Ah, pass me that book. You must look at Kokoschka—'

I shook my head, and May groaned. 'You're hopeless! Actually *listen*!'

I didn't get her. It all felt so normal that it gave me a kind of pang. It was such a nice house to be in. It was just the way Mam, Da and I used to be together, when I was a little kid – Mam whispering to herself as she learned lines, me writing a new play, Da cutting himself a sandwich and singing one of his silly songs, *Óró, sé do bheatha abhaile, anois ar theacht an tsamhraidh*—

And then I realized why I'd been reminded of that. Mrs Goodchild wasn't singing in English, any more than Da had been. They were words I didn't understand, and they jumbled up in my ears the way any language does, to people who don't know it. It can sound strange, backwards, until your ear tunes into it.

'Oh!' I gasped, and May said, 'I know! I know! You *see*!'

Mrs Goodchild came in then, carrying a silver tray piled up with nice food.

'That's a pretty song,' I said, keeping my face open and my voice light.

'Isn't it!' said Mrs Goodchild. 'My bubbe taught it me. It's just a silly Yiddish nursery rhyme. Ah, you're looking at our pictures. Weren't the children sweet when they were little? I don't know what happened to them.'

She said this loudly, and I looked up to see Cecil coming down the stairs.

'Very funny, Mum,' he said. 'I'm going out.'

'Oh, stay for tea first!' said Mrs Goodchild. 'The children were just looking at your baby photos. Cecil was such a sweet baby, and so was Anna.'

I saw Mr Goodchild look up at that. Mrs Goodchild's hand on the tea tray faltered, and the tray rattled.

'Did you say *Anna*?' asked Cecil, folding his arms in his

leather jacket. 'You're talking about her now? You never do, unless we have guests.'

'Because you know perfectly well that Anna is on a business trip,' said Mr Goodchild firmly. 'She will be home when she can.'

'Then why doesn't she *write*?' asked Cecil. 'I don't believe it.'

'Have you considered that she might not be able to write from wherever she is?' asked Mr Goodchild.

'Where is she that she couldn't write? That's nonsense, Dad, and you know it! Something's happened to Anna, but you won't admit it!'

'Nothing has happened to Anna! She's perfectly all right! I've told you, we said goodbye to her on the morning she left—'

'And I've told you that I think you're lying,' said Cecil, and he swung the door open and rushed outside. Actually, he said some stuff that was much ruder than that, but I don't think I can write it down here. I'm not totally sure how to spell some of it.

There was a rumbling outside, and a van pulled to a stop outside the window.

I heard Mr Goodchild's pencil pause on the page, and Mrs Goodchild froze halfway through cutting May's slice of cake. They both stared at each other.

'They're early,' said Mrs Goodchild softly.

'What's early?' asked May. 'Can I have that cake?'

I nudged her.

'Yes, of course, dear,' said Mrs Goodchild. 'And it's nothing. Just a few things for Mr Harris at Number Six. Art pieces that Samuel helped him buy.'

'But you said,' said May, who never can be quiet, 'that art should all be taken out of London during the war so it can be safe. Why's he bringing it here?'

'Never you mind,' said Mrs Goodchild, suddenly strict. It surprised me. I'd never heard her talk like that before. 'Go on, eat your cake.'

I was fizzing. Something was happening, I could tell. I turned my eyes to Eric and saw him staring at me. He had a really intense expression on his face, actually, and his hands – his hands were very gently moving in what I realized was semaphore code.

K – L – E – E, he motioned, and I must have looked confused because he shook his head and dropped his hands back onto his sketchbook.

And then there was a knock on the door.

Mrs Goodchild turned away from it, but Mr Goodchild got up and went ambling over to answer it. I was totally on the alert now. I knew whatever was behind that door was going to be really important.

And it was.

A man was standing there. He looked tired, and his clothes were a little dusty, but I could tell they were good. He looked polite, and friendly, like someone's uncle.

'Good afternoon, Samuel,' he said to Mr Goodchild, and he reached forward and squeezed Mr Goodchild's hand. 'All here safely, thanks to A—'

'Yakob!' said Mr Goodchild, squeezing back so hard that the man stopped halfway through the word.

He was behaving very oddly – I could tell he was thrilled to see Yakob, but he kept glancing back at us guiltily. What was this?

'Delighted, delighted,' Mr Goodchild continued. 'Well, I won't keep you – I know you're very busy.'

I saw Yakob frown.

'Mr Levy is helping arrange the pictures in Mr Harris's house,' said Mrs Goodchild in a clear voice. 'Which is very kind of him.'

She was talking too much. We hadn't asked her any of that – she was just filling up the air with chatter. That's what you do when you're nervous, and that's how people try to distract you from the fact they're lying.

'Ah, yes,' said Mr Levy, nodding and stepping away into the street again. The door closed behind him.

Right then, a picture was building up in my head. The song from the kitchen. The van and Mr Levy. The fact that Cecil hadn't said goodbye to Anna, but Mr and Mrs Goodchild had.

I finally thought I might have the answer.

64

'Do you know, I think we ought to be going,' I said to Mrs Goodchild. 'Thank you so much for the tea. It was delicious.' (I was really laying it on thick, giving her my best English Fiona.)

'It *was* nice,' said May, when I prodded her.

'Thank you so much for the lesson,' said Eric to Mr Goodchild. 'It was very useful.'

'You're welcome,' said Mr Goodchild. He was still looking at Mrs Goodchild as though something quite terrible had happened.

'Come on!' I said, and I scampered out of the house, May and Eric following me.

I was trembling with all the energy I was holding in. We ran across the mews and up into Zosia's empty flat.

'What's happened?' whispered Eric, as soon as I'd slammed the door behind us, and I knew we were safe. 'Did you see me signing to you? I found a clue!'

'No, *we* found a clue!' said May. 'It's a really big one!'

We all stared at each other, and then May said, 'Oh, come on, Nuala! Say it!'

'May spotted it first!' I said.

'Mrs Goodchild was singing a song in Yiddish,' said May, nodding. 'And it sounded strange to us, because we don't speak Yiddish. *You* know how it is.'

'Oh, yes!' said Eric, nodding. 'When I first heard English I thought I was listening wrong. I suppose that's why I didn't notice anything odd about the song – Yiddish sounds a bit like German.'

'Yes, exactly. But if you heard a language your ears *weren't* used to, especially in the middle of the night in a fog, *you might think the person was speaking backwards.*'

'OH!' said Eric. 'So . . . the person Colette heard – they were just speaking another language! But which language? It can't be English or French, because Colette's used to hearing those. Or Norwegian, either, because Mrs Mortensen's Norwegian, so she'd probably pick up a little bit. Miss Charney's mother's Czech – I heard her mention that once – oh, and Zosia knows Serbian and Polish. Then . . . is it still Zosia?'

I shook my head. 'Maybe, but . . . wait. I think we might be overcomplicating things. Colette said that she heard a man outside her window, speaking a language that she didn't know – and there's only one man in the mews who we haven't ruled out yet.'

'Mr Goodchild!' gasped May.

'And if he was talking in Yiddish, which Colette doesn't know, there's only one person who he'd be talking to, since we ruled Anna and Cecil out,' said Eric. '*Mrs* Goodchild. Do you really think it could be them?'

'It must be!' I said. 'Maybe Anna told them about Miss Fig blackmailing her, and they decided to do something about it?'

'So you think that they're part of whatever mission Anna and Zosia were on?' asked May. 'But what was it? We still don't know! Zosia wouldn't tell us.'

'I think I know,' said Eric. 'That's what I worked out when I signalled at you, just now. *Klee.*'

'Bless you,' said May.

'No, Klee! Remember, in Anna's book? K-L-E-E. May, you said you thought it might have been K. Lee, but Mr Goodchild said it to me this afternoon. There's an artist called Paul Klee.'

'So?'

'So, we thought the message we found in Miss Fig's house was about food smuggling. But we know Miss Fig was sending Anna and Zosia blackmail messages. What if this was a draft of the latest one of them? What if it wasn't food smuggling but something else? Remember Anna and Zosia's code word? *Art.*'

He opened his sketchbook again, at the page where he'd carefully taped in the scraps of paper we'd found in Miss Fig's house, and put it down on the worn wood of the kitchen table.

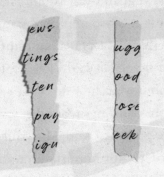

'*Paintings!*' he said, pointing. 'Look! One of the words we couldn't work out before!'

I looked, and then I had— I don't know how to describe it. Or maybe I do. It was like those moments where I can suddenly imagine where the person coding the message I've been working on had gone wrong with their spelling or the code key. I can see the kind of person they are, and how they think, and that means I can break the code.

'And if that's *paintings*, then – Oh! Look at *ood*. What if that's not *food* at all? What if that's *Goodchild*?'

We stared at each other, gasping.

'The Goodchilds are smuggling paintings into England,' I said. 'That's what Anna and Zosia were doing: helping them. That's why Mr and Mrs Goodchild haven't been worried about Anna, like Cecil is – they've known where she is. And – and Mr Harris from Number Six is helping

365

them too. That's what the van is, and the man who just came to the door – he's brought new paintings!'

'But why?' asked May. '*Art?* It's not important.'

'It is to Mr Goodchild,' I said. 'Remember what he said in the shelter, about what he's doing at work? Maybe he's trying to save more paintings from the war.'

'It still isn't important,' said May stubbornly. 'Not as important as people. Not important enough to lie to the Ministry about. It doesn't make sense. This whole thing doesn't make sense. Why *paintings?* It's silly! They're not people! Why would you kill someone for *art?*'

I was sure that wasn't right. Something was bothering me. The man we'd met just now had been called Mr Levy – I was certain I'd heard that name before somewhere. Someone had mentioned it, and I couldn't think why.

And then I looked again at the scraps of paper in Eric's book, and I spotted something else.

'Look!' I gasped. 'This, here. *Rose.* If *ood* is Goodchild, then what if this is the name of someone else from the mews? Miss Wimpress – Miss Charney calls her *Prim*, but her full name is Primrose. *Rose.* What if she's mixed up in this too?'

'Nuala, you genius!' yelped May. 'Hurry! Hurry! She'll be back from work now, won't she? We need to go talk to her! What are we waiting for? Let's go now!'

65

But it wasn't Miss Wimpress who answered the door of Number 5 – it was Miss Charney.

'Can I help you?' she asked. She looked kind of confused, and a bit distracted.

'We've come to talk to Miss Wimpress,' said May, glaring at her.

'She's still at work,' said Miss Charney. 'She must be working late today. You've got me instead. What do you want?'

'We want—' said May, and paused.

'We only wanted to see how she was,' I said quickly. 'We know she's sad about Miss Fig, and we wanted to see if she's all right.'

I saw May make a face, and Eric prod her. He nodded his head at me in encouragement.

'Prim's perfectly fine,' said Miss Charney. 'Why have you got it in your heads that she isn't? She and Miss Fig weren't on very good terms.'

'But she told us they'd begun to talk again!' said May, scowling. 'After her accident!'

'*That* was all Miss Fig,' said Miss Charney angrily. 'Playing the poor-little-me card for all it was worth. She wasn't nearly as hurt as she made out to Prim. I saw her! Walking perfectly well, then pretending she could barely hobble when Prim came by. She always did know how to get Prim on her side. She was planning something. Prim's so soft-hearted; she can't be trusted. Even after the awful rows they had last summer! Well, I knew what she was, even if Prim didn't. I told her to stay away. Not that she listened to me. But then Miss Fig's house was damaged, and she began talking about going to stay with the Lowndes family, and I hoped it would all be over. I hoped she wouldn't come back. But, of course, now she has. Awful woman!'

She ground her teeth and folded her arms.

'Huh,' said May carefully. 'Anyway, Miss Wimpress works with Mr Goodchild, doesn't she? At the museum? Are they friends, outside that? Does she spend much time with him?'

'They're neighbours,' said Miss Charney, staring at her. 'We're all in and out of each other's houses. Haven't you noticed by now?'

I looked around the living room while they talked. It was the same shape as Mr and Mrs Goodchild's. It was weird, being in all those houses. Each of them was so similar to the others that it was as though I could see the ghost of all of them when I was in each one, overlaid like panels of lace. Miss Wimpress and Miss Charney's room was darker than Mr and Mrs Goodchild's, the walls a deep blue instead of their pale green. There were prints of motor cars on the walls, one of Mr Goodchild's paintings of course, little bronze statuettes, a big leather sofa and a cut-glass drinks set. It felt quite a lot like being in a man's house – it didn't go with shy, sweet Miss Wimpress much, until I remembered that she had only moved in last year. Of course, this had been Miss Charney's house first. But I could see touches of Miss Wimpress – her pile of art books on top of one of the book cases, her fencing glove on the side table and her foil leaning against the mantelpiece, her reading glasses on a pile of magazines.

'Do you know where Anna Goodchild is?' asked May. She even took me by surprise, Diary; she was so sudden. Miss Charney flinched.

'Anna?' she asked. 'Why? She's on a business trip, isn't she? She's nothing to do with this.'

And I knew right then that another piece of the puzzle had slotted into place.

66

As we left Number 5, I saw Eric looking at his father's watch. It was five thirty, almost the end of the afternoon. In a few hours, the raids might start. And, very soon after that, Hazel would be getting on an aeroplane to France – if the mission went ahead, that is.

'Miss Charney knows where Anna is,' I said, as soon as Eric had wriggled over the side of the roof, and we were all sitting in a row leaning against the railing. The sun was starting to move down the sky, and up here the wind was a little chilly. 'The way she flinched – she *knows* something. I mean, maybe not exactly where she is, but enough. And if she knows, then she's working with Miss Wimpress, and Mr and Mrs Goodchild.'

'I still don't understand what's so important about this art stuff,' said May, scowling. 'It's just paint! Anyone can do it!'

'Not anyone, May!' said Eric. 'It's like writing a story. It's special, and personal, and important. But I agree; I don't see why half the street is involved. Mr Harris must be too, if they're using his house!'

I nodded. 'And Miss Fig noticed it was happening.' It was all making sense, at last. It felt so good, balancing ideas between the three of us like balloons.

'After Miss Charney or Miss Wimpress ran her down and hurt her, you mean!' said May. 'She watched everyone in the mews, and then she found Anna's book and worked it all out. And so Zosia and Miss Wimpress – no, wait, Zosia and Mrs Goodchild – no, wait, Miss Charney and Mr Goodchild – *I* don't know who – bumped her off by poisoning her and stabbing her. Wait, Miss Wimpress is a fencer. Is that a clue? Can you stab someone to death with a fencing sword?'

'I don't think you can. And it can't be *all* of them,' said Eric. 'We just have to work out which ones.'

And I suddenly remembered seeing different people passing each other books – people who really wouldn't have the same taste in reading at all.

I'd seen the mews as a sort of dorm for adults, hadn't I? Everyone part of everyone else's business? You might not like everyone in your dorm, but when another dorm plays a prank on someone in your dorm, the whole dorm has to retaliate. It's the principle of the thing. You work together.

'What if everyone *did*?' I asked. 'I mean – not *everyone*. Not Cecil, or Mr Abiola, or the Mortensen kids. But everyone else. What if they all helped? What if the whole street are smugglers?'

PART EIGHT

WE ARE STRUCK BY THE TRUTH

67

From the diary of Fionnuala O'Malley

Thursday 3rd April, continued

'*What?*' whispered May. Obviously, being May, she kind of blared it. 'Really? Wait – does that mean they're all murderers too? They can't be!'

I knew what she meant. 'But Mr and Mrs Goodchild are *nice*,' I said miserably.

'Mrs Mortensen isn't particularly nice,' said May.

'Yes, she is,' said Eric. 'She wouldn't let Miss Fig get rid of the General. And she stays with him during the air raids. That counts.'

'She can't get down to the shelter!' said May.

'She could ask someone to carry her,' pointed out Eric. 'But she doesn't, and not just because she wants to keep her dignity. She knows how much Colette loves him, and she wants to look after him for her. So they're all nice. Why would they kill someone just because of *paintings*—'

He stopped, then stared at us, eyes wide. Eric's not someone who usually pauses in the middle of sentences. He says what he wants to, tidily, and then waits for an answer.

'Oh,' he said. 'I think I know why. We just— We need to get up into the attics, now.'

Now it was May's turn for her eyes to go wide. 'Why?' she asked.

'If I'm right, you'll see,' said Eric. 'Come on! Hurry! Miss Fig's house.'

'What happened to you being afraid of it falling down?' I said.

'Because if I'm right, we can't use Mr Harris's house! That's part of it! Come on!'

We raced across the mews cobbles. There was no time for trickery. We all felt it – we were in a race against time now, before the planes came.

The General howled at us through the window of Number 3.

'Where are you three going so quickly?' called Colette, sticking her head out from her front door, Olivier in her arms.

'We're playing wardens!' I gasped. 'We're on a mission!'

'Funny children,' said Colette. 'Don't get yourselves hurt, all right?'

That's the good thing about parents who have little kids – they just think you're too old to worry about.

We rushed in through the wreck of Miss Fig's blasted living room and up the stairs. They creaked and groaned under us, and Eric and I grabbed hands nervously. May wasn't scared at all, especially not when we were on the trail of . . . whatever it was.

Eric and I shoved May up into the dark gap, then I pushed Eric up while May grabbed his wrists, and finally they both hung down and dragged me up. I felt splinters digging into my sweater, my feet kicked at air, and then I was lying cheek pressed against bare boards, heart beating hard in my chest.

'What's up here?' I asked.

'SHHH!' said Eric. 'We've got to be quiet. *Seriously* quiet. May, this is important. Pretend you're surrounded by enemy agents, and follow me into the crawl space. Torches off.'

'Ooh!' said May. Her eyes were still huge and round with excitement, and she was jogging from foot to foot.

'*Quiet!*' Eric whispered.

We were quiet. We crept forward into the little space, and followed Eric as he wriggled along, past the Mortensens' attic, and the Goodchilds' attic, full of Mr Goodchild's easels and paintings, and Miss Charney and Miss Wimpress's attic, and on into Mr Harris's. Eric led us out of the crawl space, towards the opening down into the house. We peered into the room below – and found it very different from the last time we'd been there.

The bed had been made, and there were towels and clothes laid out on it. A woman was sitting on the bed, and the man we'd met before, Mr Levy, was standing next to her, speaking to her in a language that sounded like French.

I understood then. Mr Levy – I *had* heard about him before. Mr Goodchild had talked about working with him. And May had been right. The smuggling operation wasn't just about paintings at all. It was also about *people* – bringing people who couldn't get to England otherwise, to make them safe from the Nazis.

This was why Anna and Zosia had wanted to keep their mission secret, and why it had mattered so much. This was why, when Miss Fig found out about it, she realized she could blackmail Anna for the money she needed after Miss Wimpress moved out – until someone decided to stop Miss Fig. And then, when the Chief Inspector turned up, Zosia decided to set the explosive trap to try to stop *him*, and stop the truth coming out.

Oh, I felt so torn, Diary. I so admired what the people in the mews had been doing. And I didn't like Miss Fig, who'd been cruel to Miss Wimpress, and who hadn't minded putting people's lives in danger just for her own gain. But murder's murder, isn't it? You just can't go around killing people.

'Go back!' hissed Eric, and the three of us wriggled backwards, through the crawl space, until we were in Miss Fig's attic again.

'So the mews has been helping bring refugees to England!' said May with a squeak. 'Illegal refugees!'

It sounds crazy, Diary, but even people who are trying to escape the Nazis aren't just allowed to turn up in England. I knew that if the police found out about Mr Levy, they'd arrive and arrest him and put them in one of those horrible internment camps in case he was a Nazi sympathizer – a camp just like the one Eric's father is in now. I knew Eric had realized that too. His eyes were damp, and his cheeks were bright pink with distress.

'It isn't right, that they're having to be hidden,' said Eric. 'Everyone should be allowed to be safe here. But, of course, if Miss Fig had gone to the police, then everyone in the mews would be in trouble. *That's* why someone wanted her dead. And that's why I don't trust the police! Thank goodness we didn't say anything to the Chief Inspector!'

'But if that's their mission,' I said, 'then they haven't been working against the Ministry at all. They're doing good things, not working for the *other side*! We have to tell Hazel. She has to get on the plane to save Daisy and Anna! What time is it?'

'Quarter past six,' said Eric, looking at his father's watch. 'There's time, if we run.'

We *ran*.

68

It was almost six thirty when we hammered on the Ministry's front door. Hazel opened it, looking harassed.

'What are you doing here?' she asked. 'Didn't we tell you to go back to the mews?'

'Yes, but listen!' May gabbled. 'We've got important information about your mission tonight! You have to go! You have to – Zosia's all right. She's not a traitor!'

Hazel stared at her – at the three of us, all panting and red-faced and frantic.

'Come in and explain properly,' she said. I told you she was the good kind of adult, Diary.

We all spilled into the front hall, where Pfote was sitting curled up on her cushion, grooming her tail.

'Explain,' said Hazel again. '*Properly*, in order.'

So we did. I think we got a little mixed up around the middle bit – and it did sound kind of made up. I mean, a whole street full of people being part of a smuggling ring? Someone committing murder because of it? But I think Hazel believed us, because she frowned (looking suddenly really like May again) and said, 'Yes, but, no matter the reason, you still can't kill people!'

Which was just what I had thought myself, and was a fair point.

By the time we'd finished, George and Ralph had come out of the downstairs office, and Miss Lessing had come down from her department. They all seemed very interested, if a bit confused.

'I vote we put this to Zosia,' said George at last. 'See if she can back it up.'

'But if she killed someone!' said Hazel reproachfully.

'She said she didn't. She might not be lying. As far as I can tell, she only held back exactly what she and Anna have been doing, and this answers that. And we're at war, Hazel. You know what it means, to be on a mission in a war. You know people have to get hurt sometimes. What do you think Daisy's been doing in France?'

'I don't *know*,' said Hazel. 'That's the point.'

We all trooped down the stairs to the basement, Hazel helping George with his crutches. Zosia was still there, squinting in the light from the Anglepoise lamp, her arms bound up behind her back. I spotted that someone had put more restraints on her, at some point since we'd been there last. I felt kind of bad for her – it couldn't have been comfortable.

'A proper interrogation,' she said when she saw us, her voice a little croaky. 'Can I have some water?'

'No,' said George, just as Hazel said, 'Yes.' They looked at each other, George with one eyebrow raised, and then Hazel went over to Zosia and gave her a sip from the water glass on the table in front of her.

'We know about Mr Levy,' said May, and I saw Zosia stiffen her arms and set her jaw.

'I don't know what you mean,' she said.

'No, listen, we know everything!' said May. 'How you've been sneaking people into England from Europe, and how Miss Fig found out about it and tried to blackmail you. And we know that Anna didn't betray the Ministry, even though she's been in hiding in France. We know *everything*!'

'May, we have to work on your interview technique,' said Hazel quietly.

'So you don't know everything,' said Zosia, tipping her head up to stare straight at May. 'You still don't know who killed Miss Fig.'

'Do you?' I asked. I felt scared for a moment.

'I have no idea,' said Zosia. 'But if you've found out about our operation, and you've passed the information to the Ministry, then there's no more point hiding.'

'There never was!' said George. 'Why haven't you told us any of this before? We'd have helped you, Zosh!'

Zosia sighed. 'Because you work for the government,'

she said. 'And what we've been doing is illegal. All right, I'll explain.

'It all started last summer, around the fall of France. Listen, before I say more – if you're recording this, you'll need to burn the recordings. Do you understand? This is secret. Do you promise?'

'Zosh, you know we can't,' said Hazel. 'But we'll be as careful as we can be. I promise that.'

Zosia nodded, wincing. 'The fall of France,' she said again. 'Colette Mortensen and her family came over on a boat. Her husband is Mrs Mortensen's son, and because she's a British citizen he and the children had British passports; they lied and said that Colette also had one, but it'd been left behind. And they brought someone else to England too. A little French Jewish boy – the son of one of Colette's friends. He had an uncle and aunt in Wales, but no passport – so the Mortensens lied, and said that he was their son, and his passport had gone missing as well.

'It all worked. The boy stayed with the Mortensens for a few days, and then his relatives collected him. His parents had sent him with a piece of art, to help pay for his board – a Degas sketch. Colette spoke to Mr Goodchild about how to go about selling it without raising suspicions – and that's how it started. The plan, I mean.'

I remembered Margot talking about the boy on the boat, who'd come back for tea. We'd heard the truth early on – we just hadn't understood what it meant.

'But *people*!' said May. 'Why does everyone care so much about stupid art? If you don't save the *people*, then none of that matters!'

'Of course,' said Zosia. 'The art was only ever the cover for what we were really doing. The people – friends and relatives, usually; we've all got people in Europe we want to get out – they're picked up and brought across the Channel by boat, and then they all arrive in Hogarth Mews before they're moved on to somewhere safe. Mr Goodchild uses all the channels that he and Miss Wimpress have established for moving valuable art around the UK. They give everyone fake identities as art curators and their families, so there are no questions asked.

'And, so far, it's worked. Colette helps – she has connections with the Free French, of course. And so does Mr Harris, the lawyer who lives in Number Six – he works on getting fake visas sorted. Mrs Mortensen provides everyone with clothes from her committees too. The first people arrived in September. We found a removals company who would deliver them to the mews. They stayed in Mr Harris's house for a few days – Mrs Winstone the housekeeper would bring food to them – and then they would be taken on into the country, to the Lowndes family and some others. We've brought across twenty-six people by now.

'And the rest – well, the rest you know. I didn't kill Miss Fig, I swear it. But she found out about the operation, and she was blackmailing us. I've still got the final note she left – it's in my handbag. I can show you.'

'But we've already looked in your handbag!' said May indignantly.

'Hidden pocket,' said Zosia, raising her eyebrows. 'I am a spy, May. Hazel, if you would? It's under the lining. There – yes, that's right.'

Hazel dug through Zosia's handbag, and exclaimed as she got to the pocket. 'Here! Oh!'

She pulled out a piece of paper and put it down on the table. We all crowded around it, and I gasped.

Anna,

As I have said before, I know that the residents of Hogarth Mews are smuggling people into the country under cover of moving art such as paintings and sculptures. Samuel and Miriam Goodchild are in charge of the efforts, with the help of Zosia Stosic, Hilda and Colette Mortensen, and Elfie Charney and Primrose Wimpress. I also know you are about to travel to Europe to help bring more people over. If you do not pay me ten pounds by Sunday, I will go to the authorities with this information. Do not doubt me.

Paula Figueroa

It was the completed version of the letter that we'd found the scraps of. She must have written a few different drafts, and destroyed the ones she didn't send. We'd been right.

'So what do you say?' asked Zosia. 'Is it enough? Do you believe me now? And will you go and help Anna?'

Hazel took a deep breath, looked her straight in the eyes, and said, 'Yes.'

69

After that, things moved fast. Hazel ran up the stairs with Miss Lessing, and then came back down again half an hour later looking totally unlike herself, her black hair in a severe bun and a pair of glasses on her nose. She checked her papers, then George pulled her into a careful hug.

'If she can be found, I'll bring her back,' she whispered to him.

'Thank you,' said George, blinking quickly.

Without another word, Hazel picked up her luggage and walked quickly out of the boring back door of the Ministry. Even her walk looked different. If you'd been watching the Ministry building, you might not even recognize her as the person who'd come to work that morning.

She was barely out of the door before the siren went.

'Go on,' said George. 'Down to the shelter in the basement.'

'No,' I said. 'I think we need to go to the Hogarth Mews shelter.'

Maybe it was silly of me, but since we'd heard Zosia's non-confession I needed to understand. I needed to *know*. We had the answer to one of the biggest secrets of Hogarth

Mews. We knew what Anna and Zosia had been doing, and why. We knew that everyone had been behind the smuggling operation. But who had been behind the murder? Was it everyone, or not? What had really happened to Miss Fig?

Instead of saying no, George just nodded. He's one of the good adults too. 'Then I'll come with you,' he said.

'I will too,' said Zosia.

'No, you won't,' said George. 'Stay here with Hetty and Ralph. You can't be a part of this.'

So it was just the four of us – May, Eric, me and George – who went hurrying through the darkening streets. You have to move with all your senses in a raid: pay attention, or you'll go over on your behind. I couldn't think about where we were going – I had to keep focusing on the pavement in front of me. I felt a tiny bit sick.

May, of course, had found a way to argue with George.

'You have to stay quiet!' I heard her hiss. 'You're only here to observe!'

'All right! This is your case, Little Wong. I won't queer your pitch.'

'Don't call me Little Wong! It's very rude! You know I'm almost eleven! Now, you have to listen to everything we say and agree with it and arrest the murderers.'

'I'll hit them with a crutch,' said George. 'That do? Remember I'm doing you a kindness, coming down to the shelter with you. You know stairs don't much agree with me these days.'

'You're being *silly*!' cried May, and someone passing us on the other side of the pavement said, 'Shh!'

'Are we ready?' May asked us when we were beside the entrance to the shelter. The sky was orange and smoky with fires.

'*Are* we ready?' asked Eric. I could hear the nerves in his voice.

I didn't think we really were. But at the same time I knew we could do it, the three of us together. If anyone could pull out the truth from the tangle, it was us.

'We're definitely ready,' I said, tucking my right hand through May's arm and my left through Eric's. 'Come on. Let's go.'

George handed one of his crutches to Eric for safekeeping, and arm in arm, again, we walked into the shelter, George moving carefully down behind us.

It was noisy as anything down there, and hot, just like always. Mr Abiola was leading a group of people in a sing-song, and some more people were practising the foxtrot next to some bunk beds (and getting shouted at by the people trying to sleep in the beds).

But there, in the corner we'd seen them in before, separated from everyone else by some bunk beds, were the Hogarth Mews group: Mr and Mrs Goodchild, Cecil, Colette, Margot and Olivier Mortensen, Miss Charney and Miss Wimpress. I had a moment where I thought, *No, it can't be!* They're all so nice and normal. At Elysium Hall, when we worked out who the murderer was, it was like we'd peeled away all the pretend nice normality from that person (I won't say who – I still hate thinking about it, much less writing it) and discovered that they were really evil. Was that what was about to happen here? Do you have to be bad, to be a murderer? Or can you just be a normal person who's stumbled? I don't think Hamlet *means* to be bad, after all, even though he does bad things.

Somehow it's even scarier thinking that anyone can become a murderer than it is thinking that the world is full of people who are secretly evil.

May marched right over to them. I could feel her trembling, just a little bit. She still hates shelters. But she was holding it together. I was proud of her then.

'Good evening,' said Mr Goodchild, smiling at us all, but especially at Eric.

'Good evening!' said May kind of shrilly. She had her chin up and her fists clenched; she was ready for battle. I tipped up my chin too, and squeezed my fingers into my palms – and, just like always, acting the emotion made me feel it. Within a couple of seconds, I was as brave as May.

'We've got something we want to say to you,' I said, doing my best English Fiona impression. A man in one of the bunk beds sat up and looked at us, and George said sternly, 'Get up! Go over there! This is police business.'

The man grumbled, but he went, and so did the other people in the bunks. We had space to talk without being overheard.

'Would you like a biscuit?' asked Mrs Goodchild. 'Or cocoa? I've got a flask here, if you don't mind sharing a mug. I've got one here you could use.'

And suddenly another piece of the puzzle fell into place. The chloral in Miss Fig's body. We knew that Mrs Goodchild brought cocoa round for everyone in the mews houses, but we'd thought, hadn't we, that no one could have poisoned it because she poured it from a big flask, and everyone had brought out their own mugs. But Miss Fig's house was the last one in the row. By the time Mrs Goodchild got to her, everyone else would have already had theirs. She could have added chloral to the flask before she knocked on Miss Fig's door.

I felt my hands shaking, and stopped them with an effort. They were totally steady as I took the mug from Mrs Goodchild and lifted it to my lips. Then I caught May's and Eric's eyes and gave my head a very gentle shake, flicking my eyes down into the cocoa and then back up. *Miss Fig*, I mouthed.

Eric got it at once. Of course he did. His mouth dropped open, and I had to take a big pretend sip of the cocoa and say, 'Oh, delicious! Thank you, Mrs Goodchild,' to cover up for him.

May took a little while longer. She reached out for the

cocoa, and I had to step on her foot pretty hard and jostle the mug.

'Hey!' she said. 'I— *Oh!*'

May works better when she's moving, and there's no room to move in an enclosed space. Although even when she's not working at her fastest she's still faster than most people I know.

I guess that was what must have made me think about enclosed spaces, and then I thought about what Eric had told us, about the way the fog shuts off everyone in their own tiny space, even if you close all the windows and doors in your house. I remembered being in Miss Fig's room with the door shut, and the way the painting – the *painting*.

I knew what to say next.

'Why did you give Miss Fig a painting just before she died if you didn't like her, Mr Goodchild?' I asked.

Everyone stared at me.

'What's that got to do with anything?' asked Miss Charney.

I'd known I was right even before it came out of my mouth, and then I looked at Mr Goodchild and the way his mouth had gone into a thin line, and the way Mrs Goodchild was suddenly staring at him, and I was totally sure.

'Well, I suppose because I painted a lot, this last year,' said Mr Goodchild slowly. 'I gave paintings to everyone in the mews.'

Eric had worked out what I was trying to say again.

'We saw it in her room,' he said, nodding.

'Whatever were you doing in there?' cried Miss Charney. 'You three get into everywhere! You need to be supervised properly.'

'Samuel is too generous, sometimes,' said Mrs Goodchild, and I could tell that annoyed Mr Goodchild, because it hadn't been what he was about to say. He glared at her over his glasses, and she glared back in a *well-you-should-have-said-it-faster* way.

'Paula saw it one day and liked the look of it, so I gave it to her,' said Mr Goodchild. 'In late November, I think it was, just before the Incident.'

'It was so nice and bright,' said Eric. 'It smelled strong, though.'

It did, I thought. It had made my head swim, even being near it for a few minutes. And that had been a clue. Because we knew, from our Ministry lessons, all the ways that you can hide poisons in things. You can put it in food and drink, you can put it into the air and on surfaces, and you can dye things with poison, so that it leaks out of clothes and fabrics. And if you can do that with dyes, you must be able to do it with *paints* too.

Those traces of arsenic in Miss Fig's body. They must have come from the painting.

It'd been big. Imagine sleeping under it during the blackout, every night, breathing in more poison with every hour you slept. No wonder Miss Fig had felt ill in the week before she died. And on the night of the sixth, she must have closed up her house even earlier than usual, because of the fog. She must have felt dreadful that night, even before the cocoa laced with chloral. And when she'd drunk it – that should have been enough to kill her.

Mr and Mrs Goodchild had killed her.

So why had she also been stabbed? It was the one thing that still didn't fit.

'This is a very strange conversation,' said Colette. 'Are you playing another game?'

'Oh, blast it,' snapped May, who'd caught up with me and Eric. (I could tell because she was beginning to bounce in her seat, not even pretending to sip the cocoa.) 'You two, stop being so polite. We *know*. We know *everything*.'

70

Then a lot of things happened at once.

Colette said, 'What are you children talking about?' Miss Wimpress gasped and pressed her hands against her chest. Miss Charney reached out and seized hold of Miss Wimpress's shoulder. And Mr and Mrs Goodchild both went very still.

'Don't lie to us!' roared May, getting into the swing of it. 'We know what you did. We know about the smuggling, and – and everything. And we know all about the murder!'

'HEY!' said Cecil, jumping up. 'You rat! You promised you wouldn't say!'

There was general confusion. Mrs Goodchild was saying, 'Cecil, what are you talking about?' and Colette was making frantic gestures at Cecil, and Cecil was shaking his fist at us and Miss Wimpress was wringing her hands and whispering in Miss Charney's ear while Miss Charney sat like a stone.

'I didn't mean the *food* smuggling!' said May quickly, which of course made everything worse.

'CECIL!' yelled Mr Goodchild, and Cecil folded his arms and said, 'Where did you think it was all coming from, Dad? You've been eating it every day!'

'I had nothing to do with that,' said Colette, which is obviously the most suspicious thing you could say in the circumstances.

'You liar!' said May. 'We know that's not true. And you were helping with the other smuggling too. We know you were. You all were!'

Now it was Cecil's turn to say, 'WHAT other smuggling?'

All the adults glanced at each other and then rose up in perfect unison, trying to drown us out.

'This is all getting very silly,' said Mrs Goodchild over everyone else. 'Drink up your cocoa and don't make up stories.'

'I would quite like to hear their story, though,' said George with authority.

'George, dear—' Mrs Goodchild began, but George smiled at her and said, 'Mrs Goodchild, I'm curious. After all, I live in the mews too.'

'Hardly,' murmured Miss Charney.

Which was kind of rude, Diary, honestly.

'I don't know why you want to hide it,' said May. 'It's the good kind of smuggling! You've been bringing people over from France, to keep them safe from the Nazis. Honestly, I think you should be quite proud.'

'This is absolute NONSENSE,' said Mr Goodchild.

'I don't know where you got this idea from, really. And do keep your voice down, please.'

'But it's true!' said May indignantly. 'Eric, Nuala, tell them!'

'We didn't make it up,' said Eric gently. 'We know Mr Levy's staying in Mr Harris's house. We know that you've all been working together to bring people over from France on boats, using Colette's connections, and then to the mews in removal vans. Then Mrs Mortensen gives them clothes she collects for her committees, and after a few days Mr Goodchild sends them off into the country, using all the channels that he and Miss Wimpress know from their official work sending paintings out of London. He pretends that the refugees are curators and their families. It's very clever, actually.'

'Yes!' I said. 'When we spoke to the Lowndes family, they thought we were from the mews, and they started to talk about the operation. They're in on it too! And we also know that Miss Fig found out about it. We discovered a book in Miss Fig's luggage that belonged to Anna, full of coded messages about meeting times, and numbers and names. We didn't know what they meant at the time, but now we've realized that they're code words to identify the people being brought over on each boat, and where they're being moved to, and the paintings going with them. We also found some scraps of paper in Miss Fig's house, in her bathroom, that we worked out were referring to the same thing: smuggling paintings, and the names of people in the mews. Miss Fig knew, and she was blackmailing Anna.

'Anna gave her the gold necklace – that's why Miss Fig was wearing it when she was found, Cecil—'

'Oh!' said Cecil, rubbing at his eyes. 'Oh!' He suddenly looked maybe even younger than May. 'So it's really not her.'

'Haven't you been listening?' asked May. 'It's not her! Anna's alive!'

'Anyway,' I continued, 'Anna gave Miss Fig the necklace, but it wasn't enough. Anna must have told Mr and Mrs Goodchild about the blackmail – they knew that Miss Fig was threatening the whole mews. On the sixth of December she left on her mission in the morning, before the fog rolled in – she was already out of London, on the train to the seaside. She went to France, to try to work out problems with the smuggling chain, and that's where she still is. So she can't have had anything to do with the murder. But she left behind a whole street full of people who wanted to protect her, and who had lots of reasons to want to stop Miss Fig from revealing what she knew. If she'd gone to the police, everyone would have been arrested, and no more people could come over to safety. So it mattered, a lot. It wasn't just about paintings. It was about people's lives.'

'If you understand that, then why are you talking about this?' asked Colette. 'We've been *helping* people! It shouldn't be a crime. I have contacts – high up. If you want money; if you want anything—'

'Quiet, Colette,' said Mr Goodchild. 'Everything is above board. There are no records—'

'We've just told you that isn't true!' said May. 'And we're *talking* about it because someone's dead. *Someone* here killed Miss Fig, and that's important.'

'Then it was self-defence,' said Colette. 'Who cares? We're at war! Bad things happen in a war sometimes.'

'It wasn't self-defence, though,' said Eric. 'It was all planned. Different people were trying to kill Miss Fig for *months* before she actually died. Someone gave her a painting that had arsenic in it. Someone tried to run her over in the blackout. And then on the night of the sixth, someone gave her a drink filled with enough chloral to kill her, and someone stabbed her to death.'

71

Miss Wimpress gasped. 'Oh!' she said. 'No!'

'This is ridiculous,' said Miss Charney. 'Who'd do all those things? It sounds like a book.'

Eric nodded at me and May, and smiled. 'We wondered that,' he said. 'It doesn't all fit together. But—'

'But it does if you realize it was lots of different people!' May cut in, too excited to wait. 'Or a few different people. You see, the painting – we know that Mr Goodchild paints. He gave paintings to lots of different people in the mews, so it's not surprising that Miss Fig should have one. But why would he give one to a woman he didn't like, and didn't think had good taste? He called her a philistine – which is someone who doesn't understand art.'

'Every time I stood near it, I got dizzy,' I said. 'Eric knows what I'm talking about. There's something in the paint – we know that you can put arsenic in things like paints, and it'll leak out and fill the room with poison. So I think that's what Mr Goodchild did. Gave Miss Fig a poisoned painting in late November. He could have used— Oh, I know! He could have used weed killer from Mrs Goodchild's flowers and put it in the top layer of paints! That's why she was sick on the night of the fog – she'd closed up her house early, and so she must have been breathing in the fumes. It must have made her feel terrible. It wasn't how she died, but it did make her ill.'

George suddenly grinned. 'Now, that does sound like a book,' he said. 'Never ask an academic to plan a murder. You know it would never have really killed her?'

'I'm not saying anything,' said Mr Goodchild sulkily. But his cheeks had gone pink with what looked an awful lot like embarrassment to me.

'And we know about the chloral too,' said May. 'We worked out that the only way it could have been taken by Miss Fig at the right time – I mean, at a time that makes sense of everything else we know – is if it was given to Miss Fig in the cocoa that Mrs Goodchild brought around at eight.'

I nodded. 'No one else could have done it. It was so simple! We almost missed it. But, of course, Miss Fig's house was the last one on the row, so Mrs Goodchild could have poured the chloral straight into the cocoa before she gave a drink to Miss Fig. It had to be her. I'm sorry.'

I said *I'm sorry* because I was watching Cecil look at his mother like his heart was breaking. That sounds overdramatic, but it's true. I remember how I felt last year when I found out the truth at Elysium Hall. I knew what it was like, and I felt so sad for him.

Mrs Goodchild stared right at me, her chin lifted, her neck straight and her arms folded. For once she wasn't sewing or darning or cooking or folding. She was just still.

'My dears,' she said at last. 'You don't have any proof of this part, do you? This is all simply a nice story you're telling.'

'But we know it's true,' said Eric. 'We know you did it for Anna, Mr and Mrs Goodchild. We know you were trying to protect her, and all the people you're helping. We know you thought you had to do it.'

I could see May opening her mouth to point out that no one ever *has* to commit murder. It was true, but I had to stop her saying so. I kicked her in the shin, hard, and her face went red and scrunched up. She stayed quiet.

'But you said the chloral didn't kill her either,' said Miss Wimpress. 'So it wasn't Mr *or* Mrs Goodchild. You said it was . . . you said she was stabbed. *Why?*'

'Because the person who stabbed her didn't know she was about to die anyway,' said Eric. 'They thought the fog was their perfect opportunity, and they took it. They crept up into the attic and down into Miss Fig's room late at night. They thought she'd be asleep, and they wanted to stab her while she couldn't defend herself. They—'

He paused and looked at me. And I had it. I could see it like a play in my head. I knew what had happened.

72

'They killed her,' I said, 'and then they tried to get rid of the body. Their plan was to hide her in the basement of Number One, so they dressed her in her day clothes to help hide the fact that she'd been stabbed. I remember, when I found her, her shirt was untucked and her shoelaces looked wrong. They started to go through the house and move everything upstairs into her luggage, to make it look as though she'd left – but then – then they heard someone else coming down through the attics. They must have been so scared, in case they were about to be caught. But it was—'

'Oooh!' said May. 'I know! I know! It was Mr Goodchild! Mrs Goodchild must have sent him up through the attics to see if Miss Fig was really dead!'

'Exactly,' I said, grinning at her. 'And, of course, Mr Goodchild must have explained everything, thinking that he'd just killed Miss Fig. The real murderer must have realized what a perfect opportunity it was – people to help them hide the crime, people who they could convince to hide what had happened because they thought *they* were guilty. So they made Mr Goodchild believe that Miss Fig had died of the arsenic, or the chloral, or both, so he'd help them carry her down into the basement. But then – then on the way back, Mrs Goodchild must have been too nervous to wait, and come out into the mews to see where they were. Mr Goodchild must have called out to her then, in Yiddish, to calm her down and tell her to go back inside, and that's what bothered the General, and what Colette heard when she woke up with Olivier. That's why the General only barked once. It all fits!'

'Except that you haven't said who the murderer is yet,' said George. 'Crucial bit of information, Nuala. Who is it?'

'Who is it?' asked Miss Wimpress, pressing her hand against Miss Charney's shoulder.

'Yes, who is it?' asked Miss Charney, laughing.

There was a pause.

Miss Wimpress turned to look at her. 'Elfie,' she said, her voice wobbling. 'Why did your voice do that thing? The – the thing it does when you cheat at cards?'

'I don't cheat at cards,' said Miss Charney. 'Don't be silly, Prim.'

'There it is again! Why are you lying? Elfie?'

'Miss Charney's the one who hit Miss Fig with her ambulance last October,' said May, folding her arms. 'Our friend Miss Temple told us so.'

I thought that was a bit mean to Lavinia, giving away that she was the one who'd told us. Shouldn't we be protecting our sources?

'ELFIE!' cried Miss Wimpress. 'But – but why? She never did a thing to you!'

'Of course she bloody didn't! She did a thing to *you*! She was rotten to you, and you would always take it. Then you left her, and I thought it was the end of it – but then she started hanging around the station. I was afraid we'd never be free of her. Living on the same street as her too. It was a nightmare. I didn't mean to do it, I swear it, but – I was out one night, and I heard her talking as she walked by. So I . . . turned the wheel. I did it without even thinking.'

Miss Wimpress stood up, brushing at her skirts as though she'd got something dirty on them.

'Elfie!' she said, tears in her eyes. 'How could you?'

'I didn't kill her!' cried Miss Charney.

'*That* time,' said May.

I nodded. 'Not that time,' I said. 'But on the night of the sixth, you did. You took your penknife – the one you're always using, the one you were cutting the apple with, that time in the shelter. You waited until Miss Wimpress was asleep – maybe you even drugged her with something too. Then you climbed up into the attics and down into Miss Fig's house. You crept into her room and – *you* were the one who actually killed her.'

'Elfie!' cried Miss Wimpress, sobbing. 'Elfie! You didn't really. I *know* you didn't really.'

Miss Charney took a deep breath and clenched her fists. 'Oh, for heaven's sake, why lie about it any more?' she snapped. 'It was what she deserved! She was trying to worm her way back into Prim's good graces, and she was going to grass on us to the authorities. I killed her, and then Mr Goodchild and I carried her down the stairs, and we hid her in the basement. And I'm *not* sorry.'

But her eyes were shining, and her teeth were clenched. She looked a lot like a kid who's been told off and won't admit they're wrong, even though they *know* they are.

'I know!' said May triumphantly. 'We've got all the evidence! We told you! You went to Post the next day and left that letter, didn't you? It would have been easy for you – when we saw you that time outside the museum, you were on your way to drop off something at Post for Mr Abiola. And you told Miss Temple and Mr Abiola that Miss Fig had spent a week saying she was going to the Lowndes family's house. No one else told us that, not directly. They all heard it from someone else. Miss Wimpress even said that Miss Fig had never told her where she was going. Why would Miss Fig tell you something and not Miss Wimpress? That doesn't make sense. And, anyway, you couldn't have heard her say anything, because Miss Fig was never supposed to go and visit! It all fits. And now George has heard you confess! Hah!'

'Why didn't you *say* anything, Mum?' asked Cecil. He'd been quiet until now. He looked like he wanted to cry too. 'You – you and Dad – you helped with a *murder.*'

'I couldn't let you be part of it,' said Mrs Goodchild. 'We made the decision – your father and I! It was for Anna, and for the people we were helping. And for all the people we can't help. Our relatives, and their friends, and their neighbours, and – so many of them! All dead! What we are doing can never be enough, but, all the same, every life is precious. And Miss Figueroa was going to stop everything. We had to – we had to do something. It felt like self-defence, even though I know the rabbi would have told us it was wrong. And we had to keep you out of it too.'

'You children – Anna and Zosia and you – deserve more than being dragged into this,' said Mr Goodchild. 'This is a war, and war changes people. But we don't want it to change you.'

'Anna and Zosia are twenty-four, Dad,' said Cecil. 'And I'm nearly seventeen. I'm almost old enough to enlist, and fight!'

'Not with your ears, darling,' said Mrs Goodchild. 'You know that.'

'What have my ears got to do with anything? There must be someone who won't care about them.'

May, Eric and I looked at each other.

'You hid this from me for four months. You lied to me! You could have told me. It wasn't even you who did it!' cried Cecil.

'But we meant to do it!' cried Mrs Goodchild. 'Isn't that enough?'

Miss Wimpress and Miss Charney were arguing too.

'But why would you do it?' Miss Wimpress was wailing. 'I never asked you to! I didn't want you to! She was— We might not have been together any more, but I didn't want anyone to hurt her!'

'*She* hurt *you*! And I asked you not to talk to her, but you kept on doing it. Even though I told you not to!'

'I think,' said George to the Hogarth Mews group, 'that when the raid is over, you'll all need to come with me.'

That shocked me, and I could tell May and Eric were confused too. Hadn't we just proved that only one person actually killed Miss Fig?

'You can't tell the police about what happened!' said Eric. 'Please! They'll stop what's going on – the refugees – it's important!'

Eric doesn't usually stumble over his words, so I knew how upset he was.

Mr Goodchild took Mrs Goodchild's hand. 'It's quite all right,' he said. 'It had to come out some time, I suppose.'

'I'm not going,' said Miss Charney. 'We're in a war. Who cares about one very unpleasant person? She'd have stayed buried – the house should have fallen on her. Why didn't it fall on her? No one would have ever known if it wasn't for *you* three!'

She lunged forward, but Miss Wimpress grabbed hold of her arm and pulled her back.

'Elfie,' she said. 'Absolutely not. I won't have you— I won't have anyone doing things for me that I didn't ask for. I won't! I know you think I'm quite silly and unworldly, but I ought to be allowed to make my own decisions about things like *murder*. I – I still cared about her, you know!'

'I know,' said Miss Charney angrily. 'That was why I did it.'

'If you'll all listen to me,' said George. 'I'm not going to tell the police yet, Eric. I want everyone to come to the Ministry, to get their statements. But there needs to be a record of what happened, and we will need to speak to the Chief Inspector. It does all tie together, the murder and the smuggling. The Ministry will have to decide what to do. And as part of that, you three –' he looked at me, Eric and May – 'I need your statements too. I'm impressed. Alex and I – we'd hardly have done as well as you. Even Daisy would be proud.'

I thought May and Eric would be proud. I felt proud right then. But I turned to look at them, and saw Eric frowning and May scowling.

'But they were trying to help,' Eric said quietly. 'Isn't that good?'

George nodded. 'Yes, but it's still a crime.'

'Well, that's not right!' said Eric. 'We've worked so hard, but – but we haven't fixed anything important. We've made it harder for more people to come over from France and be safe. It's all *wrong*.'

And he turned round and ran out of the shelter.

'Mr Jones?' Mr Abiola called after him. 'Hey! Mr Jones! It's not safe yet!'

'Come on!' I said to May. 'Hurry!'

We ran after him.

73

Eric was running so fast that we only caught up with him when he was already back in Hogarth Mews. He stood in the middle of the cobblestones, lit weirdly sideways by the fires and searchlights, and *screamed*.

A bomb swooped down somewhere away to our left, making the ground rattle, and suddenly, with a great swish and crash, Miss Fig's house collapsed in a heap. Nothing was left behind but chunks of roof and floor and, for some reason, the bathroom sink. It felt like the whole mews was screaming too.

'The war's still going on and on and we haven't made anything BETTER! I thought we were going to make the world BETTER!' Eric cried.

General Charles de Gaulle was howling, and Mrs Mortensen was dragging him out of her house, yelling and staring at the ruins of Number 2, and then May ran over next to Eric and put her arm around him and roared.

'May!' I shouted. 'Stop it!'

'SHAN'T!' yelled May. 'Eric's right! It's all gone wrong! And what if Hazel never comes back? What are we even DOING? Nothing's better at all!'

'But it is!' I said. 'We have helped!'

'HOW have we?'

'We—' I started.

'What are you three doing?' called Mrs Mortensen. She was leaning on her cane and staring at us, General Charles de Gaulle leaping around her wildly.

I remembered what we knew. Mrs Mortensen was a smuggler. She bought food on the black market, and she'd helped bring all those people over to London. Technically, she was a criminal, just like everyone else in the mews. But she looked so . . . normal, still, as stout and ferocious as ever.

'Go away!' screamed May. 'We're being upset! And you won't want to talk to us, anyway. We know what you've been doing – all the smuggling. We told . . . some people about it. We had to. We worked out who killed Miss Fig, see, and it was all tied up in that. So someone will be coming to find you as soon as the raid's over.'

Mrs Mortensen sighed. 'Well,' she said. 'That took more time than I'd thought. Who *did* kill Miss Fig?'

'Miss Charney,' I said.

'Ah, of course she did,' said Mrs Mortensen. 'And these people you had to tell – will they arrest us too?'

'I don't know,' I said. 'I hope not. I'm sorry.'

'Oh, don't worry. I've been waiting to be found out for months. The others are fools – they thought we could get away with it, but the world doesn't work like that. But I want to know why *you're* screaming?'

'Because the law is wrong!' said Eric.

'And because we're losing the war, and we can't help anyone, and my sister—' May stopped with a gasp.

'I don't pretend to understand most of that,' said Mrs Mortensen. 'But tell me why you think we're losing the war?'

'Isn't it obvious?' I asked, waving up at the sky.

'My dear child,' said Mrs Mortensen. 'All that is a sign that we've already won.'

May and Eric both went quiet. We all three gaped at her, and she nodded at us.

'The invasion hasn't happened. It was to happen in the autumn, after the fall of France. But it never came, did it? And now spring is here, and we are still not German, and the soldiers are not coming, no matter how many planes they send to trick us. *We have already won.* You can look at the darkness, if you like, and be swallowed up in it. That's very easy. But they can't blast every building. They can't destroy everything. Sometimes we have to do dark things in the war, but we can't stop looking for the light.'

'Well, there shouldn't be a war,' muttered May. 'It isn't fair.'

Mrs Mortensen sighed. 'What's fair got to do with it? Forget fair. Look at what's just happened to my house!' She pointed up at the big crack that had appeared in the wall of Number 3. 'You're here, aren't you? You're alive. Make that count.'

And, weirdly, that was the most comforting thing I'd heard for a long time.

PART NINE

WE MAKE THINGS BETTER, AFTER ALL

74

Saturday 5th April

It turned out that things weren't as hopeless as they seemed.

Very early this morning, the back door of the Ministry opened, and three people stumbled in. They were travel-worn and battered and limping, but none of that stuff mattered.

One of them was Hazel, her dark hair coming out of its bun and the sleeves of her coat torn. The second person was Daisy, looking very different from the smart young woman I'd met at Elysium Hall. Her beautiful blonde hair had been cropped raggedly short; she had cuts on her cheeks and arms, and she kept her fingers curled against her chest. And the last person was a tall, thin woman with curly dark hair, big dark eyes and great eyebrows. She looked a lot like her brother, Cecil.

'Big Sister!' said May, glaring at Hazel. 'I hate you!' And she burst into tears.

'Mei, come now,' said Hazel. 'I told you I'd be back! Look, I'm quite safe. And I got Daisy and Anna back too!'

'We did nearly die,' said Daisy. 'But it was all right in the end. I did have a plan. I was about to execute it when Anna turned up and got me out of— Well, you don't need to know that. Lucky she heard about the facility I was being kept in from her contact and realized I might be there. And then, since I couldn't exactly type, she got the Ministry to send Watson.' She raised her hands briefly, and then tucked them back against her chest. 'So it all worked out. I knew it would. No, don't hug me, don't *hug* me, you idiots!'

George and Miss Lessing and May and Eric and I all rushed her, and then Zosia came up from the basement and threw her arms around Anna. I really desperately wanted to say something to Anna – it felt like I knew her, even though obviously I didn't, which was weird.

Eventually, I snuck up to her in the midst of the celebrations – Ralph had got out some kind of wine, which the adults were drinking, and there was squash for us (I think squash is disgusting, but you have to be polite), and Zosia had turned the wireless on – and said, 'I'm Fionnuala. I found your scarf.'

Then I got embarrassed, because that wasn't what I'd wanted to say. 'I mean, I – May and Eric and I, we looked for you. We were worried about you.'

That also wasn't quite right. It left out the part where we'd thought she might be dead, or a murderer, and then the part where her parents almost *were* murderers. I felt like May. Usually I can work out how to say the thing I mean, but not then. But Anna seemed nice – as nice as Mr and Mrs Goodchild, which gave me an uncomfortable feeling.

'Thank you,' she said, smiling down at me, her eyebrows raised.

'Anna,' said Zosia. 'I have to tell you something. While you were away, some things happened. Don't *worry*, but . . . you need to know.'

She led Anna away, and I was left feeling even more uncomfortable. What if we *had* stopped the smugglers? Did that mean we were responsible for the people who couldn't be brought over? We thought we'd been helping Anna, but hadn't we just prevented her doing something good and brave and important, something that most people were too scared to do?

But then Daisy was saying, 'So, these three are proper spies now? Hazel, you know they're still very young.'

'We've been training them,' said Hazel. 'Since we were short a few agents because *you* decided to go and almost kill yourself again. And – well, they were the reason I came for you. When you didn't use your safe phrase, we thought it might not be you. They got Zosia to admit what was going on and confirm that it was Anna. I told you – they worked it all out.'

'And not just that!' said May proudly. 'We solved a murder!' Obviously, she'd already managed to forget how she'd cried in the middle of the mews.

'Not *again*,' said Daisy, flicking her eyes over us. She was still beautiful, I thought, even with the short hair.

'We are REALLY good at it!' protested May.

'I was impressed,' said George, putting his hand on May's head. She butted him away. 'I interviewed the suspects and the murderer – and I agree with their conclusion. I'll pass everything on to the Inspector to look at when he gets out of hospital.'

'Hospital?' asked Daisy sharply.

'Never mind that – he's all right,' said May. 'But see? That means we're ready to be spies! Proper spies! Spies in the field!'

Daisy's lips twisted quickly, and then went still again. 'Perhaps we wait a little while longer,' she said. 'It's quite difficult out there.'

'Grown-ups never want us to grow up,' grumbled May.

'The point is that we *do*, rather,' said Hazel.

'Um,' said Eric. 'Excuse me. Can I say something?'

We all turned towards him. He'd picked up Pfote, and she was purring in his arms, a contented ginger ball.

'I don't think I want to be a spy any more,' said Eric.

I gasped.

'I don't! There isn't any point, if we can't help people when it matters. We worked out what happened, and that means we stopped people coming over from France to be safe. So I don't want to be a spy any more.'

He was standing really sturdily, legs planted and chin up, but I saw his fingers digging into Pfote's fur, and I knew that he was clinging to her to stop himself shaking. This was big for Eric. He *never* does anything like this.

I had a sick moment of terror, because everyone leaves, don't they? Nothing ever stays the same. Every time I think I have friends, it all ends. But then I thought, *He's right, though.* So I clenched my fists and went to stand next to Eric.

'Me too,' I said. 'I'm not going to be a spy any more, either. It's not right!'

'Nuala,' said Hazel. 'It doesn't work that way. We work for the government. We have to stay within the law.'

'But it can!' I said. 'It does sometimes! You're the adults, aren't you? You got Daisy and Anna home. You can fix this.'

'What a horrifying thought,' said George. 'We *are* the adults, aren't we?'

'You're not very good at it,' said May. 'FINE. I hate this and I don't think it's fair but I *also* will stop being a spy.'

'Perhaps that would be a good thing,' said Hazel, narrowing her eyes at May.

'Stop it, Watson!' said Daisy. 'I've missed quite a lot while I've been away, haven't I? I'm going to sit down on this sofa here, and then I want you all to explain what happened. And could someone look after my hands? I don't have the time to go to a hospital.'

So we all explained. We told the whole story of the Hogarth Mews murder – the story that I've put into this diary – and George and Hazel and Zosia explained what they'd been doing, and at the end Daisy sighed and said, 'Well. I think it's quite obvious what to do. Hazel hasn't seen it, because she doesn't have the necessary ruthlessness sometimes.'

'Daisy!' said Hazel.

'Well, you don't!'

'What is it, then?' asked George.

And Daisy said, 'I am disappointed in you, George. I would have thought better of you. What's legal isn't always what's right. Why should the police have to get involved? And why shouldn't we use the contacts we have to help?'

'What?' said everyone.

'Why shouldn't we do a bad thing for good reasons? I'll make some calls in the morning, once I've had something to eat, and I'm sure we can sort it all out. *Could* I have something to eat? A bun, Hazel? Thank you.'

75

Sunday 6th April

I didn't really believe her, Diary. I was scared that we'd just ended the biggest adventure I'd ever been on, just for some people we'd never really met – but that's not right, is it? It's not *just*. They're people like Eric's father. They're important to someone.

Daisy made some calls yesterday, and said some very clipped, firm things – and then she hung up the telephone and said, 'I think that's done it. Let's wait and see. Has anyone contacted Cairo yet, by the way?'

'Hours ago,' said George with a grin that I didn't quite get. 'Don't worry.'

'I'm not worried! Hazel, take me home. We'll come back to this in the morning.'

And the thing is, this morning – I was wrong, Diary, about the Ministry and what it could do.

We had a telephone call, telling us to go to Hazel and Daisy's flat – and when we got to it we found most of the Ministry there, as well as two men I hadn't met before: one who looked very much like Daisy, and one who had George's colouring but a much softer and kinder expression.

'We've been discussing what you said,' said Hazel.

'Oh, Watson, you're being slow!' said Daisy, who still looked very battered and bruised but couldn't stop pacing around the room like a cat, or like May. 'Listen, you three are quite right. When the law's wrong, then you must just ignore it. We are the Ministry of *Unladylike* Activity, after all. So we're going to help. We've spoken to some people, and, once Miss Charney has been arrested – we had to tell Inspector Priestley about that, of course – we think we can work with the Hogarth Mews group and expand the operation. After all, Miss Charney committed the murder for reasons that were nothing to do with the smuggling. It doesn't need to come out. So, there. How does that sound?'

Eric beamed, bigger than I've seen him smile for weeks, and May squealed with excitement, and I said, 'Sure then, we'll stay.'

'Excellent,' said George. 'The correct decision, I think.'

Then we all sat down and had breakfast.

We were still eating when there was a knock on the door. Miss Lessing got up to answer it, and we heard her exclaim.

'Who is it?' called Hazel, but before she could say anything, a woman came rushing into the room. She had light brown skin, real movie-star good looks, and a mouth that looked like it was always smiling.

'Amina!' cried Hazel.

Amina dropped her bag on the floor and stormed up to Daisy.

'Stop DOING this to me!' she said angrily. 'Really, Daisy!' And then she kissed her. Daisy beamed, and two spots of colour glowed high up on her cheeks. I didn't exactly know where to look.

Amina sat down at the table and bit into a piece of toast.

'I'm Amina,' she said to me and Eric. 'I went to school with Daisy and Hazel, and I helped them on a few cases. I work for the Ministry's Cairo branch now. You must be the baby spies Daisy was telling me about.'

'We're not BABIES, Amina!' hissed May. 'And we're very good spies!'

'They did help bring Daisy and Anna home,' said Hazel, smiling at us.

'We did!' I said, grabbing May and Eric's hands.

The doorbell rang again, and Hazel got up to answer it.

We were all expecting someone else, but I heard the postwoman's voice, and Hazel answering.

She came back into the kitchen.

'Telegram from Inspector Priestley,' she said, flicking through a pile of post. 'He's getting out of the hospital this afternoon! And a letter for you, Nuala, from your mother – and, oh, there's something else in here, a letter from America. It must be your friends in the Company. And this is a bill, and another, and—'

She paused, and her face changed.

'What is it?' asked Daisy at last.

'I've been seconded to another department,' said Hazel slowly. 'Somewhere called . . . Bletchley Park. Have any of you ever heard of it?'

May's Guide to Hogarth Mews

Nuala's asked me to write this, to explain some of the words she uses in her diary. I suppose it's only fair, since she's written up the rest of this case. I was going to, but I got bored thinking about it. And she's done quite a good job, although not as good a job as I would. Anyway, here you are.

- **all-clear** – the siren that goes off at the end of an air raid, to tell everyone it's safe to come out.

- **Anglepoise lamp** – a sort of lamp that you can turn in different directions. It's useful for shining light straight into people's eyes while you're interrogating them.

- **bath chair** – a chair with wheels. Apparently it's called that because it was first made in Bath. You don't use it *in* the bath.

- **bien sûr** – a French phrase that means 'of course'.

- **Bloomsbury** – a part of London.

- **bold** – Irish slang that means rude or naughty.

- **bubbe** – a name some Jewish people call their grandmothers.

- **chignon** – a kind of hairstyle, like a low bun.

- **civil defence force** – the word for all the people who volunteer to help after a raid, wardens and ambulance drivers and so on.

- **contraband** – anything non-regulation that you try to sneak into school.

- **convalescing** – getting better from an illness.

- **coupons** – we get clothing coupons that say how much we can buy. It's all part of rationing.

- **Davy Jones** – the place where all our contraband is put at school, once mistresses discover it.

- **dorm** – the room we sleep in at school. Nuala and I are in the same dorm.

- **dote** – Nuala says this is Irish slang for someone really adorable and small.

- **eejit** – Irish slang for fool or idiot.

- **fashion plate** – a picture in a magazine of someone who's incredibly stylish.

- **flies** – the bit right above the stage in a theatre.

- **foil** – a kind of fencing sword.

- **Gráinne Ní Mháille** – an Irish pirate queen who Nuala loves.

- **gweilo** – this is a Cantonese word that means white foreigner.

- **hake** – a type of white fish that tastes disgusting.

- **Incident** – the polite way of saying a bomb strike.

- **ju-jitsu** – a combat discipline that's originally from Japan.

- **making a hames of** – Irish slang that means messing something up.

- **mews** – a small enclosed street with little tiny houses in it.

- **Mormor** – the Norwegian word for granny.

- **Nancy Drew** – an American girl detective Nuala loves.

- **no fear** – this is English slang that means the opposite of the way it sounds. It means don't worry!

- **occasional table** – not a table for a special occasion, but a small side table. I think that's a silly name for it.

- **'Óró sé do bheatha abhaile'** – this is an Irish song, and as far as Nuala's explained to me it's about the Irish pirate queen Gráinne Ní Mháille coming home and fighting her enemies. I like the sound of that a lot.

- **other side** – slang for the Nazis.

- **philistine** – someone who hates art.

- **Post** – the place where all the wardens work from, sort of like their headquarters.

- **pup** – Irish slang that means a young, silly person.

- **Quisling** – Vidkun Quisling, an awful Norwegian person who tried to do a deal with the Nazis. It's started to mean anyone who's a cowardly collaborator.

- **rations** – the government has decided how much of each food every person can have, and legally you can't buy any more than that unless you get it illegally on the black market.

- **requisition** – when the army takes a house from its owners to use it for the war effort.

- **respirator** – another word for a gas mask.

- **roadster** – a kind of American car.

- **Shabbos** – the Jewish day of rest, from Friday to Saturday night. On Friday evenings Jewish people have dinner together. They say blessings while lighting candles, and then have bread and wine before the rest of the meal.

- **shilling** – an amount of money.

- **sked** – a sort of scheduled message that agents in the field are asked to send back to the Ministry. If you miss your sked, everyone gets very worried about you!

- **spam** – delicious pressed meat from a tin.

- **synagogue** – the place where Jewish people go to pray. Also called **shul**.

- **tiffin** – a kind of cake that you don't have to cook.

- **warden** – someone who keeps everyone in their area safe during an air raid by checking on buildings and looking after shelters and so on.

- **whisht** – an Irish word that means be quiet.

- **Yiddish** – a language that some Jewish people speak.

Author's Note

I made up a lot of this book! But some parts I didn't. There really was an enormous push from art galleries around London to send the nation's most important and valuable works to safety in the countryside during the Blitz. Many pieces ended up being stored in a mountain in Wales (yes, really!), but country houses were also used, often in quite haphazard ways. I read about it in the book *National Treasures* by Caroline Shenton. I've slightly altered timelines here, and included things that did not (to the best of my knowledge!) really happen, but the art aspect of the story is fairly true. By the way, the British Museum was never used to train spies, but other London museums were, including the Natural History Museum!

The Nazis were also very focused on destroying art that they called Entartete Kunst, or 'degenerate art' – basically anything by Jewish people, gay people, Black people, trans people, or other people they hated. They wanted to destroy not just the people themselves but the work that those people made – to kill them twice, in a way. I grew up around a lot of art – my mother worked at a museum – and of course now I make a different kind of art (yes, books are art too). I'm fascinated by what art means, and why we protect or ban it. I think it's as relevant a question now as it was in 1941.

Hogarth Mews looks like any number of mews streets in London – they are gorgeous and fascinating places to come across, if you are on a walk. I based it a little on the Agatha Christie short story 'Murder in the Mews', and also on several real mews, including Gower Mews near the British Museum. In terms of the people in it, they are, of course, made up, but I was thinking (in their positive aspects only!) a little bit of my own neighbours. We moved to our street at the beginning of the pandemic, and I was struck by the sense of community we found, and how it mirrored what I was reading about the way the Blitz fostered community during the war. A huge event like a pandemic or a war breaks down barriers and forces people to rely on each other, and that's something I really wanted to write about in this book.

I was very inspired by the idea of people with dual or multiple heritages. I am one, of course, and many people I know are too. Identity in the real world is often a confusing and conflicted thing! Most of the time, though, characters in books come from one single place. That makes it easier for readers to understand their backgrounds, but it's often not particularly realistic. So, although most people in Hogarth Mews are British, they are also a mix of other national and cultural identities, and many of them have

433

parents who come from different countries just like me, and just like a lot of my readers.

I'm a big fan of General Charles de Gaulle's name – people really did seem to name, or rename, their pets with wildly patriotic names during the Second World War. It's also true that pet owners struggled to feed their animals, and that dogs and cats couldn't come into shelters – a heartbreaking Second World War fact! In terms of his appearance and character, the General is based on several real dogs who live on my street. One of them, Howl, is mine, and just like the General he barks whenever someone walks past his door. I can only apologize to my neighbours. Please don't murder me.

London fogs may be an unimaginable phenomenon to us in 2023, but they're actually shockingly recent. They only stopped in the 1950s as a result of pollution control – prior to that, Londoners were having to regularly suffer through the horrible, dangerous experiences that Eric and Cecil describe. The book *Death in the Air* by Kate Winkler Dawson was helpful to me (though absolutely not for younger readers!), as was the British Library short-story anthology *Into the London Fog*. Crime and fog seem to go together quite often . . .

A lot of fans have written to me asking me to put trans characters in my books, something that I am delighted to be able to do. It is, of course, absolutely historically accurate to have trans people in a book set in the 1940s, and just as accurate to show a trans person supported by the people around them. I have come across many stories of transitions in the early twentieth century that were treated as an interesting but ultimately uncontentious choice, and that is Anna's story here. I have chosen not to use her deadname in this book, by the way – since I am writing for readers in 2023, I can think of nothing more rude than mentioning it!

I also had a lot of requests from fans to put more disability in my books, and again I am glad to do so here. Around twenty-two per cent of people in the UK are disabled, a very large minority, and yet it's still quite uncommon to read about disabled people in books, especially people just going about their lives. There are so many different ways to be disabled, and to experience disability, that I couldn't possibly hope to capture even a fraction of them, but I hope the disabled characters in this book feel as realistic as my abled characters. The most useful and accessible book on disability I've come across recently is the phenomenally funny picture book *What Happened to You?* by James Catchpole, illustrated by Karen George. I really recommend it!

I have slightly stretched possibility with Cecil's hearing aid – the first wearable (though still very bulky – battery packs were involved, which is why Cecil wears an enormous jacket) vacuum hearing aid was created in the US in 1938, and then the technology advanced rapidly through the

1940s. So he *could* have had one, especially with parents as caring and supportive as Mr and Mrs Goodchild.

It is absolutely true that access to shelters was distressingly and dangerously lacking during the Blitz. Governments throughout time tend not to think of disabled people in their disaster planning, as can be seen by the global response to the Covid pandemic. Much changes, and much stays the same . . .

The details about the Ministry, and about poem codes and decoding work in general, I got from *Between Silk and Cyanide* by Leo Marks. It's for adults, but I really recommend it if you're interested in codes and want to experience almost unbelievable stress. Poem codes were one of the most terrible ideas the British high-ups ever had – they can be cracked almost the moment the person trying to decode them knows what poem is being used, and since a lot of spies insisted on using things like 'God Save the King', a horrible number of agents in the field had their missions compromised because their codes were broken. People literally died because British spymasters couldn't believe a Nazi might know the words to famous British poems and songs. Leo Marks spent a lot of time trying to get his bosses at the Special Operations Executive to change poem codes to something else more complicated, and eventually was successful – but that's in the future for my characters in 1941.

Details about wardens and ambulance crews were taken from various places. I first became interested in the civil defence service while reading the absolutely fantastic *The Night Watch* by Sarah Waters, a book that heavily inspired this one. Not for younger readers, but highly recommended for older Detective Society members! I found Mr Abiola in Stephen Bourne's book *Under Fire*, which mentions Ita Ekpenyon, a Black ARP warden. I also used *Raiders Overhead*, the memoir of London ARP warden Barbara Nixon. Their stories are incredible, and shocking, and painful. As I research, I keep being confronted by the fact that the truth of the Blitz was so much more terrible than it's possible to convey in a school history lesson, or a book like this. It's hard to hold on to, and harder to know what lesson to take from it. I don't think there's much you can learn from a war, apart from the universal truth that people are both better and worse than you might hope.

And, finally, a correction. For years, fans have been asking me whether Daisy is autistic. I've always said no; it wasn't something I intended for her, although I'm happy for readers to take what they need from my characters. However, I now know that these fans saw something in my books that I couldn't at the time. Daisy is autistic, and ADHD too, because I am. I realized this midway through writing this book, and it made many things a lot clearer.

It is a joy to realize who I have been all along, and to know that there are words for the way my brain works. It is also a wonder to finally be able to see my characters more fully. The Detective Society is a found family of brilliant, weird, funny, mainly neurodivergent people who are working together to try to understand the strange world they see around them. Of course, they don't have the words I now do to understand themselves – the first autism diagnosis, Donald Triplett's, only took place in 1943, and autistic people who do not fit that original diagnostic pattern were still hugely underdiagnosed in the 1990s when I was a child. Things are changing, and that is wonderful, but the fact remains that I can never say within the stories themselves that Nuala is autistic or that May is ADHD. I can say it here, though: they are! This is true! And if you are neurodivergent like me, I hope you can see a little of yourself in my characters too.

Robin Stevens, Oxford, June 2023

Acknowledgements

I got Covid in the summer of 2022, which then became Long Covid. I wasn't sure, for quite a while, whether this book would be written at all, let alone written on time. A huge thank you to the people who coached me through the days when I could barely stay awake: Courtney, Amy and Katy.

I then got my autism diagnosis in the spring of 2023, while I was working on the second draft of the book. A huge thank you to the people who helped me through from first questions to final assessment: Courtney (again), Hux, Louie, Non, and one of the twenty-first century's finest resources: kind strangers on the internet. This book has a great deal in it about disability as a part of life, for obvious reasons. This past year I have questioned everything about who I am – and, as usual, discovered that all the answers are already in the books I write.

Thanks to my neighbours, who are all over this book. We are so lucky to have found an extraordinarily kind and close-knit group of people in our neighbourhood, who have become a wonderful part of our lives.

Thanks to everyone who helped title this book, especially Colette, Tashinga and my editor Nat. Isn't it perfect!

Thanks to the fans who happened to write to me at exactly the time when I was creating the characters in this book: Paula and Kiki, who reminded me that identities are complex; Ada, who had the perfect name, and Evelyn and Jan, who very generously lent me theirs; Liora (and many others!) who asked me to put more Jewish characters in my books; and Daisy, who asked for a character who uses hearing aids.

Thanks to my readers, without whom this book would be a lot worse and less interesting: Lizzie Huxley-Jones, for help with Mrs Mortensen; Melly Carr, still the Chief Inspector's best girl (and not forgetting helpful cats Marple and Poirot, who gave important feedback on Pfote); James Catchpole, who embodies George's cool; Wei Ming Kam, resident May supporter; Courtney Smyth (again!!), who always looks after Nuala so well, and who has spotted that May is a horrible goose; Mike Smith, who gives such astonishingly thoughtful and detailed notes about history and the mystery; Claire Trevien, for help with French naming conventions; Charlie Swinbourne, for help with Cecil's character; Anne Miller, who read this in the time she absolutely does not have right now; Kathie Booth Stevens, my first fan; Keren David, for excellent thoughts about the Goodchilds; Charlie Morris, who loves Sarah Waters and Daisy Wells as much as I do; and Aoife Martin, for helpful thoughts on Anna.

Thanks to my publisher, Puffin, and the whole Team Bunbreak who worked on this book, especially my two editors, Nat and India; my editorial support, Afua; my publicists, Charlotte and Lindsay; my marketer, Michelle; my illustrator, Jan (with support from Marssaié); my designer, Sophia; my editorial manager, Josh; my copy-editor, Wendy; my proofreaders, Samantha and Petra; my sales team, Tori and Kat; and our managing director, Francesca. You are all so passionate about my books, and I am so lucky to work with you.

I had to say goodbye to the two founding members of Team Bunbreak, Nat and Harriet, this spring. I could not have survived the last ten years without them, and they deserve a lot more than this book – Nat, Harriet, thank you from the bottom of my heart.

Thanks to my agent, Gemma, who is so wise and so fierce, and whose eagle eyes have saved me many times.

Thank you to my child, for being so fantastic, and thank you to all the people who looked after my child so I could write this book, especially Becki, Poppy, Vanessa and my wonderful mother, Kathie.

Massive thanks to my partner, Dee, who really went through it with me this time. What a year! Thank you for being such a kind and loving support. You're my favourite person.

And finally, thank you to *you*, reader. You bring my characters to life in your head, and you're the reason I wrote this book.

© Chris Close, 2018

Robin Stevens was born in California and grew up in an Oxford college, across the road from the house where Alice in Wonderland lived. She has been making up stories all her life.

When she was twelve, her father handed her a copy of *The Murder of Roger Ackroyd* and she realized that she wanted to be either Hercule Poirot or Agatha Christie when she grew up. She spent her teenage years at Cheltenham Ladies' College, reading a lot of murder mysteries and hoping that she'd get the chance to do some detecting herself (she didn't). She went to university, where she studied crime fiction, and then she worked for a children's publisher.

Robin is now a full-time author and the creator of the internationally award-winning and bestselling **Murder Most Unladylike** series, starring Daisy Wells and Hazel Wong. She still hopes she might get the chance to do some detecting of her own one day. She lives in Oxford.

Read on to discover how it all began in

1

This is the first murder that the Wells & Wong Detective Society has ever investigated, so it is a good thing Daisy bought me a new casebook. The last one was finished after we solved The Case of Lavinia's Missing Tie. The solution to that, of course, was that Clementine stole it in revenge for Lavinia punching her in the stomach during lacrosse, which was Lavinia's revenge for Clementine telling everyone Lavinia came from a broken home. I suspect that the solution to this new case may be more complex.

I suppose I ought to give some explanation of ourselves, in honour of the new casebook. Daisy Wells is the President of the Detective Society, and I, Hazel Wong, am its Secretary. Daisy says that this makes her Sherlock Holmes, and me Watson. This is probably fair. After all, I am much too short to be the heroine of this story, and who ever heard of a Chinese Sherlock Holmes?

That's why it's so funny that it was me who found Miss Bell's dead body. In fact, I think Daisy is still upset about it, though of course she pretends not to be. You see, Daisy is a heroine-like person, and so it should be her that these things happen to.

Look at Daisy and you think you know exactly the sort of person she is – one of those dainty, absolutely English girls with blue eyes and golden hair; the kind who'll gallop across muddy fields in the rain clutching hockey sticks and then sit down and eat ten iced buns at tea. I, on the other hand, bulge all over like Bibendum the Michelin Man; my cheeks are moony-round and my hair and eyes are stubbornly dark brown.

I arrived from Hong Kong part way through second form, and even then, when we were all still shrimps (*shrimps*, for this new casebook, is what we call the little lower-form girls), Daisy was already famous throughout Deepdean School. She rode horses, was part of the lacrosse team, and was a member of the Drama Society. The Big Girls took notice of her, and by May the entire school knew that the Head Girl herself had called Daisy a 'good sport'.

But that is only the outside of Daisy, the jolly-good-show part that everyone sees. The inside of her is not jolly-good-show at all.

It took me quite a while to discover that.

2

Daisy wants me to explain what happened this term up to the time I found the body. She says that is what proper detectives do – add up the evidence first – so I will. She also says that a good Secretary should keep her casebook on her at all times to be ready to write up important events as they happen. It was no good reminding her that I do that anyway.

The most important thing to happen in those first few weeks of the autumn term was the Detective Society, and it was Daisy who began that. Daisy is all for making up societies for things. Last year we had the Pacifism Society (dull) and then the Spiritualism Society (less dull, but then Lavinia smashed her mug during a séance, Beanie fainted and Matron banned spiritualism altogether).

But that was all last year, when we were still shrimps.

We can't be messing about with silly things like ghosts now that we are grown-up third formers – that was what Daisy said when she came back at the beginning of this term having discovered crime.

I was quite glad. Not that I was ever afraid of ghosts, exactly. Everyone knows there aren't any. Even so, there are enough ghost stories going round our school to horrify anybody. The most famous of our ghosts is Verity Abraham, the girl who committed suicide off the Gym balcony the term before I arrived at Deepdean, but there are also ghosts of an ex-mistress who locked herself into one of the music rooms and starved herself to death, and a little first-form shrimp who drowned in the pond.

As I said, Daisy decided that this year we were going to be detectives. She arrived at House with her tuck box full of books with sinister, shadowy covers and titles like *Peril at End House* and *Mystery Mile*. Matron confiscated them one by one, but Daisy always managed to find more.

We started the Detective Society in the first week of term. The two of us made a deadly secret pact that no one else, not even our dorm mates, Kitty, Beanie and Lavinia, could be told about it. It did make me feel proud, just me and Daisy having a secret. It was awfully fun too, creeping about behind the others' backs and pretending to be ordinary when all the time *we* knew we were detectives on a secret mission to obtain information.

Daisy set all our first detective missions. In that first week we crept into the other third-form dorm and read Clementine's secret journal, and then Daisy chose a first former and set us to find out everything we could about her. This, Daisy told me, was practice – just like memorizing the licences of every motor car we saw.

In our second week there was the case of why King Henry (our name for this year's Head Girl, Henrietta Trilling, because she is so remote and regal, and has such beautiful chestnut curls) wasn't at Prayers one morning. But it only took a few hours before everyone, not just us, knew that she had been sent a telegram saying that her aunt had died suddenly that morning.

'Poor thing,' said Kitty, when we found out. Kitty has the next-door bed to Daisy's in our dorm, and Daisy has designated her a Friend of the Detective Society, even though she is still not allowed to know about it. She has smooth, light brown hair and masses of freckles, and she keeps something hidden in the bottom of her tuck box that I thought at first was a torture device but turned out to be eyelash curlers. She is as mad about gossip as Daisy, though for less scientific reasons. 'Poor old King Henry. She hasn't had much luck. She was Verity Abraham's best friend, after all, and *you* know what happened to Verity. She hasn't been the same since.'

'I don't,' said Beanie, who sleeps next to me. Her real name is Rebecca but we call her Beanie because she is very small, and everything frightens her. Lessons frighten her most of all, though. She says that when she looks at a page all the letters and numbers get up and do a jig until she can't think straight. 'What did happen to Verity?'

'*She killed herself*,' said Kitty in annoyance. 'Jumped off the Gym balcony last year. Come on, Beans.'

'Oh!' said Beanie. 'Of course. I always thought she tripped.'

Sometimes Beanie is quite slow.

Something else happened at the beginning of term that turned out to be very important indeed: The One arrived.

AND
Ration
COCOA
RATION
Biscuits
PUT THAT LIGHT OUT!
FOOD IS A WEAPON
DOHERTY
MEAT
SOUP
Purdie
Sauce